GREATHEART

ETHEL M. DELL

1st WORLD LIBRARY
Literary Society

Greatheart

Ethel M. Dell

© 1st World Library – Literary Society, 2006
PO Box 2211
Fairfield, IA 52556
www.1stworldlibrary.org
First Edition

LCCN: 2006930768

Softcover ISBN: 1-4218-2177-X
Hardcover ISBN: 1-4218-2077-3
eBook ISBN: 1-4218-2277-6

Purchase *"Greatheart"*
as a traditional bound book at:
www.1stWorldLibrary.org/purchase.asp?ISBN=1-4218-2177-X

1st World Library Literary Society is a nonprofit
organization dedicated to promoting literacy by:

- Creating a free internet library accessible from any
  computer worldwide.
- Hosting writing competitions and offering book
  publishing scholarships.

Readers interested in supporting literacy
through sponsorship, donations or
membership please contact:
literacy@1stworldlibrary.org
Check us out at: www.1stworldlibrary.ORG
and start downloading free ebooks today.

Greatheart
contributed by Tim, Ed & Rodney
in support of
1st World Library Literary Society

I Dedicate This Book To A. G. C. Friend of My
Heart and to the Memory of All the Happy Days
We have Spent Together.

"NOW MR. GREATHEART WAS A STRONG MAN."

- *The Pilgrims Progress*

CONTENTS

PART I

PART II

PART I

CHAPTER I

THE WANDERER

Biddy Maloney stood at the window of her mistress's bedroom, and surveyed the world with eyes of stern disapproval. There was nothing of the smart lady's maid about Biddy. She abominated smart lady's maids. A flyaway French cap and an apron barely reaching to the knees were to her the very essence of flighty impropriety. There was just such a creature in attendance upon Lady Grace de Vigne who occupied the best suite of rooms in the hotel, and Biddy very strongly resented her existence. In her own mind she despised her as a shameless hussy wholly devoid of all ideas of "dacency." Her resentment was partly due to the fact that the indecent one belonged to the party in possession of the best suite, which they had occupied some three weeks before Biddy and her party had appeared on the scene.

It was all Master Scott's fault, of course. He ought to have written to engage rooms sooner, but then to be sure the decision to migrate to this winter paradise in the Alps had been a sudden one. That had been Sir Eustace's fault. He was always so sudden in his ways.

Biddy sighed impatiently. Sir Eustace had always been hard to manage. She had never really conquered him even in the days when she had made him stand in the corner and go without sugar in his tea. She well remembered the shocking occasion on which he had flung sugar and basin together into the fire so that the others might be made to share his enforced abstinence. She believed he was equal to committing a similar act of violence if baulked even now. But he never was baulked. At thirty-five he reigned supreme in his own world. No one ever crossed him, unless it were Master Scott, and of course no one could be seriously angry with him, poor dear young man! He was so gentle and kind. A faint, maternal smile relaxed Biddy's grim lips. She became aware that the white world below was a-flood with sunshine.

The snowy mountains that rose against the vivid blue were dream-like in their beauty. Where the sun shone upon them, their purity was almost too dazzling to behold. It was a relief to rest the eyes upon the great patches of pine-woods that clothed some of the slopes.

"I wonder if Miss Isabel will be happy here," mused Biddy.

That to her mind was the only thing on earth that really mattered, practically the only thing for which she ever troubled her Maker. Her own wants were all amalgamated in this one great desire of her heart - that her darling's poor torn spirit should be made happy. She had wholly ceased to remember that she had ever wanted anything else. It was for Miss Isabel that she desired the best rooms, the best carriages, the best of everything. Even her love for Master Scott - poor dear young man! - depended largely upon the faculty he possessed for consoling and interesting Miss Isabel. Anyone who did that earned Biddy's undying respect and gratitude. Of the rest of the world - save for a passing disapproval - she was scarcely aware. Nothing else mattered in the same way. In fact nothing else really mattered at all.

Ah! A movement from the bed at last! Her quick ears, ever on the alert, warned her on the instant. She turned from the window with such mother-love shining in her old brown face under its severe white cap as made it as beautiful in its way as the paradise without.

"Why, Miss Isabel darlint, how you've slept then!" she said, in the soft, crooning voice which was kept for this one beloved being alone.

Two white arms were stretched wide outside the bed. Two dark eyes, mysteriously shadowed and sunken, looked up to hers.

"Has he gone already, Biddy?" a low voice asked.

"Only a little way, darlint. He's just round the corner," said Biddy tenderly. "Will ye wait a minute while I give ye your tay?"

There was a spirit-kettle singing merrily in the room. She busied herself about it, her withered face intent over the task.

The white arms fell upon the blue travelling-rug that Biddy had spread with loving care outside the bed the night before to add to her mistress's comfort. "When did he go, Biddy?" the low voice asked, and there was a furtive quality in the question as if it were designed for none but Biddy's ears. "Did he - did he leave no message?"

"Ah, to be sure!" said Biddy, turning her face for a moment. "And the likes of me to have forgotten it! He sent ye his best love, darlint, and ye were to eat a fine breakfast before ye went out."

The sad eyes smiled at her from the bed, half-gratified, half-incredulous, like the eyes of a lonely child who listens to a fairy-tale. "It was like him to think of that, Biddy. But - I wish he had stayed a little longer. I must get up and go and find him."

"Hasn't he been with ye through the night?" asked Biddy, bent again to her task.

"Nearly all night long!" The answer came on a note of triumph, yet there was also a note of challenge in it also.

"Then what more would ye have?" said Biddy wisely. "Leave him alone for a bit, darlint! Husbands are better without their wives sometimes."

A low laugh came from the bed. "Oh, Biddy, I must tell him that! He would love your *bon-mots*. Did he - did he say when he would be back?"

"That he did not," said Biddy, still absorbed over the kettle. "But there's nothing in that at all. Ye can't be always expecting a man to give account of himself. Now, mavourneen, I'll give ye your tay, and ye'll be able to get up when ye feel like it. Ah! There's Master Scott! And would ye like him to come in and have a cup with ye?"

Three soft knocks had sounded on the door. The woman in the bed raised herself, and her hair fell in glory around her, hair that at twenty-five had been raven-black, hair that at thirty-two was white as the snow outside the window.

"Is that you, Stumpy dear? Come in! Come in!" she called.

Her voice was hollow and deep. She turned her face to the door - a beautiful, wasted face with hungry eyes that watched and waited perpetually.

The door opened very quietly and unobtrusively, and a small, insignificant man came in. He was about the size of the average schoolboy of fifteen, and he walked with a slight limp, one leg being a trifle shorter than the other. Notwithstanding this defect, his general appearance was one of extreme neatness, from his colourless but carefully trained moustache and small trim beard to his well-shod feet. His clothes - -like his beard - fitted him perfectly.

His close-cropped hair was also colourless and grew somewhat

Ethel M. Dell

far back on his forehead. His pale grey eyes had a tired expression, as if they had looked too long or too earnestly upon the turmoil of life.

He came to the bedside and took the thin white hand outstretched to him on which a wedding ring hung loose. He walked without awkwardness; there was even dignity in his carriage.

He bent to kiss the uplifted face. "Have you slept well, dear?"

Her arms reached up and clasped his neck. "Oh, Stumpy, yes! I have had a lovely night. Basil has been with me. He has gone out now; but I am going to look for him presently."

"Many happy returns of the day to ye, Master Scott!" put in Biddy rather pointedly.

"Ah yes. It is your birthday. I had forgotten. Forgive me, Stumpy darling! You know I wish you always the very, very best." The clinging arms held him more closely,

"Thank you, Isabel." Scott's voice was as tired as his eyes, and yet it had a certain quality of strength. "Of course it's a very important occasion. How are we going to celebrate it?"

"I have a present for you somewhere. Biddy, where is it?" Isabel's voice had a note of impatience in it.

"It's here, darlint! It's here!" Biddy bustled up to the bed with a parcel.

Isabel took it from her and turned to Scott. "It's only a silly old cigarette-case, dear, but I thought of it all myself. How old are you now, Stumpy?"

"I am thirty," he answered, smiling. "Thank you very much, dear. It's just the thing I wanted - only too good!"

"As if anything could be too good for you!" his sister said tenderly. "Has Eustace remembered?"

"Oh yes. Eustace has given me a saddle, but as he didn't think I should want it here, it is to be presented when we get home again." He sat down on the side of the bed, still inspecting the birthday offering.

"Haven't you had anything from anyone else?" Isabel asked, after a moment.

He shook his head. "Who else is there to bother about a minnow like me?"

"You're not a minnow, Scott. And didn't - didn't Basil give you anything?"

Scott's tired eyes looked at her with a sudden fixity. He said nothing; but a piteous look came into Isabel's face under his steady gaze, and she dropped her own as if ashamed.

"Whisht, Master Scott darlint, for the Lord's sake, don't ye go upsetting her!" warned Biddy in a sibilant whisper. "I had trouble enough last night. If it hadn't been for the draught, she wouldn't have slept at all, at all."

Scott did not look at her. "You should have called me," he said, and leaning forward took his sister's hand. "Isabel, wouldn't you like to come out and see the skaters? There is some wonderful luging going on too."

She did not raise her eyes; her whole demeanour had changed. She seemed to droop as if all animation had gone; "I don't know," she said listlessly. "I think I would almost as soon stay here."

"Have your tay, darlint!" coaxed Biddy, on her other side.

"Eustace will be coming to look for you if you don't,"

said Scott.

She started at that, and gave a quick shiver. "Oh no, I don't want Eustace! Don't let him come here, Stumpy, will you?"

"Shall I go and tell him you are coming then?" asked Scott, his eyes still steadily watching her.

She nodded. "Yes, yes. But I don't want to be made. Basil never made me do things."

Scott rose. "I will wait for you downstairs. Thank you, Biddy. Yes, I'll drink that first. No tea in the world ever tastes like your brew."

"Get along with your blarney, Master Scott!" protested Biddy. "And you and Sir Eustace mustn't tire Miss Isabel out. Remember, she's just come a long journey, and it's not wonderful at all that she don't feel like exerting herself."

A red fire of resentment smouldered in the old woman's eyes, but Scott paid no attention to it. "You'd better get some sleep yourself, Biddy, if you can," he said. "No more, thanks. You will be out in an hour then, Isabel?"

"Perhaps," she said.

He paused, standing beside her. "If you are not out in an hour I shall come and fetch you," he said.

She put forth an appealing hand like a child. "I will come out, Stumpy. I will come out," she said tremulously.

He pressed the hand for a moment. "In an hour then, I want to show you everything. There is plenty to be seen."

He turned to the door, looked back with a parting smile, and went out.

Isabel did not see the smile. She was staring moodily downwards with eyes that only looked within.

CHAPTER II

THE LOOKER-ON

Down on the skating-rink below the hotel, a crowd of people were making merry. The ice was in splendid condition. It sparkled in the sun like a sheet of frosted glass, and over it the skaters glided with much mirth and laughter.

Scott stood on the road above and watched them. There were a good many accomplished performers among them, and there were also several beginners. But all seemed alike infected with the gaiety of the place. There was not one face that did not wear a smile.

It was an invigorating scene. From a slope of the white mountain-side beyond the rink the shouts and laughter of higers came through the crystal air. A string of luges was shooting down the run, and even as Scott caught sight of it the foremost came to grief, and a dozen people rolled ignominiously in the snow. He smiled involuntarily. He seemed to have stepped into an atmosphere of irresponsible youth. The air was full of the magic fluid. It stirred his pulses like a draught of champagne.

Then his eyes returned to the rink, and almost immediately singled out the best skater there. A man in a white sweater, dark, handsome, magnificently made, supremely sure of himself, darted with the swift grace of a swallow through the throng. His absolute confidence and splendid physique made him conspicuous. He executed elaborate figures with such perfect ease and certainty of movement that many turned to look at him in astonished admiration.

"Great Scott!" said a cracked voice at Scott's shoulder.

He turned sharply, and met the frank regard of a rosy-faced schoolboy a little shorter than himself.

"Look at that bloomin' swell!" said the new-comer in tones of deep disgust. "He seems to have sprouted in the night. I've no use for these star skaters myself. They're all so beastly sidey."

He addressed Scott as an equal, and as an equal Scott made reply. "P'raps when you're a star skater yourself, you'll change your mind about 'em."

The boy grinned. "Ah! P'raps! You're a new chum, aren't you?"

"Very new," said Scott.

"Can you skate?" asked the lad. "But of course you can. I suppose you're another dark horse. It's too bad, you know; just as Dinah and I are beginning to fancy ourselves at it. We began right at the beginning too."

"Consider yourself lucky!" said Scott rather briefly.

"What do you mean?" The boy's eyes flashed over him intelligently, green eyes humorously alert.

Scott glanced downwards. "I mean my legs are not a pair, so I can't even begin."

"Oh, bad luck, sir!" The equality vanished from the boy's voice. He became suddenly almost deferential, and Scott realized that he was no longer regarded as a comrade. "Still" - he hesitated - "you can luge, I suppose?"

"I don't quite see myself," said Scott, looking across once more to the merry group on the distant run.

"Any idiot can do that," the boy protested, then turned suddenly a deep red. "Oh, lor, I didn't mean that! Hi, Dinah!" He turned to cover his embarrassment and sent a deafening yell at the sun-bathed *façade* of the hotel. "Are you never coming, you cuckoo? Half the morning's gone already!"

"Coming, Billy!" at once a clear gay voice made answer, and the merriest face that Scott had ever seen made a sudden appearance at an open window. "Darling Billy, do keep your hair on for just two minutes longer! Yvonne has been trying on my fancy dress, but she's nearly done."

The neck and shoulders below the laughing face were bare and a bare arm waved in a propitiatory fashion ere it vanished.

"Looks as if the fancy dress is a minus quantity," observed Billy to his companion with a grin. "I didn't see any of it, did you?"

Scott tried not to laugh. "Your sister?" he asked.

Billy nodded affirmation. "She ain't a bad urchin," he observed, "as sisters go. We're staying here along with the de Vignes. Ever met 'em? Lady Grace is a holy terror. Her husband is a horrible stuck-up bore of an Anglo-Indian, - thinks himself everybody, and tells the most awful howlers. Rose - that's the daughter - is by way of being very beautiful. There she goes now; see? That golden-haired girl in red! She's another of your beastly star skaters. I'll bet she'll have that big bounder cutting capers with her before the day's out."

"Think so?" said Scott.

Billy nodded again. "I suppose he's a prince at least. My word, doesn't he fancy himself? Look at that now? Side - sheer side!"

The skater under discussion had just executed a most intricate figure not far from them. Having accomplished it with that unerring and somewhat blatant confidence that so revolted Billy's schoolboy soul, he straightened his tall figure, and darted in a straight line for the end of the rink above which they stood. His hands were in his pockets. His bearing was superb. He described a complete circle below them before he brought himself to a stand. Then he lifted his dark arrogant face. He wore a short clipped moustache which by no means hid the strength of a well-modelled though slightly sneering mouth. His eyes were somewhat deeply set, and shone extraordinarily blue under straight black brows that met. The man's whole expression was one of dominant self-assertion. He bore himself like a king.

"Well, Stumpy," he said, "where's Isabel?"

Scott's companion jumped, and beat a swift retreat. Scott smiled a little as he made reply.

"I have been up to see her. She will be out presently. Biddy had to give her a sleeping-draught last night."

"Damn!" said the other in a fierce undertone. "Did she call you first?"

"No."

"Then why the devil didn't she? I shall sack that woman. Isabel hasn't a chance to get well with a mischievous old hag like that always with her."

"I think Isabel would probably die without her," Stumpy responded in his quiet voice which presented a vivid contrast to his brother's stormy utterance. "And Biddy would probably die too - if she consented to go, which I doubt."

"Oh, damn Biddy! The sooner she dies the better. She's nothing but a perpetual nuisance. What is Isabel like this morning?"

Ethel M. Dell

Scott hesitated, and his brother frowned.

"That's enough. What else could any one expect? Look here, Scott! This thing has got to end. I shall take that sleeping-stuff away."

"If you can get hold of it," put in Scott drily.

"You must get hold of it. You have ample opportunity. It's all very well to preach patience, but she has been taking slow poison for seven years. I am certain of it. It's ridiculous! It's monstrous! It's got to end." He spoke with impatient finality, his blue eyes challenging remonstrance.

Scott made none. Only after a moment he said, "If you take away one prop, old chap, you must provide another. A broken thing can't stand alone. But need we discuss it now? As I told you, she is coming out presently, and this glorious air is bound to make a difference to her. It tastes like wine."

It was at this point that the golden-haired girl in red suddenly glided up and sat down on the bank a few yards away to adjust a skate.

Sir Eustace turned his head, and a sparkle came into his eyes. He watched her for a moment, then left his brother without further words.

"Can I do that for you?" he asked.

She lifted a flushed face. "Oh, how kind of you! But I have just managed it. How lovely the ice is this morning!"

She rose with the words, balancing herself with a grace as finished as his own, and threw him a dazzling smile of gratitude. Scott, from his post of observation on the bank, decided that she certainly was beautiful. Her face was almost faultless. And yet it seemed to him that there was infinitely more of witchery in the face that had laughed from the window a few minutes before. Almost unconsciously he was waiting to see the owner of that face emerge.

He watched the inevitable exchange of commonplaces between his brother and the beautiful Miss de Vigne whose graciousness plainly indicated her willingness for a nearer acquaintance, and presently he saw them move away side by side.

"What did I tell you?" said Billy's voice at his shoulder. "But you might have said that chap belonged to you. How was I to know?"

"Oh, quite so," said Scott. "Pray don't apologize! He doesn't belong to me either. It is I who belong to him."

Billy's green eyes twinkled appreciatively. "You're his brother, aren't you?"

Scott looked at him. "Now how on earth did you know that?"

He looked back with his frank, engaging grin. "Oh, there's the same hang about you. I can't tell you what it is. Dinah would know directly. You'd better ask her."

"I don't happen to have the pleasure of your sister's acquaintance," observed Scott, with his quiet smile.

"Oh, I'll soon introduce you if that's what you want," said Billy. "Come along! There she is now, just crossing the road. By the way, I don't think you told me your name."

"My name is Studley - Scott Studley, Stumpy to my friends," said Scott, in his whimsical, rather weary fashion.

Billy laughed. "You're a sport," he said. "When I know you a bit better, I shall remember that. Hi, Dinah! What a deuce of a time you've been. This is Mr. Studley, and he saw you at the window without anything on."

"I'm sure he didn't! Billy, how dare you?" Dinah's brown face burned an indignant red; she looked at Scott with instant hostility.

"Oh, please!" he protested mildly. "That's not quite fair on me."

"Serves you right," declared Billy with malicious delight. "You played me a shabby trick, you know."

Dinah's brow cleared. She smiled upon Scott. "Isn't he a horrid little pig? How do you do? Isn't it a ripping day? It makes you want to climb, doesn't it? I wish I'd got an alpenstock."

"Can't you get one anywhere?" asked Scott. "I thought they were always to be had."

"Yes, but they cost money," sighed Dinah. "And I haven't got any. It doesn't really matter though. There are lots of other things to do. Are you keen on luging? I am."

Her bright eyes smiled into his with the utmost friendliness, and he knew that she would not commit Billy's mistake and ask him if he skated.

Her smile was infectious. The charm of it lingered after it had passed. Her eyes were green like Billy's, only softer. They had a great deal of sweetness in them, and a spice - just a spice of devilry as well. The rest of the face would have been quite unremarkable, but the laughter-loving mouth and pointed chin wholly redeemed it from the commonplace. She was a little brown thing like a woodland creature, and her dainty air and quick ways put Scott irresistibly in mind of a pert robin.

In reply to her question he told her that he had arrived only the night before. "And I am quite a tyro," he added. "I have been watching the luging on that slope, and thanking all the stars that control my destiny that I wasn't there."

She laughed, showing a row of small white teeth. "Oh, you'd love it once you started. It's a heavenly sport if the run isn't bumpy. Isn't this a glorious atmosphere? It makes one feel so happy."

She came and stood by his side to watch the skaters. Billy was seated on the bank, impatiently changing his boots.

"I'm not going to wait for you any longer, Dinah," he said. "I'm fed up."

"Don't then!" she retorted. "I never asked you to."

"What a lie!" said Billy, with all a brother's gallantry.

She threw him a sister's look of scorn and deigned no rejoinder. But in a moment the incident was forgotten. "Oh, look there!" she suddenly exclaimed. "Isn't that just like Rose de Vigne? She's always sure to appropriate the most handsome man within sight. I've been watching that man from my window. He is a perfect Apollo, and skates divinely. And now she's got him!"

Deep disgust was audible in her voice. Billy looked up with a sideways grin. "You don't suppose he'd look at a sparrow like you, do you?" he said. "He prefers a swan, you bet."

"Be quiet, Billy!" commanded Dinah, making an ineffectual dig at him with her foot. "I don't want him to look at me. I hate men. But it is too bad the way Rose always chooses the best. It's just the same with everything. And I long - oh, I do long sometimes - to cut her out!"

"I should myself," said Scott unexpectedly. "But why don't you. I'm sure you could."

She threw him a whimsical smile. "I!" she said. "Why that's about as likely as -" she stopped short in some confusion.

He laughed a little. "You mean I might as soon hope to cut out Apollo? But the cases are not parallel, I assure you. Besides, Apollo happens to be my brother, which makes a difference."

"Oh, is he your brother? What a good thing you told me!" laughed Dinah. "I might have said something rude about him in a minute."

"Like me!" said Billy, stumbling to his feet. "I made a most horrific blunder, didn't I, Mr. Studley? I called him a bounder!"

Dinah looked at him witheringly. "You would!" she said. "Well, I hope you apologized."

Billy stuck out his tongue at her. "I didn't then!" he returned, and skated elegantly away on one leg.

"Billy," remarked Dinah dispassionately, "is not really such a horrid little beast as he seems."

Scott smiled his courteous smile. "I had already gathered that," he said.

Her green eyes darted him a swift look, as if to ascertain if he were in earnest. Then: "That was very nice of you," she said. "I wonder how you knew."

He still smiled, but without much mirth. "A looker-on sees a good many things, you know," he said.

Dinah's eyes flashed understanding. She said no more.

CHAPTER III

THE SEARCH

When Isabel came slowly forth at length from the hotel door whither Biddy had conducted her, Scott was sitting alone on a bench in the sunshine.

He rose at once to join her. "Why, how quick you have been! Or else the time flies here. Eustace is still skating. I had no idea he was so accomplished. See, there he is!"

But Isabel set her haggard face towards the mountain-road that wound up beyond the hotel. "I am going to look for Basil," she said.

"It is waste of time," said Scott quietly.

But he did not attempt to withstand her. They turned side by side up the hard, snowy track.

For some time they walked in silence. At a short distance from the hotel, the road ascended steeply through a pine-wood, dark and mysterious as an enchanted forest, through which there rose the sound of a rushing stream.

Scott paused to listen, but instantly his sister laid an imperious hand upon him.

"I can't wait," she said. "I am sure he is just round the corner. I heard him whistle."

He moved on in response to her insistence. "I heard that whistle too," he said. "But it was a mountain-boy."

He was right. At a curve in the road, they met a young Swiss lad who went by them with a smile and salute, and fell to whistling again when he had passed.

Isabel pressed on in silence. She had started in feverish haste, but her speed was gradually slackening. She looked neither to right nor left; her eyes perpetually strained forward as though they sought for something just beyond their range of vision. For a while Scott limped beside her without speaking, but at last as they sighted the end of the pine-wood he gently broke the silence.

"Isabel dear, I think we must turn back very soon."

"Oh, why?" she said. "Why? You always say that when -" There came a break in her voice, and she ceased to speak.

Her pace quickened so that he had some difficulty in keeping up with her, but he made no protest. With the utmost patience he also pressed on.

But it was not long before her strength began to fail. She stumbled once or twice, and he put a supporting hand under her elbow. As they neared the edge of the pines it became evident that the road dwindled to a mere mountain-path winding steeply upwards through the snow. The sun shone dazzlingly upon the great waste of whiteness.

Very suddenly Isabel stopped. "He can't have gone this way after all," she said, and turned to her brother with eyes of tragic hopelessness. "Stumpy, Stumpy, what shall I do?"

He drew her hand very gently through his arm. "We will go back, dear," he said.

A low sob escaped her, but she did not weep. "If I only had the strength to go on and on and on!" she said. "I know I should find him some day then."

"You will find him some day," he answered with grave assurance. "But not yet."

They went back to the turn in the road where the sound of the stream rose like fairy music from an unseen glen. The snow lay pure and untrodden under the trees.

Scott paused again, and this time Isabel made no remonstrance. They stood together listening to the rush of the torrent.

"How beautiful this place must be in springtime!" he said.

She gave a sharp shiver. "It is like a dead world now."

"A world that will very soon rise again," he answered.

She looked at him with vague eyes. "You are always talking of the resurrection," she said.

"When I am with you, I am often thinking of it," he said with simplicity.

A haunted look came into her face. "But that implies - death," she said, her voice very low.

"And what is Death?" said Scott gently, as if he reasoned with a child. "Do you think it is more than a step further into Life? The passing of a boundary, that is all."

"But there is no returning!" she protested piteously. "It must be more than that."

"My dear, there is never any returning," he said gravely. "None of us can go backwards. Yesterday is but a step away, but can we retrace that step? No, not one of us."

She made a sudden, almost fierce gesture. "Oh, to go back!" she cried. "Oh, to go back! Why should we be forced blindly forward when we only want to go back?"

"That is the universal law," said Scott. "That is God's Will."

"It is cruel! It is cruel!" she wailed.

"No, it is merciful. So long as there is Death in the world we must go on. We have got to get past Death."

She turned her tragic eyes upon him. "And what then? What then?"

Scott was gazing steadfastly into her face of ravaged beauty. "Then - the resurrection," he said. "There are millions of people in the world, Isabel, who are living out their lives solely for the sake of that, because they know that if they only keep on, the Resurrection will give back to them all that they have lost. My dear, it is not going back that could help anyone. The past is past, the present is passing; there is only the future that can restore all things. We are bound to go forward, and thank God for it!"

Her eyes fell slowly before his. She did not speak, but after a moment gave him her hand with a shadowy smile. They continued the descent side by side.

Another curve of the road brought them within sight of the hotel.

Scott broke the silence. "Here is Eustace coming to meet us!"

She looked up with a start, and into her face came a curious, veiled expression, half furtive, half afraid.

"Don't tell him, Stumpy!" she said quickly.

"What, dear?"

"Don't tell him I have been looking for Basil this morning. He - he wouldn't understand. And - and - you know - I must look for him sometimes. I shall lose him altogether if I don't."

"Shall we pretend we are enjoying ourselves?" said Scott with a smile.

She answered him with feverish earnestness. "Yes - yes! Let us do that! And, Stumpy, Stumpy dear, you are good, you can pray. I can't, you know. Will you - will you pray sometimes - that I may find him?"

"I shall pray that your eyes may be opened, Isabel," he answered, "so that you may know you have never really lost him."

She smiled again, her fleeting, phantom smile. "Don't pray for the impossible, Stumpy!" she said. "I - I think that would be a mistake."

"Is anything impossible?" said Scott.

He raised his hand before she could make any answer, and sent a cheery holloa down to his brother who waved a swift response. They quickened their steps to meet him.

Eustace was striding up the hill with the easy swing of a giant. He held out both hands to Isabel as he drew near. She pulled herself free from Scott, and went to him as one drawn by an unseen force.

"Ah, that's right," he said, and bent to kiss her. "I'm glad you've been for a walk. But you might have come and spoken to me first. I was only on the rink."

"I didn't want to see a lot of people," said Isabel, shrinking a little. "I - I don't like so many strangers, Eustace."

"Oh, nonsense!" he said lightly. "You have been buried too long. It's time you came out of your shell. I shan't take you home again till you have quite got over that."

His tone was kindly but it held authority. Isabel attempted no protest. Only she looked away over the sparkling world of white and blue with something near akin to despair in her eyes.

Scott took out his cigarette-case, and handed it to his brother. "Isabel's birthday present to me!" he said.

Eustace examined it with a smile. "Very nice! Did you think of it all by yourself, Isabel?"

"No," she said with dreary listlessness. "Biddy reminded me."

Eustace's face changed. He frowned slightly and gave the case back to his brother.

"Have a cigarette!" said Scott.

He took one absently, and Scott did the same.

"How did you get on with the lady in red?" he asked.

Eustace threw him a glance half-humorous, half-malicious. "If it comes to that, how did you get on with the little brown girl?"

"Oh, very nicely," smiled Scott. "Her name is Dinah. Your lady's name is Rose de Vigne, if you care to know."

"Really?" said Eustace. "And who told you that?"

"Dinah, of course, or Dinah's brother. I forget which. They belong to the same party."

"I should think that little snub-nosed person feels somewhat in the shade," observed Eustace.

"I expect she does. But she has plenty of wits to make up for it. She seems to find life quite an interesting entertainment."

"She can't skate a bit," said Eustace.

"Can't she? You'll have to give her a hint or two. I am sure she would be very grateful."

"Did she tell you so?"

"I'm not going to tell you what she told me. It wouldn't be fair."

Eustace laughed with easy tolerance. "Oh, I've no objection to giving her a hand now and then if she's amusing, and doesn't become a nuisance. I'm not going to let myself be bored by anybody this trip. I'm out for sport only."

"It's a lovely place," observed Scott.

"Oh, perfect. I'm going to ski this afternoon. How do you like it, Isabel?"

Abruptly the elder brother accosted her. She was walking between them as one in a dream. She started at the sound of her name.

"I don't know yet," she said. "It is rather cold, isn't it? I - I am not sure that I shall be able to sleep here."

Eustace's eyes held hers for a moment. "Oh, no one expects to sleep here," he said lightly. "You skate all day and dance all night. That's the programme."

Her lips parted a little. "I - dance!" she said.

"Why not?" said Eustace.

She made a gesture that was almost expressive of horror. "When I dance," she said, in her deep voice, "you may put me under lock and key for good and all, for I shall be mad indeed."

"Don't be silly!" he said sharply.

She shrank as if at a blow, and on the instant very quietly Scott intervened. "Isabel and I prefer to look on," he said, drawing her hand gently through his arm. "I fancy it suits us both best."

His eyes met his brother's quick frown deliberately, with the utmost steadiness, and for a few electric seconds there was undoubted tension between them. Isabel was aware of it, and gripped the supporting arm very closely.

Then with a shrug Eustace turned from the contest. "Oh, go your own way! It's all one to me. You're one of the slow coaches that never get anywhere."

Scott said nothing whatever. He smoked his cigarette without a sign of perturbation. Save for a certain steeliness in his pale eyes, his habitually placid expression remained unaltered.

He walked in silence for a few moments, then without effort began to talk in a general strain of their journey of the previous day. Had Isabel cared about the sleigh-ride? If so, they would go again one day.

She lighted up in response with an animation which she had not displayed during the whole walk. Her eyes shone a little, as with a far-off fire of gratitude.

"I should like it if you would, Stumpy," she said.

"Then we will certainly go," he said. "I should enjoy it very much."

Eustace came out of a somewhat sullen silence to throw a glance of half-reluctant approval towards his brother. He plainly regarded Scott's move as an achievement of some importance.

"Yes, go by all means!" he said. "Enjoy yourselves. That's all I ask."

Isabel's faint smile flitted across her tired face, but she said nothing.

Only as they reached and entered the hotel, she pressed Scott's hand for a moment in both her own.

CHAPTER IV

THE MAGICIAN

"Well, Dinah, my dear, are you ready?"

Rose de Vigne, very slim and graceful, with her beautiful hair mounted high above her white forehead and falling in a shower of golden ringlets behind after the style of a hundred years ago, stood on the threshold of Dinah's room, awaiting permission to enter. Her dress was of palest green satin brocade, a genuine Court dress of a century old. Her arms and neck gleamed with a snowy whiteness. She looked as if she had just stepped out of an ancient picture.

There came an impatient cry from within the room. "Oh, come in! Come in! I'm not nearly ready, - never shall be, I think. Where is Yvonne? Couldn't she spare me a single moment?"

The beautiful lady entered with a smile. She could afford to smile, being complete to the last detail and quite sure of taking the ballroom by storm. She found Dinah scurrying barefooted about the room with her hair in a loose bunch on her neck, her attire of the scantiest description, her expression one of wild desperation.

"I've lost my stockings. Where can they be? I know I had them this morning. Can Yvonne have taken them by mistake? She put everything ready for me, - or said she had."

The bed was littered with articles of clothing all flung together in hopeless confusion. Rose came forward. "Surely Yvonne didn't leave your things like this?" she said.

"No. I've been hunting through everything for the stockings. Where can they be? I shall have to go without them, that's all."

"My dear child, they can't be far away. You had better get on with your hair while I look for them. I am afraid you will not be able to count on any help from Yvonne to-night. She has only just finished dressing me, and has gone now to help Mother. You know what that means."

"Oh, goodness, yes!" said Dinah. "I wish I'd never gone in for this stupid fancy dress at all. I shall never be done."

Rose smiled in her indulgent way. She was always kind to Dinah. "Well, I can help you for a few minutes. I can't think how you come to be so late. I thought you came in long ago."

"Yes, but Billy wanted some buttons sewn on, and that hindered me." Dinah was dragging at her hair with impatient fingers. "What a swell you look, Rose! I'm sure no one will dare to ask you for any but square dances."

"Do you think so, dear?" said Rose, looking at herself complacently in the glass over Dinah's head.

Dinah made a sudden and hideous grimace. "Oh, drat my hair! I can't do anything with it. I believe I shall cut it all off, put on just a pinafore, and go as a piccaninny."

"That sounds a little vulgar," observed Rose. "There are your stockings under the bed. You must have dropped them under. I should think the more simply you do your hair the better if you are going to wear a coloured kerchief over it. You have natural ringlets in front, and that is the only part that will show."

"And they will hang down over my eyes," retorted Dinah, "unless I fasten them back with a comb, which I haven't got. Oh, don't stay, Rose! I know you are wanting to go, and you can't help me. I shall manage somehow."

"Are you quite sure?" said Rose turning again to survey herself.

"Quite - quite! I shall get on best alone. I'm in a bad temper too, and I want to use language - horrid language," said Dinah, tugging viciously at her dark hair.

Rose lowered her stately gaze and watched her for a moment. Then as Dinah's green eyes suddenly flashed resentful enquiry upon her she lightly touched the girl's flushed cheek, and turned away. "Poor little Dinah!" she said.

The door closed upon her graceful figure in its old-world, sweeping robe and Dinah whizzed round from the glass like a naughty fairy in a rage. "Rose de Vigne, I hate you!" she said aloud, and stamped her unshod foot upon the floor.

A period of uninterrupted misfortune followed this outburst. Everything went wrong. The costume which the French maid had so deftly fitted upon her that morning refused to be adjusted properly. The fastenings baffled her, and finally a hook at the back took firm hold of the lawn of her sleeve and maliciously refused to be disentangled therefrom.

Dinah struggled for freedom for some minutes till the lawn began to tear, and then at last she became desperate. "Billy must do it," she said, and almost in tears she threw open the door and ran down the passage.

Billy's room was round a corner, and this end of the corridor was dim. As she turned it, she almost collided with a figure coming in the opposite direction - a boyish-looking figure in evening dress which she instantly took for Billy.

"Oh, there you are!" she exclaimed. "Do come along and help

me like a saint! I'm in such a fix."

There was an instant's pause before she discovered her mistake, and then in the same moment a man's voice answered her.

"Of course I will help you with pleasure. What is wrong?"

Dinah started back, as if she would flee in dismay. But perhaps it was the kindness of his response, or possibly only the extremity of her need - something held her there. She stood her ground as it were in spite of herself.

"Oh, it is you! I do beg your pardon. I thought it was Billy. I've got my sleeve caught up at the back, and I want him to undo it."

"I'll undo it if you will allow me," said Scott.

"Oh, would you? How awfully kind! My arm is nearly broken with trying to get free. You can't see here though," said Dinah. "There's a light by my door."

"Let us go to it then!" said Scott. "I know what it is to have things go wrong at a critical time."

He accompanied her back again with the utmost simplicity, stopped by the light, and proceeded with considerable deftness to remedy the mischief.

"Oh, thank you!" said Dinah, with heart-felt gratitude as he freed her at last. "Billy would have torn the stuff in all directions. I'm dressing against time, you see, and I've no one to help me."

"Do you want any more help?" asked Scott, looking at her with a quizzical light in his eyes.

She laughed, albeit she was still not far from tears. "Yes, I want someone to pin a handkerchief on my head in the proper

Italian fashion. I don't look much like a *contadina* yet, do I?"

He surveyed her more critically. "It's not a bad get-up. You look very nice anyhow. If you like to bring me the handkerchief, I will see what I can do. I know a little about it from the point of view of an amateur artist. You want some earrings. Have you got any?"

Dinah shook her head. "Of course not."

"I believe my sister has," said Scott. "I'll go and see."

"Oh no, no! What will she think?" cried Dinah in distress.

He uttered his quiet laugh. "I will present you to her by-and-bye if I may. I am sure she will be interested and pleased. You finish off as quickly as you can! I shall be back directly."

He limped away again down the passage, moving more quickly than was his wont, and Dinah hastened back into her room wondering if this informality would be regarded by her chaperon as a great breach of etiquette.

"Rose thinks I'm vulgar," she murmured to herself. "I wonder if I really am. But really - he is such a dear little man. How could I possibly help it?"

The dear little man's return put an end to her speculations. He came back in an incredibly short time, armed with a leather jewel-case which he deposited on the threshold.

Dinah came light-footed to join him, all her grievances forgotten. Her hair, notwithstanding its waywardness, clustered very prettily about her face. There was a bewitching dimple near one corner of her mouth.

"You can come in if you like," she said. "I'm quite dressed - all except the handkerchief."

"Thank you; but I won't come in," he answered. "We mustn't shock anybody. If you could bring a chair out, I could manage quite well."

She fetched the chair. "If anyone comes down the passage, they'll wonder what on earth we are doing," she remarked.

"They will take us for old friends," said Scott in a matter of-fact tone as he opened the jewel-case.

She laughed delightedly. There was a peculiarly happy quality about her laugh. Most people smiled quite involuntarily when they heard it, though Billy compared it to the neigh of a cheery colt.

"Now," said Scott, looking at her quizzically, "are you going to sit in the chair, or am I going to stand on it?"

"Oh, I'll sit," she said. "Here's the handkerchief! You will fasten it so that it doesn't flop, won't you? May I hold that case? I won't touch anything."

He put it open into her lap. "There is a chain of coral there. Perhaps you can find it. I think it would look well with your costume."

Dinah pored over the jewels with sparkling eyes. "But are you sure - quite sure - your sister doesn't mind?"

"Quite sure," said Scott, beginning to drape the handkerchief adroitly over her bent head.

"How very sweet of her - of you both!" said Dinah. "I feel like Cinderella being dressed for the ball. Oh, what lovely pearls! I never saw anything so exquisite."

She had opened an inner case and was literally revelling in its contents.

"They were - her husband's wedding present to her," said Scott in his rather monotonous voice.

"How lovely it must be to be married!" said Dinah, with a little sigh.

"Do you think so?" said Scott.

She turned in her chair to regard him. "Don't you?"

"I can't quite imagine it," he said.

"Oh, can't I!" said Dinah. "To have someone in love with you, wanting no one but you, thinking there's no one else in the world like you. Have you never dreamt that such a thing has happened? I have. And then waked up to find everything very flat and uninteresting."

Scott was intent upon fastening an old gold brooch in the red kerchief above her forehead. He did not meet the questioning of her bright eyes.

"No," he said. "I don't think I ever cajoled myself, either waking or sleeping, into imagining that anybody would ever fall in love with me to that extent."

Dinah laughed, her upturned face a-brim with merriment. "If any woman ever wants to marry you, she'll have to do her own proposing, won't she?" she said.

"I think she will," said Scott.

"I wish Rose de Vigne would fall in love with you then," declared Dinah. "Men are always proposing to her, she leads them on till they make perfect idiots of themselves. I think it's simply horrid of her to do it. But she says she can't help being beautiful. Oh, how I wish -" Dinah broke off.

"What do you wish?" said Scott.

She turned her face away to hide a blush. "You must think me very silly and childish. So I am, but I'm not generally so. I think it's in the air here. I was going to say, how I wished I could outshine her for just one night! Isn't that piggy of me? But I am so tired of being always in the shade. She called me 'Poor little Dinah!' only to-night. How would you like to be called that?"

"Most people call me Stumpy," observed Scott, with his whimsical little smile.

"How rude of them! How horrid of them!" said Dinah. "And do you actually put up with it?"

He bent with her over the jewel-case, and picked out the coral chain. "I don't care the toss of a halfpenny," he said.

She gave him a quick, searching glance. "Not really? Not in your secret heart?"

"Not in the deepest depth of my unfathomable soul," he declared.

"Then you're a great man," said Dinah, with conviction.

Scott's laugh was one of genuine amusement. "Oh, does that follow? I've never seen myself in that light before."

But Dinah was absolutely serious and remained so. There was even a touch of reverence in her look. "You evidently don't know yourself in the least," she said. "Anyhow, you've made me feel a downright toad."

"I don't know why," said Scott. "You don't look like one if that's any comfort." He stooped to fasten the necklace. "Now for the earrings, and you are complete."

"It is good of you," she said gratefully. "I am longing to go and look at myself. But can you fasten them first? I'm sure I can't."

He complied with his almost feminine dexterity, and in a few moments a sparkling and glorified Dinah rose and skipped into her room to see the general effect of her transformation.

Scott lingered to close the jewel-case. Frankly, he had enjoyed himself during the last ten minutes. Moreover he was sure she would be pleased with the result of his labours. But he was hardly prepared for the cry of delight that reached him as he turned to depart.

He paused as he heard it, and in a moment Dinah flashed out again like a radiant butterfly and gave him both her hands.

"You - magician!" she cried. "How did you do it? How can I thank you? I've never been so nearly pretty in my life!"

He bowed in courtly fashion over the little brown hands. "Then you have never seen yourself with the eyes of others," he said. "I congratulate you on doing so to-night."

She laughed her merry laugh. "Thank you! Thank you a hundred times! I've only one thing left to wish for."

"What is that?" he said.

She told him with a touch of shyness. "That - Apollo - will dance with me!"

Scott laughed and let her go. "Oh, is that all? Then I will certainly see that he does."

"Oh, but don't tell him!" pleaded Dinah.

"I never repeat confidences," declared Scott. "Good-bye, *Signorina*!"

And with another bow, he left her.

CHAPTER V

APOLLO

The *salon* was a blaze of lights and many shifting colours. The fantastic crowd that trooped thither from the *salle-a-manger* was like a host of tropical flowers. The talking and laughter nearly drowned the efforts of the string band in the far corner.

Scott in ordinary evening-dress stood near the door talking to an immense Roman Emperor, looking by contrast even smaller and more insignificant than usual. Yet a closer observation would have shown that the same instinctive dignity of bearing characterized them both. Utterly unlike though they were, yet in this respect it was not difficult to trace their brotherhood. Though moulded upon lines so completely dissimilar, they bore the same indelible stamp - the stamp of good birth which can never be attained by such as have it not. Sir Eustace Studley was the handsomest man in the room. His imperial costume suited his somewhat arrogant carriage. He looked like a man born to command. His keen eyes glanced hither and thither with an eagle-like intensity that missed nothing. He seemed to be on the watch for someone.

"Who is it?" asked Scott, with a smile. "The lady of the rink?"

The black brows went up haughtily for a moment, then descended in an answering smile. "She is the only woman I've seen here yet that's worth looking at," he observed.

Ethel M. Dell

"Don't you be too sure of that!" said Scott. "I can show you a little Italian peasant girl who is well worth your august consideration. I think you ought to bestow a little favour on her as you have each chosen to assume the same nationality."

Sir Eustace laughed. "A *protegee* of yours, eh? That little brown girl, I suppose? Charming no doubt, my dear fellow; but ordinary - distinctly ordinary."

"You haven't seen her yet," said Scott. "You had your back to her in the *salle-a-manger.*"

"Where is she then? You had better find her before the beautiful Miss de Vigne makes her appearance. I don't mind giving her a dance or two, but you must take her off my hands if we don't get on."

"I will certainly do that," said Scott in his quiet voice that seemed to veil a touch of irony. "I believe she is in the vestibule now. No, here she is!"

Dinah, with laughing lips and sparkling eyes, had just ventured to the door with Billy. "We'll just peep," she said to her brother in the gay young tones that penetrated so much further than she realized. "But I shall never dare to dance. Why, I've never even seen the inside of a ballroom before. And as to dancing with a real live man -" She broke off as she caught sight of the two brothers standing together near the entrance.

Eustace turned his restless eyes upon her, gave her a swift, critical glance and muttered something to Scott.

The latter at once stepped forward, receiving a smile so radiant that even Eustace was momentarily dazzled. The little brown girl certainly had points.

"May I introduce my brother?" said Scott. "Sir Eustace Studley - Miss - I am afraid I don't know your surname."

"Sketchy," murmured Eustace, as he bowed.

But Dinah only laughed her ringing, merry laugh. "Of course you don't know. How could you? Our name is Bathurst. I'm Dinah and this is Billy. I am years older than he is, of course." She gave Eustace a shy glance. "How do you do?"

"She's just thirty," announced Billy, in shrill, cracked tones. "She's just pretending to be young to-night, but she ain't young really. You should see her without her warpaint."

The music became somewhat more audible at this point. Eustace bent slightly, looking down at the girl with eyes that were suddenly soft as velvet. "They are beginning to dance," he said. "May I have the pleasure? It's a pity to lose time."

Her red lips smiled delighted assent. She laid her hand with a feathery touch upon the arm he offered. "Oh, how lovely!" she said, and slid into his hold like a giddy little water-fowl taking to its own beloved element.

"Well, I'm jiggered!" said Billy. "And she's never danced with a man - except of course me - before!"

"Live and learn!" said Scott.

He watched the couple go up the great room, and he saw that, as he had suspected, Dinah was an exquisite dancer. Her whole being was merged in movement. She was as an instrument in the hand of a skilled player.

Sir Eustace Studley was an excellent dancer too, though he did not often trouble himself to dance as perfectly as he was dancing now. It was not often that he had a partner worthy of his best, and it was a semi-conscious habit of his never voluntarily to give better than he received.

But this little gipsy-girl of Scott's discovery called forth all his talent. She did not want to talk. She only wanted to dance, to spend herself in a passion of dancing that was an ecstasy beyond all speech. She was as sensitive as a harp-string to his touch; she was music, she was poetry, she was charm. The witchery of her began to possess him. Her instant response to his mood, her almost uncanny interpretation thereof, became like a spell to his senses. From wonder he passed to delight, and from delight to an almost feverish desire for more. He swayed her to his will with a well-nigh savage exultation, and she gave herself up to it so completely, so freely, so unerringly, that it was as if her very individuality had melted in some subtle fashion and become part of his. And to the man there came a moment of sheer intoxication, as though he drank and drank of a sparkling, inspiriting wine that lured him, that thrilled him, that enslaved him.

It was just when the sensation had reached its height that the music suddenly quickened for the finish. That brought him very effectually to earth. He ceased to dance and led her aside.

She turned her bright face to him for a moment, in her eyes the dazed, incredulous look of one awaking from an enthralling dream. "Oh, can't we dance it out?" she said, as if she pleaded against being aroused.

He shook his head. "I never dance to a finish. It's too much like the clown's turn after the transformation scene. It is bathos on the top of the superb. At least it would be in this case. Who in wonder taught you to dance like that?"

Dinah opened her eyes a little wider and gave him the Homage of shy admiration; but she met a look in return that amazed her, that sent the blood in a wild unreasoning race to her heart. For those eyes of burning, ardent blue had suddenly told her something, something that no eyes had told her before. It was incredible but true. Homage had met homage, aye, and more than homage. There was mastery in his look; but there was also wonder and a curious species of half-grudging reverence. She had amazed him, this witch with the sparkling eyes that shone so alluringly under the scarlet kerchief. She had swept him as it were with a fan of flame. She had made him live. And he had pronounced her ordinary!

"I have always loved to dance," she said in answer to his almost involuntary question. "Do you like my dancing? I'm so glad."

"Like it!" He laughed with an odd shamefacedness. "I could dance with you the whole evening. But I should probably end by making a fool of myself like a man who has had too much champagne."

Dinah laughed. She had an exhilarating sense of having achieved a conquest undreamed of. She also was feeling a little giddy, a little uncertain of the ground under her feet.

"Do you know," she said, dropping her eyes instinctively before the fiery intensity of his, "I've never danced with a man before? I - I was a little afraid just at first lest you should find me - gawky."

"Ye gods!" said Sir Eustace. "And you have really never danced with a man before! Tell me! How did you like it?"

"It was - heavenly!" said Dinah, drawing a deep breath.

"Will you dance with me again?" he asked.

She nodded. "Yes."

"The very next dance?"

She nodded again. "Yes."

"And again after that?" said Sir Eustace.

She threw him a glance half-shy, half-daring. "Don't you think it might be too much for you?"

He laughed. "I'll risk it if you will."

Ethel M. Dell

She turned towards him with a small, confidential gesture. "What about Rose de Vigne?" she said. "Don't you want to dance with her?"

"Oh, presently," he said. "She'll keep."

Dinah broke into her high, sweet laugh. "And what about - all my other partners?" she said, with more assurance.

He bent to her. "They must keep too. Seriously, you don't want to dance with any other fellow, do you?"

"I'm not a bit serious," said Dinah.

"Do you?" he insisted.

She lifted her eyes momentarily.

"You don't?" he insinuated.

She surrendered without conditions. "Of course I don't."

"Then you mustn't," he said. "Consider yourself booked to me for to-night, and when you're not dancing with me, you can rest. Sit out with Scott if you like! Will you do that?"

"Why?" whispered Dinah.

Again her heart was beating very fast; she wondered why.

He answered her with an impetuosity that seemed to carry her along with it. "Because your dancing is superb, magnificent, and I want to keep it for myself. It may not be the same when you've danced with another man. A flower fresh plucked is always sweeter than one that someone else has worn."

Dinah's hands clasped each other unconsciously. She had never dreamed that Apollo could so stoop to favour her.

"I will do as you like," she murmured after a moment. "But I don't suppose for an instant that anyone else would want to dance with me. I don't know anyone else."

He smiled. "I'm glad of that. It would be sheer sacrilege for you to dance with a young oaf who didn't know how. It's a bargain then. I'll give you all I can. You mustn't tell, of course."

"Oh, I won't tell," laughed Dinah.

He gave her his arm. "They are tuning up. We won't lose a minute. I always like a clear floor, before the rabble begin."

He led her to the top of the room, stood for a moment; then, as the music began, caught her to him, and they floated once more into the shining, enchanted mazes of their dreamland.

And Dinah danced as one inspired, for it seemed to her that her feet moved upon air as though winged. Apollo had drawn her up to Olympus, and she drifted in his arm in spheres unknown, far above the clouds.

CHAPTER VI

CINDERELLA

"Come and sit down!" said Scott.

Dinah gave a little start. She was standing close to him, but she had not seen him. She looked at him for a second with far-away eyes, as if she did not know him.

Then recognition flashed into them. She smiled an eager greeting. "Oh, Mr. Studley, I want to thank you for the very happiest evening of my life."

He smiled also as he sat down beside her. "You are enjoying yourself?"

"Oh yes, indeed I am!" she assured him. "Thank you a hundred million times!"

"Why thank me?" questioned Scott.

She drew a long, long breath. "Because you were the magician who pulled the strings. I should never have got dressed in the first place but for you."

He gave a laugh of amused protest. "Oh, surely! I don't feel I deserve that!"

She laughed with him. "You did it anyhow. And in the second

place you got me out of a villainous bad temper and turned an ugly goblin into a very happy butterfly. I'm downright ashamed of myself for being so horrid about Rose de Vigne. She isn't at all a bad sort though she is so impossibly beautiful. Your brother is going to dance with her now. See! There they go!"

She looked after them with a smile of complete content.

"You're feeling generous," remarked Scott.

She turned to him again, flushed and radiant. "I can afford to - though it's for the first time in my life. I've never had such a happy time, - never, never, never! Isn't your brother wonderful? His dancing is -" Words failed her. She raised her hands and let them fall with a gesture expressive of unbounded admiration.

"You mustn't let him monopolize you," said Scott. "He has plenty to choose from, you know. Others haven't."

She laughed. "He says - I wonder if it's true! - he says I am the best dancer he has ever met!"

Scott smiled at her beaming face. "That is very nice - for him," he observed. "I thought you seemed to be getting on very well."

Her eyes travelled across the room again to her late partner and the beautiful Miss de Vigne. She watched them intently for a few seconds.

"Poor Rose!" she said suddenly.

Scott was watching her. "Isn't she a good dancer?" he asked.

She turned back to him. "Oh yes, I believe she is. She always has plenty of partners anyway. At least I've always heard so. Is your sister dancing? I don't think I can have seen her yet."

"No. She is in her sitting-room upstairs. I wanted her to come down, but she wouldn't be persuaded. She -" Scott hesitated a moment - "is not fond of gaiety."

"Then I shan't see her!" said Dinah in tones of genuine disappointment. "I did so want to thank her for lending me these lovely things."

"I can take you to her if you'll come," said Scott.

"Oh, can you? Yes, I'll come. I can come now. But are you sure she will like it?" Dinah's bright eyes met his with frank directness. "I don't want to intrude on her, you know," she said.

He smiled a little. "I am sure you won't intrude. Shall we go then? Are you sure there is no one else you want to dance with here?"

"Oh, quite sure." Again momentarily Dinah's look sought her late partner; then briskly she stood up.

Scott rose also, and gave her his arm. She bestowed a small, friendly squeeze upon it. "I've never enjoyed myself so much before," she said. "And it's all your doing."

"Oh, not really!" he said.

She nodded vigorously. "But it is! I should never have been presentable but for you. And I should certainly never have danced with your brother. He has actually promised to help me with my skating to-morrow. Isn't it kind of him?"

"I wonder," said Scott.

"What do you wonder?" Dinah looked at him curiously.

But he only smiled a baffling smile, and turned the subject. "Wouldn't you like something to drink before we go up?"

Dinah declined. She was not in the least thirsty. She did not feel as if she would ever want to eat or drink again.

"Only to dance!" said Scott. "Well, I mustn't keep you long then. Who is that lady making signs to you? Hadn't you better go and speak to her?"

"Oh, bother!" said Dinah. "You come too, then. It's only Lady Grace - Rose's mother. I'm sure it can't be anything important."

Scott piloted her across the vestibule to the couch on which Lady Grace sat. She was a large, fair woman with limpid eyes and drawling speech. She extended a plump white hand to the girl.

"Dinah, my dear, I think you have had almost enough for to-night. And they were so very behind time in starting. Your mother would not like you to stay up late, I feel sure. You had better go to bed when this dance is over. You are not accustomed to dissipation, remember."

A swift cloud came over Dinah's bright face. "Oh, but, Lady Grace, I'm not in the least tired. And I'm not a baby, you know. I'm nearly twenty. I really couldn't go yet."

"You will have plenty more opportunities, dear," said Lady Grace, quite unruffled. "Rose has decided to retire after this dance, and I shall do the same. The Colonel is suffering with dyspepsia, and he does not wish us to be late."

Dinah bit her lip. "Oh, very well," she said somewhat shortly; and to Scott, "We had better go at once then."

He led her away obediently. They ascended the stairs together.

As they reached the top of the flight Dinah's indignation burst its bounds. "Isn't it too bad? Why should I go to bed just because the Colonel's got dyspepsia? I don't believe it's that at

Ethel M. Dell

all really. It's Rose who can't bear to think that I am having as good a time - or Better - than she is."

"May I say what I think?" asked Scott politely.

She stopped, facing him. "Yes, do!"

He was smiling somewhat whimsically. "I think that - like Cinderella - you may break the spell if you stay too long."

"But isn't it too bad?" protested Dinah. "Your brother too - I can't disappoint him."

Scott's smile became a laugh. "Oh, believe me, it would do him good, Miss Bathurst. He gets his own way much too often."

She smiled, but not very willingly. "It does seem such a shame. He has been - so awfully nice to me."

"That's nothing," said Scott airily. "We can all be nice when we are enjoying ourselves."

Dinah looked at him with sudden attention. "Are you pointing a moral?" she asked severely.

"Trying to," said Scott.

She tried to frown upon him, but very abruptly and completely failed. Her pointed chin went up in a gay laugh. "You do it very nicely," she said. "Thank you, Mr. Studley. I won't be grumpy any more. It would be a pity to break the spell, as you say. Will you explain to the prince?"

"Certainly," he said, leading her on again. "I shall make it quite clear to him that Cinderella was not to blame. Here is our sitting-room at the end of this passage!"

He stopped at the door and would have opened it, but Dinah,

smitten with sudden shyness, drew back.

"Hadn't you better go in first and - and explain?" she said.

"Oh no, quite unnecessary," he said, and turned the handle.

At once a woman's voice accosted him. "For the Lord's sake, Master Stumpy, come in quick and shut the door behind ye! The racket downstairs is sending Miss Isabel nearly crazy, poor lamb. And it's meself that's wondering what we'll do to-night, for there's no peace at all in this wooden shanty of a place."

"Be quiet, Biddy!" Scott's voice made calm, undaunted answer. "You can go if you like. I've come to sit with Miss Isabel for a while. And I've brought her a visitor. Isabel, my dear, I've brought you a visitor."

Dinah moved forward in response to his gentle insistence, but her shyness went with her. She was aware of something intangible in the atmosphere that startled, that almost frightened, her.

The gaunt figure of a woman clad in a long, white robe sat at a table in the middle of the room with a sheaf of letters littered before her. Her emaciated arms were flung wide over them, her white head was bowed.

But at Scott's quiet announcement, it was raised with the suddenness of eager expectancy. For the fraction of a second Dinah saw dark, sunken eyes ablaze with a hope that was almost terrible in its intensity.

It was gone on the instant. They looked at her with a species of dull wonder. "Are you a friend of Scott's? I am very pleased to meet you," a hollow voice said.

A thin hand was extended to her, and as Dinah clasped it a sudden great pity surged through her, dispelling her doubt. Something in her responded swiftly, even passionately, to the hunger of those eyes. The moment's shock passed from her like a cloud.

"My sister Mrs. Everard," said Scott's voice at her shoulder. "Isabel, this is Miss Bathurst of whom I was telling you."

"You lent me your jewels," said Dinah, looking into the wasted face with a sympathy at her heart that was almost too poignant to be borne. "Thank you so very, very much for them! It was so very kind of you to lend them to a total stranger like me."

The strange eyes were gazing at her with a curious, growing interest. A faint, faint smile was in their depths. "Are we strangers, child?" the low voice asked. "I feel as if we had met before. Why do you look at me so kindly? Most people only stare."

Dinah was suddenly conscious of a hot sensation at the throat that made her want to cry. "It is you who have been kind," she said, and her little hand closed with confidence upon the limp, cold fingers. "I am wearing your things still, and I have had such a lovely time. Thank you again for letting me have them. I am going to return them now."

"You need not do that." Isabel spoke with her eyes still fixed upon the girlish face. "Keep them if you like them! I shall never wear them again. They tell me - they tell me - I am a widow."

"Miss Isabel darlint!" Biddy spoke sibilantly from the background. "Don't be talking to the young lady of such things! Won't ye sit down then, miss? And maybe I can get ye a cup o' tay."

"Ah, do, Biddy!" Scott put in his quiet word. "There is no tea like yours. Isabel, Miss Bathurst is a keen dancer. She and Eustace have been most energetic. It was a pity you couldn't come down and see the fun."

"Oh! Did you enjoy it?" Isabel still looked into the brown, piquant face as though loth to turn her eyes away.

"I loved it," said Dinah.

"Was Eustace kind to you?"

"Oh, most kind." Dinah spoke with candid enthusiasm.

"I am glad of that," Isabel's voice held a note of satisfaction. "But I should think everyone is kind to you, child," she said, with her faint, glimmering smile. "How beautiful you are!"

"Me!" Dinah opened her eyes in genuine astonishment. "Oh you wouldn't think so if you saw me in my ordinary dress," she said. "I'm nothing at all to look at really. It's just a case of 'Fine feathers,' - nothing else."

"My dear," Isabel said, "I am not looking at your dress. I seldom notice outer things. I am looking through your eyes into your soul. It is that that makes you beautiful. I think it is the loveliest thing that I have ever seen."

"Oh, you wouldn't say so if you knew me!" cried Dinah, conscience-stricken. "I have horrid thoughts often - very often."

The dark, watching eyes still smiled in their far-off way. "I should like to know you, dear child," Isabel said. "You have helped me - you could help me in a way that probably you will never understand. Won't you sit down? I will put my letters away, and we will talk."

She began to collect the litter before her, laying the letters together one by one with reverent care.

"Can I help?" asked Dinah timidly.

But she shook her head. "No, child, your hands must not

touch them. They are the ashes of my life."

An open box stood on the table. She drew it to her, and laid the letters within it. Then she rose, and drew her guest to a lounge.

"We will sit here," she said. "Stumpy, why don't you smoke? Ah, the music has stopped at last. It has been racking me all the evening. Yes, you love it, of course. That is natural. I loved it once. It is always sweet to those who dance. But to those who sit out - those who sit out -" Her voice sank, and she said no more.

Dinah's hand slipped softly into hers. "I like sitting out too sometimes," she said. "At least I like it now."

Isabel's eyes were upon her again. They looked at her with a kind of incredulous wonder. After a moment she sighed.

"You would not like it for long, child. I am a prisoner. I sit in chains while the world goes by. They are all hurrying forward so eager to get on. But there is never any going on for me. I sit and watch - and watch."

"Surely we must all go forward somehow," said Dinah shyly.

"Surely," said Scott.

But Isabel only shook her head with dreary conviction. "Not the prisoners," she said. "They die by the wayside."

There fell a brief silence, then impetuously Dinah spoke, urged by the fulness of her heart. "I think we all feel like that sometimes. I know at home it's just like being in a cage. Nothing ever happens worth mentioning. And then quite suddenly the door is opened and out we come. That's partly why I am enjoying everything so much," she explained. "But it won't be a bit nice going back."

"What about your mother?" said Scott.

Dinah's bright face clouded again. "Yes, of course, there's Mother," she agreed.

She looked across at Scott as if she would say more; but he passed quietly on. "Where is your home, Miss Bathurst?"

"Right in the very heart of the Midlands. It is pretty country, but oh, so dull. The de Vignes are the rich people of the place. They belong to the County. We don't," said Dinah, with a sigh.

Scott laughed, and she looked momentarily hurt.

"I don't see what there is funny in that. The County people and the shop people are the only ones that get any fun. It's horrid to be between the two."

"Forgive me!" Scott said. "I quite see your point. But if you only knew it, the people who call themselves County are often the dullest of the dull."

"You say that because you belong to them, I expect," retorted Dinah. "But if you were me, and lived always under the shadow of the de Vignes, you wouldn't think it a bit funny."

"Who are the de Vignes?" asked Isabel suddenly.

Dinah turned to her. "We are staying here with them, Billy and I. My father persuaded the Colonel to have us. He knew how dreadfully we wanted to go. The Colonel is rather good-natured over some things, and he and Dad are friends. But I don't think Lady Grace wanted us much. You see, she and Rose are so very smart."

"I see," said Scott.

"Rose has been presented at Court," pursued Dinah. "They

always go up for the season. They have a house in town. We always say that Rose is waiting to marry a marquis; but he hasn't turned up yet. You see, she really is much too beautiful to marry an ordinary person, isn't she?"

"Oh, much," said Scott.

Dinah heaved another little sigh; then suddenly she laughed. "But your brother has promised to help me with my skating to-morrow anyhow," she said. "So she won't have him all the time."

"Perhaps the marquis will come along to-morrow," suggested Scott.

"I wish he would," said Dinah, with fervour.

CHAPTER VII

THE BROKEN SPELL

Biddy was in the act of handing round the tea when there came the sound of a step outside, and an impatient hand thrust open the door.

"Hullo, Stumpy!" said a voice. "Are you here? What have you done with Miss Bathurst? She's engaged to me for the next dance." Eustace entered with the words, but stopped short on the threshold. "Hullo! You are here! I thought you had given me the slip."

Dinah looked up at him with merry eyes. "So I have - practically. I am on my way to bed."

"Oh, nonsense!" he said, with his easy imperiousness. "I can't spare you yet. I must have one more dance just to soothe my nerves. I've been dancing with a faultless automaton who didn't understand me in the least. Now I want the real thing again."

"Have some tea!" said Scott.

"Thanks!" Sir Eustace sat down on the edge of the table, facing his sister and Dinah. "You're not going to let me down, now are you?" he said. "I'm counting on that dance, and I haven't enjoyed myself at all since I saw you last. That girl is machine-made. There isn't a flaw in her. She's been turned out of a mould; I'm certain of it. Miss Bathurst, why are you laughing?"

"Because I'm pleased," said Dinah.

"Pleased? I thought you'd be sorry for me. You're going to take pity on me anyway, I hope. The beautiful automaton has gone back to her band-box for the night, so we can enjoy ourselves quite unhindered. Is that for me? Thanks, Biddy! I'm needing refreshment badly."

"You would have preferred coffee," observed Isabel.

It was the first time she had spoken since his entrance. He gave her a keen, intent look. "Oh, this'll do, thanks," he said. "It is all nectar to-night. Why haven't you been down to the ballroom, Isabel? You would have enjoyed it."

Her lips twisted a little. "I have been listening to the music upstairs," she said.

"You ought to have come down," he said imperiously. "I shall expect you next time." His hand inadvertently touched the box on the table and he looked sharply downwards. "Here, Biddy! Take this thing away!" he ordered with a frown.

Isabel leaned swiftly forward. "Give it to me!" she said.

His hand closed upon it. "No. Let Biddy take it!"

"Let me!" said Dinah suddenly, and sprang to her feet.

She took it from him before he had time to protest, and gave it forthwith into Isabel's outstretched hands.

Eustace took up his cup in heavy silence, and drained it.

Then he rose. "Come along, Miss Bathurst!"

But Dinah remained seated. "I am very sorry," she said. "But I can't."

"Oh, nonsense!" He smiled very suddenly and winningly upon her. "Surely you won't disappoint me!"

She shook her head. Her eyes were wistful. "I'm disappointing myself quite as much. But I mustn't. The Colonel has gone to bed with dyspepsia, and Lady Grace and Rose have gone too by this time. I can't come down again."

"Nonsense!" he said again. "You want to. You know you do. No one pays any attention to Mrs. Grundy out here. She simply doesn't exist. Scott can come and play propriety. He's staid enough to chaperon a whole girls' school."

"Thanks, old chap," said Scott. "But I'm not coming down again, either."

Eustace looked over his head. "Then you must, Isabel. Come along! Just to oblige Miss Bathurst! It won't hurt you to sit in a safe corner for one dance."

Isabel looked up at him with a startled expression, as of one trapped. "Oh, don't ask me!" she said. "I couldn't!"

"No, don't!" said Dinah. "It isn't, fair to bother anyone else on my account! I'm dreadfully sorry to have to refuse. But - in any case - I ought not to come."

"What of that?" said Eustace lightly. "Do you always do what you ought? What a dull programme!"

Dinah flushed. "Dull but respectable," she said, with a touch of spirit.

He laughed. "But I'm not asking you to do anything very outrageous, and I shouldn't ask it at all if I didn't know you wanted to do it. Besides, you promised. It's generally considered the respectable thing to do to keep one's promises."

That reached Dinah. She wavered perceptibly. "Lady Grace will be so vexed," she murmured.

He snapped his fingers in careless disdain.

She turned appealingly to Scott. "I think I might go - just for one dance, don't you?"

Scott's pale eyes met hers with steady comradeship. "I think I shouldn't," he said.

Eustace turned as if he had not heard and strolled to the door. He opened it, and at once the room was filled with the plaintive alluring strains of waltz-music. He stood and looked back. Dinah met the look, and suddenly she was on her feet.

He held out his hand to her with a smile half-mocking, half-persuasive. The music swung on with a subtle enchantment. Dinah uttered a little quivering laugh, and went to him.

In another moment the door closed, and they stood alone in the passage.

"I knew you wanted to," said Eustace, smiling down into her eyes with the arrogance of the conqueror.

Dinah was panting a little as one who had suffered a sudden strain. "Of course I wanted to," she returned. "But that doesn't make it right."

He pressed her hand to his heart for a moment, and she caught again a glimpse of that fire in his eyes that had so thrilled her. She could not meet it. She stood in palpitating silence.

"Where is the use of fighting against fate?" he asked her softly. "A gift of the gods is never offered twice."

She did not understand him, but her heart was beating wildly, tumultuously, and an inner voice urged her to be gone.

She slipped her hand free. "Aren't we - wasting time?" she whispered.

He laughed again in that subtle, half-mocking note, but he met her wish instantly. They went downstairs to the *salon.*

There were not so many dancers now. The de Vignes had evidently retired. One rapid glance told Dinah this, and she dismissed them therewith from her mind. The rhythm and lure of the music caught her. She slid into the dance with delicious abandonment. The wonder and romance of it had got into her veins. No stolen pleasure was ever more keenly enjoyed than was that last perfect dance. Her very blood was a-fire with the strange, intoxicating joy of life. She wanted to go on for ever.

But it ended at length. She came to earth after her rapturous flight, and found herself standing with her partner in a curtained recess of the ballroom from which a glass door led on to the verandah that ran round the hotel.

"Just a glimpse of the moonlight on the mountains," he said, "before we say good-night!"

She went with him without a moment's thought. She was as one caught in the meshes of a great enchantment. He opened the door, and she passed through on to the verandah.

The music throbbed into silence behind them. Before them lay a fairy-world of dazzling silver and deepest, darkest sapphire. The mountains stood in solemn grandeur, domes of white mystery. The great vault of the sky was alight with stars, and a wonderful moon hung like a silver shield almost in the zenith.

"How - beautiful!" breathed Dinah.

The air was crystal clear, cold but not piercing. The absolute stillness held her spell-bound.

"It is like a dream-world," she whispered.

"In which you reign supreme," he murmured back.

She glanced at him with uncomprehending eyes. Her veins were still throbbing with the ecstasy of the dance.

"Oh, how I wish I had wings!" she suddenly said. "To swim through that glorious ether right above the mountain-tops as one swims through the sea! Don't you think flying must be very like swimming?"

"With variations," said Eustace.

His eyes dwelt upon her. They were fierily blue in that great flood of moonlight. His hand still rested upon her waist.

"But what a mistake to want the impossible!" he said, after a moment.

"I always do," said Dinah. "At least," she glanced up at him again, "I always have - until to-night."

"And to-night?" he questioned, dropping his voice.

"Oh, I am quite happy to-night," she said, with a little laugh, "even without the wings. If I hadn't thought of them, I should have nothing left to wish for."

"I wish I could say the same," said Sir Eustace, with the faint mocking smile at the corners of his lips.

"What can you want more?" asked Dinah innocently.

He leaned to her. "A big thing - a small thing! Would you give it to me, my elf of the mountains, if I dared to tell you what it was?"

Her eyes fluttered and fell before the flaming ardour of his. "I - I don't know," she faltered, in sudden confusion. "I expect so - if I could."

His arm slipped round her. "Would you?" he whispered. "Would you?"

She gave a little gasp, caught unawares like a butterfly on the wing. All the magic of the night seemed suddenly to be concentrated upon her like fairy batteries. Her first feeling was dismay, followed instantly by the wonder if she could be dreaming. And then, as she felt the drawing of his arm, something vehement, something almost fierce, awoke within her, clamouring wildly for freedom.

It was a blind instinct, but she obeyed it without question. She had no choice.

"Oh no!" she cried. "Oh no! I couldn't!" and wrested herself from him in a panic.

He let her go, and she heard him laugh as she broke away. But she did not wait for more. To linger was unthinkable. Urged by that imperative, inner prompting she turned and fled, not pausing for a moment's thought.

The glass door closed behind her. She burst impetuously into the deserted ballroom. And here, on the point of entering the small recess from which she was escaping, she came suddenly face to face with Scott.

So headlong was her flight that she actually ran into him. He put out a steadying hand.

"I was just coming to look for you," he said in his quiet, composed fashion.

She stopped unwillingly. "Oh, were you? How kind! I - I think I ought to go up now. It's getting late, isn't it? Good-night!"

He did not seek to detain her. She wondered with a burning sense of shame what he could have thought of her wild rush. But she was too agitated to attempt any excuse, too agitated to check her retreat. Without a backward glance she hastened away like Cinderella overtaken by fate; the spell was broken, the glamour gone.

CHAPTER VIII

MR. GREATHEART

It was a very meek and subdued Dinah who made her appearance in the *salle-a-manger* on the following morning.

She and Billy were generally in the best of spirits, and the room usually rang with their young laughter. But that morning even Billy was decorously quiet, and his sister scarcely spoke or raised her eyes.

Colonel de Vigne, white-moustached and martial, sat at the table with them, but neither Lady Grace nor Rose was present. The Colonel's face was stern. He occupied himself with letters with scarcely so much as a glance for the boy and girl on either side of him.

There was a letter by Dinah's plate also, but she had not opened it. Her downcast face was very pale. She ate but little, and that little only when urged thereto by Billy, whose appetite was rampant notwithstanding the decorum of his behaviour.

Scott, breakfasting with his brother at a table only a few yards distant, observed the trio with unobtrusive interest.

He had made acquaintance with the Colonel on the previous evening, and after a time the latter caught his eye and threw him a brief greeting. Most people were polite to Scott. But the Colonel's whole aspect was forbidding that morning, and his courtesy went no further.

Sir Eustace did not display the smallest interest in anyone. His black brows were drawn, and he looked even more haughtily unapproachable than the Colonel.

He conversed with his brother in low tones on the subject of the morning's mail which lay at Scott's elbow and which he was investigating while he ate. Now and then he gave concise and somewhat peremptory instructions, which Scott jotted down in a note-book with business-like rapidity. No casual observer would have taken them for brothers that morning. They were employer and secretary.

Only when the last letter had been discussed and laid aside did the elder abruptly abandon his aloof attitude to ask a question upon a more intimate matter.

"Did Isabel go without a sleeping-draught last night?"

Scott shook his head.

Eustace's frown became even more pronounced. "Did Biddy administer it on her own?"

"No. I authorized it." Scott's voice was low. He met his brother's look with level directness.

Eustace leaned towards him across the table. "I won't have it, Stumpy," he said very decidedly. "I told you so yesterday."

"I know." Very steadily Scott made answer. "But last night there was no alternative. It is impossible to do the thing suddenly. She has hardly got over the journey yet."

"Rubbish!" said Eustace curtly.

Scott slightly raised his shoulders, and said no more.

"It comes to this," Eustace said, speaking with stern insistence. "If you can't - or won't - assert your authority, I shall assert mine. It is all a question of influence."

"Or forcible persuasion," said Scott, with a touch of irony.

"Very well. Call it that! It is in a good cause. If you haven't the strength of mind, I have; and I shall exercise it. These drugs must be taken away. Can't you see it's the only possible thing to do?"

"Not yet," Scott said. He was still facing his brother's grim regard very gravely and unflinchingly. "I tell you, man, it is too soon. She is better than she used to be. She is calmer, more reasonable. We must do the thing gradually, if at all. To interfere forcibly would do infinitely more harm than good. I know what I am saying. I know her far better than you do now. I am in closer touch with her. You are out of sympathy. You only startle her when you try to persuade her to anything. You must leave her to me. I understand her. I know how to help her."

"You haven't achieved much in the last seven years," Eustace observed.

"But I have achieved something." Scott's answer was wholly free from resentment. He spoke with quiet confidence. "I know it's a slow process. But she is moving in the right direction. Give her time, old chap! I firmly believe that she will come back to us by slow degrees."

"Damnably slow," commented Eustace. "You're so infernally deliberate always. You talk as if it were your life-work."

Scott's eyes shone with a whimsical light. "I begin to think it is," he said. "Have you finished? Suppose we go." He gathered up the sheaf of papers at his elbow and rose. "I will attend to these at once."

Eustace strode down the long room looking neither to right nor left, moving with a free, British arrogance that served to emphasize somewhat cruelly the meagreness and infirmity of the man behind him. Yet it was upon the latter's slight, halting figure that Dinah's eyes dwelt till it finally limped out of sight, and in her look were wonder and a vagrant admiration. There was an undeniable attraction about Scott that affected her very curiously, but wherein it lay she could not possibly have said. She was furious when a murmured comment and laugh from some girls at the next table reached her.

"What a dear little lap-dog!" said one.

"Yes, I've been wanting to pat its head for a long time," said another.

"Warranted not to bite," laughed a third. "Can it really be full-grown?"

"Oh, no doubt, my dear! Look at its pretty little whiskers! It's just a toy, you know, nothing but a toy."

Dinah turned in her chair, and gazed scathingly upon the group of critics. Then, aware of the Colonel's eyes upon her, she turned back and gave him a swift look of apology.

He shook his head at her repressively, his whole air magisterial and condemnatory. "You may go if you wish," he said, in the tone of one dismissing an offender. "But be good enough to bear in mind what I have said to you!"

Billy leapt to his feet. "Can I go too, sir?" he asked eagerly.

The Colonel signified majestic assent. His mood was very far from genial that morning, and he had not the smallest desire to detain either of them. In fact, if he could have dismissed his two young charges altogether, he would have done so with alacrity. But that unfortunately was out of the question - unless by their behaviour they provoked him to fulfil the very definite threat that he had pronounced to Dinah in the privacy of his wife's room an hour before.

He was very seriously displeased with Dinah, more displeased than he had been with anyone since his soldiering days, and he had expressed himself with corresponding severity. If she could not conduct herself becomingly and obediently, he would take them both straight home again and thus put a summary end to temptation. His own daughter had never given him any cause for uneasiness, and he did not see why he should be burdened with the escapades of anyone else's troublesome offspring. It was too much to expect at his time of life.

So a severe reprimand had been Dinah's portion, to which she, very meek and crestfallen, shorn of all the previous evening's glories, had listened with a humility that had slightly mollified her judge though he had been careful not to let her know it. She had been wild and flighty, and he was determined that she should feel the rod of discipline pretty smartly.

But when he finally rose from the table and stalked out of the room, it was a little disconcerting to find the culprit awaiting him in the vestibule to slip a shy hand inside his arm and whisper, "Do forgive me! I'm so sorry."

He looked down into her quivering face, saw the pleading eyes swimming in tears, and abruptly found that his displeasure had evaporated so completely that he could not even pretend to be angry any longer. He had never taken much notice of Dinah before, treating her, as did his wife and daughter, as a mere child and of no account. But now he suddenly realized that she was an engaging minx after all.

"Ashamed of yourself?" he asked gruffly, his white moustache twitching a little.

Dinah nodded mutely.

"Then don't do it again!" he said, and grasped the little brown hand for a moment with quite unwonted kindness.

It was a tacit forgiveness, and as such Dinah treated it. She smiled thankfully through her tears, and slipped away to recover her composure.

Nearly an hour later, Scott, having finished his letters, came upon her sitting somewhat disconsolately in the verandah. He paused on his way out.

"Good morning, Miss Bathurst! Aren't you going to skate this morning?"

She turned to him with a little movement of pleasure. "Good morning, Mr. Studley! I have been waiting here for you. I have brought down your sister's trinkets. Here they are!" She held out a neat little paper parcel to him. "Please will you thank her again for them very, very much? I do hope she didn't think me very rude last night, - though I'm afraid I was."

Her look was wistful. He took the packet from her with a smile.

"Of course she didn't. She was delighted with you. When are you coming to see her again?"

"I don't know," said Dinah.

"Come to tea!" suggested Scott.

Dinah hesitated, flushing.

"You've something else to do?" he asked in his cheery way. "Well, come another time if it won't bore you!"

"Oh, it isn't that!" said Dinah, and her flush deepened. "I - I would love to come. Only -" She glanced round at an elderly couple who had just come out, and stopped.

"I'm going down to the village with my letters," said Scott. "Will you come too?"

She welcomed the idea. "Oh yes, I should like to. It's such a glorious morning again, isn't it? It's a shame not to go out."

"Sure you're not wanting to skate?" he questioned.

"Yes, quite sure. I - I'm rather tired this morning, but a walk will do me good."

They passed the rink without pausing, though Scott glanced across to see his brother skimming along in the distance with a red-clad figure beside him. He made no comment upon the sight, and Dinah was silent also. Her gay animation that morning was wholly a minus quantity.

They went on down the hill, talking but little. Speech in Scott's society was never a necessity. His silences were so obviously friendly. He had a shrewd suspicion on this occasion that the girl beside him had something to say, and he waited for it with a courteous patience, abstaining from interrupting her very evident preoccupation.

They walked between fields of snow, all glistening in the sunshine. The blue of the sky was no longer sapphire but glorious turquoise. The very air sparkled, diamond-clear in the crystal splendour of the day.

Suddenly Dinah spoke. "I suppose one always feels horrid the next morning."

"Are you feeling the reaction?" asked Scott.

"Oh, it isn't only that, I'm feeling - ashamed," said Dinah, blushing very deeply.

He did not look at her. "I don't see why," he said gently, after a moment.

"Oh, but you do!" she said impatiently. "At least you can if you try. You knew I was wrong to go down again for that last dance, just as well as I did. Why, you tried to stop me!"

"Which was very presumptuous of me," said Scott.

"No, it wasn't. It was kind. And I - I was a perfect pig not to listen. I want you to know that, Mr. Studley. I want you to know that I'm very, very sorry I didn't listen." She spoke with trembling vehemence.

Scott smiled a little. He was looking tired that morning. There were weary lines about his eyes. "I don't know why you should be so very penitent, Miss Bathurst," he said. "It was quite a small thing."

"It got me into bad trouble anyway," said Dinah. "I've had a tremendous wigging from the Colonel this morning, and if - if I ever do anything so bad again, we're to be sent home."

"I call that unreasonable," said Scott with decision. "It was not such a serious matter as all that. If you want my opinion, I think it was a mistake - a small mistake - on your part; nothing more."

"But that wasn't all," said Dinah, looking away from him and quickening her pace, "I - I have offended your brother too."

"Good heavens!" said Scott. "And is that serious too?"

"Don't laugh!" protested Dinah. "Of course it's serious. He - he won't even look at me this morning." The sound of tears came suddenly into her voice. "I was waiting for you on the verandah a little while ago, and - and he went by with Rose and never glanced my way. All because - because - oh, I am a little fool!" she declared, with an angry stamp of the foot as she walked.

"He's the fool!" said Scott rather shortly. "I shouldn't bother myself over that if I were you."

"I can't help it," said Dinah, her voice squeaking on a note half-indignant, half-piteous. "I - I behaved so idiotically, just like a raw schoolgirl. And I hate myself for it now!"

Scott looked at her for the first time since the beginning of her confidences. "Do you know, Miss Bathurst," he said, "I have a suspicion that you are much too hard on yourself. Of course I don't know what happened, but I do know that my brother is much more likely to have been in the wrong than you were. The best thing you can do is simply to dismiss the matter from your mind. Behave as if nothing had happened! Cut him next time! It's far the best way of treating him."

Dinah smiled woefully. "And he will spread himself at Rose's feet like all the rest, and never come near me again."

Scott frowned a little. "Miss de Vigne won't have the mono-poly, I can assure you."

"She will," protested Dinah. "She knows how to flirt without being caught. I don't."

"Thank the gods for that!" said Scott with fervour. "So he tried to flirt, did he? And you objected. Was that it?"

"Something like that," murmured Dinah, with hot face averted.

"Then in heaven's name, continue to object!" he said, with unusual vehemence. "You did the right thing, child. Don't be drawn into doing what others do! Strike out a straight line for yourself, and stick to it! Above all, don't be ashamed of sticking to it! No woman was ever yet the better or the more attractive for cultivating her talent for flirting. Don't you know that it is your very genuineness and straightforwardness that is your charm?"

Dinah looked at him in sheer surprise. "I haven't got any charm," she said. "That's just the trouble. It was only my dancing that made your brother fancy I had last night."

Scott's frown deepened, became almost formidable, then suddenly vanished in a laugh. "That's just your point of view," he said. "Perhaps it's a pity to open your eyes. But whatever you do, don't try to humour my brother's whims! It would be very bad for him, and you certainly wouldn't gain anything by it. Put up with me for a change, and come to tea instead!"

A flash of gaiety gleamed for a moment in Dinah's eyes. It was the first he had seen that morning. "I'll come," she said, "if Lady Grace will let me. But I think I had better ask first, don't you?"

"Perhaps it would be safer," agreed Scott. "Tell her my sister is an invalid! I don't think she will object. I made the acquaintance of the doughty Colonel last night."

"You know he isn't a bad sort," said Dinah. "He is much nicer than Lady Grace or Rose. Of course he's rather stuck up, but that's only natural. He's lived so long in India, and now he's a J.P. into the bargain. It would be rather wonderful if he were anything else. Billy can't bear him, but then Billy's a boy."

"I like Billy," observed Scott.

"Yes, and Billy likes you," she answered warmly. "He's quite an intelligent boy."

"Evidently," agreed Scott, with a smile. "Now here is the village! Where do I post my letters?"

Dinah directed him with cheerful alacrity. She was feeling much happier; her tottering self-respect was almost restored.

"He is a dear little man!" she said to herself with enthusiasm, as she waited for him to purchase some stamps.

"You've done me no end of good," she said frankly to the man himself as they turned back.

"I am very pleased to hear it," said Scott. "And it is extremely kind of you to say so."

"It's the truth," she maintained. "And, oh, you haven't been smoking all this time. Don't you want to?"

He stopped at once, and took out his cigarette-case. "Now you mention it, I think I do. But I mustn't dawdle. I have got to get back to Isabel."

Dinah waited while the cigarette kindled. Then, with a touch of shyness, she spoke.

"Mr. Studley, has - has your sister been an invalid for long?"

He looked at her. "Do you want to hear about her?"

"Yes, please," said Dinah. "If you don't mind."

He began to walk on. It was evident that the hill was something of a difficulty to him. He moved slowly, and his limp became more pronounced. "No, I should like to tell you about her," he said. "You were so good yesterday, and I hadn't prepared you in the least. I hope it didn't give you a shock."

"Of course it didn't," Dinah answered. "I'm not such a donkey as that. I was only very, very sorry."

"Thank you," he said, as if she had expressed direct sympathy with himself. "It's hard to believe, isn't it, that seven years ago she was - even lovelier than the beautiful Miss de Vigne, only in a very different style?"

"Not in the least," Dinah assured him. "She is far lovelier than Rose now. She must have been - beautiful."

"She was," said Scott. "She was like Eustace, except that she was always much softer than he is. You would scarcely believe either that she is three years younger than he is, would you?"

"I certainly shouldn't," Dinah admitted. "But then, she must have come through years of suffering."

"Yes," Scott spoke with slight constraint, as though he could not bear to dwell on the subject. "She was a girl of intensely vivid feelings, very passionate and warmhearted. She and Eustace were inseparable in the old days. They did everything together. He thought more of her than of anyone else in the world. He does still."

"He wasn't very nice to her last night," Dinah ventured.

"No. He is often like that, and she is afraid of him. But the reason of it is that he feels her trouble so horribly, and whenever he sees her in that mood it hurts him intolerably. He is quite a good chap underneath, Miss Bathurst. Like Isabel, he feels certain things intensely. Of course he is five years older than I am, and we have never been pals in the sense that he and she were pals. I was always a slow-goer, and they went like the wind. But I know him. I know what his feelings are, and what this thing has been to him. And though I am now much more to Isabel than he will probably ever be again, he has never resented it or been anything but generous and willing to give place to me. That, you know, indicates greatness. With all his faults, he is great."

"He shouldn't make her afraid of him," Dinah said.

"I am afraid that is inevitable. He is strong, and she has lost her strength. Her marriage too alienated them in the first place. She had refused so many before Basil Everard came along, and I suppose he had begun to think that she was not the marrying sort. But Everard caught her almost in a day. They met in India. Eustace and she were touring there one winter. Everard was a senior subaltern in a Ghurka regiment -

an awfully taking chap evidently. They practically fell in love with one another at sight. Poor old Eustace!" Scott paused, faintly smiling. "He meant her to marry well if she married at all, and Basil was no more than the son of a country parson without a penny to his name. However, the thing was past remedy. I saw that when they came home, and Isabel told me about it. I was at Oxford then. She came down alone for a night, and begged me to try and talk Eustace over. It was the beginning of a barrier between them even then. It has grown high since. Eustace is a difficult man to move, you know. I did my level best with him, but I wasn't very successful. In the end of course the inevitable happened. Isabel lost patience and broke away. She was on her way out again before either of us knew. Eustace - of course Eustace was furious." Scott paused again.

Dinah's silence denoted keen interest. Her expression was absorbed.

He went on, the touch of constraint again apparent in his manner. It was evident that the narration stirred up deep feelings. "We three had always hung together. The family tie meant a good deal to us for the simple reason that we were practically the only Studleys left. My father had died six years before, my mother at my birth. Eustace was the head of the family, and he and Isabel had been all in all to each other. He felt her going more than I can possibly tell you, and scarcely a week after the news came he got his things together and went off in the yacht to South America to get over it by himself. I stayed on at Oxford, but I made up my mind to go out to her in the vacation. A few days after his going, I had a cable to say they were married. A week after that, there came another cable to say that Everard was dead."

"Oh!" Dinah drew a short, hard breath. "Poor Isabel!" she whispered.

"Yes." Scott's pale eyes were gazing straight ahead. "He was killed two days after the marriage. They had gone up to the

Hills, to a place he knew of right in the wilds on the side of a mountain, and pitched camp there. There were only themselves, a handful of Pathan coolies with mules, and a *shikari*. The day after they got there, he took her up the mountain to show her some of the beauties of the place, and they lunched on a ledge about a couple of hundred feet above a great lonely tarn. It was a wonderful place but very savage, horribly desolate. They rested after the meal, and then, Isabel being still tired, he left her to bask in the sunshine while he went a little further. He told her to wait for him. He was only going round the corner. There was a great bastion of rock jutting on to the ledge. He wanted to have a look round the other side of it. He went, - and he never came back."

"He fell?" Dinah turned a shocked face upon him. "Oh, how dreadful!"

"He must have fallen. The ledge dwindled on the other side of the rock to little more than four feet in width for about six yards. There was a sheer drop below into the pool. A man of steady nerve, accustomed to mountaineering, would make nothing of it; and, from what Isabel has told me of him, I gather he was that sort of man. But on that particular afternoon something must have happened. Perhaps his happiness had unsteadied him a bit, for they were absolutely happy together. Or it may have been the heat. Anyhow he fell, he must have fallen. And no one ever knew any more than that."

"How dreadful!" Dinah whispered again. "And she was left - all alone?"

"Quite alone except for the natives, and they didn't find her till the day after. She was pacing up and down the ledge then, up and down, up and down eternally, and she refused - flatly refused - to leave it till he should come back. She had spent the whole night there alone, waiting, getting more and more distraught, and they could do nothing with her. They were afraid of her. Never from that day to this has she admitted for a moment that he must have been killed, though in her heart she knows it, poor girl, just as she knew it from the very beginning."

"But what happened?" breathed Dinah. "What did they do? They couldn't leave her there."

"They didn't know what to do. The *shikari* was the only one with any ideas among them, and he wasn't especially brilliant. But after another day and night he hit on the notion of sending one of the coolies back with the news while he and the other men waited and watched. They kept her supplied with food. She must have eaten almost mechanically. But she never left that ledge. And yet - and yet - she was kept from taking the one step that would have ended it all. I sometimes wonder if it wouldn't have been better - more merciful -" He broke off.

"Perhaps God was watching her," murmured Dinah shyly.

"Yes, I tell myself that. But even so, I can't help wondering sometimes." Scott's voice was very sad. "She was left so terribly desolate," he said. "Those letters that you saw last night are all she has of him. He has gone, and taken the mainspring of her life with him. I hate to think of what followed. They sent up a doctor from the nearest station, and she was taken away, - taken by force. When I got to her three weeks later, she was mad, raving mad, with brain fever. I had the old nurse Biddy with me. We nursed her between us. We brought her back to what she is now. Some day, please God, we shall get her quite back again; but whether it will be for her happiness He only knows."

Scott ceased to speak. His brows were drawn as the brows of a man in pain.

Dinah's eyes were full of tears. "Oh, thank you for telling me! Thank you!" she murmured. "I do hope you will get her quite back, as you say."

He looked at her, saw her tears, and put out a gentle hand that rested for a moment upon her arm. "I am afraid I have made you unhappy. Forgive me! You are so sympathetic, and I have taken advantage of it. I think we shall get her back. She is coming very, very gradually. She has never before taken such an interest in anyone as she took in you last night. She was talking of you again this morning. She has taken a fancy to you. I hope you don't mind."

"Mind!" Dinah choked a little and smiled a quivering smile. "I am proud - very proud. I only wish I deserved it. What - what made you bring her here?"

"That was my brother's idea. Since we brought her home she has never been away, except once on the yacht; and then she was so miserable that we were afraid to keep her there. But he thought a thorough change - mountain air - might do her good. The doctor was not against it. So we came."

"And do you never leave her?" questioned Dinah.

"Practically never. Ever since that awful time in India she has been very dependent upon me. Biddy of course is quite indispensable to her. And I am nearly so."

"You have given yourself up to her in fact?" Quick admiration was in Dinah's tone.

He smiled. "It didn't mean so much to me as it would have meant to some men, Miss Bathurst, - as it would have meant to Eustace, for instance. I'm not much of a man. To give up my college career and settle down at home wasn't such a great wrench. I'm not especially clever. I act as my brother's secretary, and we find it answers very well. He is a rich man, and there is a good deal of business in connection with the estate, and so on. I am a poor man. By my father's will nearly everything was left to him and to Isabel. I was something of an offence to him, being the cause of my mother's death and misshapen into the bargain."

"What a wicked shame!" broke from Dinah.

"No, no! Some people are like that. They are made so. I don't feel in the least bitter about it. He left me enough to live upon, though as a matter of fact neither he nor anyone else expected me to grow up at the time that will was made. It was solely due to Biddy's devotion, I believe, that I managed to do so." He uttered his quiet laugh. "I am talking rather much about myself. It's kind of you not to be bored."

"Bored!" echoed Dinah, with shining eyes. "I think you are simply wonderful. I hope - I hope Sir Eustace realizes it."

"I hope he does," agreed Scott with a twinkle. "He has ample opportunities for doing so. Ah, there he is! He is actually skating alone. What has become of the beautiful Miss de Vigne, I wonder."

They walked on, nearing the rink. "I'm not going to be horrid about her any more," said Dinah suddenly. "You must have thought me a perfect little cat. And so I was!"

"Oh, please!" protested Scott. "I didn't!"

She laughed. "That just shows how kind you are. It doesn't make me feel the least bit better. I was a cat. There! Oh, your brother is calling you. I think I'll go."

She blushed very deeply and quickened her steps. Sir Eustace had come to the edge of the rink.

"Stumpy!" he called. "Stumpy!"

"How dare he call you that?" said Dinah. "I can't think how you can put up with it."

Scott raised his shoulders slightly, philosophically. "Doesn't the cap fit?" he said.

"Not a bit," Dinah declared with emphasis. "I have another name for you that suits you far better."

"Oh! What is that?" he looked at her with smiling curiosity.

Dinah's blush deepened from carmine to crimson. "I call you - Mr. Greatheart," she said, her voice very low. "Because you help everybody."

A gleam of surprise crossed his face. He flushed also; but she saw that though embarrassed, he was not displeased.

He put a hand to his cap. "Thank you, Miss Bathurst," he said simply, and turned without further words to answer his brother's summons.

Dinah walked quickly on. That stroll with Scott had quite lifted her out of her depression.

CHAPTER IX

THE RUNAWAY COLT

"It really is very tiresome," complained Lady Grace. "I knew that child was going to be a nuisance from the very outset."

"What has she done now?" growled the Colonel.

He was lounging in the easiest chair in the room, smoking an excellent cigar, preparatory to indulging in his afternoon nap. His wife reclined upon a sofa with a French novel which she had not begun to read. Through the great windows that opened on to the balcony the sunshine streamed in a flood of golden light. Rose was seated on the balcony enjoying the warmth. Lady Grace's eyes rested upon her slim figure in its scarlet coat as she made reply.

"These people - these Studleys - won't leave her alone. Or else she runs after them. I can't quite make out which. Probably the latter. Anyhow the sister - who, I believe is what is termed slightly mental - has asked her to go to tea in their private sitting-room. I have told her she must decline."

"Quite right," said the Colonel. "What did she say?"

Lady Grace uttered a little laugh. "Oh, she was very ridiculous and high-flown, as you may imagine. But, as I told her, I am directly responsible to her mother for any friendships she may make out here, and I am not disposed to take any risks. We all

Ethel M. Dell

know what Mrs. Bathurst can be like if she considers herself an injured party."

"A perfect she-dragon!" agreed the Colonel. "I fancy the child herself is still kept in order with the rod. Why, even Bathurst - great hulking ox - is afraid of her. Billy isn't, but then Billy apparently can do no wrong."

"She certainly loves no one else," said Lady Grace. "I never met anyone with such an absolutely vixenish and uncontrolled temper. I am sorry for Dinah. I have always pitied her, for she certainly works hard, and gets little praise for it. But at the same time, I can't let her run wild now she is off the rein for a little. It wouldn't be right. And these people are total strangers."

"I believe they are of very good family," said the Colonel. "The title is an old one, and Sir Eustace is evidently a rich man. I had the opportunity for a little talk with the brother yesterday evening. A very courteous little chap - quite unusually so. I think we may regard them as quite passable." His eyes also wandered to the graceful, lounging figure on the balcony. "At the same time I shouldn't let Dinah accept hospitality from them, anyhow at this stage. She is full young. She must be content to stay in the background - at least for the present."

"Just what I say," said Lady Grace. "Of course if the younger brother should take a fancy to her - and he certainly seems to be attracted - it might be a very excellent thing for her. Her mother can't hope to keep her as maid of all work for ever. But I can't have her pushing herself forward. I was very glad to hear you reprimand her so severely this morning."

"She deserved it," said the Colonel judicially. "But at the same time if there is any chance of what you suggest coming to pass, I have no wish to stand in the child's way. I have a fancy that she will find the bondage at home considerably more irksome after this taste of freedom. It might, as you say, be a good thing for her if the little chap did fall in love with her. Her mother can't expect much of a match for her."

"Oh, if that really happened, her mother would be charmed," said Lady Grace. "She is a queer, ill-balanced creature, and I don't believe she has ever had the smallest affection for her. She would be delighted to get her off her hands, I should say. But things mustn't move too quickly, or they may go in the wrong direction." Again her eyes sought her daughter's graceful outline. "You say Sir Eustace is rich?" she asked, after a moment.

"Extremely rich, I should say. He has his own yacht, a house in town as well as a large place in the country, and he will probably get a seat in Parliament at the next election. I'm not greatly taken with the man myself," declared Colonel de Vigne. "He is too overbearing. At the same time," again his eyes followed his wife's, "he would no doubt be a considerable catch."

"I don't mean Dinah to have Sir Eustace," said Lady Grace very decidedly. "It would be most unsuitable. Yes, what is it?" as a low knock came at the door. "Come in!"

It opened, and Dinah, looking flushed and rather uncertain, made her appearance.

"I wish you would have the consideration not to disturb us at this hour, my dear Dinah," said Lady Grace peevishly. "What is it you want now?"

"I am sorry," said Dinah meekly. "But I heard your voices, so I knew you weren't asleep. I just came in to say that Billy and I are going luging if you don't mind."

"What next?" said Lady Grace, still fretful. "Of course I don't mind so long as you don't get up to mischief."

"Dinah, come here!" said the Colonel suddenly.

Dinah, on the point of beating a swift retreat, stood still with obvious reluctance.

"Come here!" he repeated.

She went to him hesitatingly.

He reached up a hand and grasped her by the arm. "Were you eavesdropping just now?" he demanded.

Dinah started as if stung. "I - I - of course I wasn't!" she declared, with vehemence. "How can you suggest such a thing?"

"Quite sure?" said the Colonel, still holding her.

She wrenched herself from him in a sudden fury. "Colonel de Vigne, you - you insult me! I am not the sort that listens outside closed doors. How dare you? How dare you?"

She stamped her foot with the words, gazing down at him with blazing eyes.

The Colonel stiffened slightly, but he kept his temper. "If I have done you an injustice, I apologize," he said. "You may go."

And Dinah went like a whirlwind, banging the door behind her.

"Well, really!" protested Lady Grace in genuine displeasure.

Her husband smiled somewhat grimly. "A vixen's daughter, my dear! What can you expect?"

"She behaves like a fishwife's daughter," said Lady Grace. "And if she wasn't actually eavesdropping I am convinced she heard what I said."

"So am I," said the Colonel drily. "I was about to tax her with it. Hence her masterly retreat. But she was not deliberately eavesdropping or she would not have given herself away so openly. I quite agree with you, my dear. A match between her and Sir Eustace would not be suitable. And I also think Sir Eustace would be the first to see it. Anyhow, I shall take an early opportunity of letting him know that her birth is by no means a high one, and that her presence here is simply due to our kindness. At the same time, should the rather ludicrous little younger brother take it into his head to follow her up, so far as family goes he is of course too good for her, but I am sorry for the child and I shall put no obstacle in the way."

"All the same she shall not go to tea there unless Rose is invited too," said Lady Grace firmly.

"There," said the Colonel pompously, "I think that you are right."

Lady Grace simpered a little, and opened her novel. "It really wouldn't surprise me to find that she is a born fortune-hunter," she said. "I am certain the mother is avaricious."

"The mother," said Colonel de Vigne with the deliberation of one arrived at an unalterable decision, "is the most disagreeable, vulgar, and wholly objectionable person that I have ever met."

"Oh, quite," said Lady Grace. "If she were in our set, she would be altogether intolerable. But - thank heaven - she is not! Now, dear, if you don't mind, I am going to read myself to sleep. I have promised Rose to go to the ice carnival to-night, and I need a little relaxation first."

"I suppose Dinah is going?" said the Colonel.

"Oh, yes. But she is nothing of a skater." Lady Grace suddenly broke into a little laugh. "I wonder if the redoubtable Mrs. Bathurst does really beat her when she is naughty. It would be excellent treatment for her, you know."

"I haven't a doubt of it," said the Colonel. "She is absolutely under her mother's control. That great raw-boned woman would have a heavy hand too, I'll be bound."

"Oh, there is no doubt Dinah stands very much in awe of her. I never knew she had any will of her own till she came here. I always took her for the meekest little creature imaginable."

"There is a good deal more in Miss Dinah than jumps to the eye," said the Colonel. "In fact, if you ask me, I should say she is something of a dark horse. She is just beginning to feel her feet and she'll surprise us all one of these days by turning into a runaway colt."

"Not, I do hope, while she is in my charge," said Lady Grace.

"We will hope not," agreed the Colonel. "But all the same, I rather think that her mother will find her considerably less tame and tractable when she sees her again than she has ever been before. Liberty, you know, is a dangerous joy for the young."

"Then we must be more strict with her ourselves," said Lady Grace.

CHAPTER X

THE HOUSE OF BONDAGE

Dinah ran swiftly down the corridor to her own room.

As a matter of fact, she had intruded upon the Colonel and Lady Grace in the secret hope of finding a propitious moment for once again pressing her request to be allowed to accept Scott's invitation to tea. Her failure to do so added fuel to the flame, arousing in her an almost irresistible impulse to rebel openly.

The fear of consequences alone restrained her, for to be escorted home in disgrace after only a week in this Alpine paradise was more than she could face. All her life the dread of her mother's wrath had overhung Dinah like a cloud, sometimes near, sometimes distant, but always present. She had been brought up to fear her from her cradle. All through her childhood her punishments had been bitterly severe. She winced still at the bare thought of them; and she was as fully convinced as was Lady Grace that her mother had never really loved her. To come under the ban of her displeasure meant days of harsh treatment, nor, now that her childhood was over, had the discipline been relaxed. She never attempted to rebel openly. Her fear of her mother had become an integral part of herself. Her spirit shrank before her fits of violence. But for her father and Billy she sometimes thought that home would be an impossible place.

Ethel M. Dell

But her affection for her father was of a very intense order. Lazy, self-indulgent, supremely easy-going, yet possessed of a fascination that had held her from babyhood, such was Guy Bathurst. Despised at least outwardly by his wife and adored by his daughter, he went his indifferent way, enjoying life as he found it and quite impervious to snubs.

"I never interfere with your mother," was a very frequent sentence on his lips, and by that axiom he ruled his life, looking negligently on while Dinah was bent without mercy to the wheel of tyranny.

He was fond of Dinah, - her devotion to him made that inevitable - but he never obtruded his fondness to the point of interference on her behalf; for both of them were secretly aware that the harshness meted out to her had much of its being in a deep, unreasoning jealousy of that very selfish fondness. They kept their affection as it were for strictly private consumption, and it was that alone that made life at home tolerable to Dinah.

For upon one point her father was insistent. He would not part with her unless she married. He did not object to her working at home for his comfort, but the idea of her working elsewhere and making her living was one which he refused to consider. With rare self-assertion, he would not hear of it, and when he really asserted himself, which was seldom, his wife was wont to yield, albeit ungraciously enough, to his behest.

Besides Dinah was undoubtedly useful at home, and would certainly grow out of hand if she left her.

Not very willingly had she agreed to let her go upon this Alpine jaunt with the de Vignes, but Billy had been so keen, and the invitation would scarcely have been extended to him alone.

The whole idea had originated between the heads of the two families, riding home together after a day's hunting. Dinah had chanced to come into the conversation, and the Colonel, comparing her with that of his own daughter and being stirred to pity, had suggested that the two children might like to join them on their forthcoming expedition. Bathurst had at once accepted the tentative proposal, and had blurted forth the whole matter to his assembled family on his return with the result that Billy's instant and eager delight had made it virtually impossible for his mother to oppose the suggestion.

Dinah had been delighted too, almost deliriously so; but she had kept her pleasure to herself, not daring to show it in her mother's presence till the actual arrival of the last day. Then indeed she had lost her head, had sung and danced and made merry, till some trifling accident had provoked her mother's untempered wrath and a sound boxing of ears had quite sobered her enthusiasm. She had fared forth finally upon the adventure with tearful eyes and drooping heart, her mother's frigid kiss of farewell hurting her more poignantly than her drastic punishment of an hour before. For Dinah was intensely sensitive, keenly susceptible to rebuke and coldness, and her warm heart shrank from unkindness with a shrinking that was actual pain.

She knew that the little social world of Perrythorpe looked down upon her mother though not actually refusing to associate with her. Bathurst had married a circus-girl in his green Oxford days; so the story went, - a hard, handsome woman older than himself, and fiercely, intensely ambitious. Lack of funds had prevented her climbing very high, and bitterly she resented her failure. He had never done a day's work in his life, but, unlike his wife, he had plenty of friends. He was well-bred, a good rider, a straight shot, and an entertaining guest. He knew everyone within a radius of twenty miles, and was upon terms of easy intimacy with the de Vignes and many others who received him with pleasure, but very seldom went out of their way to encounter his wife.

Dinah shrewdly suspected that this fact accounted for much of the bitterness of her mother's outlook. Her ambition had apparently died of starvation long since, but her resentment remained. Her hand was against practically all the world, including her daughter, whose fairy-like daintiness and piquancy were so obvious a contrast to the somewhat coarse and flashy beauty that had once been hers. For all that Dinah inherited from her mother was her gipsy darkness. Mrs. Bathurst was not flashy now, and any attempt at personal adornment on Dinah's part was always very sternly repressed. She had met and writhed under the eye of scornful criticism too often, and she distrusted her own taste. She was determined that Dinah should never be subjected to the same humiliation.

She humiliated her often enough herself. It was the only means she knew of asserting her authority; for she had no intention of ever being the object of her daughter's contempt. She was harsh to the point of brutality, so that the girl's heart was wont to quicken apprehensively whenever she heard her step. She scolded, she punished, she coerced. But from an outsider, the bare thought of a snub was unendurable, and the possibility that Dinah might by any means lay herself open to one was enough to bring down the vials of wrath upon her head. Dinah remembered still with shivering vividness the whipping she had received on one occasion for demeaning herself by running after the de Vignes's carriage to deliver a message. Her mother's whippings had always been very terrible, vindictively thorough. The indignity of them lashed her soul even more cruelly than the unsparing thong her body. Because of them she went in daily trepidation, submissive almost to the point of abjectness, lest this hateful and demoralizing form of punishment should be inflicted upon her. For some time now, by great wariness and circumspection she had evaded it, and she had begun to entertain the trembling hope that she was at last considered to have passed the age for such childish correction. But her mother's outbreak of violence on the day of their departure had been a painful disillusion, and she knew well what it would mean to return home in disgrace with the de Vignes. Her cheeks burned and tingled still with the shame of the discovery. She felt that another of the old dreadful chastisements would overwhelm her utterly. And yet that she would most certainly have to endure it if she were unruly now was conviction that pressed like a cold weight upon her heart. Had not the letter she had received from her mother only that morning contained a stern injunction to her to behave herself, as though she had been a naughty, wayward child?

"It would kill me!" she told herself passionately. "Oh, why, why, why can't I grow up quick and marry? But I never shall grow up at home. That's the horrible, horrible part of it. And I shall never have a chance of marrying with mother looking on. I'm just a slave - a slave. Other girls can have a good time, do as they like, flirt when they like. But I - never - never!"

Her fit of rebellion lasted long. The emancipation from the home bondage was beginning to work within her as the Colonel had predicted. Seen from a distance, the old tyranny seemed outrageous and impossible, to go back into it monstrous. And yet, so far as she could see, there was no way of escape. She was not apparently to be allowed to make any friends outside her own sphere. The freedom she had begun to enjoy so feverishly had very suddenly been circumscribed, and if she dared to overstep the bounds marked out for her, she knew what to expect.

And yet she longed for freedom as she had never longed in her life before. She was nearly desperate with longing, so sweet had been the first, intoxicating taste thereof. For the first time she had seen life from the standpoint of the ordinary, happy girl, and the contrast to the life she knew had temporarily upset her equilibrium. Her mother's treatment, harsh before, seemed unendurable now. Her cheeks burned afresh with a fierce, intolerable shame. No, no! She could never face it again. She could not! She could not! Already her brief emancipation had begun to cost her dear. She must - she must - find a way of escape ere she went back into thraldom. For she knew her mother's strength so terribly well. It would conquer all resistance by sheer, overwhelming weight. She could not remember a single occasion upon which she had ever in the smallest degree held her own against it. Her will had been broken to her mother's so often that the very thought of prolonged resistance seemed absurd. She knew herself to be incapable of it. She was bound to crumple under the strain, bound to be humbled to the dust long ere the faintest hope of outmatching her mother's iron will had begun to dawn in her soul. The very thought made her feel puny and contemptible. If she resisted to the very uttermost of her strength, yet would she be crushed in the end, and that end would be more horribly painful than she dared to contemplate. All her childhood it had been the same. She had been conquered ere she had passed the threshold of rebellion. She had never been permitted to exercise a will of her own, and the discovery that she possessed one had been something of a surprise to Dinah.

It was partly this discovery that made her long so passionately for freedom. She wanted to grow, to develop, to get beyond the stultifying influence of that unvarying despotism. She longed to get away from the perpetual dread of consequences that so haunted her. She wanted to breathe her own atmosphere, live her own life, be herself.

"I believe I could do lots of things if I only had the chance," she murmured to herself; and then she was suddenly plunged into the memory of another occasion when she had received summary and austere punishment for omitting scales from her practising. But then no one ever liked doing what they must, and she had never had any real taste for music; or if she had had, it had vanished long since under the uninspiring goad of compulsion.

All her morning depression came back while these bitter meditations racked her brain. Oh, if only - if only - her father had chosen a lady for his wife! It was disloyal, she knew, to indulge such a thought, but her mood was black and her soul was in revolt. She was sure - quite sure - that marriage presented the only possibility of deliverance, and deliverance was beginning to seem imperative. Her whole individuality, which this past week of giddy liberty had done so much to develop, cried aloud for it.

She went to the window. Billy had grown tired of waiting and gone off without her. She fancied she could see his sturdy figure on the further slope. Her eyes took in the whole lovely scene, and suddenly, effervescently, her spirits began to rise. The inherent gaiety of her bubbled to the surface. What a waste of time to stay here grizzling while that paradise lay awaiting her! The sweetness of her nature began to assert itself once more, and an almost fevered determination to live in the present, to be happy while she could, entered into her. With impetuous energy she pushed the evil thoughts away. She would be happy. She would! She would! And happiness was not difficult to Dinah. It bubbled in her, a natural spring, that ever flowed again even after the worst storms had forced it from its course.

She even laughed to herself as she prepared to join Billy. Life was good, - oh yes, life was good! And home and the trials thereof were many miles away. Who could be unhappy for long in such a world as this, where the air sparkled like champagne, and the magic of it ran riot in the blood?

The black mood passed away from her spirit like a cloud. She threw on cap and coat and ran to join the merry-makers.

CHAPTER XI

OLYMPUS

All through that afternoon Dinah and Billy played like cubs in the snow. They were very inexperienced in the art of luging, but they took their spills with much heartiness and a total disregard of dignity that made for complete enjoyment.

When the sun went down they forsook the sport, and joined in a snowballing match with a dozen or more of their fellow-visitors. But Dinah proved herself so adroit and impartial at this game that she presently became a general target, and found it advisable to retreat before she was routed. This she did with considerable skill and no small strategy, finally darting flushed and breathless into the hotel, covered with snow from head to foot, but game to the last.

"Well done!" commented a lazy voice behind her. "Now raise the drawbridge and lower the portcullis, and the honours of war are assured."

She turned with the flashing movement of a bird upon the wing, and found herself face to face with Sir Eustace.

His blue eyes met hers with deliberate nonchalance. "Sit down," he said, "while I fetch you some tea!"

Her heart gave an odd little leap that was half of pleasure and half of dread. She stammered incoherently that he must not take the trouble.

But he was evidently bent upon so doing, for he pressed her into the seat which he had just vacated. "Keep the place in the corner for me!" he commanded, and lounged away upon his errand with imperial leisureliness.

Dinah watched his tall figure out of sight. The encounter both astounded and thrilled her. She wondered if she were cheapening herself by meekly obeying his behest, wondered what Rose - that practised coquette - would have done under such circumstances; but to depart seemed so wholly out of the question that she dismissed the wonder as futile. She could only wait for the play to develop, and trust to her own particular luck, which had so favoured her the night before, to give her a cue.

He returned with tea and cake which he set before her on a little table that he had apparently secured beforehand for the purpose. "I am sure you must be ravenous," he said, in those high-bred, somewhat insolent accents of his.

"I am," Dinah admitted frankly.

"Then let me see you satisfy your hunger!" he said, seating himself in the corner he had reserved.

"Oh, but not alone!" she protested. "You - you must have some too."

He laughed. "No. I am going to smoke - with your permission. It will do me more good."

"Oh, pray do!" said Dinah, embarrassed still but strangely elated. "It makes me feel rather greedy, that's all."

"I am greedy too," he told her, his blue eyes still upon her vivid, sparkling face. "And - always with your permission - I am going to indulge my greed."

She did not understand him, but prudence restrained her from telling him so. Seated as she was he was the only person in the vestibule whom she could see, her back being turned to all beside. She wondered, again with that delightful yet half-startled thrill, if his meaning were in any way connected with this fact. He certainly absorbed the whole of her attention, if that were what he wanted. Her hunger faded completely into the background.

He lighted a cigarette and began to smoke. The space beyond them was full of moving figures and laughing voices; but the turmoil scarcely reached Dinah. An invisible barrier seemed to shut them off from all the rest. They were not merely aloof; they were alone, and a curiously intimate touch pervaded their solitude. She felt her spirit start in quivering response to the call of his, just as the night before when she had floated with him above the clouds. What was happening to her she had not the least idea, but the consciousness of his near presence pulsed magnetically through and through her. Scott's brief advice of the morning was scattered from her memory like feathers before the wind. She had no memory. She lived only in this burning splendid ardour of a moment.

She drank her tea mechanically, finding nothing enigmatic in his silence. The direct look of his blue eyes discomfited her strangely, but it was a sublime discomfiture - the discomfiture of the moth around the flame. She longed to meet it, but did not wholly dare. With veiled glances she yielded to the attraction, not yet bold enough for complete surrender.

He spoke at last, and she started.

"Well? Am I forgiven?"

The nonchalant enquiry sent the blood in another hot wave to her cheeks. Had she ever presumed to be angry with this godlike person?

"For what?" she asked, her voice very low.

He leaned towards her. "Did I only fancy that by some evil chance I had offended you?"

She kept her eyes lowered. "I thought you were the offended one," she said.

"I?" She caught the note of surprise in his voice, and it sent a very curious little sense of shame through her.

With an effort she raised her eyes. "Yes. I thought you were offended. You went by me this morning without seeing me."

His look was very intent, almost as if he were searching for something; but it did not disconcert her as she had half-expected to be disconcerted. His eyes were more caressing than dominant just then.

"What if I didn't see you because I didn't dare?" he said.

That gave her confidence. "I should think you couldn't be so silly as that," she said with decision.

He smiled a little. "Thank you, *miladi*. Then wasn't it - almost equally silly - your word, not mine! - of you to be afraid of me last night?"

She felt the thrust in a moment, and went white, conscious of the weak sick feeling that so often came over her at the sound of her mother's step when she was in disgrace.

He saw her distress, but he allowed several moments to elapse before he came to the rescue; Then lightly, "Pray don't let the matter disturb you!" he said. "Only - for your peace of mind - let me tell you that you really have nothing to fear. Out here we live in fairyland, and no one is in earnest. We just enjoy ourselves, and Mrs. Grundy simply doesn't exist. We are not ashamed of being frivolous, and we do whatever we like. And there are no consequences. Always remember that, Miss Bathurst! There are never any consequences in fairyland."

His eyes suddenly laughed at her, and Dinah was vastly reassured. Her dismay vanished, leaving a blithe sense of irresponsibility in its place.

"I shall remember that," she said, with her gay little nod. "I dreamt last night that we were in Olympus."

"We?" he said softly.

She nodded again, flushed and laughing, confident that she had received her cue. "And you - were Apollo."

She saw his eyes change magically, flashing into swift life, and dropped her own before the mastery that dawned there.

"And you," he questioned under his breath, "were Daphne?"

"Perhaps," she said enigmatically. After all, flirting was not such a difficult art, and since he had declared that there could be no consequences, she did not see why she should bury this new-found talent of hers.

"What a charming dream!" he commented lazily. "But you know what happened to Daphne when she ran away, don't you?"

She flung him a laughing challenge. "He didn't catch her anyway."

"True!" smiled Sir Eustace. "But have you never wondered whether it wouldn't have been more sport for her if he had? It wouldn't be very exciting, you know, to lead the life of a vegetable."

"It isn't!" declared Dinah, with abrupt sincerity.

"Oh, you know something about it, do you?" he said. "Then the modern Daphne ought to have too much sense to run away."

She laughed with a touch of wistfulness. "I wonder how she felt about it afterwards."

"I wonder," he agreed, tipping the ash off his cigarette. "It didn't matter so much to Apollo, you see. He had plenty to choose from."

Dinah's wistfulness vanished in a swift breath of indignation. "Really!" she said.

He looked at her. "Yes, really," he told her, with deliberation. "And he didn't need to run after them either. But, possibly," his gaze softened again, "possibly that was what made him want Daphne the most. Elusiveness is quite a fascinating quality if it isn't carried too far. Still -" he smiled - "I expect he got over it in the end, you know; but in her case I am not quite so sure."

"I don't suppose he did get ever it," maintained Dinah with spirit. "All the rest must have seemed very cheap afterwards."

"Perhaps he was more at home with the cheap variety," he suggested carelessly.

His eyes had wandered to the buzzing throng behind her, and she saw a glint of criticism - or was it merely easy contempt? - dispel the smile with which he had regarded her. His mouth wore a faint but unmistakable sneer.

But in a moment his look returned to her, kindled upon her. "Are you for the ice carnival to-night?" he asked.

She drew a quick, eager breath. "Oh, I do want to come! But I don't know - yet - if I shall be allowed."

"Why ask?" he questioned.

She hesitated, then ingenuously she told him her difficulty. "I got into trouble last night for dancing so late with you. And -

and - I may be sent to bed early to make up for it."

He frowned. "Do you mean to say you'd go?"

She coloured vividly. "I'm only nineteen, and I have to do as I'm told."

"Heavens above!" he said. "You belong to the generation before the last evidently. No girl ever does as she is told now-a-days. It isn't the thing."

"I do," whispered Dinah, in dire confusion. "At least - generally."

"And what happens if you don't?" he queried. "Do they whip you and put you to bed?"

She clenched her hands hard. "Don't!" she said. "You're only joking, I know. But - I hate it!"

His manner changed in a moment, became half-quizzical, half-caressing. "Poor little brown elf, what a shame! Well, come if you can! I shall look out for you. I may have something to show you."

"May you? Oh, what?" cried Dinah, all eagerness in a moment.

He laughed. There was a provoking hint of mystery in his manner. "Ah! That lies in the future, *miladi*."

"But tell me!" she persisted.

"Will you come then?" he asked.

"Perhaps," she said. "If I can!"

"Ah! And perhaps not!" he said. "What then?"

Dinah's mouth grew suddenly firm. "I will come," she said.

"You will?" His keen eyes held hers with smiling compulsion.

"Yes, I will."

He made a gesture as if he would take her hand, but restrained himself, and paused to tip the ash once more off his cigarette.

"Now tell me!" commanded Dinah.

"I don't think I will," he said deliberately.

"But you must!" said Dinah.

His eyes sought hers again with that look which she found it impossible to meet. She bent over her cup.

"What will you show me?" she persisted. "Tell me!"

"I didn't say I would show you anything," he pointed out. "I said I might."

"Tell me what it was anyhow!" she said.

He leaned nearer to her, and suddenly it seemed to her that they were quite alone, very far removed from the rest of the world. "It may not be to-night," he murmured. "Or even to-morrow. But some day - in this land where there are no consequences - I will show you - when the fates are propitious, not before - some of the things that Daphne missed when she ran away."

He ceased to speak. Dinah's face was burning. She could not look at him. She felt as if a magic flame had wrapped her round. Her whole body was tingling, her heart wildly a-quiver. There was a rapture in that moment that was almost too intense, too poignant, to be borne.

He was the first to move. Calmly he leaned back, and resumed his cigarette. Through the aromatic smoke his voice came to her again.

"Are you angry?"

Her whole being stirred in response. She uttered a little quivering laugh that was near akin to tears.

"No - of course - no! But I - I think I ought to go and dress! It's getting late, isn't it? Thank you for giving me tea!" She rose, her movements quick and dainty as the flight of a robin. "Good-bye!" she murmured shyly.

He rose also with a sweeping bow. "*A bientot,* - Daphne!" he said.

She gave him a single swift glance from under fluttering lashes, and turned away in silence.

She went up the stairs with the speed of a bird on the wing, but she could not outpace the wonder and the wild delight at her heart. As she entered her own room at length, she laughed, a breathless, rippling laugh. How amazing - and how gorgeous - was this new life!

CHAPTER XII

THE WINE OF THE GODS

The rink was ablaze with fairy-lights under the starry sky. Rose de Vigne, exquisitely fair in ruby velvet and ermine furs paused on the verandah, looking pensively forth.

Very beautiful she looked standing there, and Captain Brent of the Sappers striding forth with his skates jingling in his hand stopped as one compelled.

"Are you waiting for someone, Miss de Vigne? Or may I escort you?"

She looked at him with a faint smile as if in pity for his disappointment. "Too late, I am afraid, Captain Brent. I have promised Sir Eustace to skate with him."

"Who?" Brent glanced towards the rink. "Why, he's down there already dancing about with your little cousin. That's her laugh. Don't you hear it?"

Dinah's laugh, clear and ringing, came to them on the still air. Rose's slim figure stiffened very slightly, barely perceptibly, at the sound. "Sir Eustace has forgotten his engagement," she said icily. "Yes, Captain Brent, I will come with you."

"Good business!" he said heartily. "It's a glorious night. Somebody said there was a change coming; but I don't believe it. Maddening if a thaw comes before the luging competition. The run is just perfection now. I'm going up there presently. It's glorious by moonlight."

He chattered inconsequently on, happy in the fact that he had secured the prettiest girl in the hotel for his partner, and not in the least disturbed by any lack of response on her part. To skate with her hand in hand was the utmost height of his ambition just then, his brain not being of a particularly aspiring order.

Down on the rink all was gaiety and laughter. The lights shone ruby, emerald, and sapphire, upon the darting figures. The undernote of the rushing skates made magic music everywhere. The whole scene was fantastic - a glittering fairyland of colour and enchantment.

"Each evening seems more splendid than the last," declared Dinah.

"They always will if you spend them in my company," said Sir Eustace. "Do you know I could very soon teach you to skate as perfectly as you dance?"

"I believe you could teach me anything," she answered happily.

"Given a free hand I believe I could," he said. "But the gift is yours, not mine. You have the most wonderful knack of divining a mood. You adapt yourself instinctively. I never knew anyone respond so perfectly to the unspoken wish. How is it, I wonder?"

"I don't know," she answered shyly. "But I can't help understanding what you want."

"Does that mean that we are kindred spirits?" he asked, and suddenly the clasp of his hands was close and intimate.

"I expect it does," said Dinah; but she said it with a touch of uneasiness. The voice that had spoken within her the night before, warning her, urging her to be gone, was beginning to murmur again, bidding her to beware.

She turned from the subject with ready versatility, obedient to the danger-signal. "Oh, there is Rose! I am afraid I ran away from her after dinner. They went upstairs for coffee, but I was so dreadfully afraid of being stopped that I hung behind and escaped. I do hope the Colonel won't be in a wax again. But I don't see that there was anything wicked in it; for Lady Grace herself is coming to look on presently."

"I skated with Miss de Vigne nearly all the afternoon," observed Sir Eustace. "But she is a regular ice-maiden. I couldn't get any enthusiasm out of her. Tell me, is she like that all through? Or is it just a pose?"

"Oh, I don't know," Dinah said. "I've never got through the outer crust. But then of course I'm far beneath her."

"How so?" asked Sir Eustace.

She laughed up at him with the happy confidence of a child. "Can't you see it for yourself? I - I am a mere guttersnipe compared to the de Vignes. They live in a great house with lots of servants and cars. They never do a thing for themselves. I don't suppose Rose could do her hair to save her life. While we - we live in a tumble-down, ramshackle old place, and do all the work ourselves. I've never been away from home in my life before. You see, we're poor, and Billy's schooling takes up a lot of money. I had to leave school when he first went as a boarder. And that is three years ago now. So I have forgotten all I ever learnt."

"Except dancing," he suggested.

"Oh, well, that's born in me. I couldn't very well forget that. My mother -" Dinah hesitated momentarily - "my mother was a dancer before she married."

"And she taught you?" asked Sir Eustace.

"No, no! She never taught me anything except useful things - like cooking and sewing and house-work. And I detest them all," said Dinah frankly. "I like sweeping the garden and digging the potatoes far better."

"She keeps you busy then," commented Sir Eustace, with semi-humorous interest.

"Busy isn't the word for it," declared Dinah. "I'm going from morning till night. We do the washing at home too. I get up at five and go to bed at nine. I make nearly all my own clothes too. That's why I haven't got any," she ended naively.

He laughed. "Not really! But what makes you work so hard as that? You're wasting all your best time. You'll never be so young again, you know."

"I know!" cried Dinah, and suddenly a wild gust of rebellion went through her. "It's hateful! I never knew how hateful till I came here. Going back will be - too horrible for words. But - " her voice fell abruptly flat - "what am I to do?"

"I should go on strike," he said lightly. "Tell your good mother that she must find someone else to do the work! You are going to take it easy and enjoy yourself."

Dinah uttered a short, painful laugh.

"Wouldn't that do?" he asked.

"No."

"Why not?" he questioned with indolent amusement. "Surely you're not afraid of the broomstick!"

Dinah gave a great start, and suddenly, as they skated, pressed close to him with the action of some small, terrified creature seeking shelter. "Oh, don't - don't let us spoil this perfect night by talking of my home affairs!" she pleaded, her voice quick and passionate. "I want to put everything right away. I want to forget there is such a place as home."

His arm was around her in a moment. He held her caught to him. "I can soon make you forget that, my Daphne," he said. "I can lead you through such a wonderland as will dazzle you into complete forgetfulness of everything else. But you must trust me, you know. You mustn't be afraid."

He was drawing her away from the glare of coloured lights as he spoke, drawing her to the further end of the rink where stood a tiny, rustic pavilion.

She went with him with a breathless sense of high adventure, skimming the ice in time with his rhythmic movements, mesmerized into an enchanted quiescence.

They reached the pavilion, and he paused. The other skaters were left behind. They stood as it were in a magic circle all their own. And only the moon looked on.

"Ah, Daphne!" he said, and took her in his arms.

There came to Dinah then a wild and desperate sense of fear, fear that was coupled with a wholly unreasoning and instinctive shame. She strained back from him. "Oh no! Oh no!" she gasped. "I mustn't! I'm sure it's wrong!"

But he mastered her very slowly, wholly without violence, yet wholly irresistibly. His dark face with its blue, compelling eyes dominated her, conquered her. And all her life resistance had been quelled in her. Her will wavered and was down.

"Why should it be wrong?" he whispered. "I tell you that nothing matters - nothing matters. We take our pleasures, and we tell no one. It is no one's business but our own, sweetheart. And nothing is wrong, if no harm is done to anyone."

Ethel M. Dell

Subtle, alluring, half-laughing, half-relentless, he drew her closer yet, he bent and pressed his lips upon her upturned face. But she quivered still and shrank, though unresisting. She could not give her lips to his. His kiss burned through and through her, so that she longed to flee away and hide.

For though that kiss sent a thrill of wild ecstasy through her, there was anguish mingled therewith. Even while she exulted over her unexpected victory, she was smitten with the thought that it had cost her too dear. Had she told him too much about herself that he held her thus cheaply? Would he - however urgent his desire to do so - would he have dreamed of treating Rose thus? Or any other girl of his own standing?

The thought went through her like a dagger. She bent herself back over his arm avoiding his lips a second time. That one kiss had opened her eyes.

"Oh, let me go!" she said, her voice muffled and tremulous. "You mustn't - ever - do it again."

"Why not?" he whispered softly. "What does it matter? This is the land of no consequences."

"I can't help it," she whispered back. "It may not mean anything to you. But - but - it makes me feel - wicked."

He laughed at her with tender ridicule. His arms still held her, but no longer closely.

"Don't be afraid, my elf of the mountains!" he said. "I won't do it again - yet. But there is nothing in it I tell you. And what does it matter if no one knows? Why shouldn't you have all the fun you can get?"

Dinah straightened herself, and passed her hands over her face with an oddly childish gesture. He behaved as though he had conferred a favour upon her; but yet the horrible feeling of shame lingered. Her mother's most drastic punishments had never humbled her more completely.

She drew herself from his hold. "I feel it does matter," she said, her voice pathetically small and shy. "But - I know you didn't mean to - to offend me. So let's forget it, please! Let's go back!"

She gave him her hand with a timid gesture, and he took it with a smile that held arrogance as well as amusement. "We will go back certainly," he said. "But we shall not forget. We have tasted the wine of the gods, my Daphne, and there is magic in the draught. Those who drink once are bound to come again for more."

"Oh no! Oh no!" said Dinah.

But even as she said it, she felt herself to be battling against destiny.

In that moment she knew beyond all doubting that by some means of which she had no understanding he had caught her will and made it captive. Elude him though she might for a time, she was bound to be his helpless prisoner at the last.

Yet his magnetism was such that she yielded herself to him almost mechanically as they went back into the giddy vortex of the carnival. Even in the midst of her dismay and uncertainty, she was strangely, almost deliriously happy.

Romance with gold-tipped wings unfurled had suddenly descended from the high heavens and flitted before her, luring her on.

Ethel M. Dell

CHAPTER XIII

FRIENDSHIP IN THE DESERT

On the edge of the rink immediately below the hotel, a slight figure was standing, patient as the Sphinx, awaiting them.

Sir Eustace's keen eyes lighted upon it from afar. "There is my brother," he said. "We will go and speak to him if you have no objection."

Dinah received the suggestion with eagerness. She was possessed for the moment by an urgent desire to get back to the commonplace. She had been whirled off her feet, and albeit the flight had held rapture, she had a desperate longing to tread solid ground once more.

Possibly her companion shared something of this feeling. The game was his, but there was no more to be won from her that night. The time had come to descend from the heights to the dull and banal levels. He divined her wish to return to earth, and he had no reason for thwarting it. With a careless laugh he put on speed and rushed her dizzily through the throng.

To Dinah it was as a rapid fall through space. She felt as if she had been suddenly shot from the gates of Olympus. She reached Scott, flushed and breathless and quivering still with the wonder of it.

He greeted her courteously. "Are you having a good time,

Miss Bathurst?"

She answered him gaspingly. Somehow it was an immense relief to find herself by his side. "Yes; a glorious time. But I am coming off now. Have you - have you seen anything of Lady Grace or the Colonel?"

"I have just had the pleasure of making Lady Grace's acquaintance," he said. "Are you really coming off now? Have you had enough?"

She passed over his last question, for the wonder pierced her if she had not had too much. "Yes, really. I am going to change my boots. I left them somewhere here. I wonder where they are. Ah, there they are against the railing! No, please don't! I can manage quite well. I would rather."

She sat down on the bank, and bent her hot face over her task.

The two brothers remained near her. Scott was apparently waiting for her. They exchanged a few low words.

"I'll do my level best, old chap," she heard Scott say. "But if I don't succeed, it can't be helped. Rome wasn't built in a day."

Eustace made an impatient sound, and muttered something in a whisper.

"No," Scott said in answer. "Not that! Never with my consent. It wouldn't do, man! I tell you it wouldn't do. Can't you take my word for it?"

"You're as obstinate as a mule, Stumpy," his brother said, in tones of irritation. "It'll come to it sooner or later. You're only prolonging the agony."

"I am doing my best," Scott said gravely. "Give me credit for that at least!"

Sir Eustace clapped a sudden hand on his shoulder. "No one doubts that, my boy. You're true gold. But it's sheer foolishness to go on in the same old way that's proved a failure a hundred times. In heaven's name, now that we've hauled her out of that infernal groove, don't let idiotic sentimentality spoil everything! Don't shy at the consequences! I'll be responsible for them."

Dinah glanced up. She saw that for the moment she was forgotten. The light was shining upon Scott's face, and she read in it undeniable perplexity, but the eyes were steadfast and wholly calm.

He even smiled a little as he said, "My dear chap, have you ever considered the consequences of anything - counted the cost before you came to pay? No, never!"

"Don't preach to me!" Eustace said sharply.

"No. I won't. But don't you talk in that airy way about responsibility to me! Because -" Scott's smile broadened and became openly affectionate - "it just won't go down, dear fellow! I can't swallow camels - never could."

"You can strain at gnats though," commented Sir Eustace, pivoting round on his skates. "Well, you know my sentiments. I haven't put my foot down yet. But I'm going to - pretty soon. It's got to be done. And if you can't bring yourself to it, - well, I shall, that's all."

He was gone with the words, swift as an arrow, leaving behind him a space so empty that Dinah felt a sudden queer little pang of desolation.

Scott remained motionless, deep in thought, for the passage of several seconds. Then abruptly the consciousness of her presence came upon him, and he turned to her. She was sitting on the bank looking up at him with frank interest. Their eyes met.

And then a very curious thing happened to Dinah. She flinched under his look, flinched and averted her own. A great shyness suddenly surged through her, a quivering, overmastering sense of embarrassment. For in that moment she viewed the flight to Olympus as he would have viewed it, and was horribly, overwhelmingly ashamed. She could not break the silence. She had no words to utter - no possible means at hand by which to cover her discomfiture.

It was he who spoke, in his voice a tinge of restraint. "I was going to ask if it would bore you to come and see my sister again this evening. I have obtained Lady Grace's permission for you to do so."

She sprang to her feet. "Of course - of course I would love to!" she said rather incoherently. "How could it bore me? I - I should like it - more than anything."

He smiled faintly, and held out his hand for the boots she had just discarded. "That is more than kind of you," he said. "My sister was afraid you might not want to come."

"Of course I want to come!" maintained Dinah. "Oh no, thank you; I couldn't let you carry my boots. How clever of you to tackle Lady Grace! What did she say?"

"Neither she nor the Colonel made any difficulty about it at all," Scott said. "I told them my sister was an invalid. Lady Grace said that I must not keep you after ten, and I promised I wouldn't."

His manner was kindly and quizzical, and Dinah's embarrassment began to pass. But he discomfited her afresh as they walked across the road by saying, "You have made it up with my brother, I see."

Dinah's cheeks burned again. "Yes," she said, after a moment. "We made it up this afternoon."

"That was very lucky - for him," observed Scott rather dryly.

Dinah made a swift leap for the commonplace. "I hate being cross with people," she said, "or to have them cross with me; don't you?"

"I think it is sometimes unavoidable," said Scott gravely.

"Oh, surely you are never cross!" said Dinah impetuously. "I can't imagine it."

"Wait till you see it!" said Scott, with a smile.

They entered the hotel together. Dinah was tingling with excitement. She had managed to escape from her discomfiture, but she still felt that any prolonged intercourse with the man beside her would bring it back. She was beginning to know Scott as one who would not hesitate to say exactly what he thought, and not for all she possessed in the world would she have had him know what had passed in that far corner of the rink so short a time before.

She chattered inconsequently upon ordinary topics as they ascended the stairs together, but when they reached the door of Isabel's sitting-room she became suddenly shy again.

"Hadn't I better run and take off my things?" she whispered. "I feel so untidy."

He looked at her. She was clad in the white woollen cap and coat that she had worn in the day. Her eyes were alight and sparkling, her brown face flushed. She looked the very incarnation of youth.

"I think she will like to see you as you are," said Scott.

He knocked upon the door three times as before, and in a moment opened it.

"Go in, won't you?" he said, standing back.

Dinah entered.

"Ah! She has come!" A hollow voice said, and in a moment her shyness was gone.

She moved forward eagerly, saw Isabel seated in a low chair, and impulsively went to her. "How kind you are to ask me to come again!" she said.

And then all in a moment Isabel's arms came out to her, and she slipped down upon her knees beside her into their close embrace.

"How kind of you to come, dear child!" Isabel murmured. "I am afraid it is a visit to the desert for you."

"But I love to come!" Dinah told her with warm lips raised. "I can't tell you how much. I was never so happy before. Each day seems lovelier than the last."

Isabel kissed her lingeringly, tenderly. "My dear, you have a happy heart," she said. "Tell me what you have been doing since I saw you last!"

She would have let her go, but Dinah clung to her still, her cheek against her shoulder. "I have been very frivolous, dear Mrs. Everard," she said. "I have done lots of things. This afternoon we were luging, and now I have just come from the carnival, I wish you could have been there. Some people are wearing the most horrible masks. Billy - my brother - has a beauty. He made it himself. I rather wanted it to wear, but he wouldn't part with it."

"You could never wear a mask, sweetheart," Isabel said, clasping the small brown hand in hers. "Your face is too sweet a thing to hide."

Dinah hugged her in naive delight. "I always thought I was ugly before," she said.

Isabel's face wore a wan smile. She stroked the girl's soft cheek. "My dear, no one with a heart like yours could have an ugly face. How did you enjoy your dance with Eustace last night?"

Dinah bent her head a little, wishing earnestly that Scott were not in the room. "I loved it," she said in a low voice.

"And afterwards?" questioned Isabel. "No one was vexed with you, I hope?"

Dinah hesitated. "Colonel de Vigne wasn't best pleased, I'm afraid," she said, after a moment.

"He scolded you!" said Isabel, swift regret in her voice. "I am so sorry, dear child. I ought to have gone to look after you. I was selfish."

"Oh no - indeed!" Dinah protested. "It was entirely my own fault. He would have been cross in any case. They are like that."

Isabel uttered a sigh. "I shall have to try to meet them. Naturally they will not let you come to total strangers. Stumpy, remind me in the morning! I must manage somehow to meet this child's guardians."

"Of course, dear," said Scott.

Dinah, glancing towards him, saw him exchange a swift look with the old nurse in the background, but his voice held neither surprise nor gratification. He took out a cigarette and began to smoke.

Isabel leaned back in her chair with abrupt weariness as if in reaction from the strain of a sudden unwonted exertion. "Let me see! Do I know your Christian name? Ah yes, - Dinah!

What a pretty gipsy name! I think you are a little gipsy, are you not? You have the charm of the woods about you. Won't you sit in that chair, dear? You can't be comfortable on the floor."

But Dinah preferred to sit down against her knee, still holding the slender, inert hand.

"Tell me about your home!" Isabel said, closing languid eyes. "I can't talk much more, but I can listen. It does not tire me to listen."

Dinah hesitated somewhat. "I don't think you would find it very interesting," she said.

"But I am interested," Isabel said. "You live in the country, I think you said."

"At a place called Perrythorpe," Dinah said. "It's a great hunting country. My father hunts a lot and shoots too."

"Do you hunt?" asked Isabel.

"Oh no, never! There's never any time. I go for rambles sometimes on Sundays. Other days I am always busy. Fancy me hunting!" said Dinah, with a little laugh.

"I used to," said Isabel. "They always said I should end with a broken neck. But I never did."

"Are you very fond of riding?" asked Dinah.

"Not now, dear. I am not fond of anything now. Tell me some more, won't you? What makes you so busy that you never have time for any fun?"

Again Dinah hesitated. "You see, we're poor," she said. "My mother and I do all the work of the house and garden too."

"And your father is able to hunt?" Isabel's eyes opened. Her hand closed upon Dinah's caressingly.

"Oh yes, he has always hunted," Dinah said. "I don't think he could do without it. He would find it so dull."

"I see," said Isabel. "But he can't afford pleasures for you."

There was no perceptible sarcasm in her voice, but Dinah coloured a little and went at once to her father's defence.

"He sends Billy to a public school. Of course I - being only a girl - don't count. And he has sent us out here, which was very good of him - the sweetest thing he has ever done. He had a lucky speculation the other day, and he has spent it nearly all on us. Wasn't that kind of him?"

"Very kind, dear," said Isabel gently. "How long are you to have out here?"

"Only three weeks, and half the time is gone already," sighed Dinah. "The de Vignes are not staying longer. The Colonel is a J.P., and much too important to stay away for long. And they are going to have a large house-party. There isn't much more than a week left now." She sighed again.

"And then you will have no more fun at all?" asked Isabel.

"Not a scrap - nothing but work." Dinah's voice quivered a little. "I don't suppose it has been very good for me coming out here," she said. "I - I believe I'm much too fond of gaiety really."

Isabel's hand touched her cheek. "Poor little girl!" she said. "But you wouldn't like to leave your mother to do all the drudgery alone."

"Oh yes, I should," said Dinah, with a touch of recklessness. "I'd never go back if I could help it. I love Dad of course; but - " She paused.

"You don't love your mother?" supplemented Isabel.

Dinah leaned her face suddenly against the caressing hand. "Not much, I'm afraid," she whispered.

"Poor little girl!" Isabel murmured again compassionately.

CHAPTER XIV

THE PURPLE EMPRESS

Colonel De Vigne once more wore his most magisterial air when after breakfast on the following morning he drew Dinah aside.

She looked at him with swift apprehension, even with a tinge of guilt. His lecture of the previous morning was still fresh in her mind. Could he have seen her on the ice with Sir Eustace on the previous night, she asked herself? Surely, surely not!

Apparently he had, however; for his first words were admonitory.

"Look here, young lady, you're making yourself conspicuous with that three-volume-novel baronet: You don't want to be conspicuous, I suppose?"

Her face burned crimson at the question. Then he had seen, or at least he must know, something! She stood before him, too overwhelmed for speech.

"You don't, eh?" he insisted, surveying her confusion with grim relentlessness.

"Of course not!" she whispered at last.

He put a hand on her shoulder. "Very well then! Don't let

there be any more of it! You've been a good girl up till now but the last two days seem to have turned your head. I shan't be able to give a good report to your mother when we get home if this sort of thing goes on."

Dinah's heart sank still lower. The thought of the return home had begun to dog her like an evil dream.

With a great effort she met the Colonel's stern gaze. "I am very sorry," she faltered. "But - but Lady Grace did say I might go and see Mrs. Everard - the invalid sister - yesterday."

"I know she did. She thought you had been flirting with Sir Eustace long enough."

Dinah's sky began to clear a little. "Then you don't mind my going to see her?" she said.

"So long as you are not there too often," conceded the Colonel. "The younger brother is a nice little chap. There is no danger of your getting up to mischief with him."

Dinah's face burned afresh at the suggestion. He evidently did not actually know; but he suspected very strongly. Still it was a great relief to know that all intercourse with these wonderful new friends of hers was not to be barred.

"There was some talk of a sleigh-drive this afternoon," she ventured, after a moment. "Mr. Studley is taking his sister and she asked me to go too. May I?"

"You accepted, I suppose?" demanded the Colonel.

"I said I thought I might," Dinah admitted. And then very suddenly she caught a kindly gleam in his eyes, and summoned courage for entreaty. "Do please - please - let me go!" she begged, clasping his arm. "I shan't ever have any fun again when this is over."

Ethel M. Dell

"How do you know that?" said the Colonel gruffly. "Yes, you can go - you can go. But behave yourself soberly, there's a good girl. And remember - no running after the other fellow to-night! I won't have it. Is that understood?"

Dinah, too rejoiced over this concession to trouble about future prohibitions, gave cheerful acquiescence to the fiat. Perhaps she was beginning to realize that she would see quite as much of Sir Eustace as was at all advisable or even to be desired, without running after him. In fact, so shy had the previous night's flight with him made her, that she did not feel the slightest wish to encounter him again at present. To go out sleigh-driving with Scott and his sister was all that she asked of life that day.

It was a glorious morning despite all prophecies of a coming change, and she spent it joyously luging with Billy. Sir Eustace had gone ski-ing with Captain Brent, and the only glimpse she had of him was a very far one, so far that she knew him only by the magnificence of his physique as he descended the mountain-side as one borne upon wings.

She recalled the brief conversation that the brothers had held in her hearing the night before, and marvelled at the memory of Scott's attitude towards him.

"He isn't a bit afraid of him," she reflected. "In fact he behaves exactly as if he were the bigger of the two."

This phenomenon puzzled her very considerably, for Scott was wholly lacking in the pomposity that characterizes many little men. She wondered what had been the subject of their discussion. It had been connected with Isabel, she felt sure. She was glad to think that she had Scott to protect her, for there was something of tyranny about the elder brother from which she shrank instinctively, his magnetism notwithstanding, and the thought of poor, tragic Isabel being coerced by it was intolerable.

The memory of the latter's resolution to make the acquaintance of the de Vignes recurred to her as she and Billy returned for luncheon. Would she carry it out? She wondered. The look that Scott had flung at the old nurse dwelt in her mind. It would evidently be an extraordinary move if she did.

They reached the hotel, Rose and another girl had just come up from the rink together. A little knot of people were gathered on the verandah. Dinah and Billy kept behind Rose and her companion; but in a moment Dinah heard her name.

The group parted, and she saw Isabel Everard, very tall and stately in a deep purple coat, standing with Lady Grace de Vigne.

Billy gave her a push. "Go on! They're calling you."

And Dinah found the strange sad eyes upon her, alight with a smile of welcome. She went forward impetuously, and in a moment Isabel's cold hands were clasped upon her warm ones.

"I have been waiting for you, dear child," the low voice said. "What have you been doing?"

Dinah suddenly felt as if she were standing in the presence of a princess. Isabel in public bore herself with a haughtiness fully equal to that displayed by Sir Eustace, and she knew that Lady Grace was impressed by it.

"I would have come back sooner if I had known," she said, closely holding the long, slender fingers.

"My dear, you are woefully untidy now you have come," murmured Lady Grace.

But Isabel gently freed one hand to put her arm about the girl. "To me she is - just right," she said, and in her voice there sounded the music of a great tenderness. "Youth is never tidy, Lady Grace; but there is nothing in the world like it."

Lady Grace's eyes went to her daughter whose faultless apparel and perfection of line were in vivid contrast to Dinah's harum-scarum appearance.

"I do not altogether agree with you in that respect, Mrs. Everard," she said, with a smile. "I think young girls should always aim at being presentable. But I quite admit that it is more difficult for some than for others. Dinah, my dear, Mrs. Everard has been kind enough to ask you to lunch in her sitting-room with her, and to go for a sleigh-drive afterward; so you had better run and get respectable as quickly as you can."

"Oh, how kind you are!" Dinah said, with earnest eyes uplifted. "You know how I shall love to come, don't you?"

"I thought you might, dear," Isabel said. "Scott is coming to keep us company. He has arranged for a sleigh to be here in an hour. We are going for a twelve-mile round, so we must not be late starting. It gets so cold after sundown."

"I had better go then, hadn't I?" said Dinah.

"I am coming too," Isabel said. Her arm was still about her. It remained so as she turned to go. "Good-bye, Lady Grace! I will take great care of the child. Thank you for allowing her to come."

She bowed with regal graciousness and moved away, taking Dinah with her.

"Exit Purple Empress!" murmured a man in the background close to Rose. "Who on earth is she? I haven't seen her anywhere before."

Rose uttered her soft, artificial laugh. "She is Sir Eustace Studley's sister. Rather peculiar, I believe, even eccentric. But I understand they are of very good birth."

"That covers a multitude of sins," he commented. "She's been a mighty handsome woman in her day. She must be many years older than Sir Eustace. She looks more like his mother than his sister."

"I believe she is actually younger," Rose said. "They say she has never recovered from the sudden death of her husband some years ago, but I know nothing of the circumstances."

"A very charming woman," said Lady Grace, joining them. "We have had quite a long chat together. Yes, her manner is a little strange, slightly abstracted, as if she were waiting for something or someone. But a very easy companion on the whole. I think you will like her, Rose dear."

"She's dead nuts on Dinah," observed Billy with a chuckle. "She don't look at anyone else when she's got Dinah."

Lady Grace smiled over his head and took no verbal notice of the remark.

"They are a distinguished-looking family," she said. "Run and wash your hands, Billy. Are you thinking of ski-ing this afternoon, Rose?"

"You bet!" murmured Billy, under his breath. He too had seen the distant figure of Sir Eustace on the mountain-side.

"It depends," said Rose, non-committally.

"Captain Brent and Sir Eustace have been on skis all the morning," said her mother. "We must see what they say about it."

Billy spun a coin into the air behind her back. "Heads Sir Eustace and tails Captain Brent," he muttered to the man who had commented upon Isabel's beauty. "Heads it is!"

Lady Grace turned round with a touch of sharpness at the sound of his companion's laugh. "Billy! Did I not tell you to go and wash your hands?"

Billy's green eyes smiled impudent acknowledgment. "You did, Lady Grace. And I'm going. Good-bye!"

He pocketed the coin, winked at his friend, and departed whistling.

"A very unmannerly little boy!" observed Lady Grace, with severity. "Come, my dear Rose! We must go in."

"I don't like either the one or the other," said Rose, with a very unusual touch of petulance. "They are always in the way."

"I fully agree with you," said Lady Grace acidly. "But it is for the first and last time in their lives. I have already told the Colonel so. He will never ask them to accompany us again."

"Thank goodness for that!" said Rose, with restored amiability. "Of course I am sorry for poor little Dinah; but there is a limit."

"Which is very nearly reached," said Lady Grace.

CHAPTER XV

THE MOUNTAIN CREST

That sleigh-drive was to Dinah the acme of delight, and for ever after the jingle of horse-bells was to recall it to her mind. The sight of the gay red trappings, the trot of the muffled hoofs, the easy motion of the sleigh slipping over the white road, and above all, Isabel, clad in purple and seated beside her, a figure of royal distinction, made a picture in her mind that she was never to forget. She rode in a magic chariot through wonderland.

She longed to delay the precious moments as they flew, like a child chasing butterflies in the sunshine; but they only seemed to fly the faster. She chattered almost incessantly for the first few miles, and occasionally Isabel smiled and answered her; but for the most part it was Scott, seated opposite, who responded to her raptures, - Scott, unfailingly attentive and courteous, but ever watchful of his sister's face.

She gazed straight ahead when she was not looking at anything to which Dinah called her attention. Her eyes had the intense look of one who watches perpetually for something just out of sight.

Quiet but alert, he marked her attitude, marked also the emaciation which was so painfully apparent in the strong sunshine and formed so piteous a contrast to the vivid youth of the girl beside her. Presently Dinah came out of her rhapsodies

Ethel M. Dell

and observed his vigilance. She watched him covertly for a time while she still chatted on. And she noted that there were very weary lines about his eyes, lines of anxiety, lines of sleeplessness, that filled her warm heart with quick sympathy and a longing to help.

The road was one of wild beauty. It wound up a desolate mountain pass along which great black boulders were scattered haphazard like the mighty toys of a giant. The glittering snow lay all around them, making their nakedness the more apparent. And far, far above, the white crags shone with a dazzling purity in the sunlit air.

Below them the snow lay untrodden, exquisitely pure, piled here in great drifts, falling away there in wonderful curves and hollows, but always showing a surface perfect and undesecrated by any human touch. And ever the sleigh ran smoothly on over the white road till it seemed to Dinah as if they moved in a dream. She fell silent, charmed by the swift motion, and by the splendour around her.

"You are quite warm, I hope?" Scott said, after an interval.

She was wrapped in a fur cloak belonging to Isabel. She smiled an affirmative, but she saw him as through a veil. The mystery and the wonder of creation filled her soul.

"I feel," she said, "I feel as if we were being taken up into heaven."

"Oh, that we were!" said Isabel, speaking suddenly with a force that had in it something terrible. "Do you see those golden peaks, sweetheart? That is where I would be. That is where the gates of Heaven open - where the lost are found."

Dinah's hand was clasped in hers under the fur rug, and she felt the thin fingers close with a convulsive hold.

Scott leaned forward. "Heaven is nearer to us than that,

Isabel," he said gently.

She looked at him for a moment, but her eyes at once passed beyond. "No, no, Stumpy! You never understand," she said restlessly. "I must reach the mountain-tops or die. I am tired - I am tired of my prison. And I stifle in the valley - I who have watched the sun rise and set from the very edge of the world. Why did they take me away? If I had only waited a little longer - a little longer - as he told me to wait!" Her voice suddenly vibrated with a craving that was passionate. "He would have come with the next sunrise. I always knew that the dawn would bring him back to me. But" - dull despair took the place of longing - "they took me away, and the sun has never shone since."

"Isabel!" Scott's voice was very grave and quiet. "Miss Bathurst will wonder what you mean. Don't forget her!"

Dinah pressed close to her friend's side. "Oh, but I do understand!" she said softly. "And, dear Mrs. Everard, I wish I could help you. But I think Mr. Studley must be right. It is easier to get to heaven than to climb those mountain-peaks. They are so very steep and far away."

"So is Heaven, child," said Isabel, with a sigh of great weariness.

As it were with reluctance, she again met the steady gaze of Scott's eyes, and gradually her mood seemed to change. Her brief animation dropped away from her; she became again passive, inert, save that she still seemed to be watching.

Scott broke the silence, kindly and practically. "We ought to reach the *chalet* at the head of the pass soon," he said. "You will be glad of some tea."

"Oh, are we going to stop for tea?" said Dinah.

"That's the idea," said Scott. "And then back by another way.

We ought to get a good view of the sunset. I hope it won't be misty, but they say a change is coming."

"I hope it won't come yet," said Dinah fervently. "The last few days have been so perfect. And there is so little time left."

Scott smiled. "That is the worst of perfection," he said. "It never lasts."

Dinah's eyes were wistful. "It will go on being perfect here long after we have left," she said. "Isn't it dreadful to think of all the good things - all the beauty - one misses just because one isn't there?"

"It would be if there were nothing else to think of," said Scott. "But there is beauty everywhere - if we know how to look for it."

She looked at him uncertainly. "I never knew what it meant before I came here," she told him shyly. "There is no time for beautiful things in my life. It's very, very drab and ugly. And I am very discontented. I have never been anything else."

Her voice quivered a little as she made the confession. Scott's eyes were so kind, so full of friendly understanding. Isabel had dropped out of their intercourse as completely as though her presence had been withdrawn. She lay back against her cushions, but her eyes were still watching, watching incessantly.

"I think the very dullest life can be made beautiful," Scott said, after a moment. "Even the desert sand is gold when the sun shines on it. The trouble is, -" he laughed a little - "to get the sun to shine."

Dinah leaned forward eagerly, confidentially. "Yes?" she questioned.

He looked her suddenly straight in the eyes. "There is a great store of sunshine in you," he said. "One can't come near you without feeling it. Isabel will tell you the same. Do you keep it only for the Alps? If so, -" he paused.

Dinah's face flushed suddenly under his look. "If so?" she asked, under her breath.

He smiled. "Well, it seems a pity, that's all," he said. "Rather a waste too when you come to think of it."

Dinah's eyes caught the reflection of his smile. "I shall remember that, Mr. Greatheart," she said.

"Forgive me for preaching!" said Scott.

She put out a hand to him quickly, spontaneously. "You don't preach - and it does me good," she said somewhat incoherently. "Please - always - say what you like to me!"

"At risk of hurting you?" said Scott. He held the small, impulsive hand a moment and let it go.

"You could never hurt me," Dinah answered. "You are far too kind."

"I think the kindness is on your side," he answered gravely. "Most people of my acquaintance would think me a bore - if nothing worse."

"Most people have never really met you, Stumpy," said Isabel unexpectedly. "Dinah is one of the privileged few, and I am glad she appreciates it."

"Good heavens!" said Scott, flushing a deep red. "Spare me, Isabel!"

Dinah broke into her gay, infectious laugh. "Please - please don't be upset about it! I'm glad I'm one of the few. I've felt you were a prince in disguise all along."

"Very much in disguise!" protested Scott. "Remove that, and there would be nothing left."

"Except a man," said Isabel, "You can't get away, Stumpy. You're caught."

A fleeting smile crossed her face like a gleam of light and was gone. She turned her look upon Dinah, and became silent again.

Scott, much disconcerted, hunted in every pocket for his cigarette-case. "You don't mind my smoking, I hope?" he murmured.

"I like it," said Dinah. "Let me help you light up!"

She made a screen with her hands, and guarded the flame from the draught.

He thanked her courteously, recovering his composure with a smile that was not without self-ridicule, and in a moment they were talking again upon impersonal matters. But the episode, slight though it was, dwelt in Dinah's mind thereafter with an odd persistence. She felt as if Isabel had given her a flashlight glimpse of something which otherwise she would scarcely have realized. In that single fleeting moment of revelation she had seen that which no vision of knight in shining armour could have surpassed.

They reached the *chalet* at the top of the pass, and descended for tea. The windows looked right down the snow-clad valley up which they had come. The sun had begun to sink, and the greater part of it lay in shadow.

Far away, rising out of the shadows, all golden amid floating mists, was a mighty mountain crest, higher than all around. The sun-rays lighted up its wondrous peaks. The glory of it was unearthly, almost more than the eye could bear.

Dinah stood on the little wooden verandah of the *chalet* and gazed and gazed till the splendour nearly blinded her.

"Still watching the Delectable Mountains?" said Scott's voice at her shoulder.

She made a little gesture in response. She could not take her eyes off the wonder.

He came and stood beside her in mute sympathy while he finished his cigarette. There was a certain depression in his attitude of which presently she became aware. She summoned her resolution and turned herself from the great vision that so drew her.

He was leaning against a post of the verandah, and she read again in his attitude the weariness that she had marked earlier in the afternoon.

"Are you - troubled about your sister?" she asked him diffidently.

He threw away the end of his cigarette and straightened himself. "Yes, I am troubled," he said, in a low voice. "I am afraid it was a mistake to bring her here."

"I thought her looking better this morning," Dinah ventured.

His grey eyes met hers. "Did you? I thought it a good sign that she should make the effort to speak to strangers. But I am not certain now that it has done her any good. We brought her here to wake her from her lethargy. Eustace thought the air would work wonders, but - I am not sure. It is certainly waking her up. But - to what?"

His eyelids drooped heavily, and he passed his hand across his forehead with a gesture that went to her heart.

"It's rather soon to judge, isn't it?" she said.

Ethel M. Dell

"Yes," he admitted. "But there is a change in her; there is an undoubted change. She gets hardly any rest, and the usual draught at night scarcely takes effect. Of course the place is noisy. That may have something to do with it. My brother is very anxious to put a stop to the sleeping-draught altogether. But I can't agree to that. She has never slept naturally since her loss - never slept and never wept. Biddy - the old nurse - declares if she could only cry, all would come right. But I don't know - I don't know."

He uttered a deep sigh, and leaned once more upon the balustrade.

Dinah came close to him, her sweet face full of concern. "Mr. Studley," she murmured, "you - you don't think I do her any harm, do you?"

"You!" He gave a start and looked at her with that in his eyes that reassured her in a moment. "My dear child, no! You are a perfect godsend to her - and to me also, if you don't mind my saying so. No - no! The mischief that I fear will probably develop after you have gone. As long as you are here, I am not afraid for her. Yours is just the sort of influence that she needs."

"Oh, thank you!" Dinah said gratefully. "I was afraid just for a moment, because I know I have been silly and flighty. I try to be sober when I am with her, but -"

"Don't try to be anything but yourself, Miss Bathurst!" he said. "I have confided in you just because you are yourself; and I wouldn't have you any different for the world. You help her just by being yourself."

Dinah laughed while she shook her head. "I wish I were as nice as you seem to think I am."

He laughed also. "Perhaps you have never realized how nice you really are," he returned with a simplicity equal to her own. "Ah! Here comes Isabel! I expect she is ready. We had better go in."

They met her as they turned inwards. The reflection of the sunset glory was in her face recalling some of its faded beauty. She took Dinah's arm, looking at her with a strangely wistful smile.

"I want you now, sweetheart," she said. "Scott can have his turn - afterwards."

"I want you too," said Dinah instantly, squeezing her hand very closely. "Come and look at the mountains! They are so glorious now that the sun is setting."

They turned back for a few moments and Isabel's eyes went to that far and wonderful mountain crest. The gold was turning to rose. The glory deepened even as they watched.

"The peaks of Paradise," breathed Dinah softly.

Isabel was silent for a space, her eyes fixed and yearning. Then at length in a low voice that thrilled with an emotion beyond words she spoke.

"I know now where to look. That is where he is waiting for me. That is where I shall find him."

And then swiftly she turned, aware of her brother close behind her.

He looked at her with eyes of deep compassion. "Some day, Isabel!" he said gently.

She made a swift gesture as of one who brushes aside every hindrance. "Soon!" she said. "Very soon!"

Scott's eyes met Dinah's for a single instant, and she thought they held suffering as well as weariness. But they fell immediately. He stood back in silence for them to pass.

CHAPTER XVI

THE SECOND DRAUGHT

They returned to the hotel by a circuitous route that brought them by a mountain-road into the village just below the hotel. The moon was rising as they ascended the final slope. The chill of mist was in the air.

Sir Eustace was waiting for them in the porch. He helped his sister to alight, but she went by him at once with a rapt look as though she had not seen him. She had sat in almost unbroken silence throughout the homeward drive.

Dinah would have followed her in, but Sir Eustace held her back a moment. "There is to be a dance to-night," he murmured in her ear. "May I count on you?"

She looked at him, the ecstasy of the mountains still shining in her starry eyes. "Yes - yes! If I am allowed!" And then, with a sudden memory of her promise to the Colonel, "But I don't suppose I shall be. And I haven't anything to wear except my fancy dress."

"What of that?" he said lightly. "Call the fairies in to help!"

She laughed, and ran in.

Not for a moment did she suppose that she would be allowed to dance that night; but it seemed that luck was with her, for the first person she met was the Colonel, and he was looking so particularly well pleased with himself and affairs in general that she stopped to tell him of her drive.

"It's been so perfect," she said. "I have enjoyed it! Thank you ever so many times for letting me go!"

Her flushed and happy face was very fair to see, and the Colonel smiled upon her with fatherly kindness. He could not help liking the child. She was such a taking imp!

"Glad you've had a good time," he said. "I hope you thanked your friends for taking you."

"I should think I did!" laughed Dinah; and then seeing that his expression was so benignant she slipped an ingratiating hand through his arm. "Colonel, please - please - may I dance to-night?"

"What?" He looked at her searchingly, with a somewhat laboured attempt to be severe. "Now - now - who do you want to dance with?"

"Anyone or no one," said Dinah boldly. "I feel happy enough to dance by myself."

"That means you're in a mischievous mood," said the Colonel.

"It's only a Cinderella affair," pleaded Dinah. "To-morrow's Sunday, you know. There'll be no dancing to-morrow."

"And a good thing too," he commented. "A pity Sunday doesn't come oftener! What will Lady Grace say I wonder?"

"But Rose is sure to dance," urged Dinah.

"I'm not so sure of that, Sir Eustace Studley has been teaching her to ski all the afternoon, and if she isn't tired, she ought to be."

"Oh, lucky Rose!" Dinah knew an instant's envy. "But I expect she'll dance all the same. And - and - I may dance with him - just once, mayn't I? There couldn't be any harm in just one dance. No one would notice that, would they?"

She pressed close to the Colonel with her petition, and he found it hard to refuse. She made it with so childlike an earnestness, and - all his pomposity notwithstanding - he had a soft heart for children.

"There, be off with you!" he said. "Yes, you may give him one dance if he asks for it. But only one, mind! That's a bargain, is it?"

Dinah beamed radiant acquiescence. "I'll save all the rest for you. You're a dear to let me, and I'll be ever so good. Good-bye!"

She went, flitting like a butterfly up the stairs, and the Colonel smiled in spite of himself as he watched her go. "Little witch!" he muttered. "I wonder what your mother would say to you if she knew."

Dinah raced breathless to her room, and began a fevered toilet. It was true that she possessed nothing suitable for ballroom wear; but then the dance was to be quite informal, and she was too happy to fret herself over that fact. She put on the white muslin frock which she had worn for dinner ever since she had been with the de Vignes. It gave her a fairylike daintiness that had a charm of its own of which she was utterly unconscious. Perhaps fortunately, she had no time to think of her appearance. When she descended again, her eyes were still shining with a happiness so obvious that Billy, meeting her, exclaimed, "What have you got to be so cheerful about?"

She proceeded to tell him of the glorious afternoon she had spent, and was still in the midst of her description when Sir Eustace came up and joined them.

"I thought you would manage it," he said, with smiling assurance. "And now how many may I have? All the waltzes?"

Dinah's laugh rang so gaily that several heads were turned in her direction, and she smothered it in alarm.

"I can only give you one," she said, with a great effort at sobriety.

"What? Oh, nonsense!" he protested, his blue eyes dominating hers. "You couldn't be so shabby as that!"

Dinah's chin pointed merrily upwards. The situation had its humour. It was certainly rather amusing to elude him. She knew he had caught her far too easily the night before.

"It's all I have to offer," she declared.

"Meaning you're not going to dance more than one dance?" he asked.

She opened her laughing eyes wide. "Why should it mean that? You're not the only man in the room, are you?"

Sir Eustace's jaw set itself suddenly after a fashion that made him look formidable, albeit he laughed back at her with his eyes. "All right - Daphne," he murmured. "I'll have the first."

Dinah's heart gave a little throb of apprehension, but she quieted it impatiently. What had she to fear? She nodded and lightly turned away.

All through dinner she alternately dreaded and longed for the moment of his coming to claim that dance from her. That haughty confidence of his had struck a curious chord in her soul, and the suspense was almost unbearable.

She noticed that Rose was very serene and smiling, and she regarded her complacency with growing resentment. Rose could dance as often as she liked with him, and no one would find fault. Rose had had him all to herself throughout the afternoon moreover. She knew very well that had the ski-ing lesson been offered to her, she would not have been allowed to avail herself of it.

A wicked little spirit awoke within her. Why should she always be kept thus in the background? Surely her right to the joys of life was as great as - if not greater than - Rose's! With her it would all end so soon, while Rose had the whole of her youth before her like a pleasant garden in which she might wander or rest at will.

Dinah began to feel feverish. It seemed so imperative that she should miss nothing good during this brief, brief time of happiness vouchsafed her by the gods.

Her frame of mind when she entered the ballroom was curious. Mutiny and doubt, longing and dread, warred strangely together. But the moment he came to her, the moment she felt his arm about her, rapture came and drove out all beside. She drank again of the wine of the gods, drank deeply, giving herself up to it without reservation, too eager to catch every drop thereof to trouble as to what might follow.

He caught her mood. Possibly it was but the complement of his own. Freely he interpreted it, feeling her body throb in swift accord to every motion, aware of the almost passionate surrender of her whole being to the delight of that one magic dance. She was reckless, and he was determined. If this were to be all, he would take his fill at once, and she should have hers. Before the dance was more than half through, he guided her out of the labyrinth into the darkly curtained recess that led out to the verandah, and there holding her, before she so much as realized that they had ceased to dance, he gathered her suddenly and fiercely to him and covered her startled, quivering face with kisses.

She made no outcry, attempted no resistance. He had been too sudden for that. His mastery was too absolute. Holding her fast in the gloom, he took what he would, till with a little sob her arms clasped his neck and she clung to him, giving herself wholly up to him.

But when his hold relaxed at last, she hid her face panting against his breast. He smoothed the dark hair with a possessive touch, laughing softly at her agitation.

"Did you think you could get away from me, you brown elf?" he whispered.

"I - I could if I tried," she whispered back.

His hold tightened again. "Try!" he said.

She shook her head without lifting it. "No," she murmured, with a shy laugh. "I don't want to. Shan't we go back - and dance - before - before - " She broke off in confusion.

"Before what?" he said.

She made a motion to turn her face upwards, but, finding his still close, buried it a little deeper. "I - promised the Colonel - I'd be good," she faltered into his shoulder. "I think I ought to begin - soon; don't you?"

"Is that why I am to have only this one dance?" he asked.

"Yes," she admitted.

His caressing hand found and lightly pressed her cheek. "What are you going to do when it's over?" he asked.

"I don't know," she said. "There's Billy. I may dance with him."

He laughed. "That's an exciting programme. Shall I tell you what I should do - if I were in your place?"

"What?" said Dinah.

Again she raised her face a few inches and again, catching a glimpse of the compelling blue eyes, plunged it deeply into his coat.

He laughed again softly, with a hint of mockery. "I should have one dance with Billy, and one with the omnipotent Colonel. And then I should be tired and say good night."

"But I shan't be a bit tired," protested Dinah, faintly indignant.

"Of course not," laughed Sir Eustace. "You will be just ripe for a little fun. There's quite a cosy sitting-out place at the end of our corridor. I should go to bed *via* that route."

"Oh!" said Dinah, with a gasp.

She lifted her head in astonishment, and met the eyes that so thrilled her. "But - but that would be wrong!" she said.

"I've done naughtier things than that, my virtuous sprite," he said.

But Dinah did not laugh. Very suddenly quite unbidden there flashed across her the memory of Scott's look the night before and her own overwhelming confusion beneath it. What would her friend Mr. Greatheart say to such a proposal? What would he say could he see her now? The hot blood rushed to her face at the bare thought. She drew herself away from him. Her rapture was gone; she was burningly ashamed. The Colonel's majestic displeasure was as nothing in comparison with Scott's wordless disapproval.

"Oh, I couldn't do that," she said. "I - couldn't. I ought not to be here with you now."

"My fault," he said easily. "I brought you here before you

knew where you were. If you go to confession, you can mention that as an extenuating circumstance."

"Oh, don't!" said Dinah, inexplicably stung by his manner. "It - it isn't nice of you to talk like that."

He put out his hand and touched her arm lightly, persuasively. "Then you are angry with me?" he said.

Her resentment melted. She threw him a fleeting smile. "No - no! But how could you imagine I could tell anyone? You didn't seriously - you couldn't!"

"There isn't much to tell, is there?" he said, his fingers closing gently over the soft roundness of her arm. "And you don't like that plan of mine?"

"I didn't say I didn't like it," said Dinah, her eyes lowered. "But - but - I can't do it, that's all. I'm going now. Good-bye!"

She turned to go, but his fingers still held. He drew a step nearer.

"Daphne, remember - you are not to run away!"

A transient dimple showed at the corner of Dinah's mouth. "You must let me go then," she said.

"And if I do - how will you reward me?" His voice was very deep; the tones of it sent a sharp quiver through her. She felt unspeakably small and helpless.

She made a little gesture of appeal. "Please - please let me go! You know you are much stronger than I am."

He drew nearer, his face bent so low that his lips touched her shoulder as she stood turned from him. "You don't know your strength yet," he said. "But you soon will. Are you going away from me like this? Don't you think you're rather hard on me?"

It was a point of view that had not occurred to Dinah. Her warm heart had a sudden twinge of self-reproach. She turned swiftly to him.

"I didn't mean to be horrid. Please don't think that of me! I know I often am. But not to you - never to you!"

"Never?" he said.

His face was close to her, and it wore a faint smile in which she detected none of the arrogance of the conqueror. She put up a shy, impulsive hand and touched his cheek.

"Of course not - Apollo!" she whispered.

He caught the hand and kissed it. She trembled as she felt the drawing of his lips.

"I - I must really go now," she told him hastily.

He stood up to his full height, and again she quivered as she realized how magnificent a man he was.

"*A bientot*, Daphne!" he said, and let her go.

She slipped away from his presence with the feeling of being caught in the meshes of a great net from which she could never hope to escape. She had drunk to-night yet deeper of the wine of the gods, and she knew beyond all doubting that she would return for more.

The memory of his kisses thrilled her all through the night. When she dreamed she was back again in his arms.

CHAPTER XVII

THE UNKNOWN FORCE

"Arrah thin, Miss Isabel darlint, and can't ye rest at all?"

Old Biddy stooped over her charge, her parchment face a mass of wrinkles. Isabel was lying in bed, but raised upon one elbow in the attitude of one about to rise. She looked at the old woman with a queer, ironical smile in her tragic eyes.

"I am going up the mountain," she said. "It is moonlight, and I know the way. I can rest when I get to the top."

"Ah, be aisy, darlint!" urged the old woman. "It's much more likely he'll come to ye if ye lie quiet."

"No, he will not come to me." There was unalterable conviction in Isabel's voice. "It is I who must go to him. If I had waited on the mountain I should never have missed him. He is waiting for me there now."

She flung off the bedclothes and rose, a gaunt, white figure from which all the gracious lines of womanhood had long since departed. Her silvery hair hung in two great plaits from her shoulders, wonderful hair that shone in the shaded lamplight with a lustre that seemed luminous.

"Will I have to fetch Master Scott to ye?" said Biddy, eyeing her wistfully. "He's very tired, poor young man. There's two nights he's had no sleep at all. Won't ye try and rest aisy for his sake, Miss Isabel darlint? Ye can go up the mountain in the morning, and maybe that little Miss Bathurst will like to go with ye. Do wait till the morning now!" she wheedled, laying a wiry old hand upon her. "It's no Christian hour at all for going about now."

"Let me go!" said Isabel.

Biddy's black eyes pleaded with a desperate earnestness. "If ye'd only listen to reason, Miss Isabel!" she said.

"How can I listen," Isabel answered, "when I can hear his voice in my heart calling, calling, calling! Oh, let me go, Biddy! You don't understand, or you couldn't seek to hold me back from him."

"Mavourneen!" Biddy's eyes were full of tears; the hand she had laid upon Isabel's arm trembled. "It isn't meself that's holding ye back. It's God. He'll join the two of ye together in His own good time, but ye can't hurry Him. Ye've got to bide His time."

"I can't!" Isabel said. "I can't! You're all conspiring against me. I know - I know! Give me my cloak, and I will go."

Biddy heaved a great sigh, the tears were running down her cheeks, but her face was quite resolute. "I'll have to call Master Scott after all," she said.

"No! No! I don't want Scott. I don't want anyone. I only want to be up the mountain in time for the dawn. Oh, why are you all such fools? Why can't you understand?" There was growing exasperation in Isabel's voice.

Biddy's hand fell from her, and she turned to cross the room.

Scott slept in the next room to them, and a portable electric bell which they adjusted every night communicated therewith.

Biddy moved slowly to press the switch, but ere she reached it Isabel's voice stayed her.

"Biddy, don't call Master Scott!"

Biddy paused, looking back with eyes of faithful devotion.

"Ah, Miss Isabel darlint, will ye rest aisy then? I dursn't give ye the quieting stuff without Master Scott says so."

"I don't want anything," Isabel said. "I only want my liberty. Why are you all in league against me to keep me in just one place? Ah, listen to that noise! How wild those people are! It is the same every night - every night. Can they really be as happy as they sound?"

A distant hubbub had arisen in the main corridor, the banging of doors and laughter of careless voices. It was some time after one o'clock, and the merry-markers were on their way to bed.

"Never mind them!" said Biddy. "They're just a set of noisy children. Lie down again, Miss Isabel! They'll soon settle, and then p'raps ye'll get to sleep. It's not this way they'll be coming anyway."

"Someone is coming this way," said Isabel, listening with sudden close attention.

She was right. The quiet tread of a man's feet came down the corridor that led to their private suite. A man's hand knocked with imperious insistence upon the door.

"Sir Eustace!" said Biddy, in a dramatic whisper. "Will I tell him ye're asleep, Miss Isabel? Quick now! Get back to bed!"

But Isabel made no movement to comply. She only drew herself together with the nervous contraction of one about to face a dreaded ordeal.

Quietly the door opened. Biddy moved forward, her face puckered with anxiety. She met Sir Eustace on the threshold.

"Miss Isabel hasn't settled yet, Sir Eustace," she told him, her voice cracked and tremulous. "But she'll not be wanting anybody to disturb her. Will your honour say good night and go?"

There was entreaty in the words. Her eyes besought him. Her old gnarled hands gripped each other, trembling.

But Sir Eustace looked over her head as though she were not there. His gaze sought and found his sister; and a frown gathered on his clear-cut, handsome face.

"Not in bed yet?" he said, and closing the door moved forward, passing Biddy by.

Isabel stood and faced him, but she drew back a step as he reached her, and a hunted look crept into her wide eyes.

"You are late," she said. "I thought you had forgotten to say good night."

He was still in evening dress. It was evident that he had only just come upstairs. "No, I didn't forget," he said. "And it seems I am not too late for you. I shouldn't have disturbed you if you had been asleep."

She smiled a quivering, piteous smile. "You knew I should not be asleep," she said.

He glanced towards the bed which Biddy was setting in order with tender solicitude. "I expected to find you in bed nevertheless," he said. "What made you get up again?"

She shook her head in silence, standing before him like a child that expects a merited rebuke.

He put a hand on her shoulder that was authoritative rather than kind. "Lie down again!" he said. "It is time you settled for the night."

She threw him a quick, half-furtive look. "No - no!" she said hurriedly. "I can't sleep. I don't want to sleep. I think I will get a book and read."

His hand pressed upon her. "Isabel!" he said quietly. "When I say a thing I mean it."

She made a quivering gesture of appeal. "I can't go to bed, Eustace. It is like lying on thorns. Somehow I can't close my eyes to-night. They feel red-hot."

His hold did not relax. "My dear," he said, "you talk like a hysterical child! Lie down at once, and don't be ridiculous!"

She wavered perceptibly before his insistence. "If I do, Scott must give me a draught. I can't do without it - indeed - indeed!"

"You are going to do without it to-night," Eustace said, with cool decision. "Scott is worn out and has gone to bed. I made him promise to stay there unless he was rung for. And he will not be rung for to-night."

Isabel made a sharp movement of dismay. "But - but - I always have the draught sooner or later. I must have it. Eustace, I must! I can't do without it! I never have done without it!"

Eustace's face did not alter. It looked as if it were hewn in granite. "You are going to make a beginning to-night," he said. "You have been poisoned by that stuff long enough, and I am going to put a stop to it. Now get into bed, and be reasonable! Biddy, you clear out and do the same! You can leave the door ajar if you like. I'll call you if you are wanted."

He pointed to the half-open door that led into the small

adjoining room in which Biddy slept. The old woman stood and stared at him with consternation in her beady eyes.

"Is it meself that could do such a thing?" she protested. "I never leave my young lady till she's asleep, Sir Eustace. I'd sooner come under the curse of the Almighty."

He raised his brows momentarily, but he kept his hand upon his sister. He was steadily pressing her towards the bed. "If you don't do as you are told, Biddy, you will be made," he observed. "I am here to-night for a definite purpose, and I am not going to be thwarted by you. So you had better take yourself out of my way. Now, Isabel, you know me, don't you? You know it is useless to fight against me when my mind is made up. Be sensible for once! It's for your own good. You can't have that draught. You have got to manage without it."

"Oh, I can't! I can't!" moaned Isabel. She was striving to resist his hold, but her efforts were piteously weak. The force of his personality plainly dominated her. "I shall lie awake all night - all night."

"Very well," he said inexorably. "You must. Sleep will come sooner or later, and then you can make up for it."

"Oh, but you don't understand." Piteously she turned and clasped his arm in desperate entreaty. "I shall lie awake in torture. I shall hear him calling all night long. He is there beyond the mountains, wanting me. And I can't get to him. It is agony - oh, it is agony - to lie and listen!"

He took her between his hands, very firmly, very quietly. "Isabel, you are talking nonsense - utter nonsense! And I refuse to listen to it. Get into bed! Do you hear? Yes, I insist. I am capable of putting you there. If you mean to behave like a child, I shall treat you as one. Now for the last time, get into bed."

"Sir Eustace!" pleaded Biddy in a hoarse whisper. "Don't force her, Sir Eustace! Don't now! Don't!"

He paid no attention to her. His eyes were fixed upon his sister's death-white face, and her eyes, strained and glassy were upturned to his.

He said no more. Isabel's breath came in short sobbing gasps. She resisted him no longer. Under the steady pressure of his hands, her body yielded. She seemed to wilt under the compulsion of his look. Slowly, tremblingly, she crumpled in his hold, sinking downwards upon the bed.

He bent over her, laying her back, taking the bedclothes from Biddy's shaking hands and drawing them over her.

Then over his shoulder briefly he addressed the old woman. "Turn out the light, and go!"

Biddy stood and gibbered. There was that in her mistress's numb acquiescence that terrified her. "Sure, you'll kill her, Sir Eustace!" she gasped.

He made a compelling gesture. "You had better do as I say. If I want your help - or advice - I'll let you know. Do as I say! Do you hear me, Biddy?"

His voice fell suddenly and ominously to a note so deep that Biddy drew back still further affrighted and began to whimper.

Sir Eustace turned back to his sister, lying motionless on the pillow. "Tell her to go, Isabel! I am going to stay with you myself. You don't want her, do you?"

"No," said Isabel. "I want Scott."

"You can't have Scott to-night." There was absolute decision in his voice. "It is essential that he should get a rest. He looked ready to drop to-night."

Ethel M. Dell

"Ah! You think me selfish!" she said, catching her breath.

He sat down by her side. "No," he answered quietly. "But I think you have not the least idea how much he spends himself upon you. If you had, you would be shocked."

She moved restlessly. "You don't understand," she said. "You never understand. Eustace, I wish you would go away."

"I will go in half an hour," he made calm rejoinder, "if you have not moved during that time."

"You know that is impossible;" she said.

"Very well then. I shall remain." His jaw set itself in a fashion that brought it into heavy prominence.

"You will stay all night?" she questioned quickly.

"If necessary," he answered.

Biddy had turned the lamp very low. The faint radiance shone upon him as he sat imparting a certain mysterious force to his dominant outline. He looked as immovable as an image carved in stone.

A great shiver went through Isabel. "You want to see me suffer," she said.

"You are wrong," he returned inflexibly. "But I would sooner see you suffer than give yourself up to a habit which is destroying you by inches. It is no kindness on Scott's part to let you do it."

"Don't talk of Scott!" she said quickly. "No one - no one - will ever know what he is to me - how he has helped me - while you - you have only looked on!"

Her voice quivered. She flung out a restless arm. Instantly, yet without haste, he took and held her hand. His fingers pressed the fevered wrist. He spoke after a moment while he quelled her instinctive effort to free herself. "I am not merely looking on to-night. I am here to help you - if you will accept my help."

"You are here to torture me!" she flung back fiercely. "You are here to force me down into hell, and lock the gates upon me!"

His hold tightened upon her. He leaned slightly towards her. "I am here to conquer you," he said, "if you will not conquer yourself."

The sudden sternness of his speech, the compulsion of his look, took swift effect upon her. She cowered away from him.

"You are cruel!" she whispered. "You always were cruel at heart - even in the days when you loved me."

Sir Eustace's lips became a single, hard line. His whole strength was bent to the task of subduing her, and he meant it to be as brief a struggle as possible.

He said nothing whatever therefore, and so passed his only opportunity of winning the conflict by any means save naked force.

To Isabel in her torment that night was the culmination of sorrows. For years this brother who had once been all the world to her had held aloof, never seeking to pass the barrier which her widowed love had raised between them. He had threatened many times to take the step which now at last he had taken; but always Scott had intervened, shielding her from the harshness which such a step inevitably involved. And by love he had never sought to prevail. Her mental weakness seemed to have made tenderness from him an impossibility. He could not bear with her. It was as though he resented in her the likeness to one beloved whom he mourned as dead.

Possibly he had never wholly forgiven her marriage - that disastrous marriage that had broken her life. Possibly her clouded brain was to him a source of suffering which drove him to hardness. He had ever been impatient of weakness, and what he deemed hysteria was wholly beyond his endurance; and the spectacle of the one being who had been so much to him crushed beneath a sorrow the very existence of which he resented was one which he had never been able to contemplate with either pity or tolerance. As he had said, he would rather see her suffering than a passive slave to that sorrow and all that it entailed.

So during the dreadful hours that followed he held her to her inferno, convinced beyond all persuasion - with the stubborn conviction of an iron will - that by so doing he was acting for her welfare, even in a sense working out her salvation.

He relied upon the force of his personality to accomplish the end he had in view. If he could break the fatal rule of things for one night only, he believed that he would have achieved the hardest part. But the process was long and agonizing. Only by the sternest effort of will could he keep up the pressure which he knew he must not relax for a single moment if he meant to attain the victory he desired.

There came a time when Isabel's powers of endurance were lost in the abyss of mental suffering into which she was flung, and she struggled like a mad creature for freedom. He held her in his arms, feeling her strength wane with every paroxysm, till at last she lay exhausted, only feebly entreating him for the respite he would not grant.

But even when the bitter conflict was over, when she was utterly conquered at last, and he laid her down, too weak for further effort, he did not gather the fruits of victory. For her eyes remained wide and glassy, dry and sleepless with the fever that throbbed ceaselessly in the poor tortured brain behind.

She was passive from exhaustion only, and though he closed

the staring eyes, yet they opened again with tense wakefulness the moment he took his hand from the burning brow.

The night was far advanced when Biddy, creeping softly came to her mistress's side in the belief that she slept at last. She had not dared to come before, had not dared to interfere though she had listened with a wrung heart to the long and futile battle; for Sir Eustace's wrath was very terrible, too terrible a thing to incur with impunity.

But the moment she looked upon Isabel's face, her courage came upon a flood of indignation that carried all before it.

"Faith, I believe you've killed her!" she uttered in a sibilant whisper across the bed. "Is it yourself that has no heart at all?"

He looked back to her, dominant still, though the prolonged struggle had left its mark upon him also. His face was pale and set.

"This is only a phase," he said quietly. "She will fall asleep presently. You can get her a cup of tea if you can do it without making a fuss."

Biddy turned from the bed. That glimpse of Isabel's face had been enough. She had no further thought of consequences. She moved across the room to set about her task, and in doing so she paused momentarily and pressed the bell that communicated with Scott's room.

Sir Eustace did not note the action. Perhaps the long strain had weakened his vigilance somewhat. He sat in massive obduracy, relentlessly watching his sister's worn white face.

Two minutes later the door opened, and a shadowy figure slipped into the room.

He looked up then, looked up sharply. "You!" he said, with curt displeasure.

Scott came straight to him, and leaned over his sister for a moment with a hand on his shoulder. She did not stir, or seem aware of his presence. Her eyes gazed straight upwards with a painful, immovable stare.

Scott stood up again. His hand was still upon Eustace. He looked him in the eyes. "You go to bed, my dear chap!" he said. "I've had my rest."

Eustace jerked back his head with a movement of exasperation. "You promised to stay in your room unless you were rung for," he said.

Scott's brows went up for a second; then, "For the night, yes!" he said. "But the night is over. It is nearly six. I shan't sleep again. You go and get what sleep you can."

Eustace's jaw looked stubborn. "If you will give me your word of honour not to drug her, I'll go," he said. "Not otherwise."

Scott's hand pressed his shoulder. "You must leave her in my care now," he said. "I am not going to promise anything more."

"Then I remain," said Eustace grimly.

A muffled sob came from Biddy. She was weeping over her tea-kettle.

Scott took his brother by the shoulders as he sat. "Go like a good fellow," he urged. "You will do harm if you stay."

But Eustace resisted him. "I am here for a definite purpose," he said, "and I have no intention of relinquishing it. She has come through so far without it, I am not going to give in at this stage."

"And you think your treatment has done her good?" said Scott, with a glance at the drawn, motionless face on the pillow.

"Ultimate good is what I am aiming at," his brother returned stubbornly.

Scott's hold became a grip. He leaned suddenly down and spoke in a whisper. "If I had known you were up to this, I'm damned if I'd have stayed away!" he said tensely.

"Stumpy!" Eustace opened his eyes in amazement. Strong language from Scott was so unusual as to be almost outside his experience.

"I mean it!" Scott's words vibrated. "You've done a hellish thing! Clear out now, and leave me to help her in my own way! Before God, I believe she'll die if you don't! Do you want her to die?"

The question fell with a force that was passionate. There was violence in the grip of his hands. His light eyes were ablaze. His whole meagre body quivered as though galvanized by some vital, electric current more potent than it could bear.

And very curiously Sir Eustace was moved by the unknown force. It struck him unawares. Stumpy in this mood was a complete stranger to him, a being possessed by gods or devils, he knew not which; but in any case a being that compelled respect.

He got up and stood looking down at him speculatively, too astonished to be angry.

Scott faced him with clenched hands. He was white as death. "Go!" he reiterated. "Go! There's no room for you in here. Get out!"

His lips twisted over the words, and for an instant his teeth showed with a savage gleam. He was trembling from head to foot.

It was no moment for controversy. Sir Eustace recognized the fact just as surely as he realized that his brother had completely parted with his self-control. He had the look of a furious animal prepared to spring at his throat.

Greek had met Greek indeed, but upon ground that was wholly unsuitable for a tug of war. With a shrug he yielded.

"I don't know you, Stumpy," he said briefly. "You've got beyond yourself. I advise you to pull up before we meet again. I also advise you to bear in mind that to administer that draught is to undo all that I have spent the whole night to accomplish."

Scott stood back for him to pass, but the quivering fury of the man seemed to emanate from him like the scorching draught from a blast furnace. As Eustace said, he had got beyond himself, - so far beyond that he was scarcely recognizable.

"Your advice be damned!" he flung back under his breath with a concentrated bitterness that was terrible. "I shall follow my own judgment."

Sir Eustace's mouth curled superciliously. He was angry too, though by no means so angry as Scott. "Better look where you go all the same," he observed, and passed him by, not without dignity and a secret sense of relief.

The long and fruitless vigil of the night had taught him one thing at least. Rome was not built in a day. He would not attempt the feat a second time, though neither would he rest till he had gained his end.

As for Scott, he would have a reckoning with him presently - a strictly private reckoning which should demonstrate once and for all who was master.

CHAPTER XVIII

THE ESCAPE OF THE PRISONER

Dinah spent her Sunday afternoon seated in a far corner of the verandah, inditing a very laboured epistle to her mother - a very different affair from the gay little missives she scribbled to her father every other day.

The letter to her mother was a duty which must of necessity be accomplished, and perhaps in consequence she found it peculiarly distasteful. She never knew what to say, being uncomfortably aware that a detailed account of her doings would only give rise to drastic comment. The glories of the mountains were wholly beyond her powers of description when she knew that any extravagance of language would be at once termed high-flown and ridiculous. The sleigh-drive of the day before was disposed of in one sentence, and the dance of the evening could not be mentioned at all. The memory of it was like a flame in her inner consciousness. Her cheeks still burned at the thought, and her heart leapt with a wild longing. When would he kiss her again, she wondered? Ah, when, when?

There was another thought at the back of her wonder which she felt to be presumptuous, but which nevertheless could not be kept completely in abeyance. He had said that there would be no consequences; but - had he really meant it? Was it possible ever to awake wholly from so perfect a dream? Was it not rather the great reality of things to which she had suddenly come, and all her past life a mere background of shadows? How could she ever go back into that dimness now that she felt the glorious rays of this new radiance upon her? And he also - was it possible that he could ever forget? Surely it had ceased to be just a game to either of them! Surely, surely, the wonder and the rapture had caught him also into the magic web - the golden maze of Romance!

She leaned her head on her hand and gave herself up to the great enchantment, feeling again his kisses upon lips and eyes and brow, and the thrilling irresistibility of his hold. Ah, this was life indeed! Ah, this was life!

A soft footfall near her made her look up sharply, and she saw Rose de Vigne approaching. Rose was looking even more beautiful than usual, yet for the first time Dinah contemplated her without any under-current of envy. She moved slightly to make room for her.

"I haven't come to stay," Rose announced with her quiet, well-satisfied smile, as she drew near. "I have promised to sing at to-night's concert and the padre wants to look through my songs. Well, Dinah, my dear, how are you getting on? Is that a letter to your mother?"

Dinah suppressed a sigh. "Yes. I've only just begun it. I don't know in the least what to say."

Rose lifted her pretty brows. "What about your new friend Sir Eustace Studley's sister? Wouldn't she be interested to hear of her? Poor soul, it's lamentably sad to think that she should be mentally deranged. Some unfortunate strain in the family, I should say, to judge by the younger brother's appearance also."

Dinah's green eyes gleamed a little. "I don't see anything very unusual about him," she remarked. "There are plenty of little men in the world."

"And crippled?" smiled Rose.

"I shouldn't call him a cripple," rejoined Dinah quickly. "He is quite active."

"Many cripples are, dear," Rose pointed out. "He has learnt to get the better of his infirmity, but nothing can alter the fact that the infirmity exists. I call him a most peculiar little person to look at. Of course I don't deny that he may be very nice in other ways."

Dinah bit her lip and was silent. To hear Scott described as nice was to her mind less endurable than to hear him called peculiar. But somehow she could not bring herself to discuss him, so she choked down her indignation and said nothing.

Rose seated herself beside her. "I call Sir Eustace a very interesting man," she observed. "He fully makes up for the deficiencies of his brother and sister. He seems to be very kind-hearted too. Didn't I see him helping you with your skating the other night?"

Dinah's eyes shone again with a quick and ominous light. "He helped you with your ski-ing too, didn't he?" she said.

"He did, dear. I had a most enjoyable afternoon." Rose smiled again as over some private reminiscence. "He told me he thought you were coming on, in fact he seems to think that you have the makings of quite a good skater. It's a pity your opportunities are so limited, dear." Rose paused to utter a soft laugh.

"I don't see anything funny in that," remarked Dinah.

"No, no! Of course not. I was only smiling at the way in which he referred to you. 'That little brown cousin of yours' he said, 'makes me think of a water-vole, there one minute and gone the next.' He seemed to think you a rather amusing child, as of course you are." Rose put up a delicate hand and playfully caressed the glowing cheek nearest to her. "I told him you were not any relation, but just a dear little friend of mine who had never seen anything of the world before. And he laughed and said, 'That is why she looks like a chocolate baby out of an Easter egg.'"

"Anything else?" said Dinah, repressing an urgent desire to shiver at the kindly touch.

"No, I don't think so. We had more important matters to think of and talk about. He is a man who has travelled a good deal, and we found that we had quite a lot in common, having visited the same places and regarded many things from practically the same point of view. He took the trouble to be very entertaining," said Rose, with a pretty blush. "And his trouble was not misspent. I am convinced that he enjoyed the afternoon even more than I did. We also enjoyed the evening," she added. "He is an excellent dancer. We suited each other perfectly."

"Did you find him good at sitting out?" asked Dinah unexpectedly.

Rose looked at her enquiringly, but her eyes were fixed upon the distant mist-capped mountains. There was nothing in her aspect to indicate what had prompted the question.

"What a funny thing to ask!" she said, with her soft laugh. "No; we enjoyed dancing much too much to waste any time sitting out. He gave you one dance, I believe?"

"No," Dinah said briefly. "I gave him one."

She turned from her contemplation of the mountains. An odd little smile very different from Rose's smile of complacency hovered at the corners of her mouth. She gave Rose a swift and comprehensive glance, then slipped her pen into her writing-case and closed it.

"I am afraid I have interrupted you," said Rose.

"Oh no, it doesn't matter." Dinah's dimple showed for a second and was gone. "I can't write any more now. There's something about this air that makes me feel now and then that I must get up and jump. Does it affect you that way?"

"You funny little thing!" said Rose. "Why, no!"

Dinah's chin pointed upwards. She looked for the moment almost aggressively happy. But the next her look went beyond Rose, and she started. Her expression altered, became suddenly tender and anxious.

"There is Mrs. Everard!" she said softly.

Rose looked round. "Ah! Captain Brent's Purple Empress!" she said. "How haggard the poor soul looks!"

As if drawn magnetically, Dinah moved along the verandah.

Isabel was dressed in the long purple coat she had worn the previous day. She had a cap of black fur on her head. She stood as if irresolute, glancing up and down as though she searched for someone. There was an odd furtiveness in her bearing that struck Dinah on the instant. It also occurred to her as strange that though the restless eyes must have seen her they did not seem to take her in.

The fact deterred her for a second, but only for a second. Then swiftly she went forward and joined her.

"Are you looking for someone, dear Mrs. Everard?"

Isabel's eyes glanced at her, and instantly looked beyond. "I am looking for my husband," she said, her voice quick and low. "He does not seem to be here. You have not seen him, I suppose? He is tall and fair with a boyish smile, and eyes that look straight at you. He laughs a good deal. He is always laughing. You couldn't fail to notice him. He is one whom the gods love."

Again her eyes roamed over Dinah, and again they passed her to scan the mist-wreathed mountains.

Dinah slipped a loving hand through her arm. "He is not here, dear," she said. "Come and sit down for a little! The sun won't be gone yet. We can watch it go."

She tried to draw her gently along the verandah, but Isabel resisted. "No - no! I am not going that way. I have to go up the mountains to meet him. Don't keep me! Don't keep me!"

Dinah threw an anxious look around. There was no one near them. Rose had moved away to join a group just returned from the rink. The laughter and gay voices rose on the still air in merry chorus. No one knew or cared of the living tragedy so near.

Pleadingly she turned to Isabel. "Darling Mrs. Everard, need you go now? Wait till the morning! It is so late now. It will soon be dark."

Isabel made a sharp gesture of impatience. "Be quiet, child! You don't understand. Of course I must go now. I have escaped from them, and if I wait I shall be taken again. It would kill me to be kept back now. I must meet him in the dawn on the mountain-top. What was it you called it? The peaks of Paradise! That is where I shall find him. But I must start at once - at once."

She threw another furtive look around, and stepped forth. Dinah's hand closed upon her arm. "If you go, I am coming too," she said, with quick resolution. "But won't you wait a moment - just a moment - while I run and get some gloves?"

Isabel made a swift effort to disengage herself. "No, child, no! I can't wait. If you met Eustace, he would make you tell him where you were going, and then he would follow and bring me back. No, I must go now - at once. Yes, you may come too if you like. But you mustn't keep me back. I must go quickly -

quickly - before they find out. Everything depends on that."

There was no delaying her. Dinah cast another look towards the chattering group, and gave up hope. She dared not leave her, for she had no idea of the whereabouts of either of the brothers. And there was no time to make a search. The only course open to her was to accompany her friend whithersoever the fruitless quest should lead. She was convinced that Isabel's physical powers of endurance were slight, and that when they were exhausted she would be able to bring her back unresisting.

Nevertheless, she was conscious of a little tremor at the heart as they set forth. There was an air of desperation about her companion that it was impossible to overlook. Isabel's manner towards her was so wholly devoid of that caressing element that had always marked their intimacy till that moment. Without being actually frightened, she was very uneasy. It was evident that Isabel was beyond all persuasion that day.

The sun was beginning to sink towards the western peaks as they turned up the white track, casting long shadows across the snow. The pine-wood through which the road wound was mysteriously dark. The rush of the stream in the hollow had an eerie sound. It seemed to Dinah that the ground they trod was bewitched. She almost expected to catch sight of goblin-faces peering from behind the dark trunks. Now and then muffled in the snow, she thought she heard the scamper of tiny feet.

Isabel went up the steep track with a wonderful elasticity, looking neither to right nor left. Her eyes were fixed perpetually forwards, with the look in them of one who strains towards a goal. Her lips were parted, and the eagerness of her face went to Dinah's heart.

They came out above the pine-wood. They reached and passed the spot where she and Scott had turned back on their first walk together. The snow crunched crisply underfoot. The ascent was becoming more and more acute.

Dinah was panting. Light as she was, with all the activity of youth in her veins, she found it hard to keep up, for Isabel was pressing, pressing hard. She went as one in whom the fear of pursuit was ever present, paying no heed to her companion, seeming indeed to have almost forgotten her presence.

On and on, up and up, they went on their rapid pilgrimage. The winding of the road had taken them out of sight of the hotel, and the whole world seemed deserted. The sun-rays slanted ever more and more obliquely. The valley behind them had fallen into shadow.

Before them and very far above them towered the great pinnacles, clothed in the everlasting snows, beginning to turn golden above their floating wreaths of mist. Even where they were, trails like the ragged edges of a cloud drifted by them, and the coldness of the air held a clammy quality. The sparkling dryness of the atmosphere seemed to be dissolving into these thin, veil-like vapours. The cold was more penetrating than Dinah had ever before experienced.

Now and then an icy draught came swirling down upon them, making her shiver, though it was evident that Isabel was unaware of it. The harder the way became, the more set upon her purpose did she seem to be. Dinah marvelled at her strength and unvarying determination. There was about it an element of the wild, not far removed from ferocity. Her uneasiness was growing with every step, and something that was akin to fear began to knock at her heart. The higher they mounted, the more those trails of mist increased. Very soon now the sun would be gone. Already it had ceased to warm that world of snow. And what would happen then? What if the dusk came upon them while still they pressed on up that endless, difficult track?

Timidly she clasped Isabel's arm at last. "It will be getting dark soon," she said. "Shouldn't we be going back?"

For a moment Isabel's eyes swept round upon her, and she

marvelled at their intense and fiery brilliance. But instantly they sought the mountain-tops again, all rose-lit in the opal glow of sunset.

"You can go back, child," she said. "I must go on."

"But it is getting so late," pleaded Dinah. "And look at the mist! If we keep on much longer, we may be lost."

Isabel quickened her pace. "I am not afraid," she said, and her voice thrilled with a deep rapture. "He is waiting for me, there where the mountains meet the sky. I shall find him in the dawn. I know that I shall find him."

"But, dear Mrs. Everard, we can't go on after dark," urged Dinah. "We should be frozen long before morning. It is terribly cold already. And poor Biddy will be so anxious about you."

"Oh no!" Isabel spoke with supreme confidence. "Biddy will know where I have gone. She was asleep when I left, poor old soul. She had had a bad night." A sudden sharp shudder caught her. "All night I was struggling against the bars of my cage. It was only when Biddy fell asleep that I found the door was open. But you can go back, child," she added. "You had better go back. Eustace won't want to follow me if he has you."

But Dinah's hold instantly grew close and resolute. "I shall not leave you," she said, with decision.

Isabel made no further attempt to persuade her. She seemed to regard it as a matter of trifling importance. Her one aim was to reach those glowing peaks that glittered far above the floating mists like the glories half-revealed of another world.

It was nothing to her that the road by which they had come should be blotted out. She had no thought for that, no desire or intention to return. If an earthquake had rent away the ground behind them, she would not have been dismayed. It was only the forward path, leading ever upwards to the desired country, that held her mind, and the memory of a voice that called far above the mountain height.

The sun sank, the glory faded. The dark and the cold wrapped them round. But still was she undaunted. "When the dawn comes, we shall be there," she said.

And Dinah heard her with a sinking heart. She had no thought of leaving her, but she knew and faced the fact that in going on, she carried her life in her hand. Yet she kept herself from despair. Surely by now the brothers would have found out, and they would follow! Surely they would follow! And Eustace - Eustace would thank her for what she had done.

She strained her ears for their coming; but she heard nothing – nothing but their own muffled footsteps on the snow. And ever the darkness deepened, and the mist crept closer around them.

She gathered all her courage to face the falling night. She was sure she had done right to come and so she hoped God would take care of them.

CHAPTER XIX

THE CUP OF BITTERNESS

It was growing late on that same evening that Scott came through the hotel vestibule after a rehearsal of the concert which was to take place that evening and at which he had undertaken to play the accompaniments. He glanced about him as he came as though in search of someone, and finally passed on to the smoking-room. His eye were heavy and his face worn, but there was an air of resolution about him that gave purpose to his movements.

In the smoking-room several men were congregated, and in a corner of it sat Sir Eustace, writing a letter. Scott came straight to him, and bent over him a hand on the back of his chair.

"Can I have a word with you?" he asked in a low voice.

Sir Eustace did not look round or cease to write. "Presently," he said.

Scott drew back and sat down near him. He did not smoke or take up a paper. His attitude was one of quiet vigilance.

Minutes passed. Sir Eustace continued his task exactly as if he were not there. Now and then he paused to flick the ash from his cigarette, but he did not turn his head. The dressing-gong boomed through the hotel, but he paid no attention to it. One after another the men in the room got up and sauntered away,

Ethel M. Dell

but Scott remained motionless, awaiting his brother's pleasure.

Sir Eustace finished his letter, and pulled another sheet of paper towards him. Scott made no sign of impatience.

Sir Eustace began to write again, paused, wrote a few more words, then suddenly turned in his chair. They were alone.

"Oh, what the devil is it?" he said irritably. "I haven't any time to waste over you. What do you want?"

Scott stood up. "It's all right, old chap," he said gently. "I'm going. I only came in to tell you I was sorry for all the beastly things I said to you last night - this morning, rather. I lost my temper which was fairly low of me, considering you had been up all night and I hadn't."

He paused. Eustace was looking up at him from under frowning brows, his blue eyes piercing and merciless.

"It's all very fine, Stumpy," he said, after a moment. "Some people think that an apology more than atones for the offence. I don't."

"Neither do I," said Scott quietly. "But it's better than nothing, isn't it?" His eyes met his brother's very steadily and openly. His attitude was unflinching.

"It depends," Eustace rejoined curtly. "It is if you mean it. If you don't, it's not worth - that," with a snap of the fingers.

"I do mean it," said Scott, flushing.

"You do?" Eustace looked at him still more searchingly.

"I always mean what I say," Scott returned with deliberation.

"And you meant what you said this morning?" Eustace pounced without mercy upon the weak spot.

But the armour was proof. Scott remained steadfast. "I meant it - yes. But I might have put it in a different form. I lost my temper. I am sorry."

Eustace continued to regard him with a straight, unsparing scrutiny. "And you consider that to be the sort of apology I can accept?" he asked, after a moment.

"I think you might accept it, old chap," Scott made pacific rejoinder.

Eustace turned back to the table, and began to put his papers together. "I might do many things," he observed, "which, not being a weak-kneed fool, I don't. If you really wish to make your peace with me, you had better do your best to make amends - to pull with me and not against me. For I warn you, Stumpy, you went too far last night. And it is not the first time."

He paused, as if he expected a disclaimer.

Scott waited a second or two; then with a very winning movement he bent and laid his arm across his brother's shoulders. "Try and bear with me, dear chap!" he said.

His voice was not wholly steady. There was entreaty in his action.

Eustace made a sharp gesture of surprise, but he did not repel him. There fell a brief silence between them; then Scott's hand came gently down and closed upon his brother's.

"Life isn't so confoundedly easy at the best of times," he said, speaking almost under his breath. "I'm generally philosopher enough to take it as it comes. But just lately -" he broke off. "Let it be *pax*, Eustace!" he urged in a whisper.

Eustace's hand remained for a moment or two stiffly unresponsive; then very suddenly it closed and held.

"What's the matter with you?" he said gruffly.

"Oh, I'm a fool, that's all," Scott answered, and uttered a shaky laugh. "Never mind! Forget it like a dear fellow! God knows I don't want to pull against you; but, old chap, we must go slow."

It was the conclusion that events had forced upon Eustace himself during the night, but he chafed against acknowledging it. "There's no sense in drifting on in the same old hopeless way for ever," he said. "We have got to make a stand; and it's now or never."

"I know. But we must have patience a bit longer. There is a change coming. I am certain of it. But - last night has thrown her back." Scott spoke with melancholy conviction.

"You gave her the draught?" Eustace asked sharply.

"I gave her a sedative only; but it took no effect. In the middle of the morning she was still in the same unsatisfactory state, and I gave her a second sedative. After that she fell asleep, but it was not a very easy sleep for a long time. This afternoon I saw Biddy for a moment, and she told me she seemed much more comfortable. The poor old thing looked tired out, and I told her to get a rest herself. She said she would lie down in the room. If it hadn't been for this concert business, I would have relieved her. But they couldn't muster anyone to take my place. I am just going up now to see how she is getting on."

Scott straightened himself slowly, with a movement that was unconsciously very weary. Eustace gave him a keen glance.

"You're wearing yourself out over her, Stumpy," he said.

"Oh, rot!" Scott smiled upon him, a light that was boyishly affectionate in his eyes. "I'm much tougher than I look. Thanks for being decent to me, old chap! I don't deserve it. If there are any more letters to be written, bring them along, and

I'll attend to them to-night after the concert."

"No. Not this lot. I shall attend to them myself." Eustace got up, and passed a hand through his arm. "You are working too hard and sleeping too little. I'm going to take you in hand and put a stop to it."

Scott laughed. "No, no! Thanks all the same, I'm better left alone. Are you coming to the show to-night? The beautiful Miss de Vigne is going to sing."

Eustace looked supercilious. "Is there anything that young lady can't do, I wonder? Her accomplishments are legion. She told me yesterday that she could play the guitar. She can also recite, play bridge, and take cricket scores. She is a scratch golf-player, plays a good game of tennis, rides to hounds, and visits the poor. And that is by no means a complete list. I don't wonder that she gives the little brown girl indigestion. Her perfection is almost nauseating at times."

Scott laughed again. It was a relief to have diverted his brother's attention from more personal subjects. "She ought to suit you rather well," he observed. "You are something of the perfect knight yourself. I heard a lady exclaim only yesterday when you started off together on that ski-ing expedition, 'What a positively divine couple! Apollo and Aphrodite!' I think it was the parson's wife. You couldn't expect her to know much about heathen theology."

"Don't make me sick if you don't mind!" said Sir Eustace. "Look here, my friend! We shall be late if we don't go. You can't spend long with Isabel, if you are to turn up in time for this precious concert. Hullo! What's the matter?"

The door of the smoking-room had burst suddenly open, and Colonel de Vigne, very red in the face and as agitated as his pomposity would allow, stood glaring at them.

"So you are here!" he exclaimed, his tone an odd blend of relief

Ethel M. Dell

and anxiety.

"Do you mean me?" said Sir Eustace, with a touch of haughtiness.

"Yes, sir, you! I was looking for you," explained the Colonel, pulling himself together. "I thought perhaps you might be able to give me some idea as to the whereabouts of my young charge, Miss Bathurst. She is missing."

Sir Eustace raised his black brows. "What should I know about her whereabouts?" he said.

Scott broke in quickly. "I saw her in the verandah this afternoon with your daughter."

"I know. She was there." The Colonel spoke with brevity. "Rose left her there talking to your sister. No one seems to have seen her since. I thought she might have been with Sir Eustace. I see I was mistaken. I apologize. But where the devil can she be?"

Sir Eustace raised his shoulders. "She was certainly not talking to my sister," he remarked. "She has kept her room to-day. Miss Bathurst is probably in her own room dressing for dinner."

"That's just where she isn't!" exploded the Colonel. "I missed her at tea-time but thought she must be out. Now her brother tells me that he has been all over the place and can't find her. I suppose she can't be upstairs with your sister?" He turned to Scott.

"I'll go and see," Scott said. "She may be - though I doubt it. My sister was not so well, and so stayed in bed to-day."

He moved towards the stairs with the words; but ere he reached them there came the sound of a sudden commotion on the corridor above, and a wailing voice made itself heard.

"Miss Isabel! Miss Isabel! Wherever are you, mavourneen? Ah, what'll I do at all? Miss Isabel's gone!"

Old Biddy in her huge white apron and mob cap appeared at the top of the staircase and came hobbling down with skinny hands extended.

"Ah, Master Scott - Master Scott - may the saints help us! She's gone! She's gone! And meself sleeping like a hog the whole afternoon through! I'll never forgive meself, Master Scott, - never, never! Oh, what'll I do? I pray the Almighty will take my life before any harm comes to her!"

She reached Scott at the foot of the stairs and caught his hand hysterically between her own.

Sir Eustace strode forward, white to the lips. "Stop your clatter, woman, and answer me! How did Miss Isabel get away? Is she dressed?"

The old woman cowered back from the blazing wrath in his eyes. "Yes, your honour! No, your honour! I mean - Yes, your honour!" she stammered, still clinging pathetically to Scott. "I was asleep, ye see. I never knew - I never knew!"

"How long did you sleep?" demanded Sir Eustace.

"And how am I to tell at all?" wailed Biddy. "It didn't seem like five minutes, and I opened me eyes, and she was all quiet in the dark. And I said to meself, 'I won't disturb the dear lamb,' and I crept into me room and tidied meself, and made a cup o' tay. And still she kept so quiet; so I drank me tay and did a bit of work. And then - just a minute ago it was - I crept in and went to her thinking it was time she woke up, - and - and - and she wasn't there, your honour. The bed was laid up, and she was gone! Oh, what'll I do at all? What'll I do?" She burst into wild sobs, and hid her face in her apron.

Two or three people were standing about in the vestibule.

They looked at the agitated group with interest, and in a moment a young man who had just entered came up to Scott.

"I believe I saw your sister in the verandah this afternoon," he said.

"That's just what Rose said," broke in the Colonel. "And you wouldn't believe me. She came out, and Dinah went to speak to her. And now the two of them are missing. It's obvious. They must have gone off together somewhere."

"Not up the mountain. I hope," the young man said.

"That is probably where they have gone," Scott said, speaking for the first time. He was patting Biddy's shoulder with compassionate kindness. "Why do you say that?"

"It's just begun to snow," the other answered. "And the mist up the mountain path is thick."

"Damnation!" exclaimed Sir Eustace furiously. "And she may have been gone for hours!"

"Miss Bathurst was with her," said Scott. "She would keep her head. I am certain of that." He turned to the Colonel who stood fuming by. "Hadn't we better organize a search-party sir? I am afraid that there is not much doubt that they have gone up the mountain. My sister, you know -" he flushed a little - "my sister is not altogether responsible for her actions. She would not realize the danger."

"But surely Dinah wouldn't be such a little fool as to go too!" burst forth the Colonel. "She's sane enough, when she isn't larking about with other fools." He glared at Sir Eustace. "And how the devil are we to know where to look, I'd like to know? We can't hunt all over the Alps."

"There may be some dogs in the village," Scott said. "There is certainly a guide. I will go down at once and see what I can find."

"No, no, Stumpy! Not you!" Sharply Sir Eustace intervened. "I won't have you go. It's not your job, and you are not fit for it." He laid a peremptory hand upon his brother's shoulder. "That's understood, is it? You will not leave the hotel."

He spoke with stern insistence, looking Scott straight in the eyes; and after a moment or two Scott yielded the point.

"All right, old chap! I'm not much good, I know. But for heaven's sake, lose no time."

"No time will be lost." Sir Eustace turned round upon the Colonel. "We can't have any but young men on this job," he said. "See if you can muster two or three to go with me, will you? A doctor if possible! And we shall want blankets and restoratives and lanterns. Stumpy, you can see to that. Yes, and send for a guide too though he won't be much help in a thick mist. And take that wailing woman away! Have everything ready for us when we come back! They can't have gone very far. Isabel hasn't the strength. I shall be ready immediately."

He turned to the stairs and went up them in great leaps, leaving the little group below to carry out his orders.

There was a momentary inaction after his departure, then Scott limped across to the door and opened it. Thick darkness met him, the clammy darkness of fog, and the faint, faint rustle of falling snow.

He closed the door and turned back, meeting the Colonel's eyes, "It's hard to stay behind, sir," he said.

The Colonel nodded. He liked Scott. "Yes, infernally hard. But we'll do all we can. Will you find the doctor and get the necessaries together? I'll see to the rest."

"Very good, sir; I will." Scott went to the old woman who still sobbed piteously into her apron. "Come along, Biddy! There's plenty to be done. Miss Isabel's room must be quite ready for her when she comes back, and Miss Bathurst's too. We shall want boiling water - lots of it. That's your job. Come along!"

He urged her gently to the stairs, and went up with her, holding her arm.

At the top she stopped and gave him an anguished look. "Ah, Master Scott darlint, will the Almighty be merciful? Will He bring her safe back again?"

He drew her gently on. "That's another thing you can do, Biddy," he said. "Ask Him!"

And before his look Biddy commanded herself and grew calmer. "Faith, Master Scott," she said, "if it isn't yourself that's taught me the greatest lesson of all!"

A very compassionate smile shone in Scott's eyes as he passed on and left her. "Poor old Biddy," he murmured, as he went. "It's easy to preach to such as you. But, O God, there's no denying it's bitter work for those who stay behind!"

He knew that he and Biddy were destined to drink that cup of bitterness to the dregs ere the night passed.

CHAPTER XX

THE VISION OF GREATHEART

The darkness of the night lay like a black pall upon the mountain. The snow was falling thickly, and ever more thickly. It drifted in upon Dinah, as she crouched in the shelter of an empty shed that had been placed on that high slope for the protection of sheep from the spring storms. They had come upon this shelter just as the gloom had become too great for even Isabel to regard further progress as possible, and in response to the girl's insistence they had crept in to rest. They had lost the beaten track long since; neither of them had realized when. But the certainty that they had done so had had its effect upon Isabel. Her energies had flagged from the moment that it had dawned upon her. A deadly tiredness had come over her, a feebleness so complete that Dinah had had difficulty in getting her into the shelter. Return was utterly out of the question. They were hopelessly lost, and to wander in that densely falling snow was to court disaster.

Very thankful Dinah had been to find even so poor a refuge in that waste of drifting fog; but now as she huddled by Isabel's side it seemed to her that the relief afforded was but a prolonging of their agony. The cold was intense. It seemed to penetrate to her very bones, and she knew by her companion's low moaning that she was suffering keenly also.

Isabel seemed to have sunk into a state of semi-consciousness, and only now and then did broken words escape her - words

Ethel M. Dell

scarcely audible to Dinah, but which testified none the less to the bitterness of despair that had come upon her.

She sat in a corner of the desolate place with Dinah pressed close to her, while the snow drifted in through the door-less entrance and sprinkled them both. But it was the darkness rather than the cold or the snow that affected the girl as she crouched there with her arms about her companion, striving to warm and shelter her while she herself felt frozen to the very heart. It was so terrible, so monstrous, so nerve-shattering. And the silence that went with it was like a nightmare horror to her shrinking soul. For all Dinah's sensibilities were painfully on the alert. No merciful dulness of perception came to her. Responsibility had awakened in her a nervous energy that made her realize the awfulness of their position with appalling vividness. That they could possibly survive the night she did not believe. And Death - Death in that fearful darkness - was a terror from which she shrank almost in panic.

That she retained command of her quivering nerves was due solely to the fact of Isabel's helplessness - Isabel's dependence upon her. She knew that while she had any strength left, she must not give way. She must be brave. Their sole chance of rescue hung upon that.

Like Scott, she thought of the guide, though the hope was a forlorn one. He might know of this shelter; but whether in the awful darkness he would ever be able to find it she strongly doubted. Their absence must have been discovered long since, she was sure; and Scott - Scott would be certain to think of the mountain path. He would remember his sister's wild words of the day before, and he would know that she, Dinah, had had no choice but to accompany her upon the mad quest. It comforted her to think that Scott would understand, and was already at work to help them. If by any means deliverance could be brought to them she knew that Scott would compass it. His quiet and capable spirit was accustomed to grapple with difficulties, and the enormity of a task would never dismay him. He had probably organized a search-party long ere this.

He would not rest until he had done his very utmost. She wondered if he would come himself to look for them; but discarded the idea as unlikely. His infirmity made progress on the mountains a difficult matter at all times, and he would not wish to hamper the movements of the others. That was like Scott, she reflected. He would always keep his own desires in the background, subservient to the needs of others. No, he would not come himself. He would stay behind in torturing inaction while fitter men fared forth.

The thought of Eustace came again to her. He would be one of the search-party. She pictured him forcing his way upwards, all his magnificent strength bent to the work. Her heart throbbed at the memory of that all-conquering presence - the arms that had held her, the lips that had pressed her own. And he had stooped to plead with her also. She would always remember that of him with a thrill of ecstasy. He the princely and splendid - Apollo the magnificent!

Always? A sudden chill smote her heart numbing her through and through. Always? And Death waiting on the threshold to snatch her away from the wonderful joy she had only just begun to know! Always! Ah, would she remember even to-morrow - even to-morrow? And he - would he not forget?

Isabel stirred in her arms and murmured an inarticulate complaint. Tenderly she drew her closer. How cold it was! How cruelly, how bitingly cold! All her bones were beginning to ache. A dreadful stiffness was creeping over her. How long would her senses hold out, she wondered piteously? How long? How long?

It must be hours now since they had entered that freezing place, and with every minute it seemed to be growing colder. Never in her life had she imagined anything so searching, so agonizing, as this cold. It held her in an iron rigour against which she was powerless to struggle. The strength to clasp Isabel in her arms was leaving her. She thought that her numbed limbs were gradually turning to stone. Even her lips

Ethel M. Dell

were so numbed with cold that she could not move them. The steam of her breath had turned to ice upon the wool of her coat.

The need for prayer came upon her suddenly as she realized that her faculties were failing. Her belief in God was of that dim and far-off description that brings awe rather than comfort to the soul. The sudden thought of Him came upon her in the darkness like a thunderbolt. In all her life Dinah had never asked for anything outside her daily prayers which were of a strictly formal description. She had shouldered her own troubles unassisted with the philosophy of a disposition that was essentially happy. She had seldom given a serious thought to the life of the spirit. It was all so vague to her, so far removed from the daily round and the daily burden. But now - face to face with the coming night - the spiritual awoke in her. Her soul cried out for comfort.

With Isabel still clasped in her failing arms, she began a desperate prayer for help. Her words came haltingly. They sounded strange to herself. But with all the strength that remained she sent forth her cry to the Infinite. And even as she prayed there came to her - whence she knew not - the conviction that somewhere - probably not more than a couple of miles from her though the darkness made the distance seem immeasurable - Scott was praying too. That thought had a wonderfully comforting effect upon her. His prayer was so much more likely to be answered than hers. He was just the sort of man who would know how to pray.

"How I wish he were here!" she whispered piteously into the darkness. "I shouldn't be afraid of dying - if only he were here."

She was certain - quite certain - that had he been there with her, no fear would have reached her. He wore the armour of a strong man, and by it he would have shielded her also.

"Oh, dear Mr. Greatheart," she murmured through her numb

lips, "I'm sure you know the way to Heaven."

Isabel stirred again as one who moves in restless slumber. "We must scale the peaks of Paradise to reach it," she said.

"Are you awake, dearest?" asked Dinah very tenderly.

Isabel's head was sunk against her shoulder. She moved it, slightly raised it. "Yes, I am awake," she said. "I am watching for the dawn."

"It won't come yet," whispered Dinah tremulously. "It's a long, long way off."

Isabel moved a little more, feeling for Dinah in the darkness. "Are you frightened, little one?" she said. "Don't be frightened!"

Dinah swallowed down a sob. "It is so dark," she murmured through chattering teeth. "And so, so cold."

"You are cold, dear heart?" Isabel sat up suddenly. "Why should you be cold?" she said. "The darkness is nothing to those who are used to it. I have lived in outer darkness for seven weary years. But now - now I think the day is drawing near at last."

With an energy that astounded Dinah she got upon her knees and by her movements she realized, albeit too late, that she was divesting herself of the long purple coat.

With all her strength she sought to frustrate her, but her strength had become very feebleness; and when, despite resistance, Isabel wrapped her round in the garment she had discarded, her resistance was too puny to take effect.

"My dear," Isabel said, in her voice the deep music of maternal tenderness, "I am not needing it. I shall not need any earthly things for long. I am going to meet my husband in the dawning. But you - you will go back."

She fastened the coat with a quiet dexterity that made Dinah think again of Scott, and sat down again in her corner as if unconscious of the cold.

"Come and lie in my arms, little one!" she said. "Perhaps you will be able to sleep."

Dinah crept close. "It will kill you - it will kill you!" she sobbed. "Oh, why did I let you?"

Isabel's arms closed about her. "Don't cry, dear!" she murmured fondly. "It is nothing to me. A little sooner - a little later! If you had suffered what I have suffered you would say as I do, 'Dear God, let it be soon!' There! Put your head on my shoulder, dear child! See if you can get a little sleep! You have cared for me long enough. Now I am going to care for you."

With loving words she soothed her, calming her as though she had been a child in nightmare terror, and gradually a certain peace began to still the horror in Dinah's soul. An unmistakable drowsiness was stealing over her, a merciful lethargy lulling the sensibilities that had been so acutely tried. Her weakness was merging into a sense of almost blissful repose. She was no longer conscious of the anguish of the cold. Neither did the darkness trouble her. And the comfort of Isabel's arms was rest to her spirit.

As one who wanders in a golden maze she began to dream strange dreams that yet were not woven by the hand of sleep. Dimly she saw as down a long perspective a knight in golden armour climbing, ever climbing, the peaks of Paradise, from which, as from an eagle's nest, she watched his difficult but untiring progress. She thought he halted somewhat in the ascent - which was unlike Apollo, who walked as walk the gods with a gait both arrogant and assured. But still he came on, persistently, resolutely, carrying his golden shield before him.

His visor was down, and she wished that he would raise it. She yearned for the sight of that splendid face with its knightly features and blue, fiery eyes. She pictured it to herself as he came, but somehow it did not seem to fit that patient climbing figure.

And then as he gradually drew nearer, the thought came to her to go and meet him, and she started to run down the slope. She reached him. She gave him both her hands. She was ready - she was eager - to be drawn into his arms.

But he did not so draw her. To her amazement he only bowed himself before her and stretched forth the shield he bore that it might cover them both.

"It is Mr. Greatheart!" she said to herself in wonder. "Of course - it is Mr. Greatheart!"

And then, while she still gazed upon the glittering, princely form, he put up a hand and lifted the visor. And she saw the kindly, steadfast eyes all kindled and alight with a glory before which instinctively she hid her own. Never - no, never - had she dreamed before that any man could look at her so! It was not passion that those eyes held for her; - it was worship.

She stood with bated breath and throbbing heart, waiting, waiting, as one in the presence of a vision, who longs - yet fears - to look. And while she waited she knew that the sun was shining upon them both with a glowing warmth that filled her soul abrim with such a rapture as she had never known before.

"How wonderful!" she murmured to herself. "How wonderful!"

And then at last she summoned courage to look up, and all in a moment her vision was shattered. The darkness was all about her again; Greatheart was gone.

Ethel M. Dell

CHAPTER XXI

THE RETURN

What happened after the passing of her vision Dinah never fully knew, so slack had become her grip upon material things. Her spirit seemed to be wandering aimlessly about the mountain-side while her body lay in icy chains within that miserable shelter. Of Isabel's presence she was no longer even dimly aware, and she knew neither fear nor pain, only a wide desolation of emptiness that encompassed her as atmosphere encompasses the world.

Sometimes she fancied that the sound of voices came muffled through the fog that hung impenetrably upon the great slope. And when this fancy caught her, her spirit drifted back very swiftly to the near neighbourhood of that inert and frozen body that lay so helpless in the dark. For that strange freedom of the spirit seemed to her to be highly dangerous and in a fashion wrong. It would be a terrible thing if they found and buried the body, and the spirit were left alone to wander for ever homeless on that desolate mountain-side. She could not imagine a fate more awful.

At the same time, being free from the body, she knew no physical pain, and she shrank from returning before she need, knowing well the anguish of suffering that awaited her. The desolation and loneliness made her unhappy in a vague and not very comprehensible fashion, but she did not suffer actively. That would come later when return became imperative. Till then she flitted to and fro, intangible as gossamer, elusive as the snow. She wondered what Apollo would say if he could see her thus. Even he would fail to catch her now. She pictured the strong arms closing upon her, and clasping - emptiness. That thought made her a little cold, and sent her floating back to make sure that the lifeless body was still there.

And as she went, drifting through the silence, there came to her the thought that Scott would be unutterably shocked if they brought her back to him dead. It was strange how the memory of him haunted her that night. It almost seemed as if his spirit were out there in the great waste, seeking hers.

She reached the shelter and entered, borne upon snowflakes. Yes, the body was still there. She hovered over it like a bird over its nest. For Scott's sake, should she not return?

And then very suddenly there came a great sound close to her - the loud barking of a dog; - and in a second - in less - she had returned.

A long, long shiver went through the poor frozen thing that was herself, and she knew that she moaned as one awaking....

Vaguely, through dulled senses, she heard the great barking yet again, and something immense that was furry and soft brushed against her. She heard the panting of a large animal close to her in the hut, and very feebly she put out a hand.

She did not like that loud baying. It went through and through her brain. She was not frightened, only dreadfully tired. And now that she was back again in the body, she longed unspeakably to sleep.

But the noise continued, a perfect clamour of sound; and soon there came other sounds, the shouting of men, the muffled tread of feet sorely hampered by snow. A dim light began to shine, and gradually increased till it became a single, piercing eye that swept searchingly around the wretched shelter. An arc of fog surrounded it, obscuring all besides.

Dinah gazed wide-eyed at that dazzling arc, wondering numbly, whence it came. It drew nearer to her. Its brightness became intolerable. She tried to shut her eyes, but the lids felt too stiff to move. Again, more feebly, she moved her hand. It would be terrible if they thought her dead, especially after all the trouble she had taken to return.

And then very suddenly the deadly lethargy passed from her. All her nerves were pricked into activity. For someone - someone - was kneeling beside her. She felt herself gathered into strong arms.

"Quick, Wetherby! The brandy!" Ah, well she knew those brief, peremptory tones! "My God! We're only just in time!"

Fast pressed against a man's heart, a faint warmth went through her. She knew an instant of perfect serenity; but the next she uttered a piteous cry of pain. For fire - liquid, agonizing - was on her bloodless lips and in her mouth. It burned its ruthless way down her throat, setting her whole body tingling, waking afresh in her the power to suffer.

She turned, weakly gasping, and hid her face upon the breast that supported her.

Instantly she felt herself clasped more closely. "It's all right, little darling, all right!" he whispered to her with an almost fierce tenderness. "Take it like a good child! It'll pull you through."

With steady insistence he turned her face back again, chafing her icy cheek hard. And in a moment or two another burning dose was on its way.

It made her choke and gurgle, but it did its work. The frozen heart in her began to beat again with great jerks and bounds, sending quivering shocks throughout her body.

She tried to speak to him, to whisper his name; but she could only gasp and gasp against his breast, and presently from very weakness she began to cry.

He gathered her closer still, murmuring fond words, while he rubbed her face and hands, imparting the warmth of his own body to hers. His presence was like a fiery essence encompassing her. Lying there against his heart, she felt the tide of life turn in her veins and steadily flow again. Like a child, she clung to him, and after a while, with an impulse sublimely natural, she lifted her lips to his.

He pressed his lips upon them closely, lingeringly. "Better now, sweetheart?" he whispered.

And she, clinging to him, found voice to answer, "Nothing matters now you have come."

The consciousness of his protecting care filled her with a rapture almost too great to be borne. She throbbed in his arms, pressing closer, ever closer. And the grim Shadow of Death receded from the threshold. She knew that she was safe.

It was soon after this that the thought of Isabel came to her, and tremulously she begged him to go to her. But he would not suffer her out of his arms.

"The others can see to her," he said. "You are my care."

She thrilled at the words, but she would not be satisfied. "She has been so good to me," she told him pleadingly "See, I am wearing her coat."

"But for her you would never have come to this," he made brief reply, and she thought his words were stern.

Then, as she would not be pacified, he lifted her like a child and held her so that she could look down upon Isabel, lying inert and senseless against the doctor's knee.

"Oh, is she dead?" whispered Dinah, awe-struck.

"I don't know," he made answer, and by the tightening of his arms she knew that her safety meant more to him at the moment than that of Isabel or anyone else in the world.

But in a second or two she heard Isabel moan, and was reassured.

"She is coming round," the doctor said. "She is not so far gone as the other lassie."

Dinah wondered hazily what he could mean, wondered if by any chance he suspected that long and dreary wandering of her spirit up and down the mountain-side. She nestled her head down against Eustace's shoulder with a feeling of unutterable thankfulness that she had returned in time.

Her impressions after that were of a very dim and shadowy description. She supposed the brandy had made her sleepy. Very soon she drifted off into a state of semi-consciousness in which she realized nothing but the strong holding of his arms. She even vaguely wondered after a time whether this also were not a dream, for other fantasies began to crowd about her. She rocked on a sea of strange happenings on which she found it impossible to focus her mind. It seemed to have broken adrift as it were - a rudderless boat in a gale. But still that sense of security never wholly left her. Dreaming or waking, the force of his personality remained with her.

It must have been hours later, she reflected afterwards, that she heard the Colonel's voice exclaim hoarsely over her head, "In heaven's name, say she isn't dead!"

And, "Of course she isn't," came Eustace's curt response. "Should I be carrying her if she were?"

She tried to open her eyes, but could not. They seemed to be weighted down. But she did very feebly close her numbed hands about Eustace's coat. Emphatically she did not want to be handed over like a bale of goods to the Colonel.

He clasped her to him reassuringly, and presently she knew that he bore her upstairs, holding her comfortably close all the way.

"Don't go away from me!" she begged him weakly.

"Not so long as you want me, little sweetheart," he made answer. But her woman's heart told her that a parting was imminent notwithstanding.

In all her life she had never had so much attention before. She seemed to have entered upon a new and amazing phase of existence. Colonel de Vigne faded completely into the background, and she found herself in the care of Biddy and the doctor. Eustace left her with a low promise to return, and she had to be satisfied with that thought, though she would fain have clung to him still.

They undressed her and put her into a hot bath that did much to lessen the numb constriction of her limbs, though it brought also the most agonizing pain she had ever known. When it was over, the limit of her endurance was long past; and she lay in hot blankets weeping helplessly while Biddy tried in vain to persuade her to drink some scalding mixture that she swore would make her feel as gay as a lark.

In the midst of this, someone entered quietly and stood beside her; and all in a moment there came to Dinah the consciousness of an unknown force very strangely uplifting her. She looked up with a quivering smile in the midst of her tears.

"Oh, Mr. Greatheart," she whispered brokenly, "is it you?"

He smiled down upon her, and took the cup from Biddy's

Ethel M. Dell

shaky old hand.

"May I give you this?" he said.

Dinah was filled with gratified confusion. "Oh, please, you mustn't trouble! But - how very kind of you!"

He took Biddy's place by her side. His eyes were shining with an odd brilliance, almost, she thought to herself wonderingly, as if they held tears. A sharp misgiving went through her. How was it they were bestowing so much care upon her, unless Isabel - Isabel -

She did not dare to put her doubt into words, but he read it and instantly answered it. "Don't be anxious!" he said in his kindly, tired voice. "All is well. Isabel is asleep - actually sleeping quietly without any draught. The doctor is quite satisfied about her."

He spoke the simple truth, she knew; he was incapable of doing anything else. A great wave of thankfulness went through her, obliterating the worst of her misery.

"I am so glad," she told him weakly. "I was - so dreadfully afraid. I - I had to go with her, Mr. Studley. I do hope everyone understands."

"Everyone does," he made answer gently. "Now let me give you this, and then you must sleep too."

She drank from the cup he held, and felt revived.

He did not speak again till she had finished; then he leaned slightly towards her, and spoke with great earnestness. "Miss Bathurst, do you realize, I wonder, that you saved my sister's life by going with her? I do; and I shall never forget it."

She was sure now that she caught the gleam of tears in the grey eyes. She slipped her hands out to him. "I only did what I could," she murmured confusedly. "Anyone would have done it. And please, Mr. Greatheart, will you call me Dinah?"

"Or Mercy?" he suggested smiling, her hands clasped close in his.

She smiled back with shy confidence. The memory of her dream was in her mind, but she could not tell him of that.

"No," she said. "Just Dinah. I'm not nice enough to be called anything else. And thank you - thank you for being so good to me."

"My dear child," he made quiet reply, "no one who really knows you could be anything else."

"Oh, don't you think they could?" said Dinah wistfully. "I wish there were more people in the world like you."

"No one ever thought of saying that to me before," said Scott.

CHAPTER XXII

THE VALLEY OF THE SHADOW

After that interview with Scott there followed a long, long period of pain and weakness for Dinah. She who had never known before what it meant to be ill went down to the Valley of the Shadow and lingered there for many days and nights. And there came a time when those who watched beside her began to despair of her ever turning back.

So completely had she lost touch with the ordinary things of life that she knew but little of what went on around her, dwelling as it were apart, conscious sometimes of agonizing pain, but more often of a dreadful sinking as of one overwhelmed in the billows of an everlasting sea. At such times she would cling piteously to any succouring hand, crying to them to hold her up - only to hold her up. And if the hand were the hand of Greatheart, she always found comfort at length and a sense of security that none other could impart.

Her fancy played about him very curiously in those days. She saw him in many guises, - as prince, as knight, as magician; but never as the mean and insignificant figure which first had caught her attention on that sunny morning before the fancy-dress ball.

This man who sat beside her bed of suffering for hours together because she fretted when he went away, who held her up when the gathering billows threatened to overwhelm her fainting soul, who prayed for her with the utmost simplicity when she told him piteously that she could not pray for herself, this man was above and beyond all ordinary standards. She looked up to him with reverence, as one of colossal strength who had power with God.

But she never dreamed again that golden dream of Greatheart in his shining armour with the light of a great worship in his eyes. That had been a wild flight of presumptuous fancy that never could come true.

His was not the only hand to which she clung during those terrible days of fear and suffering. Another presence was almost constantly beside her night and day, - a tender, motherly presence that watched over and ministered to her with a devotion that never slackened. For some time Dinah could not find a name for this gracious and comforting presence, but one day when a figure clothed in a violet dressing-gown stooped over her to give her nourishment an illuminating memory came to her, and from that moment this loving nurse of hers filled a particular niche in her heart which was dedicated to the Purple Empress. She could think of no other name for her. That quiet and stately presence seemed to demand a royal appellation. In her calmer moments Dinah liked to lie and watch the still face with its crown of silvery hair. She loved the touch of the white hands that always knew with unerring intuition exactly what needed to be done. There seemed to be healing in their touch.

Very strangely the thought of Eustace never came to her, or coming, but flitted unrecorded and undetained across the surface of her mind. He had receded with all the rest of the world into the far, far distance that lay behind her. He had no place in this region of many shadows where these others so tenderly guided her wandering feet. No one else had any place there save old Biddy who, being never absent, seemed a part of the atmosphere, and the doctor who came and went like a presiding genie in that waste of desolation.

She did not welcome his visits, although he was invariably kind, for on one occasion she caught a low murmur from him to the effect that her mother had better come to her, and this suggestion had thrown her into a most painful state of apprehension. She had implored them weeping to let her mother stay away, and they had hushed her with soothing promises; but she never saw the doctor thereafter without a nervous dread that she might also see her mother's gaunt figure accompanying him. And she was sure - quite sure - that her mother would be very angry with her when she saw her helplessness.

Nightmares of her mother's advent began to trouble her. She would start up in anguish of soul, scarcely believing in the soothing arms that held her till their tenderness hushed her back to calmness.

"No one can come to you, sweetheart, while I am here." How often she heard the low words murmured lovingly over her head! "See, I am holding you! You are quite safe. No one can take you from me."

And Dinah would cling to her beloved empress till her panic died away.

On one of these occasions Scott was present, and he presently left the sick-room with a look in his eyes that gave him a curiously hard expression. He went deliberately in search of Billy whom he found playing a not very spirited game with the two little daughters of the establishment. The weather had broken, and several people had left in consequence.

Billy was bored as well as anxious, and his attitude said as much as he unceremoniously left his small playfellows to join Scott.

"Just amusin' the kids," he observed explanatorily. "How is she now?"

Scott linked his hand in the boy's arm. "She's pretty bad, Billy," he said. "Both lungs are affected. The doctor thinks badly of her, though he still hopes he may pull her through."

"You may you mean," returned Billy. "Can't say the de Vignes have put themselves out at all over her. There's Rose flirts all day long with your brother, and Lady Grace grumbling continually about the folly of undertaking other people's responsibilities. She swears she must get back at the end of next week for their precious house-party. And the Colonel fumes and says the same. I told him I shouldn't go unless she was out of danger, though goodness knows, sir, I don't want to sponge on you."

Scott's hand pressed his arm reassuringly. "Don't imagine such a thing possible!" he said. "Of course you must stay if she isn't very much better by that time. But now, Billy, tell me - if it isn't an unwelcome question - why doesn't your sister want your mother to come to her?"

Billy gave him one of his shrewd glances. "She's told you that, has she? Well, you know the mater is rather a queer fish, and I doubt very much if she'd come if you asked her."

"My good fellow!" Scott said. "Not if she were dying?"

"I doubt it," said Billy, unmoved. "You see, the mater hasn't much use for Dinah, except as a maid-of-all work. Never has had. It's not altogether her fault. It's just the way she's made."

"Good heavens!" said Scott, and added, as if to himself, "That little fairy thing!"

"She can't help it," said Billy. "She can't get on with the female species. It's like cats, you know, - a sort of jealousy."

"And your father?" questioned Scott, the hard look growing in his eyes.

"Oh, Dad!" said Billy, smiling tolerantly. "He's all right - quite a decent sort. But you wouldn't get him to leave home in the middle of the hunting season. He's one of the Whips."

Scott's hand had tightened unconsciously to a grip. Billy looked at him in surprised interrogation, and was amazed to see a heavy frown drawing the colourless brows. There was a fiery look in the pale eyes also that he had never seen before.

He waited in silence for developments, being of a wary disposition, and in a moment Scott spoke in a voice of such concentrated fury that Billy felt as if a total stranger were confronting him.

"An infernal and blackguardly shame!" he said. "It would serve them right if the little girl never went back to them again. I never heard of such damnable callousness in all my life before."

Billy opened his eyes wide, and after a second or two permitted himself a soft whistle.

Scott's hold upon his arm relaxed. "Yes, I know," he said. "I've no right to say it to you. But when the blood boils, you've got to let off the steam somehow. I suppose you've written to tell them all about her?"

"Oh yes, I wrote, and so did the Colonel. I had a letter from Dad this morning. He said he hoped she was better and that she was being well looked after. That's like Dad, you know. He never realizes a thing unless he's on the spot. I daresay I shouldn't myself," said Billy broadmindedly. "It's want of imagination in the main."

"Or want of heart," said Scott curtly.

Billy did not attempt to refute the amendment. "It's just the way you chance to be made," he said philosophically. "Of course I'm fond of Dinah. We're pals. But Dad's an easy-going sort of chap. He isn't specially fond of anybody. The mater, -

well, she's keen on me, I suppose," he blushed a little; "but, as I said before, she hasn't much use for Dinah. Even when she was a small kid, she used to whip her no end. Dinah is frightened to death at her. I don't wonder she doesn't want her sent for."

Scott's face was set in stern lines. "She certainly shall not be sent for," he said with decision. "The poor child shall be left in peace."

"She is going to get better, isn't she?" said Billy quickly.

"I hope so, old chap. I hope so." Scott patted his shoulder kindly and prepared to depart.

But Billy detained him a moment. "I say, can't I come and see her?"

"Not now, lad." Scott paused, and all the natural kindliness came back into his eyes. "My sister was just getting her calm again when I came away. We won't disturb her now."

"How is your sister, sir?" asked Billy. "Isn't she feeling the strain rather?"

"No, she is standing it wonderfully. In fact," Scott hesitated momentarily, "I believe that in helping Dinah, she has found herself again."

"Do you really?" said Billy. "Then I do hope for her sake that Dinah will buck up and get well."

"Thanks, old chap." Scott held out a friendly hand. "I'm sorry you're having such a rotten time. Come along to me any time when you're feeling bored! I shall be only too pleased when I'm at liberty."

"You're a brick, sir," said Billy. "And I say, you'll send for me, won't you, if - if -" He broke off. "You know, as I said before,

Dinah and I are pals," he ended wistfully.

"Of course I will, lad. Of course I will." Scott wrung his hand hard. "But we'll pull her through, please God! We must pull her through."

"If anyone can, you will," said Billy with conviction.

Like Dinah, he had caught a glimpse in that brief conversation of the soul that inhabited that weak and puny form.

CHAPTER XXIII

THE WAY BACK

It was three days later that Dinah began at last the long and weary pilgrimage back again. Almost against her will she turned her faltering steps up the steep ascent; for she was too tired for any sustained effort. Only that something seemed to be perpetually drawing her she would not have been moved to make the effort at all. For she was so piteously weak that the bare exertion of opening her eyes was almost more than she could accomplish. But ever the unknown influence urged her, very gently but very persistently, never passive, never dormant, but always drawing her as by an invisible cord back to the world of sunshine and tears that seemed so very far away from the land of shadows in which she wandered.

All active suffering had left her, and she would fain have been at peace; but the hand that clasped hers would not be denied. The motherly voice that had calmed the wildest fantasies of her fevered brain spoke now to her with tenderest encourage- ment; the love that surrounded her drew her, uplifted her, sustained her. And gradually, as she crept back from the shadows, she came to lean upon this love as upon a sure support, to count upon it as her own exclusive possession - a wonderful new gift that had come to her out of the darkness.

She still welcomed her friend Scott at her bedside, but very curiously she had grown a little shy in his presence. She could not forget that dream of hers, and for a long time she was haunted by the dread that he had in some way come to know of it. Though the steady eyes never held anything but the utmost kindness and sympathy, she was half afraid to meet them lest they should look into her heart and see the vision she had seen. She never called him Mr. Greatheart now.

With Isabel, beloved nurse and companion, she was completely at her ease. A great change had come over Isabel - such a change as turns the bare earth into a garden of spring when the bitter winter is past at last. All the ice-bound bitterness had been swept utterly away, and in its place there blossomed such a wealth of mother-love as transformed her completely.

She spent herself with the most lavish devotion in Dinah's service. There was not a wish that she expressed that was not swiftly and abundantly satisfied. Night and day she was near her, ignoring all Biddy's injunctions to rest, till the old woman, seeing the light that had dawned in the shadowed eyes, left her to take her own way in peace. She hovered in the background, always ready in case her mistress's new-found strength should fail. But Isabel did not need her care. All her being was concentrated upon the task of bringing Dinah back to life, and she thought of nothing else, meeting the strain with that strength which comes in great emergencies to all.

And as she gradually succeeded in her task, a great peace descended upon her, such as she had never known before. Biddy sometimes gazed in amazement at the smooth brow and placid countenance at Dinah's bedside.

"Sure, the young lady's been a blessing straight from the Almighty," she said to Scott.

"I think so too, Biddy," he made quiet answer.

He was much less in the sick-room now that Dinah's need of him had passed. He sometimes wondered if she even knew how many hours he had formerly spent there. He visited her every day, and it was to him that the task fell of telling her that the de Vignes had arranged to leave her in their charge.

"We have your father's permission," he said, when her brows drew together with a troubled expression. "You see, it is quite impossible to move you at present, and they must be getting home. Billy is to go with them if you think you can be happy alone with us."

She put out her little wasted hand. "I could be happy with you anywhere," she said simply. "But it doesn't seem right."

"Of course it is right," he made quiet reply. "In fact, if you ask me, I think it is our business rather than anyone else's to get you well again."

She flushed in quick embarrassment. "Oh, please, you mustn't put it like that. And I have been such a trouble to everyone ever since."

He smiled at her very kindly. "Biddy says you are a blessing from the Almighty, and I quite agree with her. It is settled then? You are content to stay with us until we take you home?"

Her hand was clasped in his, but she did not meet his look. "Oh, much more than content," she said, her voice very low. "Only -"

"Only?" he said gently.

She made an effort to lift her eyes, but dropped them again instantly. "It will make it much harder to go home," she said.

She thought he sounded somewhat grim as he said, "There is no need to meet troubles half-way, you know. You won't be strong enough for the journey for some time to come."

"I wish I could stay just as I am now," she told him tremulously, "for ever and ever and ever."

"Ah!" he said, with a faint sigh. "It is not given to any of us to bask in the sun for long."

And so, two days after, the de Vignes paid a state visit of farewell to Dinah, now pronounced out of danger but still pitiably weak, - so weak that she cried when the Colonel bade her be a good girl and get well enough to come home as soon as possible, so as not to be a burden to these kind friends of hers longer than she need.

Lady Grace's kiss was chilly and perfunctory. "I also hope you will get well quickly, Dinah," she said, "as I believe Mr. Studley and his sister are staying on mainly on your account. Sir Eustace, I understand, is returning very shortly, and I have asked him to join our house-party."

"Good-bye, dear!" murmured Rose, bending her smiling lips to kiss Dinah's forehead. "I am sorry your good time has had such a tragic end. I was hoping that you might be allowed to come to the Hunt Ball, but I am afraid that is out of the question now. Sir Eustace will be sorry too. He says you are such an excellent little dancer."

"Good-bye!" said Dinah, swallowing her tears.

She wept unrestrainedly when Billy bade her a bluff and friendly farewell, and he was practically driven from the room by Isabel; who then returned to her charge, gathered her close in her arms, and sat with her so, rocking her gently till gradually her agitation subsided.

"Do forgive me!" Dinah murmured at last, clinging round her neck.

To which Isabel made answer in that low voice of hers that so throbbed with tenderness whenever she spoke to her. "Dear child, there is nothing to forgive. You are tired and worn out. I know just how you feel. But never mind - never mind! Forget it all!"

"I know I am a burden," whispered Dinah, clinging closer.

Isabel's lips pressed her forehead. "My darling," she said, "you are such a burden as I could not bear to be without."

That satisfied Dinah for the time; but it was not the whole of her trouble, and presently, still clasped close to Isabel's heart, she gave hesitating utterance to the rest.

"It would have been - so lovely - to have gone to the Hunt Ball. I should like to dance with - with Sir Eustace again. Is he - is he really going to stay with the de Vignes?"

"I don't know, dear. Very possibly not." Isabel's voice held a hint of constraint though her arms pressed Dinah comfortingly close. "He will please himself when the time comes no doubt."

Dinah did not pursue the subject, but her mind was no longer at rest. She wondered how she could have forgotten Sir Eustace for so long, and now that she remembered him she was all on fire with the longing to see him again. Rose had spoken so possessively, so confidently, of him, as though - almost as though - he had become her own peculiar property during the long dark days in which Dinah had been wandering in another world.

Something in Dinah hotly and fiercely resented this attitude. She yearned to know if it were by any means justified. She could not, would not, believe that he had suffered himself to fall like other men a victim to Rose's wiles. He was so different from all others, so superbly far above all those other captives. And had she not heard him laugh and call Rose machine-made?

A great restlessness began to possess her. She felt she must know what had been happening during her absence from the field. She must know if Rose had succeeded in adding yet another to her long list of devoted admirers. She felt that if this were so, she could never, never forgive her. But it was not possible. She was sure - she was sure it was not possible.

Sir Eustace was not the man to grovel at any woman's feet. She recalled the arrogance of his demeanour even in his moments of greatest tenderness. She recalled the magnetic force of his personality, his overwhelming mastery. She recalled the strong holding of his arms, thrilled yet again to the burning intensity of his kisses.

No, no! He had never stooped to become one of Rose's adorers. If he had ever flirted with her, he had done it out of boredom. She was beautiful - ah yes, Rose was beautiful; but Dinah was quite convinced she had no brains. And Eustace would never seriously consider a woman without brains.

Seriously! But then had he ever taken her into his serious consideration either? Had he not rather been at pains to make her understand that what had passed between them was no more than a game to which no serious consequences were attached? She had caught his fancy, his passing fancy, and now was not her turn over? Had he not laughed and gone his way?

She chafed terribly at the thought, and ever the longing to see him again grew within her till she did not know how to hide it from those about her.

In the evening her temperature rose, and the doctor was dissatisfied with her. She passed a restless night, and was considerably weaker in the morning.

"There is something on her mind," the doctor said to Isabel. "See if you can find out what it is!"

But it was Scott who succeeded with the utmost gentleness in discovering the trouble. He came in late in the morning and sat down beside her for a few minutes.

"I have been writing letters for my brother," he said in his quiet way, "or I should have called for news of you sooner.

Isabel tells me you have had a bad night."

Dinah's face was flushed and her eyes very bright. "I heard the dance-music in the distance," she said nervously. "It - it made me want to go and dance."

"I am sorry it disturbed you," he said gently. "It was only that then? You weren't really troubled about anything?"

She hesitated, then, meeting the kindness of his look, her eyes suddenly filled with tears. She turned her head away in silence.

He leaned towards her. "Is there anything you want?" he said. "Tell me what it is! I will get it for you if it is humanly possible."

"I know - I know!" faltered Dinah, and hid her face in the pillow.

He waited a moment or two, then laid a very gentle hand upon her dark head. "Don't cry, little one!" he said softly. "Tell me what it is!"

"I can't," murmured Dinah.

"You wanted to go and dance," said Scott sympathetically. "Was it just that?"

"Not - just - that!" she whispered forlornly.

"I thought not. You were wanting something more than that. What was it?"

She tried not to tell him. She would have given almost all she had to keep silence on the subject; but somehow she had to speak. Under the pressure of that kind hand, she could not maintain her silence any longer.

"I was thinking of - of your brother," she told him with tears.

"I was wondering if - if he were dancing, and - and I not there!"

It was out at last, and she hid her face in overwhelming shame because she had given him a glimpse of her secret heart which none had ever seen before. She wondered with anguish what he thought of her, if she had forfeited his good opinion of her for ever, if indeed he would ever speak to her with kindness again.

And then very quietly he did speak, and in a moment all her anxiety was gone. "He may have been dancing," he said. "But I believe he has been very bored ever since the weather broke. I wonder if he might come and see you. Would it be too much for you? Should you mind?"

"Mind!" Dinah's tears were gone in a flash. She turned shining eyes upon him. "But would he come?" she said, with sudden misgiving. "Wouldn't that bore him too?"

Scott smiled at her in a way that set her mind wholly at rest. "No, I think not," he said. "When shall he come? This evening?"

Dinah slipped a confiding hand into his. She felt that now Scott knew and was not scandalized, there was no further need for embarrassment. "Oh, just any time," she said. "But hadn't I better get up? It would look better, wouldn't it?"

"I don't know about that," said Scott. "You had better ask the doctor."

Dinah's face flushed red. "Need the doctor know?" she asked him shyly. "I am - so afraid of his saying I am well enough to go home. And that - that will end everything."

"He shan't say that," Scott promised, still smiling in the fashion that so warmed her heart. "I will drop him a hint."

"Oh, you are good!" Dinah said very earnestly. "I think you are the kindest man I have ever met."

He laughed at that. "My dear, it is easy to be kind to you," he said.

"I'm sure I don't know why," she protested. "I'm getting very spoilt and selfish."

He patted her hand gently and laid it down. "You are - just you," he said, and rising with the words rather abruptly he left her.

Ethel M. Dell

CHAPTER XXIV

THE LIGHTS OF A CITY

"May I come in?" said Sir Eustace.

He stood in the doorway, a gigantic figure to Dinah's unaccustomed eyes, and looked in upon her with a careless smile on his handsome face.

"Oh, please do!" she said.

She was lying on a couch under a purple rug belonging to Isabel. Very fragile and weak she looked, but her face was flushed and eager, her eyes alight with welcome. She thought he had never looked so splendid, so godlike, as at that moment. She wanted to hold out both her arms to him and be borne upward to Olympus in his embrace.

He came forward with his easy carriage and stood beside her. His smile was one of kindly indulgence. He looked down at her as he might have looked upon an infant.

An uneasy sense of her own insignificance went through Dinah. She could not remember that he had ever regarded her thus before. A faint, faint throb of resentment also pulsed through her. His attitude was so suggestive of the mere casual acquaintance. Surely - surely he had not forgotten!

"Won't you sit down?" she asked in a small voice that was

quite unconsciously formal.

He seated himself in the chair that had been placed at her side. "So they have left you behind to be mended, have they?" he said. "I hope it is a satisfactory process, is it?"

She had meant to give him her hand, but as he did not seem to expect it she refrained from doing so. A great longing to cover her face and burst into tears took possession of her; she resisted it frantically, with all her strength.

"Oh yes, I am getting better, thank you," she said, in a voice that quivered in spite of her. "I am afraid I have been a great nuisance to everybody. I am sure the de Vignes thought so; and - and - I expect you do too."

She could not keep the tears from springing to her eyes, strive as she would. He was so different - so different. He might have been a total stranger, sitting there beside her.

Yet as he looked at her, she felt something of the old quick thrill; for the blue eyes regarded her with a slightly warmer interest as he said, "I can't answer for the de Vignes of course, but it doesn't seem to me that either they or I have had much cause for complaint. I shouldn't fret about that if I were you."

She commanded herself with an effort. "I don't. Only it isn't nice to feel a burden to anyone, is it? You wouldn't like it, would you?"

"Oh, I don't know," he said, with his easy arrogance. "I think I should expect to be waited on if I were ill. You've had rather a bad time, I'm afraid. But you haven't missed much. The weather has been villainous."

"I've missed all the dances," said Dinah, stifling a sob.

He began to smile. "I wish I had. I haven't enjoyed one of them."

That comforted her a little. At least Rose had not scored an unqualified victory! "You've been bored?" she asked.

"Horribly bored," said Sir Eustace. "There's been no fun for anyone since the weather broke."

She gathered her courage in both hands. "And so you're going home?" she said, and lay in quivering dread of his answer.

He did not make one immediately. He seemed to be considering the matter. "There doesn't seem to be much point in staying on," he said finally, "unless things improve."

"But they will improve," said Dinah quickly. "At least - at least they ought to."

"A fortnight of bad weather isn't particularly encouraging," he remarked.

"Of course it isn't! It's horrid," she agreed. "But every day makes it less likely that it will last much longer. And I expect it's much worse in England," she added.

"I wonder," said Sir Eustace. "There's the hunting anyway."

"Oh no; it would freeze directly you got there," she said, with a shaky little laugh. "And then you would wish you had stayed here."

"I could shoot," said Sir Eustace.

"And there is the Hunt Ball, isn't there?" said Dinah with more assurance.

He looked at her keenly. "What Hunt Ball?"

She met his eyes with a faint challenge in her own. "I heard you were going to stay with the de Vignes. They always go to the Hunt Ball every year."

"Do you go?" asked Sir Eustace.

She shook her head. "No. I never go anywhere."

She saw his eyes soften unexpectedly as he said, "Then there isn't much inducement for me to go, is there?"

Her heart gave a wild throb of half-incredulous delight. She made a small movement of one hand towards him, and quite suddenly she found it grasped in his. He bent to her with a laugh in his eyes.

"Shall we go on with the game, - Daphne?" he whispered. "Are you well enough?"

Her eyes answered him. Was he not irresistible? "Oh," she whispered, "I thought - I thought you had forgotten."

He glanced round, as if to make sure that they were alone, and then swiftly bent and kissed her quivering lips. "But the past has no claims," he said. "Remember, it is a game without consequences!"

She laughed very happily, clasping his hand. "I was afraid it was all over," she said. "But it isn't, is it?"

He laughed too under his breath. "I am under the very strictest orders not to excite you," he said, passing the question by. "If the doctor were to come and feel your pulse now, there would be serious trouble. And I shouldn't be allowed within a dozen yards of you again for many a long day."

"What nonsense!" murmured Dinah. "Why, you have done me so much good that I feel almost well." She squeezed his hand with all the strength she could muster. "Don't go away till I'm quite well!" she begged him wistfully. "We must have - one more dance."

His eyes kindled suddenly with that fire which she dared not meet. "I will grant you that," he said, "on condition that you promise - mind, you promise - not to run away afterwards."

His intensity embarrassed her, she knew not wherefore. "Why - why should I run away?" she faltered.

"You ran away last time," he said.

"Oh, that was only - only because I was afraid the Colonel might be angry with me," she murmured.

"Oh well, there is no Colonel to be angry now," he said. "It's a promise then, is it?"

But for some reason wholly undefined she hesitated. She felt as if she could not bring herself thus to cut off her own line of retreat. "No, I don't think I can quite promise that," she said, after a moment.

"You won't?" he said.

His tone warned her to reconsider her decision. "I - I'll tell you to-morrow," she said hastily.

"I may be gone by to-morrow," he said.

She looked up at him with swift daring. "Oh no, you won't," she said, with conviction. "Or if you are, you'll come back."

"How do you know that?" he demanded, frowning upon her while his eyes still gleamed with that lambent fire that made her half afraid.

She dropped her own. "There's someone coming," she whispered. "It doesn't matter, does it? I do know. Good-bye!"

She slipped her hand from his with a little secret sense of triumph; for though he had so arrogantly asserted himself she was conscious of a certain power over him which gave her confidence. She was firmly convinced in that moment that he would not go.

He rose to leave her as Isabel came softly into the room, and between the brother and sister there flashed a look that was curiously like the crossing of blades.

Isabel came straight to Dinah's side. "You must settle down now, dear child," she said, in that low, musical voice of hers that Dinah loved. "It is getting late, and you didn't sleep well last night."

Dinah smiled, and drew the hand that had so often smoothed her pillow to her cheek. But her eyes were upon Eustace, and she caught a parting gleam from his as with a gesture of farewell he turned away.

"I am much better," she said to Isabel later, as she composed herself to rest. "I feel as if I am going to sleep well."

Isabel stooped to kiss her. "Sleep is the best medicine in the world," she said.

"Do you sleep better now?" Dinah asked, detaining her.

Isabel hesitated for a second. "Oh yes, I sleep," she said then. "I am able to sleep now that you are safe, my darling."

Dinah clung to her. "I can't think what I would do without you," she murmured. "No one was ever so good to me before."

Isabel held her closely. "Don't you realize," she said fondly, "that you have been my salvation."

"Not - not really?" faltered Dinah.

"Yes, really." There was a throb of passion in Isabel's voice. "I have been a prisoner for years, but you - you, little Dinah, - have set me free. I am travelling forward again now - like the rest of the world." She paused a moment, and her arms clasped Dinah more closely still. "I do not think I have very far to go," she said, speaking very softly. "My night has been so long that I think the dawn cannot be far off now. God knows how I am longing for it."

"Oh, darling, don't - don't!" whispered Dinah piteously.

"I won't, dearest." Very tenderly Isabel kissed her again. "I didn't mean to distress you. Only I want you to know that you are just all the world to me - the main-spring of what life there is left to me. I shall never forgive myself for leading you away on that terrible Sunday, and causing you all this suffering."

"Oh, but I should have been home again by now if that hadn't happened," said Dinah quickly. "See what I should have missed! I'd far, far rather be ill with you than well at home."

"Yours isn't a happy home, sweetheart," Isabel said gently.

"Not very," Dinah admitted. "But being away makes it seem much worse. I have been so spoilt with you."

Isabel smiled. "I only wish I could keep you always, dear child."

Dinah drew a sharp breath. "Oh, if you only could!" she said.

Isabel pressed her to her heart, and laid her down. "I must get you back to bed, dear," she said. "We have talked too long already."

Late that night Isabel went softly to the door in answer to a low knock, and found Scott on the threshold.

She lifted a warning finger. "She is asleep."

"That's right," he said quietly. "I only came to say good night to you. Are you going to bed now?"

She looked at him with a faint smile in her shadowed eyes. "I daresay I shall go some time," she said; then seeing the concern in his eyes: "Don't worry about me, Stumpy dear. I don't sleep a great deal, you know; but I rest."

He took her arm and drew her gently outside the room. "I want you to take care of yourself now that she is safe," he said. "Will you try?"

The smile still lingered in her eyes. She bent her stately neck to kiss him. "Oh yes, dear; I shall be all right," she said. "It does me good to have the little one to think of."

"I know," he said. "But don't wear yourself out! Remember, you are not strong."

"Nothing I can do for her would be too much," she answered with quick feeling. "Think - think what she has done for me!"

"For us all," said Scott gently. "But all the same, dear, you can spare a little thought for yourself now." He hesitated momentarily, then: "I think Eustace would like to see more of you," he said, speaking with a touch of diffidence.

She made a sharp gesture of impatience. "Why did you send him to disturb the child's peace?"

"She wanted him," said Scott simply.

"Ah!" Isabel stood tense for a second. "And he?" she questioned.

"He was quite pleased to see her again," said Scott.

She grasped his arm suddenly. "Stumpy, don't let him break her heart!"

He met her look with steadfast eyes. "He shall not do that," he said, with inflexible resolution.

Her hold became a grip. "Can you prevent it? You know what he is"

"Oh yes, I know," very steadily Scott made answer. "But you needn't be afraid, Isabel. He shall not do that."

A measure of relief came into her drawn face. "Thank you, Stumpy," she said. "I was horribly afraid - when I saw him just now - and she, poor child, so innocently glad to have him!"

"You needn't be afraid," he reiterated. "Eustace is too much of a sportsman to amuse himself at the expense of an unsophisticated child like that."

Isabel suppressed a shiver. "I don't think he is so scrupulous as you imagine," she said. "We must watch, Stumpy; we must watch."

He patted her arm with his quiet smile. "And we mustn't let ourselves get over-anxious," he said. "Now go to bed, like a dear girl! You are looking absolutely worn out."

Her lips quivered as she smiled back. "At least you are getting better nights," she said.

"Yes, I sleep very well," he answered. "I want to know you are doing the same."

Her face shone as though reflecting the lights of a city seen from afar. "Oh yes, I sleep," she said. "And sometimes I dream that I have really found the peaks of Paradise. But before I reach the summit - I am awake."

He drew her to him, and kissed her. "It is better that you should wake, dear," he said.

She returned his kiss with tenderness, but her eyes were fixed and distant. "Some day the dream will come true, Stumpy," she said softly. "And I shall find him there where he has been waiting for me all these years."

"But not yet, Isabel," murmured Scott, and there was pleading in his voice.

She looked at him for a moment ere she turned to re-enter the room in which Dinah lay. "Not just yet," she answered softly. "Good night, dear! Good night!"

The strange light was still upon her face as she went, and Scott looked after her with a faint, wistful smile about his mouth. As he went to his own room, he passed his hand across his forehead with a gesture of unutterable weariness.

CHAPTER XXV

THE TRUE GOLD

The actual turning-point in Dinah's illness seemed to date from that brief interview with Sir Eustace. They had drawn her back half against her will from the land of shadows, but from that day her will was set to recover. The old elasticity came back to her, and with every hour her strength increased. The joy of life was hers once more. She was like a flower opening to the sun.

Sir Eustace presented himself every evening for admittance and sat with her for a little while. Isabel was generally present, and their conversation was in consequence of a strictly common-place order; but the keen blue eyes told Dinah more than the proud lips ever uttered. She came to watch for that look which she could not meet, and though at times it sent a wild dart of fear through her, yet it filled her also with a rapture indefinable but unspeakably precious. She felt sure that he had never turned that look on Rose or any other girl. It was kept exclusively for her, and its fiery intensity thrilled her soul. It was the sign of a secret understanding between them which she believed none other suspected.

It was a somewhat terrible joy, for the man's strength had startled her more than once, but in moments of dread she reassured herself with the memory of his reiterated declaration that the magic bond that existed between them was no bond at all in reality - only a game without consequences. She would not look forward to the time when that game should be over. She was not looking forward at all, so sublimely happy was she in the present. The period of convalescence which to most patients is the hardest of all to bear was to her a dream of delight.

A week after the departure of the de Vignes she was well enough to be moved into Isabel's sitting-room, and here on that first day both Sir Eustace and Scott joined them at tea.

The weather had cleared again, and Sir Eustace came in from an afternoon's ski-ing attired in the white sweater in which Dinah always loved to see him. She lay on her couch and watched him with shining eyes, telling herself that no prince had ever looked more royal.

It was Scott who waited upon her, but she was scarcely aware of his presence. Even Isabel seemed to have faded into the background. She could think only of Eustace lounging near her in careless magnificence, talking in his deep voice of the day's sport.

"There are several new people arrived," he said, "both ancient and modern. The place was getting empty, but it has filled up again. There is to be a dance to-night," his eyes sought Dinah's. "I am going down presently to see if any of the new-comers have any talents worth cultivating."

She met his look with a flash of daring. "I wish you luck," she said.

He made her a bow. "You are very generous. But I scarcely expect any. My star has not been in the ascendant for a long time."

Scott uttered a laugh that sounded faintly derisive. "You'll have to make the best of the second best for once, my dear chap," he said. "You can't always have your cake iced."

Eustace glanced at him momentarily. "I am not you, Stumpy," he said. "The philosophy of the second best is only for those who have never tasted the best."

There was in his tone a touch of malice that caught Dinah very oddly, like the flick of a lash intended for another. She awoke very suddenly to the realization of Scott sitting near Isabel with the light shining on his pale face and small, colourless beard. How insignificant he looked! And yet the narrow shoulders had an independent set about them as though they were not without a certain strength.

The smile still lingered about his lips as he made quiet rejoinder. "It sometimes needs a philosopher to tell what is the best."

Eustace gave an impatient shrug. "The philosopher is not always a wise man," he observed briefly.

"But seldom an utter fool," returned Scott.

The elder brother's face was contemptuous as he said, "A philosopher may recognize what is best, but it is seldom within his reach."

"And so, being a philosopher, he does without it." Scott spoke thoughtfully; he was gazing straight before him.

Isabel suddenly leaned forward. "He is not always the loser, Stumpy," she said.

He looked at her. "Certainly a man can't lose what he has never had," he said.

"Every man has his chance once," she insisted.

"And - if he's a philosopher - he doesn't take it," laughed Eustace. "Don't you know, my dear Isabel, that that is the very cream and essence of philosophy?"

She gave him a swift look that was an open challenge. "What do you know of philosophy and the greater things of life?" she said.

He looked momentarily surprised. Dinah saw the ready frown gather on his handsome face; but before he could speak Scott intervened.

"How on earth did we get onto this abstruse subject?" he said easily. "Miss Bathurst will vote us all a party of bores, and with reason. What were we talking about before? Iced cake, wasn't it? Are you a cook Miss Bathurst?"

"I can make some kinds of cakes," Dinah said modestly, "but I like making pastry best. I often make sausage-rolls for Dad to take hunting."

"That sounds more amusing for him than for you," observed Eustace.

"Oh no, I love making them," she assured him. "And he always says he likes mine better than anyone's. But I'm not a particularly good cook really. Mother generally does that part, and I do all the rest."

"All?" said Isabel.

"Yes. You see, we can't afford to keep a servant," said Dinah. "And I groom Rupert - that's the hunter - too, when Billy isn't at home. I like doing that. He's such a beauty."

"Do you ever ride him?" asked Eustace.

She shook her head. "No. I'd love to, of course, but there's never any time. I can't spend as long as I like over grooming him because there are so many other things. But he generally looks very nice," she spoke with pride; "quite as nice as any of the de Vignes's horses."

"You must have a very busy time of it," said Scott.

"Yes." Dinah's bright face clouded a little. "I often wish I had more time for other things; but it's no good wishing. Anyway, I've had my time out here, and I shall never forget it."

"You must come out again with us," said Isabel.

Dinah beamed. "Oh, how I should love it!" she said. "But -" her face fell again - "I don't believe mother will ever spare me a second time."

"All right. I'll run away with you in the yacht," said Eustace. "Come for a trip in the summer!"

She looked at him with shining eyes. "It's not a bit of good thinking about it," she said. "But oh, how lovely it would be!"

He laughed, looking at her with that gleam in his eyes that she had come to know as exclusively her own. "Where there's a will, there's a way," he said. "If you have the will, you can leave the way to me."

She drew a quick breath. Her heart was beating rather fast. "All right," she said. "I'll come."

"Is it a promise?" said Eustace.

She shook her head instantly. "No. I never make promises. They have a way of spoiling things so."

"Exactly my own idea," he said. "Never turn a pleasure into a duty, or it becomes a burden at once. Well, I must go and make myself pretty for this evening's show. If I'm very bored, I shall come and sit out with you."

"Not to-night," said Isabel with quick decision. "Dinah is going to bed very soon."

"Really?" He stood by Dinah's couch, looking down at her with his faint supercilious smile. "Do you submit to that sort of tyranny?" he said.

She held up her hand to him. "It isn't tyranny. It is the very dearest kindness in the world. Don't you know the difference?"

He held the little, confiding hand a moment or two, and she felt his fingers close around it with a strength that seemed as if it encompassed her very soul. "There are two ways of looking at everything," he said. "But I shouldn't be too docile if I were you; not, that is, if you want to get any fun out of life. Remember, life is short."

He let her go with the words, straightened himself to his full, splendid height, and sauntered with regal arrogance to the door.

"I want you, Stumpy," he said, in passing. "There are one or two letters for you to deal with. You can come to my room while I dress."

"In that case, I had better say good night too," said Scott, rising.

"Oh no," said Dinah, with her quick smile. "You can come in and say good night to me afterwards - when I'm in bed. Can't he, Isabel?"

She had fallen into the habit of calling Isabel by her Christian name from hearing Scott use it. It had begun almost in delirium, and now it came so naturally that she never dreamed of reverting to the more formal mode of address.

Scott smiled in his quiet fashion, and turned to join his brother. "I will with pleasure," he said.

Eustace threw a mocking glance backwards. "It seems that philosophers rush in where mere ordinary males fear to tread," he observed. "Stumpy, allow me to congratulate you on your privileges!"

"Thanks, old chap!" Scott made answer in his tired voice. "But there is no occasion for the ordinary male to envy me my compensations."

"What did he mean by that?" said Dinah, as the door closed.

Isabel moved to her side and sat down on the edge of the couch. "Scott is very lonely, little one," she said.

"Is he?" said Dinah, wonderingly. "But - surely he must have lots of friends. He's such a dear."

Isabel smiled at her rather sadly. "Yes, everyone who knows him thinks that."

"Everyone must love him," protested Dinah. "Who could help it?"

"I wonder," said Isabel slowly, "if he will ever meet anyone who will love him best of all."

Dinah was suddenly conscious of a rush of blood to her face. She knew not wherefore, but she felt it beat in her temples and sing in her ears. "Oh, surely - surely!" she stammered in confusion.

Isabel looked beyond her. "You know, Dinah," she said, her voice very low, "Scott is a man with an almost infinite greatness of soul. I don't know if you realize it. I have thought sometimes that you did. But there are very few - very few - who do."

"I know he is great," whispered Dinah. "I told him so almost - almost the first time I saw him."

Isabel's smile was very tender. She stooped and gathered Dinah to her bosom. "Oh, my dear," she murmured, "never prefer the tinsel to the true gold! He is far, far the greatest man I know. And you - you will never meet a greater."

Dinah clung to her in quick responsiveness. Her strange agitation was subsiding, but she could feel the blood yet pulsing in her veins. "I know it," she whispered. "I am sure of it. He is very much to you, dear, isn't he?"

"For years he has been my all," Isabel said. "Listen a moment! I will tell you something. In the first dreadful days of my illness, I was crazy with trouble, and - and they bound me to keep me from violence. I have never forgotten it. I never shall. Then - he came. He was very young at that time, only twenty-three. He had his life before him, and mine - mine was practically over. Yet he gave up everything - everything for my sake. He took command; he banished all the horrible people who had taken possession of me. He gave me freedom, and he set himself to safe-guard me. He brought me home. He was with me night and day, or if not actually with me, within call. He and Biddy between them brought me back. They watched me, nursed me, cared for me. Whenever my trouble was greater than I could bear, he was always there to help me. He never left me; and gradually he became so necessary to me that I couldn't contemplate life without him. I have been terribly selfish." A low sob checked her utterance for a moment, and Dinah's young arms tightened. "I let my grief take hold of me to the exclusion of everything else. I didn't see - I didn't realize - the sacrifice he was making. For years I took it all as a right, living in my fog of misery and blind to all beside. But now - now at last - thanks to you, little one, whom I nearly killed - my eyes are open once more. The fog has rolled away. No, I can never be happy. I am of those who wait. But I will never again, God helping me, deprive others of happiness. Scott shall live his own life now. His devotion to me must come to an end. My greatest wish in life now is that he may meet a woman worthy of him, who will love him as he deserves to be loved, before I climb the peaks of Paradise and find my beloved in the dawning." Isabel's voice sank. She pressed Dinah close against her heart. "It will not be long," she whispered. "I have had a message that there is no mistaking, I know it will not be long. But oh, darling, I do want to see him happy first."

Dinah was crying softly. She could find no words to utter.

So for awhile they clung together, the woman who had suffered and come at last through bitter tribulation into peace, and the child whose feet yet halted on the threshold of the enchanted country that the other had long since traversed and left behind.

Nothing further passed between them. Isabel had said her say, and for some reason Dinah was powerless to speak. She could think of no words to utter, and deep in her heart she was half afraid to break the silence. That sudden agitation of hers had left her oddly confused and embarrassed. She shrank from pursuing the matter further.

Yet for a long time that night she lay awake pondering, wondering. Certainly Scott was different from all other men, totally, undeniably different. He seemed to dwell on a different plane. She could not grasp what it was about him that set him thus apart. But what Isabel had said showed her very clearly that the spirit that dwelt behind that unimposing exterior was a force that counted, and could hold its own against odds.

She slept at last with the thought of him still present in her mind. And in her dreams the vision of Greatheart in his shining armour came to her again, filling her with a happiness which even sleeping she did not dare to analyse, scarcely to contemplate.

CHAPTER XXVI

THE CALL OF APOLLO

Dinah's strength came back to her in leaps and bounds, and three weeks after the de Vignes's departure she was almost herself again. The season was drawing to a close. The holidays were over, and English people were turning homeward. Very reluctantly Isabel had to admit that her charge was well enough for the journey back. Mrs. Bathurst wrote in an insistent strain, urging that the time had come for her to return, and no further excuse could be invented for keeping her longer.

They decided to return themselves and take Dinah to her home, Isabel having determined to make the acquaintance of the redoubtable Mrs. Bathurst, and persuade her to spare her darling to them again in the summer. The coming parting was hard to face, so hard that Dinah could not bear to speak of it. She shed a good many tears in private, as Isabel was well aware; but she never willingly made any reference to the ordeal she so dreaded.

The only time she voluntarily broached the subject was when she entreated to be allowed to go down to the last dance that was to be held in the hotel. It chanced that this was fixed for the night before their own departure, and Isabel demurred somewhat; for though Dinah had shaken off most of her invalid habits, she was still far from robust.

"You will be so tired in the morning, darling," she protested

Ethel M. Dell

gently, while Dinah knelt beside her, earnestly pleading. "You will get that tiresome side-ache, and you won't be fit to travel."

"I shall - I shall," Dinah assured her. "Oh, please, dear, just this once - just this once - let me have this one more fling! I shall never have another chance. I'm sure I never shall."

Isabel's hand stroked the soft dark hair caressingly. She saw that Dinah was very near to tears. "I don't believe I ought to say Yes, dear child," she said. "You know I hate to deny you anything. But if it were to do you harm, I should never forgive myself."

"It couldn't! It shan't!" declared Dinah, almost incoherent in her vehemence. "It isn't as if I wanted to dance every dance. I'd come and sit out with you in between. And if I got tired, you could take me away. I would go directly if you said so. Really I would."

She was hard to resist, kneeling there with her arms about Isabel and her bright eyes lifted. Isabel took the sweet face between her hands and kissed it.

"Let me ask Scott what he thinks!" she said. "I want to give in to you, Dinah darling, but it's against my judgment. If it is against his judgment too, will you be content to give it up?"

"Oh, of course," said Dinah instantly. She was confident that Scott - that kind and gentle friend of hers - would deny her nothing. It seemed almost superfluous to ask him.

The words had scarcely left her lips when his quiet knock came at the sitting-room door, and he entered.

She looked round at him with a smile of quick welcome. "I'll give it up in a minute if he says so," she said.

Isabel turned in her chair. "Come here, Stumpy!" she said. "We want your advice. We are talking about the dance to-night. Dinah has set her heart on going. Would it - do you think it would - do her any harm?"

Scott came up to them in his halting way. He looked at Dinah pressed close to his sister's side, and his smile was very kindly as he said, "Poor little Cinderella! It's hard lines; but, you know, the doctor's last words to you were a warning against over-exerting yourself."

"But I shouldn't," she assured him eagerly. "Really, truly, I shouldn't! I walked all the way to the village with you yesterday, and wasn't a bit tired - or hardly a bit - when I got back."

"You looked jaded to death," he said.

"I am afraid it is thumbs down," said Isabel, a touch of regret in her voice.

"Oh no, - no!" entreated Dinah. "Mr. Studley, please - please say I may go! I promise I won't dance too much. I promise I'll stop directly I'm tired."

"My dear child," Scott said, "it would be sheer madness for you to attempt to dance at all. Isabel," he turned to his sister with most unusual sharpness, "how can you tantalize her in this way? Say No at once! You know perfectly well she isn't fit for it."

Isabel made no attempt to argue the point. "You hear, Dinah?" she said.

A quick throb of anger went through Dinah. She disengaged herself quickly, and stood up. "Mr. Studley," she said in a voice that quivered, "it's not right - it's not fair! How can you know what is good for me? And even if you did, what - what right - " She broke off, trembling and holding to Isabel's chair to steady herself.

Scott's eyes, very level, very kind, were looking straight at her in a fashion that checked the hot words on her lips. "My child, no right whatever," he said. "I have no more power to control your actions than the man in the moon. But if you want my approval to your scheme, I can't give it you. I don't approve, and because I don't, I tell Isabel that she ought to refuse to carry it through. I have no right to control her either, but I think my opinion means something to her. I hope it does at least."

He looked at Isabel, but she said nothing. Only she put her arm about Dinah as she stood.

There followed a few moments of very difficult silence; then abruptly the mutiny went out of Dinah's face and attitude.

"I'm horrid," she said, in a voice half-choked. "Forgive me! You - you shouldn't spoil me so."

"Oh, don't, please!" said Scott. "I am infernally sorry. I know what it means to you."

He took out his cigarette-case and turned away with a touch of embarrassment. She saw that for some reason he was moved.

Impulsively she left Isabel and came to him. "Don't think any more about it!" she said. "I'll go to bed and be good."

"You always are," said Scott, faintly smiling.

"No, no, I'm not! What a fib! You know I'm not. But I'm going to be good this time - so that you shall have something nice to remember me by." Dinah's voice quivered still, but she managed to smile.

He gave her a quick look. "You will always be the pleasantest memory I have," he said.

The words were quietly spoken, so quietly that they sounded

almost matter-of-fact. But Dinah flushed with pleasure, detecting the sincerity in his voice.

"It's very nice of you to say that," she said, "especially as I deserve it so little. Thank you, Mr. - Scott!" She uttered the name timidly. She had never ventured to use it before.

He held out his hand to her. "Oh, drop the prefix!" he said. "Call me Stumpy like the rest of the world!"

But Dinah shook her head with vehemence. There were tears standing in her eyes, but she smiled through them. "I will not call you Stumpy!" she declared. "It doesn't suit you a bit. I never even think of you by that name. It - it is perfectly ludicrous applied to you!"

"Some people think I am ludicrous," observed Scott.

His hand grasped hers firmly for a moment, and let it go. The steadfast friendliness in his eyes shone out like a beacon. And there came to Dinah a swift sense of great and uplifting pride at the thought that she numbered this man among her friends.

The moment passed, but the warmth at her heart remained. She went back to Isabel, and slipped down into the shelter of her arm, feeling oddly shy and also inexplicably happy. Her disappointment had shrunk to a negligible quantity. She even wondered at herself for having cared so greatly about so trifling a matter.

There came the firm tread of a man's feet outside the door, and it swung open. Eustace entered with his air of high confidence.

"Ah, Stumpy, there you are! I want you. Well, Miss Bathurst, what about to-night?"

She faced him bravely from Isabel's side. "I've promised to go to bed early, as usual," she said.

Ethel M. Dell

"What? You're not dancing?" She saw his ready frown. "Well, you will come and look on anyway. Isabel, you must show for once."

He spoke imperiously. Isabel looked up. "I am sorry, Eustace. It is out of the question," she said coldly. "Both Dinah and I are retiring early in preparation for to-morrow."

He bit his lip. "This is too bad. Miss Bathurst, don't you want to come down? It's for the last time."

Dinah hesitated, and Scott came quietly to her rescue.

"She is being prudent against her own inclination, old chap. Don't make it hard for her!"

"What a confounded shame!" said Eustace.

"No, no, it isn't!" said Dinah. "It is quite right. I am not going to think any more about it."

He laughed with a touch of mockery. "Which means you will probably think about it all night. Well, you will have the reward of virtue anyhow, which ought to be very satisfying. Come along, Stumpy! I want you to catch the post."

He bore his brother off with him, and Dinah went rather wistfully to help Biddy pack. She had done right, she knew; but it was difficult to stifle the regret in her heart. She had so longed for that one last dance, and it seemed to her that she had treated Sir Eustace somewhat shabbily also. She was sure that he was displeased, and the thought of it troubled her. For she had almost promised him that last dance.

"Arrah thin, Miss Dinah dear, don't ye look so sad at all!" counselled Biddy. "Good times pass, but there's always good times to come while ye're young. And it's the bonny face ye've got on ye. Sure, there'll be a fine wedding one of these days. There's a prince looking for ye, or me name's not

Biddy Maloney."

Dinah tried to smile, but her heart was heavy. She could not share Biddy's cheery belief in the good times to come, and she was quite sure that no prince would ever come her way.

Sir Eustace - that king among men - might think of her sometimes, but not seriously, oh no, not seriously. He had so many other interests. It was only her dancing that drew him, and he would never have another opportunity of enjoying that.

She rested in the afternoon at Isabel's desire, but she did not sleep. Some teasing sprite had set a waltz refrain running in her brain, and it haunted her perpetually. She went down to the vestibule with Isabel for tea, and here Scott joined them; but Sir Eustace did not put in an appearance. In their company she sought to be cheerful, and in a measure succeeded; but the thought of the morrow pressed upon her. In another brief twenty-four hours this place where she had first known the wonder and the glory of life would know her no more. In two days she would be back in the old bondage, chained once more to the oar, with the dread of her mother ever present in her heart, however fair the world might be.

She could keep her depression more or less at bay in the presence of her friends, but when later she went to her room to prepare for dinner something like desperation seized her. How was she going to bear it? One last wild fling would have helped her, but this inaction made things infinitely worse, made things intolerable.

While she dressed, she waged a fierce struggle against her tears. She knew that Isabel would be greatly distressed should she detect them, and to hurt Isabel seemed to her the acme of selfish cruelty. She would not give way! She would not!

And then - suddenly she heard a step in the corridor, and her heart leapt. Well she knew that careless, confident tread! But what was he doing there? Why had he come to her door?

With bated breath she stood and listened. Yes, he had paused. In a moment she heard a rustle on the floor. A screw of paper appeared under the door as though blown in by a wandering wind. Then the careless feet retreated again, and she thought she heard him whistling below his breath.

Eagerly she swooped forward and snatched up the note. Her hands shook so that she could scarcely open it. Trembling, she stood under the light to read it.

It was headed in a bold hand: "To Daphne." And below in much smaller writing she read: "Come to the top of the stairs when the band plays *Simple Aveu*, and leave the rest to me.

"APOLLO."

A wild thrill went through her. But could she? Dared she? Had she not practically promised Isabel that she would go to bed?

Yet how could she go, and leave this direct invitation, which was almost a command, unanswered? And it was only one dance - only one dance! Would it be so very wrong to snatch just that one?

The thought of Scott came to her and the look of sincerity in his eyes when he had told her that she would always be the pleasantest memory he had. But she thrust it from her almost fiercely. Ah no, no, no! She could not let him deprive her thus of this one last gaiety. Apollo had called her. It only remained for her to obey.

She dressed in a fever of excitement, and hid the note - that precious note - in her bosom. She would meet him at dinner, and he would look for an answer. How should she convey it? And oh, what answer should she give?

Looking back afterwards, it seemed to her that Fate had pressed her hard that night, - so hard that resistance was impossible. When she was dressed in the almost childishly simple muslin she looked herself in the eyes and fancied that there was something in her face that she had never seen there before. It was something that pleased her immensely giving her a strangely new self-confidence. She did not wot that it was the charm of her coming womanhood that had burst into sudden flower.

At the last moment she cast all her scruples away from her, and snatched up a slip of paper.

"I will be there. Daphne," were the words she wrote, and though her conscience smote her as she did it, she stifled it fiercely. Had she not promised him that one dance long ago?

She met him at dinner with a face of smiling unconcern. The new force within had imbued her with a wondrous strength. She exulted in the thought of her power over him, transient though she knew it to be. Deep down in her heart she was afraid, yet was she wildly daring. It was her last night, and she was utterly reckless.

She left her note in his hand with the utmost coolness when she bade him good night in the vestibule. She bade good night to Scott also, but she met his eyes for no more than a second; and then she had to stifle afresh the sharp pang at her heart.

She went away up the stairs with Isabel, leaving them smoking over their coffee, leaving also the dreamy strains of the band, the gay laughter and movement of the happy crowd that drifted towards the ballroom.

Isabel accompanied her to her room. "You are a dear, good child," she said tenderly, as she held her for a last kiss. "I shall never forget how sweetly you gave up the thing you wanted so much."

Dinah clung to her fast for a moment or two, and her hold was passionate. "Oh, don't praise me for that!" she whispered into Isabel's neck. "I am not good at all. I am very bad."

She almost tore herself free a second later, and Isabel, divining that any further demonstration from her would cause a breakdown, bade her a loving good night and went away.

Dinah stood awhile struggling for self-control. She had been perilously near to baring her soul to Isabel in those moments of tenderness. Even now the impulse urged her to run after her and tell her of the temptation to which she was yielding. She forced it down with clenched hands, telling herself over and over that it was her last chance, her last chance, and she must not lose it. And so at length it passed; and with it passed also the pricks of conscience that had so troubled her. She emerged from the brief struggle with a sense of mad triumph. The spirit of adventure had entered into her, and she no longer paused to count the cost.

"I expect I shall be sorry in the morning," she said to herself. "But to-night - oh, to-night - nothing matters except Apollo!"

She whisked to the door and set it ajar. The dance-music drew her, drew her, like the voice of a siren. For that one night she would live again. She would feel his arm about her and the magic in her brain. Already her feet yearned to the alluring rhythm. She leaned against the door-post, and gave herself up to her dream. Yet once more the wine of the gods was held to her lips. She would drink deeply, deeply.

CHAPTER XXVII

THE GOLDEN MAZE

Softly the strains of *Simple Aveu* floated along the corridor. It came like fairy music, now near, now far, haunting as a dream, woven through and through with the gold of Romance.

Someone was coming along the passage with the easy swing of the born dancer, and pressed against her door-post in the shadows, another born dancer awaited him with a wildly throbbing heart.

The die was cast, and there was no going back. She heard the deep voice humming the magic melody as he came. In a moment the superb figure came into sight, moving with that royal ease of carriage so characteristic and so wonderful.

He drew near. He spied the small white figure lurking in the dimness. With a low laugh he opened his arms to her.

And then there came to Dinah, not for the first time, a strange, wholly indefinable misgiving. It was a warning so insistent that she suddenly and swiftly drew back, as if she would flee into the room behind her.

But he was too quick for her. He caught her on the threshold. "Oh no, no!" he laughed. "That's not playing the game." He drew her to him, holding her two wrists. "Daphne! Daphne!" he said. "Still running away? Do you call that fair?"

She did not resist him, for the moment she felt his touch she knew herself a captive. The magic force of his personality had caught her; but she did not give herself wholly to him. She stood and palpitated in his hold, her head bent low.

"I - I'm not running away," she told him breathlessly. "I was just - just coming. But - but - shan't we be seen? Your brother -"

"What?" He was stooping over her; she felt his breath upon her neck. "Oh, Scott! Surely you're not afraid of Scott, are you? You needn't be. I've sent him off to write some letters. He'll be occupied for an hour at least. Come! Come! You promised. And we're wasting time."

There was a subtle caressing note in his voice. It thrilled her as she stood, and ever the soft music drifted on around them, pulsing with a sweetness almost too intense to be borne.

He held her with the hold of a conqueror. She was quivering from head to foot, but all desire to free herself was gone. Still she would not raise her face.

Panting, she spoke. "Yes, we - we are wasting time. Let us go!"

He laughed above her head - a low laugh of absolute assurance. "Are you too shy to look at me, - Daphne?"

She laughed also very tremulously. "I think I am - just at present. Let us dance first anyway! Must we go down to the salon? Couldn't we dance in the corridor?"

His arm was round her. He led her down the passage. "No, no! We will go down. And afterwards -"

"Afterwards," she broke in breathlessly, "we will just peep at the moonlight on the mountains, and then I must come back."

"I will show you something better than the moonlight on the

mountains," said Sir Eustace.

She did not ask him what he meant, though her whole being was strung to a tense expectancy. He had brought her once more to the heights of Olympus, and each moment was full of a vivid life that had to be lived to the utmost. She lacked the strength to look forward; the present was too overwhelming. It was almost more than she could bear.

They reached the head of the stairs. His arm tightened about her. She descended as though upon wings. Passing through the vestibule, her feet did not seem to touch the ground. And then like a golden maze the ballroom received them.

Before she knew it, they were among the dancers and the magic of her dream had merged into reality. She closed her eyes, for the glare of light and moving figures dazzled her, and gave herself up to the rapture of that one splendid dance. Her heart was beating wildly, as though it would choke her. A curious thirst that yet was part of her delight made her throat burn. A weakness that exulted in the man's supporting strength held her bound and entranced by such an ecstasy as she had never known before. She laughed, a gurgling laugh through panting lips. She wondered whether he realized that she was floating through the air, held up by his arm alone above the glitter and the turmoil all around them. She wondered too how soon they would find their way to the heart of that golden maze, and what nameless treasure awaited them there. For that treasure was for them, and them alone, she never doubted. It was the gift of the gods, bestowed upon no others in all that merry crowd.

The magic deepened and grew within her. She felt that the climax was drawing near. He would not dance to a finish, she knew, and already the music was quickening. She was too giddy, too spent had she but known it, to open her eyes. Only by instinct did she know that he was bearing her, sure and swift as a swallow, to the curtained recess whither he had led her twice before. This, she told herself, this was the heart of the maze. All things began and ended here. Her lips quivered and tingled. She would never escape him now. He had her firmly in the net. Nor did she seriously want to escape. Only she felt desperately afraid of him. His strength, his determination, above all, his silence, sent tumultuous fear throbbing through her heart. And when at length the pause came, when she knew that they were alone in the gloom with the music dying away behind them, a last wild dread that was almost anguish made her hide her face deep, deep in his arm while her body hung powerless in his embrace.

He laughed a little - a laugh that thrilled her with its exultation, its passion. And then, whether she would or not, he turned her face upwards to meet his own.

His kisses descended upon her hotly, suffocatingly. He held her pressed to him in such a grip as seemed to drive all the breath out of her quivering frame. His lips were like a fierce flame on face and neck - a flame that grew in intensity, possessing her, consuming her. The mastery of his hold was utterly irresistible.

She gasped and gasped for breath as one suddenly plunged in deep waters. His violence appalled her, well-nigh quenching her rapture. She was more terrified in those moments than she had ever been before. She almost felt as if the godlike being she had so humbly adored from afar had turned upon her with the demand for human sacrifice. Those devouring kisses sent unimagined apprehensions through her heart. They seemed to satisfy him so little while they sapped from her every atom of vitality, leaving her helpless as an infant, her body drawn to his as a needle to the magnet, not of her own volition, but simply by his strength. And ever the fire of his passion grew hotter till she felt as one bound on the edge of a mighty furnace which scorched her mercilessly from head to foot.

She was near to fainting when she felt his arms relax, and suddenly above her upturned face she heard his voice, low and deep, like the growl of an angry beast.

"What have you come here for? Go! You're not wanted."

In a flash she realized that they were no longer alone. She would have disengaged herself, but she was too weak to stand. She could only cling feebly to the supporting arm.

In that moment a great wave of humiliation burst over her, sweeping away her last foothold. For without turning she knew who it was who stood behind her; she knew to whom those furious words had been addressed.

Before her inner sight with overwhelming vividness there arose a vision - the vision of Greatheart in his shining armour with a drawn sword in his hand; and in his eyes - But no, she could not look into his eyes.

She hid her face instead, burning and quivering still from the touch of those passionate lips, hid it low against her lover's breast, too shamed even for speech.

There came a movement, the halting movement of a lame man, and she heard Scott's voice. It pierced her intolerably, perfectly gentle though it was.

"I am sorry to intrude," he said. "But Isabel begged me to come and look for - Dinah." His pause before the name was scarcely perceptible, but that also pierced her through and through. "I don't think she is quite equal to this."

Sir Eustace uttered his faint, contemptuous laugh. "You hear, Dinah?" he said. "This gallant knight has come to your rescue. Look up and tell him if you want to be rescued!"

But she could not look up. She could, only cling to him in voiceless abasement. There was a brief silence, and then she felt his hand upon her head. He spoke again, the sneering note gone from his voice though it still held a faint inflection of sardonic humour.

"You needn't be anxious, most worthy Scott. Leave her to me for five minutes, and I will undertake to return her to Isabel in good condition! You're not wanted for the moment, man. Can't you see it?"

That moved Dinah. She lifted her head from its shelter, and found her voice.

"Oh, don't send him away:" she entreated. "He - he - it was very kind of him to come and look for me."

Eustace's hand caressed her dark hair for a moment. His eyes looked down, into hers, and she saw that the glowing embers of his passion still smouldered there.

She caught her breath with a sob. "Tell him - not to go away!" she begged.

He smiled a little, but electricity lingered in the pressure of his arm. "I think it is time we broke up the meeting," he said. "You had better run back to Isabel. If you wish to keep this episode a secret, Scott is, I believe, gentleman enough to hold his peace."

She was free, and very slowly she released herself. She turned round to Scott, but still she could not - dared not - meet his eyes.

Her limbs were trembling painfully. She felt weak and dizzy. Suddenly she became aware of his hand held out to her, proffering silent assistance.

Thankfully she accepted it, feeling it close firmly, reassuringly, upon her own. "Shall we go upstairs?" he asked, in his quiet, matter-of-fact way. "Isabel is a little anxious about you."

"Oh yes," she whispered tremulously. "Let us go!"

She tottered a little with the words, and he transferred his hold to her elbow. He supported her steadily and sustainingly.

Eustace stepped forward, and lifted the heavy curtain for them with a mask-like ceremony. She glanced up at him as she went through.

"Good night!" he said.

Her lips quivered in response.

He suddenly bent to her. "Good night!" he said again.

There was imperious insistence in his voice. His eyes compelled.

Mutely she responded to the mastery that would not be denied. She lifted her trembling lips to his; and deliberately - in Scott's presence - he kissed her.

"Sleep well!" he said lightly.

She returned his kiss, because she could not do otherwise. She felt as if he had so merged her will into his that she was deprived of all power to resist.

But the hand that held her arm urged her with quiet strength. It led her unfalteringly away.

CHAPTER XXVIII

THE LESSON

Ten minutes later Scott descended the stairs alone and returned to the salon.

A dance was in progress. He stood for a space in the doorway, watching. Finally, having satisfied himself that his brother was not among the dancers, he turned away.

With his usual quietness of demeanour, he crossed the vestibule, and looked into the smoking-room. Sir Eustace was not there either, and he was closing the door again when the man himself came up the passage behind him, and clapped a careless hand on his shoulder.

"Are you looking for me, most doughty knight?" he asked.

Scott turned so sharply that the hand fell. "Yes, I am looking for you," he said, and his voice was unusually curt. "Come outside a minute, will you? I want to speak to you."

"I am not going outside," Sir Eustace said, with exasperating coolness. "If you want to talk, you can come in here and smoke with me."

"I must be alone with you," Scott said briefly. "There are two or three men in there."

His brother gave him a look of amused curiosity. "Do you want to do something violent then? There's plenty of room for a quiet talk in there without disturbing or being disturbed by anyone."

But Scott stood his ground. "I must see you alone for a minute," he said stubbornly. "You can come to my room, or I will come to yours, - whichever you like."

Sir Eustace shrugged his shoulders. "You are damned persistent. I don't know that I am specially anxious to hear what you have to say. In any case it can keep till the morning. I can't be bothered now."

Scott's hand grasped his arm. A queer gleam shone in his pale eyes. "Man," he said, "I think you had better hear me now."

Eustace looked down at him, half-sneering, half-impressed. "What a mule you are, Stumpy! Come along then if you must! But you had better mind how you go. I'm in no mood for trifling."

"Nor I," said Scott, with very unaccustomed bitterness.

He kept his hand upon his brother's arm as they turned. He leaned slightly upon him as they ascended the stairs. Eustace's room was the first they reached, and they turned into that.

Scott was very pale, but there was no lack of resolution about him as he closed the door and faced the elder man.

"Well, what is it?" Eustace demanded.

"Just this." Very steadily Scott made answer. "I want to know how far this matter has gone between you and Miss Bathurst. I want to know - what you are going to do."

"My intentions, eh?" Eustace's sneer became very pronounced as he put the question. He pulled forward a chair and sat down with an arrogant air as though to bring himself thus to Scott's level.

Scott's eyes gleamed again momentarily at the action, but he stood like a rock. "Yes, your intentions," he said briefly.

Sir Eustace's black brows went up, he looked him up and down. "Can you give me any reason at all why I should hold myself answerable to you?" he asked.

Scott's hands clenched as he stood. "I can," he said. "I regard Miss Bathurst as very peculiarly our charge - under our protection. We are both in a great measure responsible for her, though possibly -" he hesitated slightly - "my responsibility is greater than yours, in so far as I take it more seriously. I do not think that either of us is in a position to make love to her under existing circumstances. But that, I admit, is merely a matter of opinion. Most emphatically neither of us has the right to trifle with her. I want to know - and I must know - are you trifling with her, as you have trifled with Miss de Vigne for the past fortnight? Or are you in earnest? Which?"

He spoke sternly, as one delivering an ultimatum. His eyes, steel-bright and unwavering, were fixed upon his brother's face.

Sir Eustace made a sharp gesture, as of one who flings off some stinging insect. "It is not particularly good form on your part to bring another lady's name into the discussion," he said. "At least you have no responsibilities so far as Miss de Vigne is concerned."

"I admit that," Scott answered shortly. "Moreover, she is fully capable of taking care of herself. But Miss Bathurst is not. She is a mere child in many ways, but she takes things hard. If you are merely amusing yourself at her expense -" He stopped.

"Well?" Sir Eustace threw the question with sudden anger. His great, lounging figure stiffened. A blue flame shot up in his eyes.

Scott stood silent for a moment or two; then with a great effort
he unclenched his hands and came forward. "I am not going to
believe that of you unless you tell me it is so," he said.

Sir Eustace reached out an unexpected hand without rising,
and took him by the shoulder. "You may be small of stature,
Stumpy," he said, "but you're the biggest fool I know. You're
making mountains out of molehills, and you'll get yourself
into trouble if you're not careful."

Scott looked at him. "Do you imagine I'm afraid of you, I
wonder?" he said, a faint tremor of irony in his quiet voice.

Sir Eustace's hold tightened. His mouth was hard. "I imagine
that I could make things highly unpleasant for you if you
provoked me too far," he said. "And let me warn you, you have
gone quite far enough in a matter in which you have no
concern whatever. I never have stood any interference from
you and I never will. Let that be understood - once for all!"

He met Scott's look with eyes of smouldering wrath. There
was more than warning in his hold; it conveyed menace.

Yet Scott, very pale, supremely dignified, made no motion to
retreat. "You have not answered me yet," he said. "I must have
an answer."

Sir Eustace's brows met in a thick and threatening line. "You
will have very much more than you bargain for if you persist,"
he said.

"Meaning that I am to draw my own conclusions?" Scott
asked, unmoved.

The smouldering fire suddenly blazed into flame. He pulled
Scott to him with the movement of a giant, and bent him
irresistibly downwards. "I will show you what I mean," he said.

Scott made a swift, instinctive effort to free himself, but the

Ethel M. Dell

next instant he was passive. Only as the relentless hands forced him lower he spoke, his voice quick and breathless.

"You can hammer me to your heart's content, but you'll get nothing out of it. That sort of thing simply doesn't count - with me."

Sir Eustace held him in a vice-like grip. "Are you going to take it lying down then?" he questioned grimly.

"I'm not going to fight you certainly." Scott's voice had a faint quiver of humour in it, as though he jested at his own expense. "Not - that is - in a physical sense. If you choose to resort to brute force, that's your affair. And I fancy you'll be sorry afterwards. But it will make no actual difference to me." He broke off, breathing short and hard, like a man who struggles against odds yet with no thought of yielding.

Sir Eustace held him a few seconds as if irresolute, then abruptly let him go. "I believe you're right," he said. "You wouldn't care a damn. But you're a fool to bait me all the same. Now clear out, and leave me alone for the future!"

"I haven't done with you yet," Scott said. He straightened himself, and returned indomitably to the attack. "I asked you a question, and - so far - you haven't answered it. Are you ashamed to answer it?"

Sir Eustace got up with a movement of exasperation, but very oddly his anger had died down. "Oh, confound you, Stumpy! You're worse than a swarm of mosquitoes!" he said. "I dispute your right to ask that question. It is no affair of yours."

"I maintain that it is," Scott said quietly. "It matters to me - perhaps more than you realize - whether you behave honourably or otherwise."

"Honourably!" His brother caught him up sharply. "You're on dangerous ground, I warn you," he said. "I won't stand that from you or any man."

"I've no intention of insulting you," Scott answered. "But I must know the truth. Are you hoping to marry Miss Bathurst, or are you not?"

Sir Eustace drew himself up with a haughty gesture. "The time has not come to talk of that," he said.

"Not when you are deliberately making love to her?" Scott's voice remained quiet, but the glitter was in his eyes again - a quivering, ominous gleam.

"Oh, that! My dear fellow, you are disquieting yourself in vain. She knows as well as I do that that is a mere game." Eustace spoke scoffingly, looking over his brother's head, ignoring his attitude. "I assure you she is not so green as you imagine," he said. "It has been nothing but a game all through."

"Nothing but a game!" Scott repeated the words slowly as if incredulous. "Do you actually mean that?"

Sir Eustace laughed and took out his cigarettes. "What do you take me for, you old duffer? Think I should commit myself at this stage? An old hand like me! Not likely!"

Scott stood up before him, white to the lips. "I take you for an infernal blackguard, if you want to know!" he said, speaking with great distinctness. "You may call yourself a man of honour. I call you a scoundrel!"

"What?" Eustace put back his cigarette-case with a smile that was oddly like a snarl. "It looks to me as if you'll have to have that lesson after all," he said. "What's the matter with you now-a-days? Fallen in love yourself? Is that it?"

He took Scott by the shoulders, not roughly, but with power.

Scott's eyes met his like a sword in a master-hand. "The matter

Ethel M. Dell

is," he said, "that this precious game of yours has got to end. If you are not man enough to end it - I will."

"Will you indeed?" Eustace shook him to and fro as he stood, but still without violence. "And how?"

"I shall tell her," Scott spoke without the smallest hesitation, "the exact truth. I shall tell her - and she will believe me - precisely what you are."

"Damn you!" said Sir Eustace.

With the words he shifted his grasp, took Scott by the collar, and swung him round.

"Then you may also tell her," he said, his voice low and furious, "that you have had the kicking that a little yapping cur like you deserves."

He kicked him with the words, kicked him thrice, and flung him brutally aside.

Scott went down, grabbing vainly at the bed to save himself. His face was deathly as he turned it, but he said nothing. He had said his say.

Sir Eustace was white also, white and terrible, with eyes of flame. He stood a moment, glaring down at him. Then, as though he could not trust himself, wheeled and strode to the door.

"And when you've done," he said, "you can come to me for another, you beastly little cad!"

He went, leaving the door wide behind him. His feet resounded along the passage and died away. The distant waltz-music came softly in. And Scott pulled himself painfully up and sat on the end of the bed, panting heavily.

Minutes passed ere he moved. Then at last very slowly he got up. He had recovered his breath. His mouth was firm, his eyes resolute and indomitable, his whole bearing composed, as with that dignity that Dinah had so often remarked in him he limped to the door and passed out, closing it quietly behind him.

The dance-music was still floating through the passages with a mocking allurement. The tramp of feet and laughter of many voices rose with it. A flicker of irony passed over his drawn face. He straightened his collar with absolute steadiness, and moved away in the direction of his own room.

CHAPTER XXIX

THE CAPTIVE

Isabel uttered no reproaches to her charge as, quivering with shame, she returned from her escapade. She exchanged no more than a low "Good night!" with Scott, and then turned back into the room with Dinah. But as the latter stood before her, crest-fallen and humiliated, expecting a reprimand, she only laid very gentle hands upon her and began to unfasten her dress.

"I wasn't spying upon you, dear child," she said. "I only looked in to see if you would care for a cup of milk last thing."

That broke Dinah utterly and overwhelmingly. In her contrition, she cast herself literally at Isabel's feet. "Oh, what a beast I am! What a beast!" she sobbed. "Will you ever forgive me? I shall never forgive myself!"

Isabel was very tender with her, checking her wild outburst with loving words. She asked no question as to what had been happening, for which forbearance Dinah's gratitude was great even though it served to intensify her remorse. With all a mother's loving care she soothed her, assuring her of complete forgiveness and understanding.

"I did wild things in my own girlhood," she said. "I know what it means, dear, when temptation comes."

And so at last she calmed her agitation, and helped her to bed, waiting upon her with the utmost gentleness, saying no word of blame or even of admonition.

Not till she had gone, did it dawn upon Dinah that this task had probably been left to Scott, and with the thought a great dread of the morrow came upon her. Though he had betrayed no hint of displeasure, she felt convinced that she had incurred it; and all her new-born shyness in his presence, returned upon her a thousandfold. She did not know how she would face him when the morning came.

He would not be angry she knew. He would not scold her like Colonel de Vigne. But yet she shrank from the thought of his disappointment in her as she had never before shrunk from the Colonel's rebuke. She was sure that she had forfeited his good opinion for ever, and many and bitter were the tears that she shed over her loss.

Her thoughts of Eustace were of too confused a nature to be put into coherent form. The moment they turned in his direction her brain became a flashing whirl in which doubts, fears, and terrible ectasies ran wild riot. She lay and trembled at the memory of his strength, exulting almost in the same moment that he had stooped with such mastery to possess her. His magnificence dazzled her, deprived her of all powers of rational judgment. She only realized that she - and she alone - had been singled out of the crowd for that fiery worship; and it seemed to her that she had been created for that one splendid purpose.

But always the memory of Scott shot her triumph through with a regret so poignant as to deprive it of all lasting rapture. She had hurt him, she had disappointed him; she did not know how she would ever look him in the eyes again.

Her sleep throughout that last night was broken and unrefreshing, and ever the haunting strains of *Simple Aveu* pulsed through her brain like a low voice calling her perpetually, refusing to be stilled. Only one night more and she would be back in her home; this glittering, Alpine dream would be over, never to return. And again she turned on her pillow and wept. It was so hard, so hard, to go back.

In the morning she arose white-faced and weary, with dark shadows under her eyes, and a head that throbbed tormentingly. She breakfasted with Isabel in the latter's room, and was again deeply grateful to her friend for forbearing to comment upon her subdued manner. She could not make any pretence at cheerfulness that day, being in fact still so near to tears that she could scarcely keep from breaking down.

"Don't wait for me, dear!" Isabel said gently at length. "I see you are not hungry. We are taking some provisions with us; perhaps you will feel more like eating presently."

Dinah escaped very thankfully and returned to her own room.

Here she remained for awhile till more sure of herself; then Biddy came in to finish her packing and she slipped away to avoid the old woman's shrewd observation. She feared to go downstairs lest she should meet Scott; but presently, as she hovered in the passage, she heard his halting tread in the main corridor.

He was evidently on his way to his sister's room, and seizing her opportunity, she ran like a hare in the opposite direction and managed to slip downstairs without adventure.

She was not to escape unnoticed, however. The first person she encountered in the vestibule came forward instantly at sight of her with the promptitude of one who has been lying in wait.

She recoiled with a gasp, but she could not run away. She was caught as surely as she had been the night before.

"Hullo!" smiled Sir Eustace, with extended hand. "Going out for a last look round? May I come too?"

She felt the dominance of his grip. It was coolly, imperially possessive. To answer his request seemed superfluous, even bordering upon presumption. It was obvious that he had every intention of accompanying her.

She gave a confused murmur of assent, and they passed through the vestibule side by side. She was conscious of curious glances from several strangers who were standing about, and Eustace exchanged a few words with a species of regal condescension here and there as they went. And then they were out in the pure sunlight of the mountains, alone for the last time in their paradise of snow.

Almost instinctively Dinah turned up the winding track. They had half an hour before them, and she felt she could not bear to stand still. He strolled beside her, idly smoking, not troubling to make conversation, now as ever sublimely at his ease.

The snow sparkled around them like a thousand gems Dinah's eyes were burning and smarting with the brightness. And still that tender waltz-music ran lilting through her brain, drifting as it were through the mist of her unshed tears.

Suddenly he spoke. They were nearing the pine-wood and quite alone. "Is there anything the matter?"

She choked down a great lump in her throat before she could speak in answer. "No," she murmured then. "I - I am just - rather low about leaving; that's all."

"Quite all?" he said.

His tone was so casual, so normal, that it seemed impossible now to think of last night's happening save as an extravagant dream. She almost felt for the moment as if she had imagined it all. And then he spoke again, and she caught a subtle note of tenderness in his voice that brought it all back upon her in an overwhelming rush.

Ethel M. Dell

"That's really all, is it? You're not unhappy about anything else? Scott hasn't been bullying you?"

She gasped at the question. "Oh no! Oh no! He wouldn't! He couldn't! I - haven't even seen him today."

He received the information in silence; but in a moment or two he tossed away his cigarette with the air of a man having come to an abrupt resolution.

"And so you're fretting about going home?" he said.

She nodded mutely. The matter would not bear discussion.

"Poor little Daphne!" he said. "It's been a good game, hasn't it?"

She nodded again. "Just like the dreams that never come true," she managed to say.

"Would you like it to come true?" he asked her unexpectedly.

She glanced up at him with a woeful little smile. "It's no good thinking of that, is it?" she said.

"I have an idea we could make it come true between us," he said.

She shook her head. That brief glimpse of his intent eyes had sent a sudden and overwhelming wave of shyness through her. She remembered again the fiery holding of his arms, and was afraid.

He paused in his walk and turned aside to the railing that bounded the side of the track above the steep, pine-covered descent. "Wish hard enough," he said, "and all dreams come true!"

Dinah went with him as if compelled. She leaned against the

railing, glad of the support, while he sat down upon it. His attitude was supremely easy and self-possessed.

"Do you know, Daphne," he said, "I've taken a fancy to that particular dream myself? Now I've caught you, I don't see myself letting you go again."

Her heart throbbed at his words. She bent her head, fixing her eyes upon the rough wood upon which she leaned.

"But it's no good, is it?" she said, almost below her breath. "I've just got to go."

He put his hand on her shoulder, and she was conscious afresh of the electricity of his touch. She shrank a little - a very little; for she was frightened, albeit curiously aware of a magnetism that drew her irresistibly.

"Yes, I suppose you've got to go," he said. "But - there's nothing to prevent me following you, is there?"

She quivered from head to foot. That hand upon her shoulder sent such a tumult of emotions through her that she could not collect her thoughts in any coherent order. "I - I don't know," she whispered, bending her head still lower. "They - I don't know what they would say at home."

"Your people?" His hand was drawing her now with an insistent pressure that would not be denied. "They'd probably dance on their heads with delight," he said, his tone one of slightly supercilious humour. "I assure you I am considered something of a catch by a good many anxious mammas."

She started at that, started and straightened herself, lifting shy eyes to his. "Oh, but we've only been - playing," she said rather uncertainly. "Just - just pretending to flirt, that's all."

He laughed, bending his handsome, imperious face to hers. "It's been a fairly solid pretence, hasn't it?" he said. "But I'm proposing something slightly different now. I'm offering you my hand - as well as my heart."

Dinah was trembling all over. She gasped for breath, drawing back slightly from the nearness of his lips. "Do you mean - you'd like - to marry me?" she whispered tremulously, and hid her face on the instant; for the bald words sounded preposterous.

He laughed again, softly, half-mockingly, and drew her into his arms. "Whatever made you think of that, my elf of the mountains? I'll vow it came into your head first. Ah, you needn't hide your eyes from me. I know you're mine - all mine. I've known it from the first - ever since you began to run away. But I've caught you now. Haven't I? Haven't I?"

She clung to him desperately. It seemed the only way; for she was for the moment swept off her feet, terribly afraid of arousing that storm of passion which had so overwhelmed her the night before. Instinct warned her what to expect if she attempted to withdraw herself. Moreover, the tumult of her feeling was such that she did not want to do so. She wanted only to hide her head for a space, and be still.

He pressed her close, still laughing at her shyness. "What a good thing I'm not shy!" he said. "If I were, to-day would be the end of everything instead of the beginning. Can't you bring yourself to look at your new possession? Did you think you could laugh and run away for all time?"

Then, as in muffled accents she besought him to be patient with her, he softened magically and for the first time spoke of love.

"Don't you know you have wrenched the very heart out of me, you little brown witch? I loved you from the very first moment of our dance together. You've been too much for me all through. I had to have you. I simply had to have you."

She trembled afresh at his words, but she clung closer. If the fear deepened, so also did the fascination. She tried to picture him as hers - hers, and failed. He was so fine, so splendid, so much too big for her.

He went on, dropping his voice lower, his breath warm upon her neck. "Are you going to take all and give - nothing, Daphne? Did they make you without a heart, I wonder? Like a robin that mates afresh a dozen times in a season? Haven't you anything to give me, little sweetheart? Are you going to keep me waiting for a long, long time, and then send me empty away?"

That moved her. That he should stoop to plead with her seemed so amazing, almost a fabulous state of affairs.

With a little sob, she lifted her face at last. "Oh, Apollo!" she said brokenly. "Apollo the magnificent! I am all yours - all yours! But don't - don't take too much - at a time!"

The plea must have touched him, accompanied as it was by that full surrender. He held her a moment, looking down into her eyes with the fiery possessiveness subdued to a half-veiled tenderness in his own.

Then, very gently, even with reverence, he bent his face to hers. "Give me - just what you can spare, then, little sweetheart!" he said. "I can always come again for more now."

She slipped her arms around his neck, and shyly, childishly, she kissed the lips that had devoured her own so mercilessly the night before.

"Yes - yes, I will always give you more!" she said tremulously.

He took her face between his hands and kissed her in return, not violently, but with confidence. "That seals you for my very own," he said. "You will never run away from me again?"

But she would not promise that. The memory of the previous night still scorched her intolerably whenever her thoughts turned that way.

"I shan't want to run away if - if you stay as you are now," she told him confusedly.

He laughed in his easy way. "Oh, Daphne, I shall have a lot to teach you when we are married. How soon do you think you can be ready?"

She started in his hold at the question, and then quickly gave herself fully back to him again. "I don't know a bit. You'll have to ask mother. P'raps - she may not allow it at all."

"Ho! Won't she?" said Sir Eustace. "I think I know better. What about that trip on the yacht in July? Can you be ready in time for that?"

"Oh, I expect I could be ready sooner than that," said Dinah naively.

"You could?" He smiled upon her. "Well, next week then! What do you say to next week?"

But she shrank again at that. "Oh no! Not possibly! Not possibly! You - you're laughing!" She looked at him accusingly.

He caught her to him. "You baby! You innocent! Yes, I'm going to kiss you. Where will you have it? Just anywhere?"

He held her and kissed her, still laughing, yet with a heat that made her flinch involuntarily; kissed the pointed chin and quivering lips, the swift-shut eyes and soft cheeks, the little, trembling dimple that came and went.

"Yes, you are mine - all mine," he said. "Remember, I have a right to you now that no one else has. Not all the mammas in the world could come between us now."

She laughed, half-exultantly, half-dubiously, peeping at him through her lowered lashes. "I wonder if you'll still say that when - when you've seen - my mother," she murmured.

He kissed her again, kissed anew the dimples that showed and vanished so alluringly. "You will see presently, my Daphne," he said. "But I'm going to have you, you know. That's quite understood, isn't it?"

"Yes," whispered Dinah, with docility.

"No more running away," he insisted. "That's past and done with."

She gave him a fleeting smile. "I couldn't if - if I wanted to."

"I'm glad you realize that," he said.

She clung to him suddenly with a little movement that was almost convulsive. "Oh, are you sure - quite sure - that you wouldn't rather marry Rose de Vigne?"

He uttered his careless laugh. "My dear child, there are plenty of Roses in the world. There is only one - Daphne - Daphne, the fleet of foot - Daphne, the enchantress!"

She clung to him a little faster. "And there is only one Apollo," she murmured. "Apollo the magnificent!"

"We seem to be quite a unique couple," laughed Eustace, with his lips upon her hair.

CHAPTER XXX

THE SECOND SUMMONS

When they went down the hill again to the hotel, Dinah felt as if she were treading on air. The whole world had magically changed for her. Fears still lurked in the background, such fears as she did not dare to turn and contemplate; but she herself had stepped into such a blaze of sunshine that she felt literally bathed from head to foot in the glow.

Her dread of returning to the old home-life had dwindled to a mere shadow. Sir Eustace's absolute confidence on the subject of his desirability as a husband had accomplished this. There would be paens of rejoicing, he told her, and she had actually begun to think that he spoke the truth. She was quite convinced that her mother would be pleased. It was Cinderella and the prince indeed. Who could be otherwise?

Her escapade of the night before had also shrunk to a matter of small importance. Eustace in his grand, easy way had justified her, and she was no longer tormented by the thought of the mute reproach she would encounter in Scott's eyes. She was triumphantly vindicated, and no one would dream of reproaching her now. Isabel too - surely Isabel would be glad, would welcome her as a sister, though the realization of this nearness of relationship made her blush in sheer horror at her presumption.

She to be Lady Studley! She - little, insignificant, moneyless

Dinah! The thought of Rose's soft patronage flashed through her brain, and she chuckled aloud. Poor dear Rose, waiting for him at the Court, expecting every day to hear of his promised advent! What a shock for them all! Why, she would rank with the County now! Even Lady Grace would scarcely be in a position to patronize her! Again, quite involuntarily, she chuckled.

"What's the joke?" demanded Sir Eustace.

She blushed very deeply, realizing that she had allowed her thoughts to run away with her.

"There isn't a joke really," she told him. "It wasn't important anyhow. I was only thinking how - how surprised the de Vignes would be."

He frowned momentarily; then he laughed. "Proud of your conquest, eh?" he asked.

She blushed still more deeply. "It's easy to laugh now, but I shall never dare to face them," she murmured.

He took her hand as they walked, linking his fingers in hers with a careless air of possession. "When you are Lady Studley," he said, "I shall not allow you to knock under to anyone - except your husband."

She gave a faint laugh. "I - shall have to learn to swagger," she said. "But I'm afraid I shall never do it as well as you do."

"What? Swagger?" He frowned again. "How dare you accuse me of that?"

"Oh, I didn't! I don't!" Hastily she sought to avert his displeasure. "No, no! I only meant that you were born to it. I'm not. I - I'm very ordinary; not nearly good enough for you."

His frown melted again. "You are - Daphne," he said. "Ah! Here is Scott, coming to look for us! Who is going to break the news to him?"

She made a small, ineffectual attempt to release her hand. Then, under her breath, "He - saw you kiss me last night," she whispered. "Don't you think he may have guessed already?"

A very cynical look came into Eustace's face. "I wonder," he said briefly.

They went on side by side down the white, shining track; but Dinah was no longer treading on air. She could see the slight, insignificant figure that awaited them close to the hotel-entrance, and her heart felt oddly weighted within her. It was not the memory of the night before that oppressed her. That episode had faded almost into nothingness. But the ordeal of facing him, of telling him of the wonderful thing that had just happened to her, seemed suddenly more than she could bear. Something within her seemed to cry out against it. She had a curious feeling of looking out at him across great billows of seething uncertainty that rolled ever higher and higher between them, threatening to separate them for all time.

Yet when she neared him, the tumult of feeling sank again as the quietness of his presence reached her. Out of the tempest she found herself drifting into a safe harbour of still waters.

He moved to meet them, and she heard his voice greet her as he raised his cap. "So you have been for your farewell stroll!"

She did not answer in words, only she freed her hand from Eustace with a resolute little tug and gave it to him.

Eustace spoke, a species of half-veiled insolence in his tone. "Like the psalmist she went forth weeping and has returned bearing her sheaf with her - in the form of a fairly substantial *fiance*."

Dinah ventured to cast a lightning-glance at Scott to see how he took the information and was conscious of an instant's shock. He looked so grey, so ill, like a man who had received a deadly wound.

But the impression passed in a flash as she felt his hand close upon hers.

"My dear," he said simply, "I'm awfully pleased."

The warm grasp did her good. It brought her swiftly back to a normal state of mind. She drew a hard breath and met his eyes, reassuring herself in a moment with the conviction that after all he looked quite as usual. Somehow her imagination had tricked her. His kindly smile seemed to make everything right.

"Oh, it is kind of you not to mind," she said impulsively.

Whereat Sir Eustace laughed. "He is rather magnanimous, isn't he? Well, come along and tell Isabel!"

Scott's eyes came swiftly to him. He released Dinah, and offered his hand to his brother. "Let me congratulate you, old chap!" he said, his voice rather low. "I hope you will both have - all happiness."

"Thanks!" said Eustace. He took the hand, looking at the younger man with keen, hawk-eyes. "We mean to make a bid for it anyway. Dinah is lucky in one thing at least. She will have an ideal brother-in-law."

The words were carelessly spoken, but they were not without meaning. Scott flushed slightly; even while for an instant he smiled. "I shall do my best in that capacity," he said. "But before you go in, I want you to wait a moment. Isabel has had a slight fainting attack. We mustn't take her by surprise."

"A fainting attack!" Sharply Eustace echoed the words. "How did it happen?" he demanded.

Scott raised his shoulders. "We were talking together. I can't tell you exactly what caused it. It came rather suddenly. Biddy and I brought her round almost immediately, and she declares that she will make the journey. She did not wish me to tell you of it, but I thought it better."

"Of coarse." Sir Eustace's voice was short and stern; his face wore a heavy frown. "But something must have caused it. What were you talking about?"

Scott hesitated for a second. "I can't tell you that, old fellow," he said then.

Eustace uttered a brief laugh. "Too personal, eh? Well, how did it happen? Did she suddenly lose consciousness?"

"She suddenly gasped, and said her heart had stopped. She fell across the table. I called to Biddy, and we lifted her and gave her brandy. That brought her to very quickly. I left her lying down in her room. But she says she feels much better, and she is very set upon leaving the arrangements for the journey unaltered."

Scott spoke rather wearily. Dinah's heart went out to him in swift sympathy which she did not know how to express.

"May I - could I - go to her?" she suggested, after a moment timidly.

Scott turned to her instantly. "Please do! I know she would like to see you. We ought to be starting in another quarter of an hour. The sleigh will be here directly."

"May I do as I like about - about telling her?" Dinah asked, pausing.

Scott's eyes shone with a very kindly gleam. "Of course, I know you will not startle her. You always do her good."

The words followed her as she turned away. How good he was to her! How full of understanding and human sympathy! Her heart throbbed with a warmth that filled her with an odd desire to weep. She wished that Eustace did not treat him quite so arrogantly.

And then, looking back, she reproached herself for the thought; for Eustace had linked a hand in his arm, and she saw that they were walking together in complete accord.

"But I will never - no, never - call him Stumpy!" she said to herself, as she passed into the hotel.

She went up the stairs rapidly, and hastened to Isabel's room. That look she had caught in Scott's face - that stricken look - had doubtless been brought there by his sudden anxiety for his sister. That would fully account for it, she was sure.

On the threshold of Isabel's room an overwhelming nervousness assailed her. How was she going to tell her of the wonderful event that had taken place in the last half-hour? On the other hand, how could she possibly suppress so tremendous a matter? And again, the disquieting question arose; could she be ill - really ill? Scott had looked so troubled - so unutterably sad.

With an effort she summoned her courage, and softly knocked.

Instantly a low voice answered her, bidding her enter. She opened the door and went in, feeling as though she were treading sacred ground.

But Isabel's voice spoke again instantly, greeting her; and in a moment all her doubts, all her forebodings, were gone.

"Come in, little sweetheart!" Isabel said.

And she advanced with quickened steps to find Isabel lying propped on the sofa, looking at her, smiling up at her, with such a glory on her wasted face as made it "as it had been the face of an angel."

In an instant Dinah was on her knees beside her, with loving arms clasping her close. "Oh, darling, I've only just heard. Are you better? Are you better?" she said yearningly.

Isabel held her, and fondly kissed the upturned lips. "Why, I believe Scott has been frightening you," she said. "Silly fellow! Yes, dear. I am well - quite well."

"You are sure?" Dinah insisted. "You are really not ill?"

Isabel's smile had in it - had she but known it - a gleam of the Divine. "My dearest, all is well with me," she said. "I lay down for a little to please Scott. But I am going to get up now. Where have you been since *dejeuner*? I missed you."

Dinah clung closer, hiding her face.

Instantly Isabel's arms tightened. The passionate tenderness of them thrilled her through and through. "Why, child, what has happened?" she whispered. "Tell me! Tell me!"

But Dinah only hid her face a little deeper. "I don't know how," she murmured.

There fell a silence. Then, under her breath, Isabel spoke. "My darling, whisper - just whisper! Who - is it?"

And very, very faintly, at last Dinah made answer. "It - it is - Sir Eustace."

There fell another silence, longer, deeper, than the first. Then Isabel uttered a short, hard sigh, and, stooping, kissed the bowed, curly head. "God bless and keep you always, dearest!" she said.

Something in the words - or was it the tone? - pierced Dinah.

She turned her face slightly upwards. "I - I was afraid you wouldn't be pleased," she faltered. "Do - do forgive me - if you can!"

"Forgive you!" All the wealth of Isabel's love was in the words. "Why, darling, I have been wanting you for my own little sister ever since I first saw you."

"Oh, have you?" Eagerly Dinah lifted her head. Her eyes were shining, her cheeks very flushed. "Then you are pleased?" she said earnestly. "You really are pleased?"

Isabel smiled at her very sadly, very fondly. "My darling, if you are happy, I am more than pleased," she said.

Yet Dinah was puzzled, not wholly satisfied. She received Isabel's kiss with a certain wistfulness. "I feel - somehow - as if I've done wrong," she said. "Yet - yet - Scott -" she halted over the name, uttering it shyly - "said he was - awfully pleased."

"Ah! You have told Scott!" There was a sharp, almost a wrung, sound in Isabel's voice; but the next moment she controlled it, and spoke with steady resolution. "Then, my dear, you needn't have any misgivings. If you love Eustace and he loves you, it is the best thing possible for you both." She held Dinah to her again and kissed her; then very tenderly released her. "You must run and get ready, dear child. It is getting late."

Dinah went obediently, still with that bewildered feeling of having somehow taken a wrong turning. She was convinced in her own mind that the news had not been welcome to Isabel, disguise it how she would. And suddenly through her mind there ran the memory of those words she had uttered a few weeks before. "Never prefer the tinsel to the true gold!" She had not fully understood their meaning then. Now very vividly it flashed upon her. Isabel had compared her two brothers in that brief sentence. Isabel's estimate of the one was as low as that of the other was high. Isabel did not love Eustace - the handsome, debonair brother who had once been all the world to her.

A little, sick feeling of doubt went through Dinah! Had she - by any evil chance - had she made a mistake?

And then the man's overwhelming personality swung suddenly through her consciousness, filling all her being, possessing her, dominating her. She flung the doubt from her, as one flings away a poisonous insect. He was her own - her very own; her lover, the first, the best, - Apollo the Magnificent!

In Isabel's room old Biddy Maloney stood, gazing down at her mistress with eyes of burning devotion.

"And is it yourself that's feeling better now?" she questioned fondly.

Isabel raised herself, smiling her sad smile. "Oh, Biddy," she said, "for myself I feel that all is well - all will be well. The dawn draws nearer - every hour."

Biddy shook her head with pursed lips. "Ye shouldn't talk so, mavourneen. It's the Almighty who has the ruling. Ye wouldn't wish to go before your time?"

"Before my time! Oh, Biddy! When I have lingered in the prison-house so long!" Slowly Isabel rose to her feet. She looked at Biddy almost whimsically. "I think He will take that into the reckoning," she said. "Do you know, Biddy, this is the second summons that has come to me? And I think - I think," her face was glorified again as the face of one who sees a vision - "I think the third will be the last."

Biddy's black eyes screwed up suddenly. She turned her face away.

"Will we be getting ready to go now, Miss Isabel?" she asked after a moment, in a voice that shook.

The glory died out of Isabel's face, though the reflection of it still lingered in her eyes. "I am very selfish, Biddy," she said. "Can you guess what Miss Dinah has just told me?"

"Arrah thin, I can," said Biddy, with a touch of aggressiveness. "I've seen it coming for a long time past. And ye didn't ought to allow it at all, Miss Isabel. It's a mistake, that's what it is. It's just a bad mistake."

"Not if he loves her, Biddy." Isabel spoke gently, but there was a hint of reproof in her voice.

Biddy, however, remained quite unabashed. "He love her!" she snorted. "As if he ever loved anybody besides himself! Talk about the lion and the lamb, Miss Isabel! It's a cruel shame to let her go to such as him. And what'll poor Master Scott do at all? And he worshipping the little fairy feet of her!"

"Hush, Biddy, hush!" Isabel spoke with decision. "I hope - I trust - that he isn't very grievously disappointed. But if he is, it is the one thing that neither you nor I must ever seem to suspect."

"Ah!" grumbled Biddy mutinously. "And isn't that just like Sir Eustace, with all the world to pick from, to choose the one thing - the one little wild rose - as Master Scott had set his heart on? He's done it from his cradle. Always the one thing someone else wanted he must grab for himself. But is it too late, Miss Isabel darlint?" Sudden hope shone in the old woman's eyes. "Is it really too late? Couldn't ye drop a hint to the dear lamb? Sure and she's fond of Master Scott! Maybe she'd turn to him after all if she knew."

Isabel shook her head almost sternly. "Biddy, no! This is no affair of ours. If Master Scott suspected for a moment what you have just said to me, he would never forgive you."

"May I come in?" said Scott's voice at the door. "My dear, you are looking better. Are you well enough to start?"

"Yes, of course." Isabel moved towards him, her hands extended in mute affection.

He took and held them. "Dinah has told you? I am sure you are glad. Eustace is waiting downstairs. Come and tell him how glad you are!"

His eyes, very straight and steadfast, met hers.

Isabel tried to speak in answer, but caught her breath in a sudden sob.

He waited a second. Then, "Isabel!" he said gently.

Sharply she controlled herself. "Yes. Yes. Let us go!" she said. "I must - congratulate Eustace."

They went; and old Biddy was left alone.

She looked after them with a piteous expression on her wrinkled face; then suddenly, with a wistful gesture, she clasped her old worn hands.

"I pray the Almighty," she said, with great earnestness, "to open the dear young lady's eyes, before it is too late. And if He wants anyone to help Him - sure it's meself that'll be only too pleased."

It was the most impressive prayer that Biddy had ever uttered.

PART II

CHAPTER I

CINDERELLA'S PRINCE

The early dusk of February was falling, together with a fine, drenching rain. The trees that over-hung the muddy lane were beating their stark branches together as though in despair over the general hopelessness of the outlook. The west wind that raced across the brown fields had the sharpness of snow in its train.

"We shall catch it before we've done," said Bathurst to his hunter.

Rupert the hunter, a dapple grey with powerful hindquarters, cocked a knowing ear in a fashion that Dinah always described as "his smile."

It had not been a good day for either of them. The meet had been at a considerable distance, there had been no run worth mentioning; and now that it was over they were returning, thoroughly tired, from the kennels.

Bathurst's pink coat clung to him like a sack, all streaked and darkened with rain. It had weathered a good many storms in its time, as its many varieties of tint testified; but despite this fact, its wearer never failed to look a sportsman and a gentleman. There was nothing of the vagabond about

Bathurst, but he had the vagabond's facility for making himself at home wherever he went. He was never at a loss, never embarrassed, never affronted. He took life easily, as he himself put it; and on the whole he found it good.

Riding home at a jog-trot in that driving rain with the prospect of having to feed and rub down Rupert at the end of it before he could attend to his own needs was not a particularly entrancing prospect; but he faced it philosophically. After today the little girl would be at home, and she could do it for him again. She loved to wait on him hand and foot, and it really was a pleasure to let her.

He whistled cheerily to himself as he wended his leisurely way through the dripping lane that made the shortest cut to his home. It would be nice to have the little girl home again. Lydia was all very well - a good wife, as wives went - but there was no doubt about it that Dinah's presence made a considerable difference to his comfort. The child was quick to forestall his wants; he sometimes thought that she was even more useful to him than a valet would have been. He had missed her more than he would have dreamed possible.

Lydia had missed her too; he was sure of that. She had been peculiarly short of temper lately. Not that he ever took much notice; he was too used to her tantrums for that. But it certainly was more comfortable when Dinah was at home to bear the brunt of them. Yes, on the whole he was quite pleased that the little girl was coming back. It would make a difference to him in many ways.

He wondered what time she would arrive. He had known, but he had forgotten. He believed it was to be some time in the evening. Her grand friends had arranged to stay at Great Mallowes, three miles, away for the night, and one of them - the maid probably - was to bring Dinah home. He had smiled over this arrangement, and Lydia had openly scoffed at it. As if a girl of Dinah's age were not capable of travelling alone! But then of course she had been ill, very ill according to all

Ethel M. Dell

accounts; and it was quite decent of them to bestow so much care upon her.

He fell to wondering if the child had got spoilt at all during her long absence from home and the harsh discipline thereof. If so, there was a hard time before her; for Lydia was never one to stand any nonsense. She had always been hard on her first-born, unreasonably hard, he sometimes thought; though it was not his business to interfere. The task of chastising the daughter of the family was surely the mother's exclusive prerogative; and certainly Lydia had carried it out very thoroughly. And if at times he thought her over-severe, he could not deny that the result achieved was eminently satis-factory. Dinah was always docile and active in his service - altogether a very good child; and this was presumably due to her mother's training. No, on the whole he had not much fault to find with either of them. Doubtless Lydia understood her own sex best.

He was nearing the end of the long lane; it terminated close to his home. Rupert quickened his pace. They were both splashed with mud from shoulder to heel. They had both had more than enough of the wet and the slush.

"That's right, Rupert, my boy!" the man murmured. "Finish in style!"

They came out from beneath the over-arching trees, emerging upon the high road that led from Great Mallowes to Perrythorpe. The hoot of a motor-horn caused Rupert to prick his ears, and his master reined him back as two great, shining head-lights appeared round a curve. They drew swiftly near, flashed past, and were gone meteor-like into the gloom.

"Whose car was that, I wonder?" mused Bathurst.

"The de Vignes's? It didn't look like one of the Court cars, but the old bird is always buying something new. Lucky devil!"

The thought of the Colonel renewed his thoughts of Dinah. Certain hints the former had dropped had made him wonder a little if the child were always as demure as she seemed. Not that Colonel de Vigne had actually found fault with her. He was plainly fond of her. But he had not spoken as if Dinah had effaced herself as completely abroad as she did at home.

"Oh, yes, the little baggage enjoyed herself - was as gay as a lark - till she got ill," he had said. "You may find her something of a handful when she gets back, Bathurst. She's stretched her wings a bit since she left you."

Bathurst shrugged his shoulders with the comforting reflection that he would not have the trouble of dealing with her. If she had been giddy, after all, it was but natural. Her mother had not been particularly steady in the days of her wild youth. And anyhow he was sure her mother would speedily break her in again. She had a will of iron before which Dinah was *always* forced to bend.

He rode on along the highroad. It was not more than half a mile farther to his home on the outskirts of the village. Somewhere in the gloom ahead of him church-bells were pealing. It was practice-night, he remembered. Dinah loved the sound of the bells. She would feel that they were ringing in her honour. Funny little Dinah! The child was full of fancies of that sort. Just as well perhaps, for it was the only form of amusement that ever came into her home life.

The gay peal turned into a deafening clashing as at length he neared his home. The old church stood only a stone's throw further on. They were ringing the joy-bells with a vengeance. And then very suddenly he caught sight of the tail-lamp of a car close to his own gate.

Dinah had returned then. They had actually chartered that car to convey her from Great Mallowes. He pursed his lips to a whistle. The little girl had been in clover indeed.

"She certainly won't think much of the home crusts after this," he murmured to himself.

He walked Rupert round to the tumble-down stable, and dismounted.

For the next quarter of an hour he was busy over the animal. He thought it a little strange that Dinah did not spy the stable-lamp from the kitchen and come dancing out to greet him. He also wondered why the car lingered so long. It looked as if someone other than the maid had accompanied her, and were staying to tea.

He never took tea after a day's hunting; hot whisky and water and a bath formed his customary programme, and then a tasty supper and bed.

He supposed on this occasion that he would have to go in and show himself, though he was certainly not fit to be seen. Reluctantly he pulled the bedraggled pink coat on again. After all, it did not greatly matter. Hunting was its own excuse. No sportsman ever returned in the apple-pie order in which he started.

Carelessly he sauntered in by way of the back premises, and was instantly struck by the sound of a man's voice, well-bred, with a slightly haughty intonation, speaking in one of the front rooms of the little house.

"Dinah seemed to think that she could not keep it in till to-morrow," it said, with easy assurance. "So I thought I had better come along with her to-night and get it over."

The words reached Bathurst as he arrived in the small square hall, and he stopped dead. "Hullo! Hullo!" he murmured softly to himself.

And then came his wife's voice, a harsh, determined voice, "Do I understand that you wish to marry my daughter?"

"That's the idea," came the suave reply. "You don't know me, of course, but I think I can satisfy you that I am not an undesirable *parti*. My family is considered fairly respectable, as old families go. I am the ninth baronet in direct succession; and I have a very fair amount of worldly goods to offer my wife."

Mrs. Bathurst broke in upon him, a tremor of eagerness in her hard voice. "If that is the case, of course I have no objection," she said. "Dinah won't do any better for herself than that. It seems to me that she will have the best of the bargain. But that is your affair. She's full young. I don't suppose you want to marry her yet, do you?"

"I'd marry her to-night if I could," said Sir Eustace, with his careless laugh.

But Mrs. Bathurst did not laugh with him. "We'll have the banns published and everything done proper," she said. "Hasty marriages as often as not aren't regular. Here, Dinah! Don't stand there listening! Go and see if the kettle boils!"

It was at this point that Bathurst deemed that the moment had arrived to present himself. He entered, almost running into Dinah about to hurry out.

"Hullo!" he said. "Hullo!" and taking her by the shoulders, kissed her.

She clung to him for a moment, her sweet face burning. "Oh, Dad!" she murmured in confusion, "Oh, Dad!"

With his arm about her, he turned her back into the room. "You come back and introduce me to your new friend!" he said. "I've got to thank him, you know, for taking such care of you."

She yielded, but not very willingly. She was painfully embarrassed, almost incoherent, as she obeyed Bathurst's behest.

"This - this is Dad," she murmured.

Sir Eustace came forward with his leisurely air of confidence. His great bulk seemed to fill the low room. He looked even more magnificent than usual.

"Ah, sir, you have just come in from hunting," he said. "I hope I don't intrude. It's a beastly wet evening. I should think you're not sorry to get in."

Mrs. Bathurst, tall, bony, angular, with harsh, gipsy features that were still in a fashion boldly handsome, broke in upon her husband's answering greeting.

"Ronald, this gentleman tells me he wants to marry Dinah. It is very sudden, but these things often are. You will give your consent of course. I have already given mine."

"Easy, easy!" laughed Bathurst. "Why exceed the speed limit in this reckless fashion? You are Sir Eustace Studley? I am very pleased to meet you."

He held out his hand to Sir Eustace, and gave him the grasp of good-fellowship. It seemed to Dinah that the very atmosphere changed magically with the coming of her father. No difficult situation ever dismayed him. He and Sir Eustace were not dissimilar in this respect. Whatever the circumstances, they both knew how to hold their own with absolute ease. It was a faculty which she would have given much to possess.

Sir Eustace was laughing in his careless, well-bred way. "It's rather a shame to spring the matter on you like this," he said. "I ought to have waited to ask your consent to the engagement, but I am afraid I am not a very patient person, and I wanted to make sure of your daughter before we parted. We are staying at Great Mallowes - at the Royal Stag. May I come over to-morrow and put things on a more business-like footing?"

"Oh, don't hurry away!" said Bathurst easily. "Sit down and have some tea with us! It is something of a surprise certainly but a very agreeable one. Lydia, what about tea? Or perhaps you prefer a whisky and soda?"

"Tea, thanks," said Sir Eustace, and seated himself with his superb air of complete assurance.

Mrs. Bathurst turned upon her daughter. "Dinah, how many more times am I to tell you to go and see if the kettle boils?"

Dinah started, as one rudely awakened from an entrancing dream. "I am sorry," she murmured in confusion. "I forgot."

She fled from the room with the words, and her mother, with dark brows drawn, looked after her for a moment, then sat down facing Sir Eustace.

"I should like to know," she said aggressively, "what you are prepared to do for her."

Sir Eustace smiled in his aloof, slightly supercilious fashion. He had been more or less prepared for Dinah's mother, but the temptation to address her as "My good woman" was almost more than he could withstand.

"Will you not allow me," he said, icily courteous, "to settle this important matter with Mr. Bathurst to-morrow? He will then be in a position to explain it to you."

Mrs. Bathurst made a movement of fierce impatience. She had been put in her place by this stranger and furiously she resented it. But the man was a baronet, and a marvellous catch for a son-in-law; and she did not dare to put her resentment into words.

She got up therefore, and flounced angrily to the door. Sir Eustace arose without haste and with a stretch of his long arm opened it for her.

She flung him a glance, half-hostile, half-awed, as she went through. She had a malignant hatred for the upper class, despite the fact that her own husband was a member thereof. And yet she held it in unwilling respect. Sir Eustace's nonchalantly administered snub was far harder to bear than any open rudeness from a man of her own standing would have been.

Fiercely indignant, she entered the kitchen, and caught Dinah peeping at herself in the shining surface of the warming-pan after having removed her hat.

"Ah, that's your game, my girl, is it?" she said. "You've come back the grand lady, have you? You've no further, use for your mother, I daresay. She may work her fingers to the bone for all you care - or ever will care again."

Dinah whizzed round, scarlet and crestfallen. "Oh, Mother! How you startled me! I only wanted to see if - if my hair was tidy."

"And that's one of your lies," said Mrs. Bathurst, with a heavy hand on her shoulder. "They've taught you how to juggle with the truth, that's plain. Oh yes, Lady Studley that is to be, you've learnt a lot since you've been away, I can see - learnt to despise your mother, I'll lay a wager. But I'll show you she's not to be despised by a prinking minx like you. What did I send you in here for, eh?"

"To - to see to the kettle," faltered Dinah, shrinking before the stern regard of the black eyes that so mercilessly held her own.

"And there it is ready to boil over, and you haven't touched it, you worthless little hussy, you! Take that - and dare to disobey me again!"

She dealt the girl a blow with her open hand as she spoke, a swinging, pitiless blow, on the cheek, and pushed her fiercely from her.

Dinah reeled momentarily. The sudden violence of the attack bewildered her. Actually she had almost forgotten how dreadful her mother could be. Then, recovering herself, she went to the fire and stooped over it, without a word. She had a burning sensation at the throat, and she was on the verge of passionate tears. The memory of Isabel's parting embrace, the tender drawing of her arms only a brief half-hour before made this home-coming almost intolerable.

"What's that thing you're wearing?" demanded Mrs. Bathurst abruptly.

Dinah lifted the kettle and turned. "It is a fur-lined coat that - that he bought for me in Paris."

"Then take it off!" commanded Mrs. Bathurst. "And don't you wear it again until I give you leave! How dare you accept presents from the man before I've even seen him?"

"I couldn't help it," murmured Dinah, as she slipped off the luxurious garment that Isabel had chosen for her.

"Couldn't help it!" Bitterly Mrs. Bathurst echoed the words. "You'll say you couldn't help him falling in love with you next! As if you didn't set out to catch him, you little artful brown-faced monkey! Oh, I always knew you were crafty, for all your simple ways. Mind, I don't say you haven't done well for yourself, you have - a deal better than you deserve. But don't ever say you couldn't help it to me again! For if you do, I'll trounce you for it, do you hear? None of your coy airs for me! I won't put up with 'em. You'll behave yourself as long as you're in this house, or I'll know the reason why."

To all of which Dinah listened in set silence, telling herself with desperate insistence that it would not be for long. Sir Eustace did not mean to be kept waiting, and he would deliver her finally and for all time.

She did not know exactly why her mother was angry. She

supposed she resented the idea of losing her slave. There seemed no other possible reason, for love for her she had none. Dinah knew but too cruelly well that she had been naught but an unwelcome burden from the very earliest days of her existence. Till she met Isabel, she had never known what real mother-love could be.

She wondered if her *fiance* would notice the red mark on her cheek when she carried in the teapot; but he was holding a careless conversation with her father, and only gave her a glance and a smile.

During the meal that followed he scarcely addressed her or so much as looked her way. He treated her mother with a freezing aloofness that made her tremble inwardly. She wondered how he dared.

When at length he rose to go, however, his attention returned to Dinah. He laid a dominating hand upon her shoulder. "Are you coming to see me off?"

She glanced at her mother in involuntary appeal, but failed to catch her eye. Silently she turned to the door.

He took leave of her parents with the indifference of one accustomed to popularity. "I shall be round in the morning," he said to her father. "About twelve? That'll suit me very well; unless I wait till the afternoon and bring my sister. I know she hopes to come over if she is well enough. That is, of course, if you don't object to an informal call."

He spoke as if in his opinion the very fact of its informality conferred a favour, and again Dinah trembled lest her mother should break forth into open rudeness.

But to her amazement Mrs. Bathurst seemed somewhat overawed by the princely stranger. She even smiled in a grim way as she said, "I will be at home to her."

Sir Eustace made her a ceremonious bow and went out sweeping Dinah along with him. He closed the door with a decision there was no mistaking, and the next moment he had her in his arms.

"You poor little frightened mouse!" he said. "No wonder - no wonder you never knew before what life, real life, could be!"

She clung to him with all her strength, burying her face in the fur collar of his coat. "Oh, do marry me, quick - quick - quick!" she besought him, in a muffled whisper. "And take me away!"

He gathered her close in his arms, so close that she trembled again. Her nerves were all on edge that night.

"If they won't let me have you in a month from now," he said, in a voice that quivered slightly, "I swear I'll run away with you."

There was no echo of humour in his words though she tried to laugh at them, and ever he pressed her closer and closer to his heart, till panting she had to lift her face. And then he kissed her in his passionate compelling way, holding her shy lips with his own till he actually forced them to respond. She felt as if his love burned her, but, even so, she dared not shrink from it. There was so much at stake. Her mother's lack of love was infinitely harder to endure.

And so she bore the fierce flame of his passion unflinching even though her spirit clamoured wildly to be free, choosing rather to be consumed by it than left a beaten slave in her house of bondage.

His kisses waked in her much more of fear than rapture. That untamed desire of his frightened her to the very depths of her being, but yet it was infinitely preferable to the haughty indifference with which he regarded all the rest of the world. It meant that he would not let her go, and that in itself was comfort unspeakable to Dinah. He meant to have her at any price, and she was very badly in need of deliverance, even though she might have to pay for it, and pay heavily.

It was at this point, actually while his fiery kisses were scorching her lips, that a very strange thought crept all unawares into her consciousness. If she ever needed help, if she ever needed escape, she had a friend to whom she could turn - a staunch and capable friend who would never fail her. She was sure that Scott would find a way to ease the burden if it became too heavy. Her faith in him, his wisdom, his strength, was unbounded. And he helped everyone - the valiant servant Greatheart, protector of the helpless, sustainer of the vanquished.

When her lover was gone at last, she closed the door and leaned against it, feeling weak in every fibre.

Bathurst, coming out a few moments later, was struck by her spent look. "Well, Dinah lass," he said lightly, "you look as if it had cost something of an effort to land your catch. But he's a mighty fine one, I will say that for him."

She went to him, twining her arm in his, forcing herself to smile. "Oh, Dad," she said, "he is fine, isn't he?" But - but - she uttered the words almost in spite of herself - "you should see his brother. You should see - Scott."

"What? Is he finer still?" laughed Bathurst, pinching her cheek. "Have you got the whole family at your feet, you little baggage?"

She flushed very deeply. "Oh no! Oh no! I didn't mean that. Scott - Scott is not a bit like that. He is - he is - " And there she broke off, for who could hope to convey any faithful impression of this good friend of hers? There were no words that could adequately describe him. With a little sigh she turned from the subject. "I'm glad you like Eustace," she said shyly.

Bathurst laughed a little, then bent unexpectedly, and kissed her. "It's a case of Cinderella and the prince," he said lightly. "But the luck isn't all on Cinderella's side, I'm thinking."

She clung to him eagerly. "Oh, Daddy, thank you! Thank you! Do you know - it's funny - Scott used to call me Cinderella!"

Bathurst crooked his brows quizzically. "How original of him! This Scott seems to be quite a wonderful person. And what was your pet name for him I wonder, eh, sly-boots?"

She laughed in evident embarrassment. There was something implied in her father's tone that made her curiously reluctant to discuss her hero. And yet, in justification of the man himself, she felt she must say something.

"His brother and sister call him - Stumpy," she said, "because he is little and he limps. But I -" her face was as red as the hunting-coat against which it nestled - "I called him - Mr. Greatheart. He is - just like that."

Mr. Bathurst laughed again, tweaking her ear. "Altogether an extraordinary family!" he commented. "I must meet this Mr. Stumpy Greatheart. Now suppose you run upstairs and turn on the hot water. And when you've done that, you can take my boots down to the kitchen to dry. And mind you don't fall foul of your mother, for she strikes me as being a bit on the ramp tonight!"

He kissed her again, and she clung to him very fast for a moment or two, tasting in that casual, kindly embrace all the home joy she had ever known.

Then, hearing her mother's step, she swiftly and guiltily disengaged herself and fled up the stairs like a startled bird. As she prepared his bath for him, the wayward thought came to her that if only he and she had lived alone together, she would never have wanted to get married at all - even for the delight of being Lady Studley instead of "poor little Dinah Bathurst!"

CHAPTER II

WEDDING ARRANGEMENTS

It was certainly not love at first sight that prompted Mrs. Bathurst to take a fancy to Isabel Everard.

Secretly Dinah had dreaded their meeting, fearing that innate antagonism which her mother invariably seemed to cherish against the upper class. But within a quarter of an hour of their meeting she was aware of a change of attitude, a quenching of the hostile element, a curious and wholly new sensation of peace.

For though Isabel's regal carriage and low, musical voice, marked her as one of the hated species, her gentleness banished all impression of pride. She treated Dinah's mother with an assumption of friendliness that had in it no trace of condescension, and she was so obviously sincere in her wish to establish a cordial relation that it was impossible to remain ungracious.

"I can't feel that we are strangers," she said, with her rare smile when Dinah had departed to fetch the tea. "Your little Dinah has done so much for me - more than I can ever tell you. That I am to have her for a sister seems almost too good to be true."

"I wonder you think she's good enough," remarked Mrs. Bathurst in her blunt way. "She isn't much to look at. I've done my best to bring her up well, but I never thought of her turning into a fine lady. I question if she's fit for it."

"If she were a fine lady, I don't think I should think so highly of her," Isabel said gently. "But as to her being unfit to fill a high position, she is only inexperienced and she will learn very quickly. I am willing to teach her all in my power."

"Aye, learn to despise her mother," commented Mrs. Bathurst, with sudden bitterness, "after all the trouble I've taken to make her respect me."

"I should never teach her that," Isabel answered quietly. "And I am sure that she would be quite incapable of learning it. Mrs. Bathurst, do you really think that worldly position is a thing that greatly matters to anyone in the long run? I don't."

It was then that a faint, half-grudging admiration awoke in the elder woman's resentful soul, and she looked at Isabel with the first glimmer of kindliness. "You're right," she said slowly, "it don't matter to those who've got it. But to those who haven't - " her eyes glowed red for a moment - "you don't know how it galls," she said.

And then she flushed dully, realizing that she had made a confidante of one of the hated breed.

But Isabel's hand was on hers in a moment; her eyes, full of understanding, looked earnest friendship into hers. "Oh, I know," she said. "It is the little things that gall us all, until - until some great - some fundamental - sorrow wrenches our very lives in twain. And then - and then - one can almost laugh to think one ever cared about them."

Her voice throbbed with feeling. She had lifted the veil for a moment to salve the other woman's bitterness.

And Mrs. Bathurst realized it, and was touched. "Ah! You've suffered," she said.

Isabel bent her head. "But it is over," she said. "I married a man who, they said, was beneath me. But - God knows - he was above me - in every way. And then - I lost him." Her voice sank.

Mrs. Bathurst's hand came down with a clumsy movement upon hers. "He died?" she said.

"Yes." Almost in a whisper Isabel made answer. "For years I would not face it - would not believe it. He went from me so suddenly - oh, God, so suddenly -" a tremor of anguish sounded in the low words; but in a moment she raised her head, and her eyes were shining with a brightness that no pain could dim. "It is over," she said. "It is quite, quite over. My night is past and can never come again. I am waiting now for the full day. And I know that I have not very long to wait. I have not seen him - no, I have not seen him. But - twice now - I have heard his voice."

"Poor soul! Poor soul!" said Mrs. Bathurst.

It was all the sympathy she could express; but it came from her heart. She no longer regretted her own burst of confidence. The spontaneous answer that it had evoked had had a magically softening effect upon her. In all her life no one had ever charmed her thus. She was astonished herself at the melting of her hardness.

"You've suffered worse than I have," she said, "for I never cared for any man like that. I was let down badly when I was a girl, and I've never had any opinion of any of 'em since. My husband's all right, so far as he goes. But he isn't the sort of man to worship. Precious few of 'em are."

Whereat Isabel laughed, a soft, sad laugh. "That is why worldly position matters so little," she said. "If by chance the right man really comes, nothing else counts. He is just everything."

"Maybe you're right," said Mrs. Bathurst, with gloomy

acquiescence. "Anyhow, it isn't for me to say you're wrong."

And this was why when Dinah brought in the tea, she found a wholly new element in the atmosphere, and missed the customary sharp rebuke from her mother's lips when she had to go back for the sugar-tongs.

She had been disappointed that her friend Scott had not been of the party. Isabel's explanation that he had gone home at Eustace's wish to attend to some business had not removed an odd little hurt sense of having been defrauded. She had counted upon seeing Scott that day. It was almost as if he had failed her when she needed him, though why she seemed to need him she could not have said, nor could he possibly have known that she would do so.

Sir Eustace was in her father's den. She was sure that they were getting on very well together from the occasional bursts of laughter with which their conversation was interspersed. They were not apparently sticking exclusively to business. And now that Isabel had won her mother, deeply though she rejoiced over the conquest, she felt a little - a very little - forlorn. They were all talking about her, but if Scott had been there he would have talked to her and made her feel at ease. She could not understand his going, even at his brother's behest. It seemed incredible that he should not want to see her home.

She sat meekly in the background, thinking of him, while she drank her tea; and then, just as she finished, there came the sound of voices at the door, and her father and Sir Eustace came in. They were laughing still. Evidently the result of the interview was satisfactory to both. Sir Eustace greeted his hostess with lofty courtesy, and passed on straight to her side.

She turned and tingled at his approach; he was looking more princely than ever. Instinctively she rose.

"What do you want to get up for?" demanded her mother sharply.

Sir Eustace reached his little trembling *fiancee*, and took the eager hand she stretched to him. His blue eyes flashed their fierce flame over her upturned, quivering face. "Take me into the kitchen - anywhere!" he murmured. "I want you to myself."

She nodded. "Don't you want any tea? All right. Dad doesn't either. I'll clear away."

"No, you don't!" her mother said. "You sit down and behave yourself! You'll clear when I tell you to; not before."

Sir Eustace wheeled round to her, the flame of his look turning to ice. "With your permission, madam," he said with extreme formality, "Dinah and I are going to retire to talk things over."

He had his way. It was obvious that he meant to have it. He motioned to Dinah with an imperious gesture to precede him, and she obeyed, not daring to glance in her mother's direction.

Mrs. Bathurst said no more. Something in Sir Eustace's bearing seemed to quell her. She watched him go with eyes that shone with a hot resentment under drawn brows. It took Isabel's utmost effort to charm her back to a mood less hostile.

As for Dinah, she led her *fiance* back to her father's den in considerable trepidation. To be compelled to resist her mother's will was a state of affairs that filled her with foreboding.

But the moment she was alone with him she forgot all but the one tremendous fact of his presence, for with the closing of the door he had her in his arms.

She clung to him desperately close, feeling as one struggling in deep waters, caught in a great current that would bear her swiftly, irresistibly, - whither?

He laughed at her trembling with careless amusement. "What,

still scared, my brown elf? Where is your old daring? Aren't you allowed to have any spirit at all in this house?"

She answered him incoherently, straining to keep her face hidden out of reach of his upturning hand. "No, - no, it's not that. You don't understand. It's all so new - so strange. Eustace, please - please, don't kiss me yet!"

He laughed again, but he did not press her for the moment. "Your father and I have had no end of a talk," he said. "Do you know what has come of it? Would you like to know?"

"Yes," she murmured shyly.

He was caressing the soft dark ringlets that clustered about her neck.

"About getting married, little sweetheart," he said. "You want to get it over quickly and so do I. There's no reason why we shouldn't in fact. How about the beginning of next month? How about April?"

"Oh, Eustace!" She clung to him closer still; she had no words. But still that sense of being caught, of being borne against her will, possessed her, filling her with dread rather than ecstasy. Whither was she going? Ah, whither?

He went on with his easy self-assurance, speaking as if he held the whole world at his disposal. "We will go South for the honeymoon. I've crowds of things to show you - Rome, Naples, Venice. After that we'll come back and go for that summer trip in the yacht I promised you."

"And Isabel too - and Scott?" asked Dinah, in muffled accents.

He laughed over her head, as at the naive prattling of a child. "What! On our honeymoon? Oh, hardly, I think. I'll see to it that you're not bored. And look here, my elf! I won't have you shy with me any more. Is that understood? I'm not an ogre."

"I think you are - rather," murmured Dinah.

He bent over her, his lips upon her neck. "You - midget! And you think I'm going to devour you? Well, perhaps I shall some day if you go on running away. There's a terrible threat! Now hold up your head, Daphne - Daphne - and let me have that kiss!"

She hesitated a while longer, and then feeling his patience ebbing she lifted her face impulsively to his. "You will be good to me? Promise! Promise!" she pleaded tremulously.

He was laughing still, but his eyes were aflame. "That depends," he declared. "I can't answer for myself when you run away. Come! When are you going to kiss me first? Isn't it time you began?"

She slipped her arms about his neck. Her face was burning. "I will now," she said.

Yet the moment her lips touched his, the old wild fear came upon her. She made a backward movement of shrinking.

He caught her to him. "Daphne!" he said, and kissed her quivering throat.

She did not resist him, but her arms fell apart, and the red blush swiftly died. When he released her, she fell back a step with eyes fast closed, and in a moment her hands went up as though to shield face and neck from the scorching of a furnace.

He watched her, a slight frown drawing his brows. The flame still glittered in his eyes, but his mouth was hard. "Look here, child! Don't be silly!" he said. "If you treat me like a monster, I shall behave like one. I'm made that way."

His voice was curt; it held displeasure. Dinah uncovered her face and looked at him.

"Oh, you're angry!" she said, in tragic accents.

He laughed at that. "About as angry as I could get with a piece of thistledown. But you know, you're not very wise, my Daphne. You've got it in you to madden me, but it's a risky thing to do. Now see here! I've brought you something to make those moss-agate eyes of yours shine. Can you guess what it is?"

His hand was held out to her. She laid her own within it with conscious reluctance. He drew her into the circle of his arm, pressing her to him.

She leaned her head against him with a bewildered sense of self-reproach. "I'm sorry I'm silly, Eustace," she murmured "I expect I'm made that way too. Don't - don't take any notice!"

He touched her forehead lightly with his lips. "You'll get over it, sweetheart," he said. "It won't matter so much after we're married. I can do as I like with you then."

"Oh, I shan't like that," said Dinah quickly.

His arm pressed her closer. "Yes, you will. I'll give you no end of a good time. Now, sweetheart, give me that little hand of yours again! No, the left! There! I wonder if it's small enough. Rather a loose fit, eh? How do you like it?"

He was fitting a ring on to the third finger. Dinah looked and was dazzled. "Oh, Eustace, - diamonds!" she said, in an awed whisper.

"The best I could find," he told her, with princely arrogance. "I hunted through Bond Street for it this morning. Will it do?"

"You went up on purpose? Oh, Eustace!" she laid her cheek with a winning movement against his hand. "You are too good! You are much too good!"

He laughed carelessly. "I'm glad you're satisfied. It's a bond, remember. You must wear it always - till I give you a wedding-ring instead."

She lifted her face and looked at him with shining eyes. "I shall love to wear it," she said. "But I expect I shall have to keep it for best. Mother wouldn't let me wear it always."

"Never mind what your mother says!" he returned. "It's what I say that matters now. We're going to have you to stay at Willowmount in a few days. Isabel is arranging it with your mother now."

"Your home! Oh, how lovely!" Genuine delight was in Dinah's voice. "Scott is there, isn't he?"

He frowned again. "Bother Scott! You're coming to see me - no one else."

She flushed. "Oh yes, I know. And I shall love it - I shall love it! But - do you think I shall be allowed to come?"

"You must come," he said imperiously.

But Dinah looked dubious. "I expect I shall be wanted at home now. And I don't believe we shall get married in April either. I've been away so long."

He laughed, flicking her cheek. "Haven't I always told you that where there's a will there's a way? If necessary, I can run away with you."

She shook her head. "Oh no! I'd rather not. And if - if we're really going to be married in April, I ought to stay at home to get ready."

"Nonsense!" he said carelessly. "You can do that from Willowmount. Isabel will help you. It's less than an hour's run to town."

Dinah opened her eyes wide. "But I shan't shop in town. I shall have to make all my things. I always do."

He laughed again easily, indulgently. "That simplifies matters. You can do that anywhere. What are you going to be married in? White cotton?"

She laughed with him. "I would love to have a real grand wedding," she said, "the sort of wedding Rose de Vigne will have, with bridesmaids and flowers and crowds and crowds of people. Of course I know it can't be done." She gave a little sigh. "But I would love it. I would love it."

He was laughing still. "Why can't it be done? Who's going to prevent it?"

Dinah had become serious. "Dad hasn't money enough for one thing. And then there's Mother. She wouldn't do it."

"Ho! Wouldn't she? I've a notion she'd enjoy it even more than you would. If you want a smart wedding you'd better have it in town. Then the de Vignes and everyone else can come."

"Oh no! I want it to be here." Dinah's eyes began to shine. "Dad knows lots of people round about - County people too. Those are the sort of people I'd like to come. Even Mother might like that," she added reflectively.

"You prefer a big splash in your own little pond to a small one in a good-sized lake, is that it?" questioned Eustace. "Well, have it your own way, my child! But I shouldn't make many clothes if I were you. We will shop in Paris after we are married, and then you can get whatever you fancy."

Dinah's eyes fairly danced at the thought. "I shall love that. I'll tell Daddy, shall I, to keep all his money for the wedding, and then we can buy the clothes afterwards; that is, if you can afford it," she added quickly. "I ought not to let you really."

Ethel M. Dell

"You can't prevent me doing anything," he returned, his hand pressing her shoulder. "No one can."

She leaned her head momentarily against his arm. "You - you wouldn't want to do anything that anyone didn't like," she murmured shyly.

"Shouldn't I?" he said and for a moment his mouth was grim. "I am not accustomed to being regarded as an amiable nonentity, I assure you. It's settled then, is it? The first week in April? And you are to come to us for at least a fortnight beforehand."

Dinah nodded, her head bent. "All right, - if Mother doesn't mind."

"What would happen if she did?" he asked curiously.

"It just wouldn't be done," she made answer.

"Wouldn't it? Not if you insisted?"

"I couldn't insist," she said, her voice very low.

"Why couldn't you? I should have thought you had a will of your own. Don't you ever assert yourself?"

"Against her? No, never!" Dinah gave a little shudder. "Don't let's talk of it!" she said. "Isn't it time to go back? I believe I ought to be clearing away."

He detained her for a moment. "You're not going to work like a nigger when you are married to me," he said.

She smiled up at him, a merry, dimpling smile. "Oh no, I shall just enjoy myself then - like Rose de Vigne. I shall be much too grand to work. There! I really must go back. Thank you again ever so much - ever so much - for the lovely ring. I hope you'll never find out how unworthy I am of it."

She drew his head down with quivering courage and bestowed a butterfly kiss upon his cheek. And then in a second she was gone from his hold, gone like a woodland elf with a tinkle of laughter and the skipping of fairy feet.

Sir Eustace followed her flight with his eyes only, but in those eyes was the leaping fire of a passion that burned around her in an ever-narrowing circle. She knew that it was there, but she would not look back to see it. For deep in her heart she feared that flame as she feared nothing else on earth.

Ethel M. Dell

CHAPTER III

DESPAIR

"If I had known that this was going to happen, I would never have troubled to cultivate their acquaintance," said Lady Grace fretfully. "I knew of course that that artful little minx was running after the man, but that he could ever be foolish enough to let himself be caught in such an obvious trap was a possibility that I never seriously contemplated."

"It doesn't matter to me," said Rose.

She had said it many times before with the same rather forced smile. It was not a subject that she greatly cared to discuss. The news of Dinah's conquest had come like a thunderbolt. In common with her mother, she had never seriously thought that Sir Eustace could be so foolish. But since the utterly unexpected had come to pass, it seemed to her futile to talk about it. Dinah had secured the finest prize within reach for the moment, and there was no disputing the fact.

"The wedding is to take place so soon too," lamented Lady Grace. "That, I have no doubt, is the doing of that scheming mother of hers. What shall we do about going to it, Rose? Do you want to go, dear?"

"Not in the least, but I am going all the same." Rose was still smiling, and her eyes were fixed. "I think, you know, Mother," she said, "that we might do worse than ask Sir Eustace and his party to stay here for the event."

"My dear Rose!" Lady Grace gazed at her in amazement.

Rose continued to stare into space. "It would be much more convenient for them," she said. "And really we have no reason for allowing people to imagine that we are other than pleased over the arrangement. We shall not be going to town before Easter, so it seems to me that it would be only neighbourly to invite Sir Eustace to stay at the Court for the wedding. Great Mallowes is not a particularly nice place to put up in, and this would be far handier for him."

Lady Grace slowly veiled her astonishment. "Of course, dear; if you think so, it might be managed. We will talk to your father about it, and if he approves I will write to Sir Eustace - or get him to do so. I do not myself consider that Sir Eustace has behaved at all nicely. He was most cavalier about the Hunt Ball. But if you wish to overlook it - well, I shall not put any difficulty in the way."

"I think it would be a good thing to do," said Rose somewhat enigmatically.

The letter that reached Sir Eustace two days later was penned by the Colonel's hand, and contained a brief but cordial invitation to him and his following to stay at Perrythorpe Court for the wedding.

He read it with a careless smile and tossed it over to Scott. "Here is magnanimity," he commented. "Shall we accept the coals of fire?"

Scott read with all gravity and laid it down. "If you want my opinion, I should say 'No,'" he said.

"Why would you say No?" There was a lazy challenge in the question, a provocative gleam in Sir Eustace's blue eyes.

Scott smiled a little. "For one thing I shouldn't enjoy the coals of fire. For another, I shouldn't care to be at too close quarters with the beautiful Miss de Vigne again, if I had your very highly susceptible temperament. And for a third, I believe Isabel would prefer to stay at Great Mallowes."

"You're mighty clever, my son, aren't you?" said Eustace with a supercilious twist of the lips. "But - as it chances - not one of those excellent reasons appeals to me."

"Very well then," said Scott, with the utmost patience. "It is up to you to accept."

"Why should Isabel prefer Great Mallowes?" demanded Sir Eustace. "She knows the de Vignes. It is far better for her to see people, and there is more comfort in a private house than in a hotel."

"Quite so," said Scott. "I am sure she will fall in with your wishes in this respect, whatever they are. Will you write to Colonel de Vigne, or shall I?"

"You can - and accept," returned Sir Eustace imperially.

Scott took a sheet of paper without further words.

His brother leaned back in his chair, his black brows slightly drawn, and contemplated him as he did it.

"By the way, Scott," he said, after a moment, "Dinah's staying here need not make any difference to you in any way. She can't expect to have you at her beck and call as she had in Switzerland. You must make that clear to her."

"Very well, old chap." Scott spoke without raising his head. "You're going to meet her at the station, I suppose?"

"Almost immediately, yes." Eustace got up with a movement of suppressed impatience. "We shall have tea in Isabel's room.

You needn't turn up. I'll tell them to send yours in here."

"Oh, don't trouble! I'm going to turn up," very calmly Scott made rejoinder. He had already begun to write; his hand moved steadily across the sheet.

Sir Eustace's frown deepened. "You won't catch the post with those letters if you do."

Scott looked up at last, and his eyes were as steady as his hand had been. "That's my business, old chap," he said quietly. "Don't you worry yourself about that!"

There was a hint of ferocity about Sir Eustace as he met that steadfast look. He stood motionless for a moment or two, then flung round on his heel. Scott returned to his work with the composure characteristic of him, and almost immediately the banging of the door told of his brother's departure.

Then for a second his hand paused; he passed the other across his eyes with the old gesture of weariness, and a short, hard sigh came from him ere he bent again to his task.

Sir Eustace strode across the hall with the frown still drawing his brows. An open car was waiting at the door, but ere he went to it he turned aside and knocked peremptorily at another door.

He opened without waiting for a reply and entered a long, low-ceiled room through which the rays of the afternoon sun were pouring. Isabel, lying on a couch between fire and window, turned her head towards him.

"Haven't you started yet? Surely it is getting very late," she said in her low, rather monotonous voice.

He came to her. "I prefer starting a bit late," he said. "You will have tea ready when we return?"

Ethel M. Dell

"Certainly," she said.

He stood looking down at her intently. "Are you all right today?" he asked abruptly.

A faint colour rose in her cheeks. "I am - as usual," she said.

"What does that mean?" Curtly he put the question. "Why don't you go out more? Why don't you get old Lister to make you up a tonic?"

She smiled a little, but there was slight uneasiness behind her smile. Her eyes had the remote look of one who watches the far horizon. "My dear Eustace," she said, "*cui bono?*"

He stooped suddenly over her. "It is because you won't make the effort," he said, speaking with grim emphasis. "You're letting yourself go again, I know; I've been watching you for the past week. And by heaven, Isabel, you shan't do it! Scott may be fool enough to let you, but I'm not. You've only been home a week, and you've been steadily losing ground ever since you got back. What is it? What's the matter with you? Tell me what is the matter!"

So insistent was his tone, so almost menacing his attitude, that Isabel shrank from him with a gesture too swift to repress. The old pathetic furtive look was in her eyes as she made reply.

"I am very sorry. I don't see how I can help it. I - I am getting old, you know. That is the chief reason."

"You're talking nonsense, my dear girl." Impatiently Eustace broke in. "You are just coming into your prime. I won't have you ruin your life like this. Do you hear me? I won't. If you don't rouse yourself I will find a means to rouse you. You are simply drifting now - simply drifting."

"But into my desired haven," whispered Isabel, with a piteous quiver of the lips.

He straightened himself with a gesture of exasperation. "You are wasting yourself over a myth, an illusion. On my soul, Isabel, what a wicked waste it is! Have you forgotten the days when you and I roamed over the world together? Have you forgotten Egypt and all we did there? Life was worth having then."

"Ah! I thought so." She met his look with eyes that did not seem to see him. "We were children then, Eustace," she said, "children playing on the sands. But the great tide caught us. You breasted the waves, but I was broken and thrown aside. I could never play on the sands again. I can only lie and wait for the tide to come again and float me away."

He clenched his hands. "Do you think I would let you go - like that?" he said.

"It is the only kindness you can do me," she answered in her low voice of pleading.

He swung round to go. "I curse the day," he said very bitterly, "that you ever met Basil Everard! I curse his memory!"

She flinched at the words as if they had been a blow. Her face turned suddenly grey. She clasped her hands very tightly together, saying no word.

He went to the door and paused, his back towards her. "I came in," he said then, "to tell you that the de Vignes have offered to put us up at their place for the wedding. And I have accepted."

He waited for some rejoinder but she made none. It was as if she had not heard. Her eyes had the impotent, stricken look of one who has searched dim distances for some beloved object - and searched in vain.

He did not glance round. His temper was on edge. With a fierce movement he pulled open the door and departed. And behind him like a veil there fell the silence of a great despair.

CHAPTER IV

THE NEW HOME

A small figure was already standing outside the station when the car Sir Eustace drove whirled round the corner of the station yard. He was greeted by the waving of a vigorous hand, as he dashed up, grinding on the brakes in the last moment as was his impetuous custom. Everyone knew him from afar by his driving, and the village children were wont to scatter like rabbits at his approach.

Dinah however stood her ground with a confidence which his wild performance hardly justified, and the moment he alighted sprang to meet him with the eagerness of a child escaped from school.

"Oh, Eustace, it is fun coming here! I was so horribly afraid something would stop me just at the last. But everything has turned out all right, and we are going to have ever such a fine wedding with crowds and crowds of people. Did you know Isabel wrote and said she would give me my wedding dress? Isn't it dear of her? How is she now?"

"Where is your luggage?" said Eustace.

She pointed to a diminutive dress-basket behind her. "That's all there is. I'm not to stay more than a week as the time is getting so short I don't feel as if I shall ever be ready as it is. I've never been so rushed before. I sometimes wonder if it wouldn't be almost better to put it off a few weeks."

"Jump up!" commanded Eustace, with a curt sign to a porter to pick up his *fiancee's* humble impediments.

Dinah sprang up beside him and slipped a shy hand onto his knee. "You look more like Apollo than ever," she whispered, awe-struck, "when you frown like that. Is anything the matter?"

His brow cleared magically at her action. "I began to think I should have to come down to Perrythorpe and fetch you," he said, grasping the little nervous fingers. "I thought you meant to give me the slip - if you could."

"Oh no!" said Dinah, shocked at the suggestion. "I wanted to come; only - only - I couldn't be spared sooner. It wasn't my fault," she urged pleadingly. "Truly it wasn't!"

He smiled upon her. "All right, - Daphne. I'll forgive you this time," he said. "But now I've got you, my nymph of the woods, I am not going to part with you again in a hurry. And if you talk of putting off the wedding again, I'll simply run away with you. So now you know what to expect."

Dinah uttered her giddy little laugh. The excitement of this visit - the first she had ever paid to anyone - had turned her head. "Do you know Rose is actually going to be my chief bridesmaid?" she said. "Isn't that - magnanimous of her? She is pretending to be pleased, but I know she is frightfully jealous underneath. The other bridesmaid is the Vicar's daughter. She is quite old, nearly thirty but I couldn't think of anyone else, except the infant schoolmistress, and they wouldn't let me have her. I shall feel rather small, shan't I? Even Rose is twenty-five. I wonder if I shall feel grown up when I'm married. Do you think I shall?"

"Not till you cease to be - Daphne," said Sir Eustace enigmatically.

He started the car with the words, and they shot forward with a suddenness that made Dinah hold her breath.

But in a few moments she was chattering again, for she was never quiet for long. How was Scott? Was he at home? And Isabel - he hadn't told her. She did hope dear Isabel was keeping better. Was she? Was she?

She pressed the question as he did not seem inclined to answer it, and saw again the frown that had darkened his handsome face upon arrival.

"Do tell me!" she begged. "Isn't she so well?"

And at last with the curtness of speech which always denoted displeasure with him, he made reply.

"No, she has gone back a good deal since she got home. She lies on a sofa and broods all day long. I am looking to you to wake her up. For heaven's sake be as lively as you can!"

"Oh, poor Isabel!" Quick concern was in Dinah's voice. "What is it, do you think? Doesn't the place suit her?"

"Heaven knows," he answered gloomily, "I have a house down at Heath-on-Sea where we keep the yacht, but I doubt if it would do her much good to go there this time of the year. She and Scott might try it later - after the wedding."

"Couldn't we all go there?" suggested Dinah ingenuously.

He gave her a keen glance. "For the honeymoon? No I don't think so," he said.

"Only for the first part of it," said Dinah coaxingly; "till Isabel felt better."

He uttered a brief laugh. "No, thanks, Daphne. We're going to be alone - quite alone, for the first part of our honeymoon. I

Ethel M. Dell

am going to take you in this car to the most out-of-the-way corner in England, where - even, if you run away - there'll be nowhere to run to. And there you'll stay till -" he paused a moment - "you realize that you are all mine for ever and ever, till in fact, you've shed all your baby nonsense and become a wise little married woman."

Dinah gave a sudden sharp shiver, and pulled her coat closer about her.

He glanced at her again. "You'll like it better than being a maid-of-all-work," he said, with his swift, transforming smile.

She smiled back at him with ready responsiveness. "Oh, I shall! I'm sure I shall. I've always wanted to be married - always. Only - it'll seem a little funny, just at first. You won't get impatient with me, will you, if - if sometimes I forget how to behave?"

He laughed and abruptly slackened speed. They were running down a narrow lane bordered with bare trees through which the spring sunshine filtered down. On a brown upland to one side of them a plough was being driven. On the other the ground sloped away to deep meadows where wound a willow-banked river.

The car stopped. "How pretty it is!" said Dinah.

And then very suddenly she found that it was not for the sake of the view that he had brought her to a standstill in that secluded place. For he caught her to him with the hot ardour she had learned to dread and kissed with passion the burning face she sought to hide.

She struggled for a few seconds like a captured bird, but in the end she yielded palpitating, as she had yielded so often before, mutely bearing that which her whole soul clamoured inarticulately to escape. When he let her go, her cheeks were on fire. He was laughing, but she was on the verge of tears.

He started on again without words, and in a very brief space they were racing forward at terrific speed, seeming scarcely to touch the ground so rapid was their progress.

Dinah sat with her two hands clutched upon her hat, thankful for the cold rush of air that gave her relief after the fiery intensity of those unsparing kisses. Her heart was beating in great thumps. Somehow the fierceness of him always exceeded either memory or expectation. He was so terribly strong, so disconcertingly absolute in his demands upon her. And every time he seemed to take more.

She hardly noticed anything further of the country through which they passed. Her agitation possessed her over-whelmingly. She felt exhausted, unnerved, very curiously ashamed. It was good to have so princely a lover, but his tempestuous wooing was altogether too much for her. She wondered how Rose, the sedate and composed beauty, would have met those wild gusts of passion. They would not have disconcerted her; nothing ever did. She would probably have endured all with a smile. No form of adoration could come amiss with her. She did not fancy that Rose's heart was capable of beating at more than the usual speed. Her very blushes savoured of a delicate complacency that enhanced her beauty without disturbing her serenity. A great wave of envy went through Dinah. "Ah, why had she not been blessed with such a temperament as that?"

His voice broke in upon her disjointed meditations. "Well, Daphne? Feeling better?"

She glanced at him with the confused consciousness that she dared not meet his eyes. She was glad that he was laughing, but the turbulent feeling of uncertainty that his nearness always brought to her was with her still. She was as one who had passed by a raging fire, and the scorching heat of the flame yet remained with her. Breathlessly she spoke. "I can't think - or do anything - in this wind. Are we nearly there?"

"We are there," he made answer.

And she discovered that which in her distress of mind she had failed to notice. They were running smoothly along a private avenue of fir-trees towards an old stone mansion that stood on a slope overlooking the long river valley.

She drew a hard breath. "But this is better - ever so much - than the Court!" she said.

"Your future home, my queen!" said Sir Eustace royally.

She breathed again deeply, wonderingly. "Is it real?" she said.

He laughed. "I almost think so. You see that other house right away in the distance, across that further slope? That is the Dower House where Isabel and Scott are to live when we are married."

"Oh!" There was a quick note of disappointment in Dinah's voice. "I thought they would live with us."

"I don't know why," said Sir Eustace with a touch of sharpness, and then softening almost immediately, "It's practically the same thing, my sprite of the woods. But I wish you to be mistress in your own home - when we do settle down, which won't be at present. For we're not coming back from our honeymoon till you have learnt that I am the only person in the world that matters."

Again a slight shiver caught Dinah, but she repressed it instantly. "I expect it won't take me very long to learn that, Apollo," she said, with her shy, fleeting smile.

And then they glided up to the wide steps of his home and the door opened to receive them, showing Scott - Scott her friend - standing in the opening, awaiting her.

CHAPTER V

THE WATCHER

She sprang to meet him with a cry of delight, both hands extended.

"Oh, it is good to see you again! It is good! It is good!" she panted. "Why didn't you come to Perrythorpe? I did want you there!"

He grasped her hands very tightly. His pale eyes smiled their welcome, but - it came to her afterwards - he scarcely said a word in greeting. In a second or two he set her free.

"Come and see Isabel!" he said.

She went with him eagerly, forgetful of Sir Eustace striding in her wake. As Scott opened the door of Isabel's room, she pressed forward, and the next moment she was kneeling by Isabel's side, gathered close, close to her breast in a silence that was deeper than any speech.

Dinah's arms clung fast about the elder woman's neck. She was conscious of a curious impulse to tears, but she conquered it, forcing herself somewhat brokenly to laugh.

"Isn't it lovely to be together again?" she whispered. "You can't think what it means to me. I lay in bed last night and counted the hours and then the minutes. I was so dreadfully afraid

Ethel M. Dell

something might happen to prevent my coming. And, oh, Isabel, I had no idea your home was so beautiful."

Isabel's hold slackened. "Sit on the sofa beside me, my darling!" she said. "I am so glad you like Willowmount. Was Eustace in time for your train?"

Dinah laughed again with more assurance. "Oh no! I got there first. He came swooping down as if he had dropped from the clouds. We had a very quick run back, and I'm blown all to pieces." She put up impetuous hands to thrust back the disordered clusters of dark hair.

"Take off your hat!" said Scott.

She obeyed, with shining eyes upon him. "Now, why didn't you come over to Perrythorpe? You haven't told me yet."

"I was busy," he answered. "I had to get home."

His eyes were shining also. She did not need to be told that he was glad to see her. He rang for tea and sat down somewhere near in his usual unobtrusive fashion. Eustace occupied the place of honour in an easy-chair drawn close to the end of the sofa on which Dinah sat. He was watching her, she knew but she could not meet his look as she met Scott's. His very nearness made her feel again the scorching of the flame.

She slipped her hand into Isabel's as though seeking refuge and as she did so she heard Eustace address his brother, his tone brief and peremptory, - the voice of the employer.

"You have finished that correspondence?"

"I shall finish it in time for the post," Scott made answer.

Eustace made a sound expressive of dissatisfaction. "You'll miss it sure as a gun!"

Scott said nothing further, but his silence was not without a certain mastery that sent an odd little thrill of triumph through Dinah.

Eustace frowned heavily and turned from him.

The entrance of Biddy with the tea made a diversion, for her greeting of Dinah was full of warmth.

"But sure, ye're not looking like I'd like to see ye, Miss Dinah," was her verdict. "It's meself that'll have to feed ye up."

"But I'm always thin!" protested Dinah. "It's just the way I'm made."

Biddy pursed her lips and shook her head. "It's not the sign of a contented mind," she commented.

"I never was contented before I went to Switzerland," said Dinah; she turned to Isabel. "Wasn't it all lovely? It's just like a dream to me now - all glitter and romance. I'd give anything to have it over again."

"I'll show you better things than winter in the Alps," said Eustace in his free, imperial fashion.

Her bright eyes glanced up to his for a moment. "Do you know I don't believe you could," she said.

He laughed. "You won't say that six months hence. The Alps will be no more than an episode to you then."

"Rather an important episode," remarked Scott.

Her look came to him, settled upon him like a shy bird at rest. "Very, very important," she said softly. "Do you remember that first day - that first night - how you helped me dress for the ball? Eustace would never have thought of dancing with me if it hadn't been for you."

"I seem to have a good deal to answer for," said Scott, with his rather tired smile.

"I owe you - everything," said Dinah.

"Stumpy has many debtors," said Isabel.

Eustace uttered a brief laugh. "Stumpy scores without running," he observed. "He always has. Saves trouble, eh, Stumpy?"

"Quite so," said Scott with precision. "It's easy to be kind when it costs you nothing."

"And it pays," said Eustace.

Dinah's green eyes went back to him with something of a flash. "Scott would never have thought of that," she said.

"I am sure he wouldn't," said Eustace dryly.

Her look darted about him like an angry bird seeking some vulnerable point whereat to strike. But before she could speak, Scott leaned forward and intervened.

"My thoughts are my own private property, if no one objects," he said whimsically. "Judge me - if you must - by my actions! But I should prefer not to be judged at all. Have you told Dinah about the invitation to the de Vignes's, Eustace?"

"No! They haven't asked you for the wedding surely!" Dinah's thoughts were instantly diverted. "Have they really? I never thought they would. Oh, that will be fun! I expect Rose is trying to pretend she isn't -" She broke off, colouring vividly. "What a pig I am!" she said apologetically to Scott. "Please forget I said that!"

"But you didn't say it," said Scott.

"A near thing!" commented Eustace. "I had no idea Miss de Vigne was so smitten. Stumpy, you'll be best man. You'll have to console her."

"I believe the best man has to console everybody," said Scott.

"You are peculiarly well fitted for the task," said his brother, setting down his cup and pulling out a cigarette-case. "Be quick and quench your thirst, Dinah. I want to trot you round the place before dark."

Dinah looked at Isabel. "You'll come too?"

Isabel shook her head. "No, dear, I can't walk much. Besides, Eustace will want you to himself."

But a queer little spirit of perversity had entered into Dinah. She shook her head also. "We will go round in the morning," she said, with a resolute look at her *fiance*. "I am going to stay with Isabel to-night. You have had quite as much of me as is good for you; now haven't you?"

There was an instant of silence that felt ominous before somewhat curtly Sir Eustace yielded the point. "I won't grudge you to Isabel if she wants you. You can both of you come up to the picture-gallery when you have done. There's a fine view of the river from there."

He got up with the words and Scott rose also. They went away together, and Dinah at once nestled to Isabel's side.

"Now we can be cosy!" she said.

Isabel put an arm about her. "You mustn't make me monopolize you, sweetheart," she said. "I think Eustace was a little disappointed."

"I'll be ever so nice to him presently to make up," said Dinah. "But I do want you now, Isabel!"

Ethel M. Dell

"What is it, dearest?"

Dinah's cheek rubbed softly against her shoulder. "Isabel - darling, I never thought that you and Scott were going to leave this place because Eustace was marrying me."

Isabel's arm pressed her closer. "We are not going far away, darling. It will be better for you to be alone."

"I don't think so," said Dinah. "We shall be alone quite long enough on our honeymoon." She trembled a little in Isabel's hold. "I do wish you were coming too," she whispered.

"My dear, Eustace will take care of you," Isabel said.

"Oh yes, I know. But he's so big. He wants such a lot," murmured Dinah in distress. "I don't know quite how to manage him. He's never satisfied. If - if only you were coming with us, he'd have something else to think about."

"Oh no, he wouldn't, dear. When you are present, he thinks of no one else. You see," Isabel spoke with something of an effort, "he's in love with you."

"Yes - yes, of course. I'm very silly." Dinah dabbed her eyes and began to smile. "But he makes me feel all the while as if - as if he wants to eat me. I know it's all my silliness; but I wish you weren't going to the Dower House all the same. Shall you be quite comfortable there?"

"It is being done up, dear. You must come round with us and see it. We shall move in directly the wedding is over, and then this place is to be done up too, made ready for you. I believe you are to choose wall-papers and hangings while you are here. You will enjoy that."

"If you will help me," said Dinah.

"Of course I will help you, dear child. I will always help you with anything so long as it is in my power."

Very tenderly Isabel reassured her till presently the scared feeling subsided.

They went up later to the picture-gallery and joined Eustace whom they found smoking there. His mood also had changed by that time, and he introduced his ancestors to Dinah with complete good humour.

Isabel remained with them, but she talked very little in her brother's presence; and when after a time Dinah turned to her she was startled by the deadly weariness of her face.

"Oh, I am tiring you!" she exclaimed, with swift compunction.

But Isabel assured her with a smile that this was not so. She was a little tired, but that was nothing new.

"But you generally rest before dinner!" said Dinah, full of self-reproach, "Eustace, ought she not to rest?"

Eustace glanced at his sister half-reluctantly, and a shade of concern crossed his face also. "Are you feeling faint?" he asked her. "Do you want anything?"

"No, no! Of course not!" She averted her face sharply from his look. "Go on talking to Dinah! I am all right."

She moved to a deep window-embrasure, and sat down on the cushioned seat. The spring dusk was falling. She gazed forth into it with that look of perpetual searching that Dinah had grown to know in the earliest days of their acquaintance. She was watching, she was waiting, - for what? She longed to draw near and comfort her, but the presence of Eustace made that impossible. She did not know how to dismiss him.

And then to her relief the door opened, and Scott came quietly in upon them. He seemed to take in the situation at a glance, for after a few words with them he passed on to Isabel, sitting aloof and silent in the twilight.

She greeted him with a smile, and Dinah's anxiety lifted somewhat. She turned to Eustace.

"Show me your den now!" she said. "I can see the rest of the house to-morrow."

And with a feeling that she was doing Isabel a service she went away with him, alone.

CHAPTER VI

THE WRONG ROAD

When Dinah descended to breakfast the next morning, she encountered Scott in the hall. He had evidently just come in from an early ride, and he was looking younger and more animated than his wont.

"Ah, there you are!" he said, coming to meet her. "I've got some shocking news for you this morning. Eustace has had to go to town to see his solicitor. An urgent telephone message came through this morning. He has just gone up by the early train in the hope of getting back in good time. He charged me with all sorts of messages for you, and I have promised to take care of you in his absence, if you will allow me."

"Oh, that will be great fun!" exclaimed Dinah ingenuously, "I hope you are not very busy. I'd like you to show me everything."

He laughed. "No, I can't do that. We must keep that for Eustace. But I will take you to the Dower House, and show you that."

"I shall love that," said Dinah.

He took her into a room that overlooked terrace and river-valley and the sunny southern slope that lay between.

Ethel M. Dell

Breakfast was laid for two, and a cheery fire was burning. "How cosy it looks!" said Dinah.

"It does, doesn't it?" said Scott. "We always breakfast here in the winter for that reason. Not that it is winter to-day. It is glorious spring. You seem to have brought it with you. Take the coffee-pot end, won't you? What will you have to eat?"

He spoke with a lightness that Dinah found peculiarly exhilarating. He was evidently determined that she should not be dull. Her spirits rose. She suddenly felt like a child who has been granted an unexpected holiday.

She smiled up at him as he brought her a plate. "Isn't it a perfect morning? I'm so glad to be here. Don't let us waste a single minute; will we?"

"Not one," said Scott.

He went to his own place. He was plainly in a holiday mood also. She saw it in his whole bearing, and her heart rejoiced. It was so good to see him looking happy.

"Have you seen Isabel this morning?" he asked her presently.

"No. I went to her door, but Biddy said she was asleep, so I didn't go in."

"She often doesn't sleep much before morning," Scott said. "I expect she will be down to luncheon if you can put up with me only till then."

He evidently did not want to discuss Isabel's health just then, and Dinah was quite willing also to let the subject pass for the time. It was a morning for happy thoughts only. She and Scott would pretend that they had not a care in the world.

They breakfasted together as if it were a picnic. She had never seen him so cheery and inconsequent. It was as if he also were engaged in some species of make-believe. Or was it the enchantment of spring that had fallen upon them both? Dinah could not have said. She only knew that she had never felt so happy in all her life before.

The walk to the Dower House was full of delight. It was all so exquisite, the long, grassy slopes, the dark woods, the bare trees stark against the blue. The path led through a birch copse, and here in sheltered corners were primroses. She gathered them eagerly, and Scott helped her, even forgetting to smoke.

She did not remember later what they talked about, or even if they talked at all. But the amazing gladness of her heart on that spring morning was to be a vivid memory to her for as long as she lived.

They reached the Dower House. Like Willowmount, it overlooked the river, but from a different angle. Dinah was charmed with the old place. It was full of unexpected corners and old-fashioned contrivances. Blue patches of violets bloomed in the garden. Again with Scott's help, she gathered a great dewy bunch.

There were workmen in one or two of the rooms, and she stood by or wandered at will while Scott talked to the foreman.

They found themselves presently in the room that was to be Isabel's, - a large and sunlit apartment that had a turret window that looked to the far hills beyond the river. Dinah stood entranced with her eyes upon the blue distance. Finally, with a sigh, she spoke.

"How I wish I were going to live here too!"

"What! You like it better than Willowmount?" said Scott.

She made a little gesture of the hands, as if she pleaded for understanding. "I feel so small in big places. This is spacious, but it's cosy too. I - I should feel lost alone at Willowmount."

"But you won't be alone," he pointed out, with his kindly smile. "You will be very much the reverse, I can assure you."

She gave that sharp, uncontrollable little shiver of hers. "You mean Eustace -" she said haltingly.

"Yes, Eustace, and all the people round who will want to know his bride," said Scott. "I don't think you will have much time to be lonely. If you have, you can always come along to us, you know. We shall be only too delighted to see you."

Dinah turned to him impulsively. "You are good!" she said. "I wonder you don't look upon me as a horrid little interloper, turning you out of your home where you have always lived! I do hate the thought of it! Really it isn't my fault."

She spoke with tears in her eyes; but Scott still smiled. "My dear child," he said, "such an idea never entered my head. Isabel and I have often thought we should like to make this our home. We have always intended to as soon as Eustace married."

"Did you never think of marrying?" Dinah asked him suddenly.

There was an instant's pause, and then, as he was about to speak, she broke in quickly.

"Oh, please don't tell me! I was a pig to ask! I didn't mean to. It just slipped out. Do forgive me!"

"But why shouldn't you ask?" said Scott gently. "We are friends. I don't mind answering you. I've had my dream like the rest of the world. But it was very soon over. I never seriously deluded myself into the belief that anyone could care to marry a shrimp like me."

"Oh, Scott!" Almost fiercely Dinah cut him short. "How can you - you of all people - say a thing like that?"

Scott looked at her quizzically for a moment. "I should have thought I was the one person who could say it," he observed.

Dinah turned from him sharply. Her hands were clenched. "Oh no! Oh no!" she said incoherently. "It's not right! It's not fair! You - you - Mr. Greatheart!" Quite suddenly, as if the utterance of the name were too much for her, she broke down, covered her face, and wept.

"Dinah!" said Scott.

He came to her and took her very gently by the arm. Dinah's shoulders were shaking. She could not lift her face.

"Why - why shouldn't your dream come true too?" she sobbed. "You - who help everybody - to get what they want!"

"My dear," Scott said, "my dream is over. Don't you grieve on my account! God knows I'm not grieving for myself." His voice was low, but very steadfast.

"You wouldn't!" said Dinah.

"No; because it's futile, unnecessary, a waste of time. I've other things to do - plenty of other things." Scott braced himself with the words, as one who manfully lifts a burden. "Cheer up, Dinah! I didn't mean to make you sad."

"But - but - are you sure - quite sure - she didn't care?" faltered Dinah, rubbing her eyes woefully.

"Quite sure," said Scott, with decision.

Dinah threw him a sudden, flashing glance of indignation. "Then she was a donkey, Scott, a fool - an idiot!" she declared, with trembling vehemence. "I'd like - oh, how I'd like - to tell her so."

Scott was smiling, his own, whimsical smile. "Yes, wouldn't

you?" he said. "And it's awfully nice of you to say so. But do you know, you're quite wrong. She wasn't any of those things. On the other hand, I was all three. But where's the use of talking? It's over, and a good thing too!"

Dinah slipped a quivering hand over his. "We'll always be friends, won't we, Scott?" she said tremulously.

"Always," said Scott.

She squeezed his hand hard, and in response his fingers pressed her arm. His steady eyes looked straight into hers.

And in the silence, there came to Dinah a queer stirring of uncertainty, - the uncertainty of one who just begins to suspect that he is on the wrong road.

The moment passed, and they talked again of lighter things, but the mood of irresponsible light-heartedness had gone. When they finally left the Dower House, Dinah felt that she trod the earth once more.

"I shall come and see you very often when we come back," she said rather wistfully. "I hope Eustace won't want to be away a very long time."

"Aren't you looking forward to your honeymoon?" asked Scott.

"I don't know," said Dinah, and paused. "I really don't know. But," brightening, "I'm sure the wedding will be great fun."

"I hope it will," said Scott kindly.

It was not till they were nearing Willowmount that Dinah asked him at length hesitatingly about Isabel.

"Do you mind telling me? Is she worse?"

Scott also hesitated a little before he answered. Then: "In one sense she is much better," he said. "But physically," he paused, "physically she is losing ground."

"Oh, Scott!" Dinah looked at him with swift dismay. "But why - why? Can nothing be done?"

His eyes met hers unwaveringly. "No, nothing," he said, and he spoke with that decision which she had come to know as in some fashion a part of himself. His words carried conviction, and yet by some means they quieted her dismay as well. He went on after a moment with that gentle philosophy of his that seemed to soften all he said. "She is as one nearing the end of a long journey, and she is very tired, poor girl. We can't grudge her her rest - when it comes. Eustace wants to rouse her, but I think the time for that is past. It is kinder - it is wiser - to let her alone."

Dinah drew a little nearer to him. "Do you mean - that you think she won't live very long?" she whispered.

"If you like to put it that way," Scott answered quietly.

"Oh, but what of you?" she said.

She uttered the words almost involuntarily, and the next moment she would have recalled them, for she saw his face change. For a second - only a second - she read suffering in his eyes. But he answered her without hesitation.

"I shall just keep on, Dinah," he said. "It's the only way. But, as I think I've mentioned before, it's no good meeting troubles half-way. The day's work is all that really matters."

They walked on for a space in silence; then as they drew near the house he changed the subject. But that brief shadow of a coming desolation dwelt in Dinah's memory with a persistence that defied all lesser things. He was brave enough, cheery enough, in the shouldering of his burden; but her heart ached when she realized how heavy that burden must be.

A message awaited her at the house that she would go to Isabel in her sitting-room, and she went, half-eager, half-diffident. But as soon as she was with her friend her doubts were all gone. For Isabel looked and spoke so much as usual that it seemed impossible to believe that she was indeed nearing the end of the journey.

She wanted to know all that Dinah had been doing, and they sat and discussed the decorations of the Dower House till the luncheon-hour.

When luncheon was over they repaired to a sheltered corner of the terrace, looking down over the garden to the river, while Scott went away to write letters; and here they talked over the serious matter of the trousseau with regard to which neither Dinah nor her mother had made any very definite arrangements.

Perhaps Mrs. Bathurst had foreseen the possibility of Isabel desiring to undertake this responsibility. Perhaps Isabel had already dropped a hint of her intention. In any case it seemed the most natural thing in the world that Isabel should be the one to assist and advise, and when Dinah demurred a little on the score of cost she found herself gently but quite effectually silenced. Sir Eustace's bride must have a suitable outfit, Isabel told her. The question of ways and means was not one which need trouble her.

So Dinah obediently put the matter from her, and entered into the delightful discussion with keen zest. Isabel's ideas were so entrancing. She knew exactly what she would need. Her taste also was so simple, and so unerring. Dinah had never before pictured herself as possessing such things as Isabel calmly proclaimed that she must have.

"We must go up to town to-morrow," Isabel said, "and get things started. It will mean the whole day, I am afraid. Can you bear to be parted from Eustace for so long?"

Dinah laughed merrily at the question. "Of course - of course! What fun it will be! I always knew I should like to be married, but I never dreamt it could be so exciting as this."

Isabel smiled at her with a touch of pity in her eyes. "Marriage isn't only new clothes and wedding presents, Dinah," she said.

"No, no! I know!" Dinah spoke with swift compunction. "It is far more than that. But I've never had such lovely things before. I can't help feeling a little giddy about it. You do understand, don't you? I'm not like that all through - really."

"My darling!" Isabel answered fondly. "Of course I know it. I sometimes think that it would be better for you if you were."

"Isabel, why - why?" Dinah pressed close to her, half-curious, half-frightened.

But Isabel did not answer her. She only kissed the vivid, upturned face with all a mother's tenderness, and turned back in silence, to the fashion-book on her knee.

CHAPTER VII

DOUBTING CASTLE

When Sir Eustace returned, he found his bride-elect awaiting him with a radiant face. She sprang to greet him with an eagerness that outwent all shyness.

"Oh, Eustace, I have had such a lovely time!" she told him. "It has been a perfect day."

She offered him her lips with a child's simplicity, but blushed deeply when she felt the hot pressure of his, turning her face aside the moment he released her.

He laughed a little, keeping his arm about her shoulders. "You haven't missed me then?" he said.

"Oh, not a bit," said Dinah truthfully; and then quickly, "but what a horrid thing to say! Why did you put it like that?"

"I wanted to know," said Sir Eustace.

She turned back to him. "I should have missed you if I hadn't been so busy. Isabel is going to help me with my trousseau. And oh, Eustace, I am to have such a crowd of lovely things."

He pinched her cheek. "What should a brown elf need beyond a shift of thistle-down? Where is Isabel?"

"She is resting now. She got so tired. Biddy said she must lie down, and we mustn't disturb her for tea. I do hope it wasn't too much for her, Eustace."

"Too much for her! Nonsense! It does her good to think of someone else besides herself," said Eustace. "If Biddy didn't coddle her so in the day time, she would sleep better at night. Well, where is tea? In the drawing-room? Come along and have it!"

Dinah clung to his arm. "It - it's in a place called my lady's boudoir," she told him shyly.

He looked at her. "Where? Oh, I know. That inner sanctuary with the west window. You've taken a fancy to it, have you? Then we will call it Daphne's Bower."

Dinah's laugh was not without a hint of restraint. "I haven't been in any other room. Scott said you would show me everything. But I just wandered in there, and he found me and showed me the dear little boudoir. He said you were going to have it done up."

"So I am," said Eustace. "Everything that belongs to you must be new. Have you decided what colour will suit you best?"

They were passing through the long drawing-room towards the curtained doorway that led into the little boudoir. The drawing-room was a palatial apartment with stately French furniture that Dinah surveyed with awe. She could not picture herself as hostess in so magnificent a setting. She could only think of Rose de Vigne. It would have suited her flawless beauty perfectly, and she knew that Rose's self-contained heart would have revelled in such an atmosphere.

But it made her feel a stranger, and she hastened through it to the cosier nest beyond.

This was a far more homely spot. The furniture here was

French also, and exquisitely delicate; but it was designed for comfort, and the gilded state of the outer room was wholly absent.

A tea-table stood near a deeply-cushioned settee, and the kettle sang merrily over a spirit-lamp.

Eustace dropped on to the settee and drew her suddenly and wholly unexpectedly down upon his knee.

"Oh, Eustace!" she gasped, turning crimson.

He wound his arms about her, holding her two hands imprisoned. "Oh, Daphne!" he mocked softly. "I've caught you - I've caught you! Here in your own bower with no one to look on! No, you can't even flutter your wings now. You've got to stay still and be worshipped."

He spoke with his face against her neck. She felt the burning of his breath, and something; - an urgent, inner prompting - warned her to submit. She sat there in his grasp in quivering silence.

His arms drew her nearer, nearer. It was as if he were gradually merging her whole being into his. In a moment, with a little gasp, she gave him her trembling lips.

He uttered a low laugh of mastery and gave his passion the rein, overwhelming her with those devouring kisses that from the very outset had always filled her with an indefinable sense of shame. She was quite powerless to frustrate him. The delicate barrier of her reserve was rudely torn away. The burning blush on face and neck served but to feed the flame. He kissed the panting throat as if he would draw the very life out of it. There was fierce possession in the holding of his arms. She thought she would never be free again.

The first fiery wave spent itself at last, but even then he did not let her go. He held her pressed to him, and she lay against his breast trembling but wholly passive, overcome by an inexplicable longing to hide, to hide.

After a few seconds he spoke to her, his voice oddly unsteady, very deep. "You're driving me mad, Daphne. Do you know that?"

"I - I'm sorry," she faltered, trying to shelter her tingling face in his coat.

His arms were tense about her. "I want you more and more every day," he said. "I don't know how to wait for you. How long is it to our wedding?"

"Three weeks and four days," she told him faintly.

He gave his low, quivering laugh, "What! You are counting the days too! Daphne! My Daphne! Need we wait - all that time?"

Dinah's thumping heart gave a great start and seemed to stop. "Oh yes," she gasped desperately. "Yes, I couldn't possibly - be ready sooner."

He put his face down to hers, as one who breathes the essence of a flower. "You are ready now," he said. "You will never be lovelier than you are to-night."

She tried to laugh, but his lips were too near. Her voice quavered piteously.

"Why do I wait for you?" he said, and in his words there beat a fierce unrest. "Why am I such a fool? I lie awake night after night consumed with the want of you. When I sleep, I am always chasing you, you will-o'-the-wisp; and you always manage to keep just out of reach." His arms tightened. His voice suddenly sank to a deep whisper. "Daphne! Shall I tell you what I am going to do?"

"What?" panted Dinah.

"I am going to take you right away over the hills to-morrow to a place I know of where it is as lonely as the Sahara, and we will have a picnic there all to ourselves - all to ourselves, and make up for to-day."

His lips pressed hers again, but she withdrew herself with a sharp effort. There was nameless terror in her heart.

"Oh, I can't, Eustace! I can't indeed!" she said, and now she was striving, striving impotently, for freedom. "I'm going up to town with Isabel."

"Isabel can wait," he said.

"No! No! I must go. You don't understand. There are no end of things to be done." Dinah was as one encircled by fire, searching wildly round for a means of escape. "I must go!" she said again. "I must go!"

"You can go the next day," he said with arrogance. "I want you to-morrow and I mean to have you. Look at me, Dinah!"

She glanced at him, compelled by the command of his tone, met the fiery intensity of his look, and sank helpless, conquered.

He kissed her again. "There! That's settled. You silly little thing! Why do you always beat your wings against the inevitable? Do you think you are going to get away from me now?"

She hid her face against his shoulder. She was almost in tears. "You - you hurt me! You frighten me!" she whispered.

"Do I?" he said, and still in his voice she heard that deep note that made her whole being quiver. "It's your own fault, my Daphne. You shouldn't run away."

"I - I can't help it," she said tremulously. "I sometimes think -

I'm not big enough for you."

"You'll grow," he said.

"I don't know," she answered in distress. "I may not. And if I do, I feel - I feel as if I shan't be myself any longer, but just - but just - a bit of you!"

He laughed. "Daphne, - you oddity! Don't you want to be a bit of me?"

"I'd rather be myself," she murmured shyly.

His hold was not so close, and she longed, but did not dare, to get off his knee and breathe. But in that moment there came the sound of a halting step in the drawing-room beyond, and swiftly she raised her head.

"Oh, Eustace, let me go! Here is Scott!"

He did not release her instantly. Scott was already in the doorway before, like a frightened fawn, she leapt from his grasp. She heard Eustace laugh again, and somehow his laugh had a note of insolence.

"Come in, my good brother!" he said. "My lady is just about to make tea. I presume that is what you have come for."

"The presumption is correct," said Scott.

He came forward in his quiet, unhurried fashion, and paused at the table to open the tea-caddy for Dinah.

She thanked him with trembling lips, her eyes cast down, her face on fire.

Eustace lounged back on the settee and watched her. He frowned momentarily when Scott sat down beside him, leaving her a low chair by the tea-tray.

Dinah's hands fluttered among the cups. She was painfully ill at ease. But in a second or two Scott's placid voice came into the silence, and at once her distress began to subside.

"Have you decided about the decoration of this room yet?" he asked. "I always thought this dead-white rather cold."

"Dinah is to have her own choice," said Sir Eustace.

"I would like shell-pink," said Dinah, without looking up. "Don't you think that would be nice with those pretty water-colour sketches?"

She spoke diffidently. No one had ever deferred to her taste before.

Sir Eustace laughed in his slightly supercilious way. "Do you know who is responsible for those pretty sketches, my red, red rose?"

She glanced up nervously. "Not - not - are they yours, Scott?"

"They are," said Scott, with a smile.

She met his eyes for an instant, and was surprised by their gravity. "Oh, I do like them," she said. "I wonder I didn't guess. They are so beautifully finished, so - complete."

"I am glad you like them," said Scott. "I thought you might want to turn them out as lumber."

"As if I should!" she said. "I love them - every one of them. I shall love them better still now I know they are yours."

"Thank you," said Scott.

Eustace turned his attention to him. "No one ever paid you such a compliment as that before, my good Stumpy," he observed. "If everyone saw you in that light, you'd be a great artist by now."

"I wonder," said Scott.

Dinah sent him another swift glance. She seemed on the verge of speech, but checked herself, and there fell a brief silence.

It was broken by the entrance of a servant. "If you please, Sir Eustace, Mr. Grey is in the library and would be glad if you could spare him a few minutes."

Sir Eustace uttered an impatient exclamation. "You go and see what he wants, Stumpy!" he said.

But Scott remained seated. "I know what he wants, my dear chap, and it's something that only you can give. He has come about Bob Jelf who was caught poaching last week. He wants you to give the fellow as light a sentence as possible on account of his wife."

Sir Eustace frowned. "I never give a light sentence for poaching. He's always at it, I'd give him the cat if I could."

Scott raised his shoulders slightly. "Well, don't ask me to say that to Mr. Grey! He's taking the whole business badly to heart, as he was beginning to look on Jelf as a reformed character."

"I'll reform him!" said Sir Eustace. He turned to the servant. "Ask Mr. Grey to join us here!"

"You had better see him alone first," said Scott.

"Why?" His brother turned upon him almost savagely.

Scott took up his tea-cup. "You can't refuse to give him a hearing," he observed. "He has come up on purpose."

Sir Eustace murmured something under his breath and rose.

His look fell upon Dinah. "It's the village padre," he said. "I shall have to bring him in here. I hope you don't mind?"

She gave him a quick, half-startled smile. "Of course not."

He turned to the door which the waiting servant was holding open, and strode out with annoyed majesty.

Dinah watched him till the door closed; then very suddenly and urgently she turned to Scott.

"Oh, please, will you help me?" she said.

He gave her a straight, keen look that seemed to penetrate to her soul. "If it lies in my power," he said slowly.

She caught her breath, pierced by a sharp uncertainty. "You can. I'm sure you can," she said.

He set down his cup. "Dinah," he said gently, "don't ask me to interfere in your affairs if you can by any means manage without!"

"But that's just it!" she said in distress. "I can't."

He leaned forward. "My dear, don't be agitated!" he said. "Tell me what is the matter!"

Dinah leaned forward also, her hands tightly clasped, and spoke in a rapid whisper.

"Scott, Eustace wants me to go for an all-day picnic alone with him to-morrow. I - don't want to go."

He was still looking at her with that straight, almost stern regard. An odd little quiver went through her as she met it. She felt as if she were in a fashion on her trial.

"Why don't you want to go?" he asked.

She hesitated. "I was to have gone up to town with Isabel to shop," she said.

"No, that isn't the reason," he said. "Tell me the reason!"

She made a quick gesture of appeal. "I - wish you wouldn't ask," she faltered, and suddenly she could meet his eyes no longer. She lowered her own, and sat before him in burning confusion.

"Have you asked yourself?" he said, his voice very low.

She was silent; the quiet question seemed to probe her through and through. There was no evading it.

Scott was still watching her very closely, very intently. He spoke at length, just as she was beginning to feel his scrutiny to be more than she could bear.

"If you are just shy with him - as I think you are - I think you ought to try and get over it, as much for his sake as for your own. You don't want to hurt him, do you? You wouldn't like him to be disappointed?"

Dinah shook her head. "If you could come too!" she suggested, in a very small voice.

"No, I can't," said Scott firmly.

She sent him a darting glance. "Are you angry with me?" she said.

"I!" said Scott in amazement.

"You - spoke as if you were," she said. "And you looked - quite grim."

He laughed a little. "If you are afraid of me, you must indeed be easily frightened. No, of course I am not angry. Dinah!

Ethel M. Dell

Dinah! Don't be silly!"

Her lips were quivering, but in response to his admonishing tone she forced them to smile. "I know I am silly," she said, with an effort. "I - I'm not nearly good enough for Eustace. And I'm a dreadful little coward, I know. But he does frighten me. When he kisses me - I always want to run away."

"But you wouldn't like it if he didn't," said Scott, in the voice of the philosopher.

"Shouldn't I?" said Dinah. "I wonder. It - wouldn't be him, would it?"

"And what are you going to do when you are married?" said Scott, point blank. "You'll see much more of him then."

"Oh, I expect I shall feel different then," said Dinah. "Married people are different, aren't they? They are not always going off by themselves and kissing in corners."

"Not as a rule," admitted Scott. "But I've been told that there is usually a good deal of that sort of thing done during the honeymoon."

"That's different too," Dinah's voice was slightly dubious notwithstanding. "But we are not on our honeymoon yet. Scott, couldn't you - just for once - help me to - to find an excuse not to go? It would be - so dear of you."

She spoke with earnest entreaty, her eyes frankly raised to his.

Scott looked into them with steady searching before he finally responded. "I will speak to him if you like. I don't know that I shall be successful. But - if you wish it - I will try."

"Oh, thank you," she said. "Thank you." And then quickly, "You're sure you don't mind? Sure you're not afraid?"

"Oh, quite sure of that," said Scott.

Her eyes expressed open admiration. "I can't think how you manage not to be," she said.

He smiled with a touch of sadness. "Perhaps I am not so weak as I look," he said.

"You - weak!" said Dinah. "Why, you are the strongest man I ever met."

Scott smothered a sudden sigh. "Which only proves how very little you know about me," he said.

But Dinah shook her head, wholly unconvinced. Here at least she was absolutely sure of her ground.

"'Mr. Greatheart was a strong man,'" she quoted, "'and he was not afraid of a Lion.'"

"There are sometimes worse things than lions in the path," said Scott gravely.

CHAPTER VIII

THE VICTORY

The return of Sir Eustace, marshalling the Vicar before him, put an end to further confidences.

Dinah rose nervously to receive the new-comer - a tall, thin man, elderly, with a grave, intellectual face and courteous manner, who looked at her with a gleam of surprise as he took her shyly proffered hand.

"It is a great privilege to meet you," he said then, and Dinah perceived at once that he had prepared that remark for someone much more imposing than herself, and had not time to readjust it.

She thanked him, and he sat down at Scott's invitation and fell into a troubled silence.

Sir Eustace was looking decidedly formidable, and it was not difficult to see that he had just given an unqualified refusal to his visitor's earnest request.

It was Scott as usual who came to the rescue, breaking through the Vicar's abstraction to ask for details concerning certain additions that were being made to the Cottage Hospital. He drew Dinah also into the conversation, taking it for granted that she would be interested; and presently Mr. Grey brightened somewhat, launching into what was evidently a favourite topic.

"We are hoping," he said, "that the new wing will be completed by the end of June, and it is expected that the Parish Council will request Lady Studley to be good enough to declare it open."

He looked at Dinah with the words, and she realized their significance with a sharp shock. "Oh, do you mean me?" she said. "I don't think I could."

"It wouldn't be a very difficult business," said Scott reassuringly.

"Oh, I couldn't!" she said. "Why - why, there would be crowds of people, wouldn't there?"

"I hope to get a few of the County," said Mr. Grey, "to support you."

"That makes it worse," said Dinah.

Scott laughed. "Eustace and I will come too and take care of you. You see, the Lady of the Manor has to do these tiresome things."

"Oh! I'll come if you want me," said Dinah. "But I've never done anything like that before and I can't think what the County will say. You see, I don't belong."

"Snap your fingers in its face, and it won't bite you!" said Eustace. "You will belong by that time."

Mr. Grey smiled a very kindly smile that had in it a touch of compassion. He said nothing, but in a few minutes he rose to take his leave, and then, with Dinah's hand held for a moment in his, he said in a low voice, "I wish I might enlist your sympathy on behalf of one of my parishioners. His wife is dying of cancer, and he is to be sent to gaol for poaching."

"Oh!" Dinah exclaimed in distress.

She looked quickly across at her *fiance*, and saw that his brow was dark.

He said nothing whatever, and she went to him impulsively. "Eustace, must you send him to prison?"

He looked at her for a second, then turned, without responding, to the Vicar. "That was a very unnecessary move on your part, sir," he said icily. "I have told you my decision in the matter, and there it must rest. Justice is justice."

Dinah was looking at him very pleadingly; he laid his hand upon her arm, and she felt his fingers close with a strong, restraining pressure.

Mr. Grey turned to go. "I make no excuse, Sir Eustace," he said. "I am begging for mercy, not justice. My cause is urgent. If one weapon fails, I must employ another."

He went out with Scott, and Dinah was left alone with Sir Eustace.

He spoke at once, sternly and briefly, before she had time to open her lips. "Dinah, this is no matter for your interference. I forbid you to pursue it any further."

His tone was crushingly absolute; she saw that he was white with anger.

She felt the colour die out of her own cheeks as she faced him. But the Vicar's few words had made a deep impression upon her; she forced back her fear.

"But, Eustace, is it true?" she said. "Is the man's wife really dying? If so - if so - surely you will let him off!"

His grasp upon her arm tightened. "Are you going to disobey

me?" he said warningly.

His look was terrible, but she braved it. "Yes - yes, I am," she said, with desperate courage. "Eustace, I've never asked you to do anything before. Couldn't you - can't you - do this one thing?"

She met the blazing wrath of his eyes though her heart felt stiff with fear. It had come so suddenly, this ordeal, but she braced herself to meet it. Horrible though it was to withstand him, the thought came to her that if she did not make the effort just once she would never have the strength again.

"You think me very impertinent," she said, speaking quickly through quivering lips. "But - but - I have a right to speak. If I am to be - your wife, you must not treat me as - a servant."

She saw his look change. The anger went out of it, but something that was more terrible to her took its place, something that she could not meet.

She flinched involuntarily, and in the same moment he drew her close to him. "Ah, Daphne, the adorable!" he said. "I've never seen you at bay before! You claim your privileges, do you? You think I can refuse you nothing?"

She shrank at his tone - the mastery of it, the confidence, the caress.

"You needn't be afraid," he said, and bent his face to hers. "Whatever you wish is law. But don't forget one thing! If I refuse you nothing, I must have everything in exchange. 'Love the gift is Love the debt,' my Daphne. You must give me freely all that you have in return."

She trembled in his embrace. Those passionate words of his frightened her anew. Was it possible - would it ever be possible - to give him - freely - all that she had?

Ethel M. Dell

The doubt shot through her like the stab of a dagger even while she gave him the kiss he demanded for her audacity. Her victory over him amazed her, so appalling had seemed the odds. But in a fashion it dismayed her too. He was too mighty a giant to kneel at her feet for long. He would exact payment in full, she was sure, she was sure, for all that he gave her now.

She was thankful when a ceremonious knock at the door compelled him to release her. Biddy presented herself very upright, primly correct.

"If ye please, Miss Dinah, Mrs. Everard is awake and will be pleased to see ye whenever it suits ye to go to her at all."

"Oh, I'll go now," said Dinah with relief. She glanced at Eustace. "You don't mind? You don't want me?"

"No, I have some business to discuss with Stumpy," he said. "Perhaps I will join you presently."

He took out a cigarette and lighted it, and Dinah turned; and went away with the old woman.

"And it's to be hoped he'll do nothing of the kind," remarked Biddy, as they walked through the long drawing-room. "For the very thought of him is enough to drive poor Miss Isabel scranny, specially in the evening."

"Is - is Miss Isabel so afraid of him?" asked Dinah under her breath.

Biddy nodded darkly. "She is that, Miss Dinah, and small blame to her."

Dinah pressed suddenly close. "Biddy, why?"

Biddy pursed her lips. "Faith, and it's meself that's afraid, ye'll find the answer to that only too soon, Miss Dinah dear!" she said solemnly. "I can't tell ye the straight truth. Ye wouldn't believe me if I did. Ye must watch for yourself, me jewel. Ye've got a woman's intelligence. Don't ye be afraid to use it!"

It was the soundest piece of advice that she had ever heard from Biddy's lips, and Dinah accepted it in silence. She had known for some time that Biddy had small love for Sir Eustace, but it was evident that the precise reason for this was not to be conveyed in words. She wished she could have persuaded her to be more explicit, but something held her back from attempting to gain the information that Biddy withheld. It was better - surely it was sometimes better - not to know too much.

They met Scott as they turned out of the drawing-room, and Biddy's grim old face softened at the sight of him.

He paused: "Hullo! Going to Isabel? Has she had a good rest, Biddy?"

"Glory to goodness, Master Scott, she has!" said Biddy fervently.

"That's all right." Scott prepared to pass on. "Eustace hasn't gone, I suppose?"

"No, he is in there, waiting for you." Dinah detained him for a moment. "Scott, he - I think he is going to - to let that man off with a light sentence."

"What?" said Scott. "Dinah, you witch! How on earth did you do it?"

He looked so pleased that her heart gave a throb of triumph. It had been well worth while just to win that look from him.

She smiled back at him. "I don't know. I really don't know. But, - Scott" - she became a little breathless - "if - if he really wants me to-morrow, I think - p'raps - I'd better go."

Ethel M. Dell

Scott gave her his straight, level look. There was a moment's pause before he said, "Wait till to-morrow comes anyway!" and with that he was gone, limping through the great room with that steady but unobtrusive purpose that ever, to Dinah's mind, redeemed him from insignificance.

"Ah! He's the gentleman is Master Scott," said Biddy's voice at her side. "Ye'll never meet his like in all the world. It's a sad life he leads, poor young gentleman, but he keeps a brave heart though never a single joy comes his way. May the Almighty reward him and give him his desire before it's too late."

"What desire?" asked Dinah.

Biddy shot her a lightning glance from her beady eyes ere again mysteriously she shook her head.

"And it's the innocent lamb that ye are entirely, Miss Dinah dear," she said.

With which enigmatical answer Dinah was forced to be content.

CHAPTER IX

THE BURDEN

Sir Eustace was standing by the window of the little boudoir when his brother entered, and Scott joined him there. He also lighted a cigarette, and they smoked together in silence for several seconds.

Finally Eustace turned with his faint, supercilious smile. "What's the matter, Stumpy? Something on your mind?"

Scott met his look. "Something I've got to say to you anyway, old chap, that rather sticks in my gullet."

Sir Eustace laughed. "You carry conscience enough for the two of us. What is it? Fire away!"

Scott puffed at his cigarette. "You won't like it," he observed. "But it's got to be said. Look here, Eustace! It's all very well to be in love. But you're carrying it too far. The child's downright afraid of you."

"Has she told you so?" demanded Eustace. A hot gleam suddenly shone in his blue eyes. He looked down at Scott with a frown.

Scott shook his head. "If she had, I shouldn't tell you so. But the fact remains. You're a bit of an ogre, you know, always have been. Slack off a bit, there's a good fellow! You'll find it's

Ethel M. Dell

worth it."

He spoke with the utmost gentleness, but there was determination in his quiet eyes. Having spoken, he turned them upon the garden again and resumed his cigarette.

There fell a brief silence between them. Sir Eustace was no longer smoking. His frown had deepened. Suddenly he laid his hand upon Scott's shoulder.

"It's my turn now," he said. "I've something to say to you."

"Well?" said Scott. He stiffened a little at the hold upon him, but he did not attempt to frustrate it.

"Only this." Eustace pressed upon him as one who would convey a warning. "You've interfered with me more than once lately, and I've borne with it - more or less patiently. But I'm not going to bear with it much longer. You may be useful to me, but - you're not indispensable. Remember that!"

Scott started at the words, as a well-bred horse starts at the flicker of the whip. He controlled himself instantly, but his eyelids quivered a little as he answered, "I will remember it."

Sir Eustace's hand fell. "I think that is all that need be said," he observed. "We will get to business."

He turned from the window, but in the same moment Scott wheeled also and took him by the arm. "One moment!" he said. "Eustace, we are not going to quarrel over this. You don't imagine, do you, that I interfere with you in this way for my own pleasure?"

He spoke urgently, an odd wistfulness in voice and gesture.

Sir Eustace paused. The sternness still lingered in his eyes though his face softened somewhat as he said, "I haven't gone into the question of motives, Stumpy. I have no doubt they are

- like yourself - very worthy, though it might not soothe me greatly to know what they are."

Scott still held his arm. "Oh, man," he said very earnestly, "don't miss the best thing in life for want of a little patience! She's such a child. She doesn't understand. For your own sake give her time!"

There was that in his tone that somehow made further offence impossible. A faint, half-grudging smile took the place of the grimness on his brother's face.

"You take things so mighty seriously," he said. "What's the matter? What has she been saying?"

Scott hesitated. "I can't tell you that. I imagine it is more what she doesn't say that makes me realize the state of her mind. I can tell you one thing. She would rather go shopping with Isabel to-morrow than picnicking in the wilderness with you, and if you're wise, you'll give in and let her go. You'll run a very grave risk of losing her altogether if you ask too much."

"What do you mean?" Eustace's voice was short and stern; the question was like a sword thrust.

Again Scott hesitated. Then very steadily he made reply. "I mean that - with or without reason, you know best - she is beginning not to trust you. It is more than mere shyness with her. She is genuinely frightened."

His words went into silence, and in the silence he took out his handkerchief and wiped his forehead. It had been a more difficult interview for him than Eustace would ever realize. His powers of endurance were considerable, but he had an almost desperate desire now to escape.

But some instinct kept him where he was. To fail at the last moment for lack of perseverance would have been utterly uncharacteristic of him. It was his custom to stand his ground

Ethel M. Dell

to the last, whatever the cost.

And so he forced himself to wait while his brother contemplated the unpleasant truth that he had imparted. He knew that it was not in his nature to spend long over the process, but he was still by no means sure of the final result.

Eustace spoke at length very suddenly. "See here, Stumpy!" he said. "There may be something in what you say, and there may not. But in any case, you and Dinah are getting altogether too intimate and confidential to please me. It's up to you to put the brake on a bit. Understand?"

He smiled as he said it, but there was a gleam as of cold steel behind his smile.

Scott straightened himself. It was as if something within him leapt to meet the steel. Spent though he was, this was a matter no man could shirk.

"I shall do nothing of the kind," he said. "Do you think I'd destroy her trust in me too? I'd sell my soul sooner."

The words were passionate, and the man as he uttered them seemed suddenly galvanized with a new force, a force irresistible, elemental, even sublime. The elder brother's brows went up in amazement. He did not know Stumpy in that mood. He found himself confronted with a power colossal manifested in the meagre frame, and before that power instinctively, wholly involuntarily, he gave ground.

"I see you mean to please yourself," he said, and turned to go with a sub-conscious feeling that if he lingered he would have the worst of it. "But I warn you if you get in my way, you'll be kicked. So look out!"

It was not a conciliatory speech, but it was the outcome of undoubted discomfiture. He was so accustomed to submission from Scott that he had come to look upon it as inevitable. His sudden self-assertion was oddly disconcerting.

So also was the laugh that followed his threat, a careless laugh wholly devoid of bitterness which yet in some fashion inexplicable pierced his armour, making him feel ashamed.

"You know exactly what I think of that sort of thing, don't you?" Scott said. "That's the best of having no special physical attractions. One doesn't need to think of appearances."

Sir Eustace made no rejoinder. He could think of nothing to say; for he knew that Scott's attitude was absolutely sincere. For physical suffering he cared not one jot. The indomitable spirit of the man lifted him above it. He was fashioned upon the same lines as the men who faced the lions of Rome. No bodily pain could ever daunt him.

He went from the room haughtily but in his heart he carried an odd misgiving that burned and spread like a slow fire, consuming his pride. Scott had withstood him, Scott the weakling, and in so doing had made him aware of a strength that exceeded his own.

As for Scott, the moment he was alone he drew a great breath of relief, and almost immediately after opened the French window and passed quietly out into the garden.

The dusk was falling, and the air smote chill; yet he moved slowly forth, closing the window behind him and so down into the desolate shrubberies where he paced for a long, long time....

When he went to Isabel's room more than an hour later, his eyes were heavy with weariness, and he moved like a man who bears a burden.

She was alone, and looked up at his entrance with a smile of welcome. "Come and sit down, Stumpy! I've seen nothing of you. Dinah has only just left me. She tells me Eustace is talking of a picnic for to-morrow, but really she ought to give her mind to her trousseau if she is ever to be ready in time. Do you think Eustace can be induced to see reason?"

"I don't know," Scott said. He seated himself by Isabel's side and leaned back against the cushions, closing his eyes.

"You are tired," she said gently.

"Oh, only a little, Isabel!" He spoke without moving, making no effort to veil his weariness from her.

"What is it, dear?" she said.

"I am very anxious about Dinah." He spoke the words deliberately; his face remained absolutely still and expressionless.

"Anxious, Stumpy!" Isabel echoed the word quickly, almost as though it gave her relief to speak. "Oh, so am I - terribly anxious. She is so young, so utterly unprepared for marriage. I believe she is frightened to death when she lets herself stop to think."

"I blame myself," Scott said heavily.

"My dear, why?" Isabel's hand sought and held his. "How could you be to blame?"

"I forced it on," he said. "I - in a way - compelled Eustace to propose. He wasn't serious till then. I made him serious."

"Oh, Stumpy, you!" Incredulity and reproach mingled in Isabel's tone.

She would have withdrawn her hand, but his fingers closed upon it. "I made a mistake," he said, with dreary conviction, "a great mistake, though God knows I meant well; and now it is out of my power to set it right. I thought her heart was involved. I know now it was not. It's hard on him too in a way, because he is very much in earnest now, whatever he was before. I was a fool - I was a fool - not to let things take their course. She would have suffered, but it would have been soon over. Whereas now -" He stopped himself abruptly. "It's no good talking. There's nothing to be done. He may - after marriage - break her in to loving him, but if he does - if he does - " his hand clenched with sudden force upon Isabel's - "it won't be Dinah any more," he said. "It'll be - another woman; one who is satisfied with - a very little."

His hand relaxed as suddenly as it had closed. He lay still with a face like marble.

Isabel sat motionless by his side for several seconds. She was gazing straight before her with eyes that seemed to read the future.

"How did you compel him to propose?" she asked presently.

He shrugged his narrow shoulders slightly. "I can do these things, Isabel, if I try. But I wish I'd killed myself now before I interfered. As I tell you, I was a fool - a fool."

He ceased to speak and sat in the silence of a great despair.

Isabel said nought to comfort him. Her tragic eyes still seemed to be gazing into the future.

After many minutes Scott turned his head and looked at her. "Isabel, I wish you would try to keep her with you as much as possible. Tell Eustace what you have just told me! There is certainly no time to lose if she is really to be married in three weeks from now!"

"I suppose he would never consent to put it off," Isabel said slowly.

"He certainly would not." Scott rose with a restless movement

Ethel M. Dell

that said more than words. "He is on fire for her. Can't you see it? There is nothing to be done unless she herself wishes to be released. And I don't think that is very likely to happen."

"He would never give her up," Isabel said with conviction.

"If she desired it, he would," Scott's reply held an even more absolute finality.

Isabel looked at him for a moment; then: "Yes, but the poor little thing would never dare," she said. "Besides - besides - there is the glamour of it all."

"Yes, there is the glamour." Scott spoke with a kind of grim compassion. "The glamour may carry her through. If so, then - possibly - it may soften life for her afterwards. It may even turn into romance. Who knows? But - in any case - there will probably be - compensations."

"Ah!" Isabel said. A wonderful light shone for a moment in her eyes and died; she turned her face aside. "Compensations don't come to everyone, Stumpy," she said. "What if the glamour fades and they don't come to take its place?"

Scott was standing before the fire, his eyes fixed upon its red depths. His shoulders were still bent, as though they bore a burden well-nigh overwhelming. An odd little spasm went over his face at her words.

"Then - God help my Dinah!" he said almost under his breath.

In the silence that followed the words, Isabel rose impulsively, came to him, and slipped her hand through his arm.

She neither looked at him nor spoke, and in silence the matter passed.

CHAPTER X

THE HOURS OF DARKNESS

Dinah could not sleep that night. For the first time in all her healthy young life she lay awake with grim care for a bed-fellow. When in trouble she had always wept herself to sleep before, but to-night she did not weep. She lay wide-eyed, feeling hot and cold by turns as the memory of her lover's devouring passion and Biddy's sinister words alternated in her brain. What was the warning that Biddy had meant to convey? And how - oh, how - would she ever face the morrow and its fierce, prolonged courtship, from the bare thought of which every fibre of her being shrank in shamed dismay?

"There won't be any of me left by night," she told herself, as she sought to cool her burning face against the pillow. "Oh, I wish he didn't love me quite so terribly."

It was no good attempting to bridle wish or fears. They were far too insistent. She was immured in the very dungeons of Doubting Castle, and no star shone in her darkness.

Towards morning her restlessness became unendurable. She arose and tremblingly paced the room, sick with a nameless apprehension that seemed to deprive her alike of the strength to walk or to be still.

Her whole body was in a fever as though it had been scourged with thongs; in fact, she still seemed to feel the scourge,

Ethel M. Dell

goading her on.

To and fro, to and fro, she wandered, scarcely knowing what she wanted, only urged by that unbearable restlessness that gave her no respite. Of the future ahead of her she did not definitely think. Her marriage still seemed too intangible a matter for serious contemplation. She still in her child's heart believed that marriage would make a difference. He would not make such ardent love to her when they were married. They would both have so many other things to think about. It was the present that so weighed upon her, her lover's almost appalling intensity of worship and her own utter inadequacy and futility.

Again, as often before, the question arose within her, How would Rose have met the situation? Would she have been dismayed? Would she have shrunk from those fiery kisses? Or could she - could she possibly - have remained calm and complacent and dignified in the midst of those surging tempests of love? But yet again she failed completely to picture Rose so mastered, so possessed, by any man; Rose the queen whom all men worshipped with reverence from afar. She wondered again how Sir Eustace had managed to elude the subtle charm she cast upon all about her. He had actually declared that her perfection bored him. It was evident that she left him cold. Dinah marvelled at the fact, so certain was she that had he humbled himself to ask for Rose's favour it would have been instantly and graciously accorded to him.

It would have saved a lot of trouble if he had fallen in love with Rose, she reflected; and then the old thrill of triumph went through her, temporarily buoying her up. She had been preferred to Rose. She had beaten Rose on her own ground, she the little, insignificant adjunct of the de Vigne party! She was glad - oh, she was very glad! - that Rose was to have so close a view of her final conquest.

She began to take comfort in the thought of her approaching wedding and all its attendant glories, picturing every detail with girlish zest. To be the queen of such a brilliant ceremony as that! To be received into the County as one entering a new world! To belong to that Society from which her mother had been excluded! To be in short - her ladyship.

A new excitement began to urge Dinah. She picked up a towel and draped it about her head and shoulders like a bridal veil. Her mother would have rated her for such vanity, but for the moment vanity was her only comfort, and the thought of her mother did not trouble her. This was how she would look on her wedding-day. There would be a wreath of orange-blossoms of course; Isabel would see to that. And - yes, Isabel had said that her bouquet should be composed of lilies-of-the-valley. She even began to wish it were her wedding morning.

The glamour spread like a rosy dawning; she forgot the clouds that loomed immediately ahead. Standing there in her night attire, poised like a brown wood-nymph on the edge of a pool, she asked herself for the first time if it were possible that she could have any pretensions to beauty. It was not in the least likely, of course. Her mother had always railed at her for the plainness of her looks. Did Eustace - did Scott - think her plain? She wondered. She wondered.

A slight sound, the opening of a window, in the room next to hers, made her start. That was Isabel's room. What was happening? It was three o'clock in the morning. Could Isabel be ill?

Very softly she opened her own window and leaned forth. It was one of those warm spring nights that come in the midst of March gales. There was a scent of violets on the air. She thought again for a fleeting second of Scott and their walk through fairyland that morning. And then she heard a voice, pitched very low but throbbing with an eagerness unutterable, and at once her thoughts were centred upon Isabel.

"Did you call me, my beloved? I am waiting! I am waiting!" said the voice.

It went forth into the sighing darkness of the night, and Dinah held her breath to listen, almost as if she expected to hear an answer.

There fell a long, long silence, and then there came a sound that struck straight to her warm heart. It seemed to her that Isabel was weeping.

She left her window with the impetuosity of one actuated by an impulse irresistible; she crossed her own room, and slipped out into the dark passage just as she was. A moment or two she fumbled feeling her way; and then her hand found Isabel's door. Softly she turned the handle, opened, and peeped in.

Isabel was on her knees by the low window-sill. Her head with its crown of silver hair was bowed upon her arm and they rested upon the bundle of letters which Dinah had seen on the very first night that she had seen Isabel. Old Biddy hovered shadow-like in the background. She made a sign to Dinah as she entered, but Dinah was too intent upon her friend to notice.

Fleet-footed she drew near, and as she approached a long bitter sigh broke from Isabel and, following it, low-toned entreaties that pierced her anew with the utter abandonment of their supplication.

"Oh God," she prayed brokenly. "I am so tired - so tired - of waiting. Open the door for me! Let me out of my prison! Let me find my beloved in the dawning - in the dawning!"

Her voice sank, went into piteous sobbing. She crouched lower in the depth of her woe.

Dinah stooped over her with a little crooning murmur of pity, and gathered her close in her arms.

Isabel gave a great start. "Child!" she said, and then she clasped Dinah to her, leaning her face against her bosom.

Dinah was crying softly, but she saw that Isabel had no tears. That sobbing came from her broken heart, but it brought no relief. The dark eyes burned with a misery that found no vent, save possibly in the passionate holding of her arms.

"My darling," she whispered presently, "did I wake you?"

"No, dearest, no!" Dinah was tenderly caressing the snowy hair; she spoke with an almost motherly fondness. "I happened to be awake, and I heard you at the window."

"Why were you awake, darling? Aren't you happy?"

Quick anxiety was in the words. Dinah flushed with a sense of guilt.

"Of course I am happy," she made answer. "What more could I have to wish for? But, Isabel, you - you!"

"Ah, never mind me!" Isabel said. She rose with the movement of one who would shield another from harm. "You ought to be in bed, sweetheart. Shall I come and tuck you up?"

"Come and finish the night with me!" whispered Dinah. "We shall both be happy then."

She scarcely expected that Isabel would accede to her desire, but it seemed that Isabel could refuse her nothing. She turned, holding Dinah closely to her.

"My good angel!" she murmured tenderly. "What should I do without you? It is always you who come to lift me out of my inferno."

She left the letters forgotten on the window-sill. By the simple outpouring of her love, Dinah had drawn her out of her place of torment; and she led her now, leaning heavily upon her, through the passage to her own room.

Biddy crept after them like a wise old cat alert for danger. "She'll sleep now, Miss Dinah darlint," she murmured. "Ye won't be anxious at all, at all? It's meself that'll be within call."

"No, no! Go to your own room and sleep, Biddy!" Isabel said. "We are both going to do the same."

She sank into the great double bed that Dinah had found almost alarmingly capacious, with a sigh of exhaustion, and Dinah slipped in beside her. They clasped each other, each with a separate sense of comfort.

Biddy tucked up first one side, then the other, with a whispered blessing for each.

"Ah, the poor lambs!" she murmured, as she went away.

But Isabel's voice had reassured her; she did not linger even outside the door.

Mumbling still below her breath her inarticulate benisons, Biddy passed through her mistress's room into her own. She was very tired, for she had been watching without intermission for nearly five hours. She almost dropped on to her bed and lay as she fell, deeply sleeping.

The letters on the window-sill were forgotten for the rest of that night.

CHAPTER XI

THE NET

When Dinah met her lover in the morning she found him in a surprisingly indulgent mood. The day was showery, and he announced his intention of accompanying them in the car up to town.

"An excellent opportunity for selecting the wedding-ring," he told her lightly. "You will like that better than a picnic."

And Dinah in her relief admitted that this was the case.

Up to the last moment she hoped that Scott would accompany them also, but when she came down dressed for the expedition she found that he had gone to the library to write letters. She pursued him thither, but he would not be persuaded to leave his work.

"Besides, I should only be in the way," he said. And when she vehemently negatived this, he smiled and fell back upon the plea that he was busy.

Just at the last she tried to murmur a word of thanks to him for intervening on her behalf to induce Eustace to abandon the picnic, but he gently checked her.

"Oh, please don't thank me!" he said. "I am not a very good meddler, I assure you. I hope you are going to have a good

Ethel M. Dell

day. Take care of Isabel!"

Dinah would have lingered to tell him of the night's happening, but Sir Eustace called her and with a smile of farewell she hastened away.

She enjoyed that day with a zest that banished all misgivings. Sir Eustace insisted upon the purchase of the ring at the outset, and then she and Isabel went their way alone, and shopped in a fashion that raised Dinah's spirits to giddy heights. She had never seen or imagined such exquisite things as Isabel ordered on her behalf. The hours slipped away in one long dream of delight. Sir Eustace had desired them to join him at luncheon, but Isabel had gravely refused. There would not be time, she said. They would meet for tea. And somewhat to Dinah's surprise he had yielded the point.

They met for tea in a Bond Street restaurant and here Sir Eustace took away his *fiancee's* breath by presenting her with a pearl necklace to wear at her wedding.

She was almost too overwhelmed by the gift to thank him. "Oh, it's too good - it's too good!" she said, awestruck by its splendour.

"Nothing is too good for my wife," he said in his imperial fashion.

Isabel smiled the smile that never reached her shadowed eyes. "A chain of pearls to bind a bride!" she said.

And the thought flashed upon Dinah that there was truth in her words. Whether with intention or not, by every gift he gave her he bound her the more closely to him. An odd little sensation of dismay accompanied it, but she put it resolutely from her. Bound or not, what did it matter - since she had no desire to escape?

She thanked him again very earnestly that night in the

conservatory, and he pressed her to him and kissed the neck on which his pearls rested with the hot lips of a thirsty man. But he had himself under control, and when she sought to draw herself away he let her go. She wondered at his forbearance and was mutely grateful for it.

At Isabel's suggestion she went up to her room early. She was certainly weary, but she was radiantly happy. It had been a wonderful day. The beauty of the pearls dazzled her. She kissed them ere she laid them out of sight. He was good to her. He was much too good.

There came a knock at the door just as she was getting into bed, and Biddy came softly in, her brown face full of mystery and, Dinah saw at a glance, of anxiety also.

She put up a warning finger as she advanced. "Whisht, Miss Dinah darlint! For the love of heaven, don't ye make a noise! I just came in to ask ye a question, for it's worried to death I am."

"Why what's the matter, Biddy?" Dinah questioned in surprise.

"And ye may well ask, Miss Dinah dear!" Tragedy made itself heard in Biddy's rejoinder. "Sure it's them letters of Miss Isabel's that's disappeared entirely, and left no trace. And what'll I do at all when she comes to ask for them? It's not meself that'll dare to tell her as they've gone, and she setting such store by them. She'll go clean out of her mind, Miss Dinah, for sure, they've been her only comfort, poor lamb, these seven years."

"But, Biddy!" Impulsively Dinah broke in upon her, her eyes round with surprise and consternation. "They can't be - gone! They must be somewhere! Have you hunted for them? She left them on the window-sill, didn't she? They must have got put away."

"That they have not!" declared Biddy solemnly. "It's my belief that the old gentleman himself must have spirited them away. The window was left open, ye know, Miss Dinah, and it was a dark night."

"Oh, Biddy, nonsense, nonsense! One of the servants must have moved them when she was doing the room. Have you asked everyone?"

"That couldn't have happened, Miss Dinah dear." Unshakable conviction was in Biddy's voice. "I got up late, and I had to get Miss Isabel up in a hurry to go off in the motor. But I missed the letters directly after she was gone, and I hadn't left the room - except to call her. No one had been in - not unless they slipped in in those few minutes while me back was turned. And for what should anyone take such a thing as them letters, Miss Dinah? There are no thieves in the house. And them love-letters were worth nothing to nobody saving to Miss Isabel, and they were the very breath of life to her when the black mood was on her. Whatever she'll say - whatever she'll do - I don't dare to think."

Poor Biddy flourished her apron as though she would throw it over her head. Her parchment face was working painfully.

Dinah sat on the edge of her bed and watched her, not knowing what to say.

"Where is Miss Isabel?" she asked at last.

"She's still downstairs with Master Scott, and I'm expecting her up every minute. It's herself that ought to be in bed by now, for she's tired out after her long day; but he'll be bringing her up directly and then she'll ask for her love-letters. There's never a night goes by but what she kisses them before she lies down. When ye were ill, Miss Dinah dear, she'd forget sometimes, but ever since she's been alone again she's never missed, not once."

"Have you told Master Scott?" asked Dinah.

Biddy shook her head. "Would I add to his burdens, poor young gentleman? He'll know soon enough."

"And are you sure you've looked everywhere - everywhere?" insisted Dinah. "If no one has taken them -"

"Miss Dinah, I've turned the whole room upside down and shaken it," declared Biddy. "I'll take my dying oath that them letters have gone."

"Could they - could they possibly have fallen out of the window?" hazarded Dinah.

"Miss Dinah dear, no!" A hint of impatience born of her distress was perceptible in the old woman's tone; she turned to the door. "Well, well, it's no good talking. Don't ye fret yourself! What must be, will be."

"But I think Scott ought to know," said Dinah.

"No, no, Miss Dinah! We'll not tell him before we need. He's got his own troubles. But I wonder - I wonder - " Biddy paused with the door-handle in her bony old fingers - "how would it be now," she said slowly, "if ye was to get Miss Isabel to sleep with ye again? She forgot last night. It's likely she may forget again - unless he calls her."

"Biddy!" exclaimed Dinah, startled.

Biddy's beady eyes gleamed mysteriously. "Arrah, but it's the truth I'm telling ye, Miss Dinah. He does call her. I've known him call her when she's been lying in a deep sleep, and she'll rise up with her arms stretched out and that look in her eyes!" Biddy's face crumpled momentarily, but was swiftly straightened again. "Will ye do it then, Miss Dinah? Ye needn't be afraid. I'll be within call. But when she's got you, she don't seem to be craving for anyone else. What was it she called ye only last night? Her good angel! And so ye be, me jewel; so ye be!"

Dinah stood debating the matter. Biddy's expedient was of too temporary an order to recommend itself to her. She wondered why Scott should not be consulted, and it was with some vague intention of laying the matter before him if an opportunity should occur that she finally gave her somewhat hesitating consent.

"I will do it of course, Biddy. I love her to sleep with me. But, you know, it is bound to come out some time, unless you manage to find the letters again. They must be somewhere."

Biddy shook her head. "We must just leave that to the Almighty, Miss Dinah dear," she said piously. "There's nothing else we can do at all. I'll get back to her room now, and when she comes up, I'll tell her ye're feeling lonely, and will she please to sleep with ye again. She won't think of anything else then ye may be sure. Why, she worships the very ground under your feet, mavourneen, like - like someone else I know."

She was gone with the words, leaving upon Dinah a dim impression that her last words were intended to convey something which she would have translated into simpler language had she been at liberty to do so.

She did not pay much attention to them. She was too troubled over her former revelation to think seriously of anything else. Into her mind, all unbidden, had flashed a sudden memory, and it held her like a nightmare-vision. She saw Sir Eustace with that imperious frown on his face holding out Isabel's treasure with a curt, "Take this thing away!" She saw herself leap up and seize it from his intolerant grasp. She saw Isabel's outstretched, pleading hands, and the piteous hunger in her eyes....

When Isabel came to her that night, her face was all softened with mother-love. She drew Dinah to her breast, kissing her very tenderly.

"Did you want me to come and take care of you, my darling?"

Dinah's heart smote her for the deception, but she answered bravely enough, "Oh, Isabel, yes, yes! You are so good to me, I want you always."

"Dear heart!" Isabel said, with a sigh, and folded her closer as though she would guard her against all the world.

She was the first to fall asleep notwithstanding, while Dinah lay motionless and troubled far into the night. She wished that Biddy would give her permission to tell Scott, for without that permission such a step seemed like a betrayal of confidence. But for some reason Biddy evidently thought that Scott had enough on his shoulders just then. And so it seemed, she could only wait - only wait.

She did not want to burden Scott unduly either, and there was something about him just now, something of a repressing nature, that held her back from confiding in him too freely. He seemed to have raised a barrier between them since their return to England which no intimacy ever quite succeeded in scaling. Full of brotherly kindness though he was, the old frank fellowship was gone. It was as though he had realized her dependence upon him, and were trying with the utmost gentleness to make her stand alone.

Dinah slept at last from sheer weariness, and forgot her troubles. She must not tell Scott, she could not tell Eustace, and so there was no other course but silence. But the anxiety of it weighed upon her even through her slumber. Life was far more interesting than of yore. But never, never before had it been so full of doubts and fears. The complexity of it all was like an endless net, enmeshing her however warily she stepped.

And always, and always, at the back of her mind there lurked the dread conviction that one day the net would be drawn close, and she would find herself a helpless prisoner in the grip of a giant.

CHAPTER XII

THE DIVINE SPARK

With the morning Dinah found her anxieties less oppressive. Isabel was becoming so much more like herself that she was able to put the matter from her and in a measure forget it. Like Biddy, she began to hope that by postponing the evil hour they might possibly evade it altogether. For there was nothing abnormal about Isabel during that day or those that succeeded it. The time passed quickly. There was much to be done, much to be discussed and decided, and their thoughts were fully occupied. Dinah felt as one whirled in a torrent. She could not think of the great undercurrent. She could deal only with the things on the surface.

How that week sped away she never afterwards fully recalled. It passed like a fevered dream. Two more journeys to town with Isabel, the ordeal of a dinner at the house of a neighbouring magnate, a much less formidable tea at the Vicarage, on which occasion Mr. Grey drew her aside and thanked her for using her influence over Sir Eustace in the right direction and earnestly exhorted her to maintain and develop it as far as possible when she was married, a few riding-lessons with Scott who always seemed so much more imposing in the saddle than out of it and knew so exactly how to instruct her, a few wild races in Sir Eustace's car from which she always returned in a state of almost delirious exultation, and then night after night the sleep of utter weariness, with Isabel lying by her side.

Ethel M. Dell

The last night came upon her almost with a sense of shock. It had become a custom for her to sit in the conservatory with Sir Eustace after dinner, and here with the lights turned low he was wont to pour out to her all the fiery worship which throughout the day he curbed. No one ever disturbed them, but they were close to Isabel's sitting-room where Scott was wont to sit and read while his sister lay on her couch resting and listening. The murmur of his voice was audible to Dinah, and the knowledge of his close proximity gave her a courage which surely had not been hers otherwise. She was learning how to receive her lover's demonstrations without starting away in affright. If he ever startled her, the sound of Scott's voice in the adjoining room would always reassure her. She knew that Scott was at hand and would never fail her.

But on that last night Sir Eustace was more ardent than she had ever known him. He seemed to be almost fiercely resentful of the coming separation, brief though it was to be, and he would not suffer her out of reach of his hand.

Wedding presents had begun to arrive, and in some fashion they seemed to increase his impatience.

"I can't think what we are waiting for," he said, with his arm about her, drawing her close. "All this pomp and circumstance is nothing but a hindrance. It's you I want, not your wedding finery. You had better be married first and get the finery afterwards, as it isn't to be in town."

"Oh, but I want a big wedding," protested Dinah. "It's going to be such fun."

He laughed, holding her pointed chin between his finger and thumb. "I believe that's all you care about, you little heartless witch. I don't count at all. You'd have enjoyed this week every bit as well if I hadn't been here."

She winced a little at his words, for somehow they went home. "There hasn't been much time for anything, has there?" she said. "But - but I've enjoyed the motor rides, and - and I ought to thank you for being so very good to me."

He kissed the quivering lips, and she slipped a shy arm round his neck with the feeling that she owed it to him. But she did not return his kisses, for she was afraid to feed the flame that already leapt so high.

"You've nothing to thank me for," he said presently, when she turned her face at last abashed into his shoulder. "I may be giving more than you at this stage, but it won't be so later. You shall have the opportunity of paying me back in full. How does that appeal to you, Daphne the demure? Are you going to be a good little wife to me?"

"I'll try," she whispered.

"And give me all I ask - always?"

"I'll try," she whispered again more faintly, conscious of that terrifying sense of being so merged into his overwhelming personality that the very breath she drew seemed not her own.

He lifted her into his arms, holding her hard pressed against the throbbing of his heart. "You wisp of thistledown!" he said. "You feather! How have you managed to set me on fire like this? I think of nothing but you - the fairy wonder of you - day and night. If you were to slip out of my reach now, I believe I should follow and kill you."

Dinah lay across his breast in palpitating submission to his will. She could hear his heart beating like a rising tempest, and the force of his passion overcame her like a tornado. His kisses were like the flames of a fiery furnace. She felt stifled, shattered by his violence. But in the room beyond she still heard that steady voice reading aloud, and it kept her from panic. She knew that she had only to raise her own voice, and he would be with her, - Greatheart of the golden armour, strong and fearless in her defence.

Ethel M. Dell

Sir Eustace heard that quiet voice also, as one hears the warning of conscience. He slackened his hold upon her, with a quivering, half-shamed laugh.

"Only another fortnight," he said, "and I shall have you to myself - all day and all night too." He looked at her with sudden critical attention. "You had better go to bed, child. You look like a little tired ghost."

She did not feel like a ghost, for she was burning from head to foot. But as she slipped from his arms the ground seemed to be rocking all around her. She stretched out her hands blindly, gasping, feeling for support.

He was up in a moment, holding her. "What is it? Aren't you well?"

She sank against him for she could not stand. He held her with a tenderness that was new to her.

"My darling, have I tired you out? What a thoughtless brute I am!"

It was the first time she had ever heard a word of self-reproach upon his lips; the first time, though she knew it not, that actual love inspired him, entering as it were through that breach in the wall of overbearing pride that girt him round.

She leaned against him with more confidence than she had ever before known, dizzy still, and conscious of a rush of tears behind her closed lids. For that sudden compunction of his hurt her oddly. She did not know how to meet it.

He bent over her. "Getting better, little sweetheart? Oh, don't cry! What happened? Did I hurt you - frighten you?"

He was stroking her hair soothingly, persuasively, his dark face so close to hers that when she opened her eyes they looked up straight into his. But she saw nought to frighten her there, and after a moment she reached up and kissed him apologetically.

"I'm only silly - only silly," she murmured confusedly. "Good night - good night - Apollo!"

And with the words she stood up, summoning her strength, smiled upon him, and slipped free from his encircling arm.

He did not seek to detain her. She flitted from his presence like a fluttering white moth, and he was left alone. He stood quite motionless in the semi-darkness, breathing deeply, his clenched hands pressed against his sides.

That moment had been a revelation to him also. He was abruptly conscious of the spirit so dominating the body that the fierce, ungoverned heart of him drew back ashamed as a beast will shrink from the flare of a torch, and he felt strangely conquered, almost cowed, as though an angel with a flaming sword had suddenly intervened between him and his desire.

The madness of his passion was yet beating in his veins, but this - this was another and a stronger element before which all else became contemptible. The soul of the man had sprung from sleep like an awaking giant. Half in wonder and half in awe, he watched the kindling of the Divine Spark that outshineth every earthly fire.

Ethel M. Dell

CHAPTER XIII

THE BROKEN HEART

The return home was to Dinah like a sudden plunge into icy depths after a brief sojourn in the tropics. The change of atmosphere was such that she seemed actually to feel it in her bones, and her whole being, physical and mental contracted in consequence. Her mother treated her with all her customary harshness, and Dinah, grown sensitive by reason of much petting, shrank almost with horror whenever she came in contact with the iron will that had subjugated her from babyhood.

Before the first week was over, she was counting the days to her deliverance; but of this fact she hinted nothing in her letters to her lover. These were carefully worded, demure little epistles that gave him not the smallest inkling of her state of mind. She was far too much afraid of him to betray that.

Had she been writing to Scott she could scarcely have repressed it. In one letter to Isabel indeed something of her yearning for the vanished sunshine leaked out; but very strangely Isabel did not respond to the pathetic little confidence, and Dinah did not venture to repeat it. Perhaps Isabel was shocked.

The last week came, and with it the arrival of wedding-presents from her father and friends that lifted Dinah out of her depression and even softened her mother into occasional good humour. Preparations for the wedding began in earnest. Billy, released somewhat before the holidays for the occasion, returned home, and everything took a more cheerful aspect.

Dinah could not feel that her mother's attitude towards herself had materially altered. It was sullen and threatening at times, almost as if she resented her daughter's good fortune, and she lived in continual dread of an outbreak of the cruel temper that had so embittered her home life. But Billy's presence made a difference even to that. His influence was entirely wholesome, and he feared no one.

"Why don't you stand up to her?" he said to his sister on one occasion when he found her weeping after an overwhelming brow-beating over some failure in the kitchen. "She'd think something of you then."

Dinah had no answer. She could not convince him that her spirit had been broken for such encounters long ago. Billy had never been tied up to a bed-post and whipped till limp with exhaustion, but such treatment had been her portion more times than she could number.

But every hour brought her deliverance nearer, and so far she had managed to avoid physical violence though the dread of it always menaced her.

"Why does she hate me so?" Over and over again she asked herself the question, but she never found any answer thereto; and she was fain to believe her father's easy-going verdict: "There's no accounting for your mother's tantrums; they've got to be visited on somebody."

She wondered what would happen when she was no longer at hand to act as scapegoat, and yet it seemed to her that her mother longed to be rid of her.

"I'll get things into good order when you're out of the way," she said to her on the last evening but one before the wedding-day, the evening on which the Studleys were to arrive at the Court. "You're just a born muddler, and you'll never be anything else, Lady Studley or no Lady Studley. Get along upstairs and dress yourself for your precious dinner-party, or your father will be ready first! Oh, it'll be a good thing when it's all over and done with, but if you think you'll ever get treated as a grand lady here, you're very much mistaken. Home broth is all you'll ever get from me, so you needn't expect anything different. If you don't like it, you can stop away."

Dinah escaped from the rating tongue as swiftly as she dared. She knew that her mother had been asked to dine at the Court also - for the first time in her life - and had tersely refused. She wasn't going to be condescended to by anybody, she had told her husband in Dinah's hearing, and he had merely shrugged his shoulders and advised her to please herself.

Billy had not been asked, somewhat to his disgust; but he looked forward to seeing Scott again in the morning and ordered Dinah to ask him to lunch with them.

So finally Dinah and her father set forth alone in one of the motors from the Court to attend the gathering of County magnates that the de Vignes had summoned in honour of Sir Eustace Studley and his chosen bride.

She wore one of her trousseau gowns for the occasion, a pale green gossamer-like garment that made her look more nymph-like than ever. Her mother had surveyed it with narrowed eyes and a bitter sneer.

"Ok yes, you'll pass for one of the quality," she had said. "No one would take you for a child of mine any way."

"That's no fault of the child's, Lydia," her father had rejoined good-humouredly, and in the car he had taken her little cold hand into his and asked her kindly enough if she were happy.

She answered him tremulously in the affirmative, the dread of her mother still so strong upon her that she could think of nothing but the relief of escape. And then before she had time to prepare herself in any way for the sudden transition she found herself back in that tropical, brilliant atmosphere in which thenceforth she was to move and have her being.

She could not feel that she would ever shine there. There were so many bright lights, and though her father was instantly and completely at home she felt dazzled and strange, till all-unexpectedly someone came to her through the great lamp-lit hall, haltingly yet with purpose, and held her hand and asked her how she was.

The quiet grasp steadied her, and in a moment she was radiantly happy, all her troubles and anxieties swept from her path. "Oh, Scott!" she said, and her eyes beamed upon him the greeting her lips somehow refused to utter.

He was laughing a little; his look was quizzical. "I have been on the look-out for you," he told her. "It's the best man's privilege, isn't it? Won't you introduce me to your father?"

She did so, and then Rose glided forward, exquisite in maize satin and pearls, and smilingly detached her from the two men and led her upstairs.

"We are to have a little informal dance presently," she said. "Did I tell you in my note? No? Oh, well, no doubt it will be a pleasant little surprise for you. How very charming you are looking, my dear! I didn't know you had it in you. Did you choose that pretty frock yourself?"

Dinah, with something of her mother's bluntness of speech, explained that the creation in question had been Isabel's choice, and Rose smiled as one who fully understood the situation.

"She has been very good to you, poor soul, has she not?" she said. "She is not coming down to-night. The journey has fatigued her terribly. That funny, old-fashioned nurse of hers has asked very particularly that she may not be disturbed, except to see you for a few minutes later."

"Is she worse?" asked Dinah, startled.

Whereat Rose shook her dainty head. "Has she ever been better? No, poor thing, I am afraid her days are numbered, nor could one in kindness wish it otherwise. Still, I mustn't sadden you, dear. You have got to look your very best to-night, or Sir Eustace will be disappointed. There are quite a lot of pretty girls coming, and you know what he is." Rose uttered a little self-conscious laugh. "Put on a tinge of colour, dear!" she said, as Dinah stood before the mirror in her room. "You look such a little brown thing; just a faint glow on your cheeks would be such an improvement."

"No, thank you," said Dinah, and flushed suddenly and hotly at the thought of what she had once endured at her mother's hands for daring to pencil the shadows under her eyes. It had been no more than a girlish trick - an experiment to pass an idle moment. But it had been treated as an offence of immeasurable enormity, and she winced still at the memory of all that that moment's vanity had entailed.

Rose looked at her appraisingly. "No, perhaps you don't need it after all, not anyhow when you blush like that. You have quite a pretty blush, Dinah, and you are wise to make the most of it. Are you ready, dear? Then we will go down."

She rustled forth with Dinah beside her, shedding a soft fragrance of some Indian scent as she moved that somehow filled Dinah with indignation, like a resentful butterfly in search of more wholesome delights.

Eustace was in the hall when they descended. He came forward to meet his *fiancee*, and her heart throbbed fast and hard at the sight of him. But his manner was so strictly casual and impersonal that her agitation speedily passed, and by the time they were seated side by side at dinner - for the last time in their lives, as the Colonel jocosely remarked - she could not feel that she had ever been anything nearer to him than a passing acquaintance.

She was shy and very quiet. The hubbub of voices, the brilliance of it all, overwhelmed her. If Scott had been on her other side, she would have been much happier, but he was far away making courteous conversation for the benefit of a deaf old lady whom no one else made the smallest effort to entertain.

Suddenly Sir Eustace disengaged himself from the general talk and turned to her. "Dinah!" he said.

Her heart leapt again. She glanced at him and caught the gleam of the hunter in those rapier-bright eyes of his.

He leaned slightly towards her, his smile like a shining cloak, hiding his soul. "Daphne," he said, and his voice came to her subtle, caressing, commanding, through the gay tumult all about them, "there is going to be dancing presently. Did you hear?"

"Yes," she whispered with lowered eyes.

"You will dance with only one to-night," he said. "That is understood, is it?"

"Yes," she whispered again.

"Good!" he said. And then imperiously, "Why don't you drink some wine?"

She made a slight, startled movement. "I never do, I don't like it."

"You need it," he said, and made a curt sign to one of the servants.

Wine was poured into her glass, and she drank submissively. The discipline of the past two weeks had made her wholly docile. And the wine warmed and cheered her in a fashion that made her think that perhaps he was right and she had needed it.

When the dinner came to an end she was feeling far less scared and strange. Guests were beginning to assemble for the dance, and as they passed out people whom she knew by sight but to whom she had never spoken came up and talked with her as though they were old friends. Several men asked her to dance, but she steadily refused them all. Her turn would come later.

"I am going up to see Mrs. Everard," was her excuse. "She is expecting me."

And then Scott came, and she turned to him with eager welcome. "Oh, please, will you take me to see Isabel?"

He gave her a straight, intent look, and led her out of the throng.

His hand rested upon her arm as they mounted the stairs and she thought he moved with deliberate slowness. At the top he spoke.

"Dinah, before you see her I ought to prepare you for a change. She has been losing ground lately. She is not - what she was."

Dinah stopped short. "Oh, Scott!" She said in breathless dismay.

His hand pressed upon her, but it seemed to be imparting strength rather than seeking it. "I think I told you that day at the Dower House that she was nearing the end of her journey. I don't want to sadden you. You mustn't be sad. But you couldn't see her without knowing. It won't be quite yet; but it will be - soon."

He spoke with the utmost quietness; his face never varied. His eyes with their steady comradeship looked straight into hers, stilling her distress.

"She is so tired," he said gently. "I don't think it ought to grieve us that her rest is drawing near at last. She has so longed for it, poor girl."

"Oh, Scott!" Dinah said again, but she said it this time without consternation. His steadfast strength had given her confidence.

"Shall we go to her?" he said. "At least, I think it would be better if you went alone. She is quite determined that nothing shall interfere with your coming happiness, so you mustn't let her think you shocked or grieved. I thought it best to prepare you, that's all."

He led her gravely along the passage, and presently stopped outside a closed door. He knocked three times as of old, and Dinah stood waiting as one on the threshold of a holy place.

The door, was opened by Biddy, and he pressed her forward. "Don't stay long!" he said. "She is very tired to-night, and Eustace will be wanting you."

She squeezed his hand in answer and passed within.

Biddy's wrinkled brown face smiled a brief welcome under its snowy cap. She motioned her to approach. "Ye'll not stay long, Miss Dinah dear," she whispered. "The poor lamb's very tired to-night."

Dinah went forward.

The window was wide open, and the rush of the west wind filled the room. Isabel was lying in bed with her face to the night, wide-eyed, intent, still as death.

Noiselessly Dinah drew near. There was something in the

Ethel M. Dell

atmosphere - a ghostly, hovering presence - that awed her. In the sound of that racing wind she seemed to hear the beat of mighty wings.

She uttered no word, she was almost afraid to speak. But when she reached the bed, when she bent and looked into Isabel's face, she caught her breath in a gasping cry. For she was shocked - shocked unutterably - by what she saw. Shrivelled as the face of one who had come through fiery tortures, ashen-grey, with eyes in which the anguish of the burnt-out flame still lingered, eyes that were dead to hope, eyes that were open only to the darkness, such was the face upon which she looked.

Biddy was by her side in a moment, speaking in a rapid whisper. "Arrah thin, Miss Dinah darlint, don't ye be scared at all! She'll speak to ye in a minute, sure. It's only that she's tired to-night. She'll be more herself like in the morning."

Dinah hung over the still figure. Biddy's whispering was as the buzzing of a fly. She heard it with the outer sense alone.

"Isabel!" she said; and again with a passionate earnestness, "Isabel - darling - my darling - what has happened to you?"

At the sound of that pleading voice Isabel moved, seeming as it were to return slowly from afar.

"Why, Dinah dear!" she said.

Her dark eyes smiled up at her in welcome, but it was a smile that cut her to the heart with its aloofness, its total lack of gladness.

Dinah stooped to kiss her. "Are you so tired, dearest? Perhaps I had better go away."

But Isabel put up a trembling, skeleton hand and detained her. "No, dear, no! I am not so tired as that. I can't talk much; but I can listen. Sit down and tell me about yourself!"

Dinah sat down, but she could think of nothing but the piteous, lined face upon the pillow and the hopeless suffering of the eyes that looked forth from it.

She held Isabel's hand very tightly, though its terrible emaciation shocked her anew, and so for a time they were silent while Isabel seemed to drift back again into the limitless spaces out of which Dinah's coming had for a moment called her.

It was Biddy who broke the silence at last, laying a gnarled and quivering hand upon Dinah as she sat.

"Ye'd better come again in the morning, mavourneen," she said. "She's too far off to-night to heed ye."

Dinah started. Her eyes were full of tears as she bent and kissed the poor, wasted fingers she held, realizing with poignant certainty as she did it the truth of the old woman's statement. Isabel was too far off to heed.

Then, as she rose to go, a strange thing happened. The tender strains of a waltz, *Simple Aveu*, floated softly in broken snatches in on the west wind, and again - as one who hears a voice that calls - Isabel came back. She raised herself suddenly. Her face was alight, transfigured - the face of a woman on the threshold of Love's sanctuary.

"Oh, my dearest!" she said, and her voice thrilled as never Dinah had heard it thrill before. "How I have waited for this! How I have waited!"

She stretched out her arms in one second of rapture unutterable; and then almost in the same moment they fell. The youth went out of her, she crumpled like a withered flower.

"Biddy!" she said. "Oh, Biddy, tell them to stop! I can't bear it! I can't bear it!"

Dinah went to the window and closed it, shutting out the haunting strains. That waltz meant something to her also, something with which for the moment she felt she could not cope.

Turning, she saw that Isabel was clinging convulsively to the old nurse, and she was crying, crying, crying, as one who has lost all hope.

"But it's too late to do her any good," mourned Biddy over the bowed head. "It's the tears of a broken heart."

CHAPTER XIV

THE WRATH OF THE GODS

The paroxysm did not last long, and in that fact most poignantly did Dinah realize the waning strength.

Dumbly she stood and watched Biddy lay the inanimate figure back upon the pillows. Isabel had sunk into a state of exhaustion that was almost torpor.

"She'll sleep now, dear lamb," said Biddy, and tenderly covered her over as though she had been a child.

She turned round to Dinah, looking at her with shrewd darting eyes. "Ye'd better be getting along to your lover, Miss Dinah," she said. "He'll be wanting ye to dance with him."

But Dinah stood her ground with a little shiver. The bare thought of dancing at that moment made her feel physically sick. "Biddy! Biddy!" she whispered, "what has happened to make her - like this?"

"And ye may well ask!" said Biddy darkly. "But it's not for me to tell ye. Ye'd best run along, Miss Dinah dear, and be happy while ye can."

"But I'm not happy!" broke from Dinah. "How can I be? Biddy, what has happened? You must tell me if you can. She wasn't like this a fortnight ago. She has never been - quite like this - before."

Biddy pursed her lips. "Sure, we none of us travel the same road twice, Miss Dinah," she said.

But Dinah would not be satisfied with so vague an axiom.

"Something has happened," she said. "Come into the next room and tell me all about it! Please, Biddy!"

Biddy glanced at the bed. "She'll not hear ye in here, Miss Dinah," she said. "And what for should I be telling ye at all? Ye'll be Sir Eustace's bride in less than forty-eight hours from now, so it's maybe better ye shouldn't know."

"I must know," Dinah said, and with the words a great wave of resolution went through her, uplifting her, inspiring her. "I've got to know," she said. "Whatever happens, I've got to know."

Biddy left the bedside and came close to her. "If ye insist, Miss Dinah -" she said.

"I do - I do insist." Never in her life before had Dinah spoken with such authority, but a force within was urging her - a force irresistible; she spoke as one compelled.

Biddy came closer still. "Ye'll not tell Master Scott - nor any of 'em - if I tell ye?" she whispered.

"No, no; of course - no!" Dinah's voice came breathlessly; she had not the power to draw back.

"Ye promise, Miss Dinah?" Biddy could be insistent too; her eyes burned like live coals.

"I promise, yes." Dinah held out an impulsive hand. "You can trust me," she said.

Biddy's fingers closed claw-like upon it. "Whist now, Miss

Dinah!" she said. "If Sir Eustace was to hear me, sure, he'd wring the neck on me like as if I was an old fowl. But ye've asked me what's happened, mavourneen, and sure, I'll tell ye. For it's the pretty young lady that ye are and a cruel shame that ye should ever belong to the likes of him. It's his doing, Miss Dinah, every bit of it, and it's the truth I'm speaking, as the Almighty Himself could tell ye if He'd a mind to. The poor lamb was fading away aisy like, but he came along and broke her heart. It was them letters, Miss Dinah. He took 'em. And he burned 'em, my dear, he burned 'em, and when ye were gone she missed 'em, and then he told her what he'd done, told her brutal-like that it was time she'd done with such litter. He said it was all damn' nonsense that she was wasting her life over 'em and over the dead. Oh, it was wicked, it was cruel. And she - poor innocent - she locked herself up when he'd gone and cried and cried and cried till the poor heart of her was broke entirely. She said she'd lost touch with her darling husband and he'd never come back to her again."

"Biddy!" Horror undisguised sounded in Dinah's low voice. "He never did such a thing as that!"

"He did that!" A queer species of triumph was apparent in Biddy's rejoinder; malice twinkled for a second in her eyes. "I've told ye! I've told ye!" she said. And then, with sharp anxiety. "But ye'll not tell anyone as ye know, Miss Dinah. Ye promised, now didn't ye? Miss Isabel wouldn't that any should know - not even Master Scott. He was away when it happened, dining down at the Vicarage he was. And Miss Isabel she says to me, 'For the life of ye, don't tell Master Scott! He'd be that angry,' she says, 'and Sir Eustace would murder him entirely if it came to a quarrel.' She was that insistent, Miss Dinah, and I knew there was truth in what she said. Master Scott has the heart of a lion. He never knew the meaning of fear from his babyhood. And Sir Eustace is a monster of destruction when once his blood's up. And he minds what Master Scott says more than anyone. So I promised, Miss Dinah dear, the same as you have. And so he doesn't know to this day. Sir Eustace, ye see, has been in a touchy mood all along, ever since ye left.

Like gunpowder he's been, and Master Scott has had a difficult enough time with him; and Miss Isabel has kept it from him so that he thinks it was just your going again that made her fret so. There, now ye know all, Miss Dinah dear, and don't ye for the love of heaven tell a soul what I've told ye! Miss Isabel would never forgive me if she came to know. Ah, the saints preserve us, what's that?"

A brisk tap at the door had made her jump with violence. She went to parley with a guilty air.

In a moment or two she shut the door and came back. "It's that flighty young French hussy, Miss Dinah; her they call Yvonne. She says Sir Eustace is waiting for ye downstairs."

A great revulsion of feeling went through Dinah. It shook her like an overwhelming tempest and passed, leaving her deadly cold. She turned white to the lips.

"I can't go to him, Biddy," she said. "I can't dance to-night. Yvonne must tell him."

Biddy gave her a searching look. "Ye won't let him find out, Miss Dinah?" she urged. "Won't he guess now if ye stay up here?"

The earnest entreaty of the old bright eyes moved her. She turned to the door. "Oh, very well. I'll go myself and tell him."

"Ye won't let him suspect, mavourneen - mavourneen?" pleaded Biddy desperately.

"No, Biddy, no! Haven't I sworn it a dozen times already?" Dinah had reached the door; she looked back for a moment and her look was steadfast notwithstanding the deathly pallor of her face. Then she passed slowly forth, and heard old Biddy softly turn the key behind her, making assurance doubly sure.

Slowly she moved along the passage. It was deserted, but the sound of laughing voices and the tuning of violins floated up from below. Again that feeling that was akin to physical sickness assailed Dinah. Down there he was waiting for her, waiting to be intoxicated into headlong, devouring passion by her dancing. She seemed to feel his arms already holding her, straining her to him, so that the warmth of him was as a fiery atmosphere all about her, encompassing her, possessing her. Her whole body burned at the thought, and then again was cold - cold as though she had drunk a draught of poison. She stood still, feeling too sick to go on.

And then, while she waited, she heard a step. Her heart seemed to spring into her throat, throbbing wildly like a caged bird seeking freedom. She drew back against the wall, trembling from head to foot.

He came along the passage, magnificent, princely, confident, swinging his shoulders with that semi-conscious swagger she knew so well. He spied her where she stood, and she heard his brief, half-mocking laugh as he strode to her.

"Ah, Daphne! Hiding as usual!" he said.

He took her between his hands, and she felt the mastery of him in that free hold. She stood as a prisoner in his grasp. Her new-found resolution was gone at the first contact with that overwhelming personality of his. She hung her head in quivering distress.

He bent down, bringing his face close to hers. He tried to look into the eyes that she kept downcast.

And suddenly he spoke again, softly into her ear. "Why so shy, little sweetheart? Are you getting frightened now the time is so near?"

Her breathing quickened at his tone. Possessive though it was, it held that tender note that was harder to bear than all his fiercest passion. She could not speak in answer. No words would come.

He put his arm around her and held her close. "But you mustn't be afraid of me," he said. "Don't you know I love you? Don't you know I am going to make you the happiest little woman in the world?"

Dinah choked down some scalding tears. She longed to escape from the holding of his arm, and yet her torn spirit felt the comfort of it. She stood silent, shaken, unnerved, piteously conscious of her utter weakness - the weakness wrought by that iron discipline that had never suffered her to have any will of her own.

He put up a hand and pressed her drooping head against his shoulder. "There's nothing very dreadful in being married, dear," he told her. "I'm not such a devouring monster as I may seem. Why, I wouldn't hurt a hair of your head. They are all precious to me."

She quivered at his use of the word that Biddy had employed with such venom only a few minutes before; but still she said nothing. What could she say? Against this new weapon of his she was more helpless than ever. She hid her face against him and strove for self-control.

He kissed her temple and the clustering hair above it. "There now! You are not going to be a silly little scared fawn any more. Come along and dance it off!"

His arm encircled her shoulders; he began to lead her to the stairs.

And Dinah went, slave-like in her submission, but hating herself the more for every step she took.

They went to the ballroom, and presently they danced. But the old subtle charm was absent. Her feet moved to the rhythm of the music, her body swayed and pulsed to the behest of his;

but her spirit stood apart, bruised and downcast and very much alone. Her gilded palace had fallen all about her in ruins. The deliverance to which she had looked forward so eagerly was but another bondage that would prove more cruel and more enslaving than the first. She longed with all her quivering heart to run away and hide.

He was very kind to her, more considerate than she had ever known him. Perhaps he missed the fairy abandonment which had so delighted him in her dancing of old; but he found no fault; and when the dance was over he did not lead her away to some private corner as she had dreaded, but took her instead to her father and stood with him for some time in talk.

She saw Scott in the distance, but he did not approach her while Eustace was with them, and when her *fiance* turned away at length he had disappeared.

They were left comparatively alone, and Dinah slipped an urgent hand into her father's. "I want to go home, Daddy. I'm so tired."

He looked at her in surprise, but she managed to muster a smile in reply, and he was not observant enough to note the distress that lay behind it.

"Had enough of it, eh?" he questioned. "Well, I think you're wise. You'll be busy to-morrow. By all means, let's go!"

It was not till the very last moment that she saw Scott again. He came forward just as she was passing through the hall to the front door.

He took the hand she held out to him, looking at her with those straight, steady eyes of his that there was no evading, but he made no comment of any sort.

"Mr. Grey is coming by a morning train to-morrow," he said. "May I bring him to call upon you in the afternoon? I believe he wants to run through the wedding-service with you beforehand."

He smiled as he said it, but Dinah could not smile in answer. There was something ominous to her in that last sentence, something that made her think of the clanking of chains. She was relieved to hear her father answer for her.

"Come by all means! Nothing like a dress rehearsal to make things go smoothly. I'll tell my wife to expect you."

Scott's hand relinquished hers, and she felt suddenly cold. She murmured a barely audible "Good night!" and turned away.

From the portico she glanced back and saw Sir Eustace leading Rose de Vigne to the ballroom. The light shone full upon them. They made a splendid couple. And a sudden bizarre thought smote her. This was what the gods had willed. This had been the weaving of destiny; and she - she - had dared to intervene, frustrating, tearing the gilded, smooth-wrought threads apart.

Ah well! It was done now. It was too late to draw back. But the wrath of the gods remained to be faced. Already it was upon her, and there was no escape.

As one who hears a voice speaking from a far distance, she heard herself telling her father that all was well with her and she had spent an enjoyable evening.

Then she lay back in the car with clenched hands, and listened trembling to the thundering wheels of Destiny.

CHAPTER XV

THE SAPPHIRE FOR FRIENDSHIP

No girl ever worked harder in preparation for her own wedding than did Dinah on the following day.

That she had scarcely slept all night was a fact that no one suspected. Work-a-day Dinah, as her father was wont to call her, was not an object of great solicitude to any in her home-circle, and for the first time in her life she was thankful that such was the case.

Her mother's hard gipsy eyes watched only for delinquencies, and her rating tongue was actually a relief to Dinah after the dread solitude of those long hours. She was like a prisoner awaiting execution, and even that harsh companionship was in a measure helpful to her.

The time passed with appalling swiftness. When the luncheon hour arrived she was horrified to find that the morning had gone. She could eat nothing, a fact which raised a jeering laugh from her mother and a chaffing remonstrance from her father. Billy had gone riding on Rupert and had not returned. Billy always came and went exactly as he pleased.

One or two more presents from friends of her father's had arrived by the midday post. Mrs. Bathurst unpacked them, admiring them with more than a touch of envy, assuring Dinah that she was a very lucky girl, luckier than she deserved

Ethel M. Dell

to be; but Dinah, though she acquiesced, had no heart for presents. She could only see - as she had seen all through the night - the piteous, marred face of a woman who had passed through such an intensity of suffering as she could only dimly guess at into the dark of utter despair. She could only hear, whichever way she turned, the clanking of the chains that in so brief a time were to be welded irrevocably about herself.

Luncheon over, she went up to dress and to finish the packing of the new trunks which were to accompany her upon her honeymoon. She had not even yet begun to realize these strange belongings of hers. She could no longer visualize herself as a bride. She looked upon all the finery as destined for another, possibly Rose de Vigne, but emphatically not for herself.

The wedding-dress and veil lying in their box, swathed in tissue-paper, had a gossamer unreality about them that even the sense of touch could not dispel. No - no! The bride of to-morrow was surely, surely, not herself!

They were to spend the first part of their honeymoon at a little place on the Cornish coast, very far from everywhere, as Sir Eustace said. She thought of that little place with a vague wonder. It was the stepping-stone between the life she now knew and that new unknown life that awaited her. She would go there just Dinah - work-a-day Dinah - her own ordinary self. She would leave a fortnight after, possibly less, a totally different being - a married woman, Lady Studley, part and parcel of Sir Eustace's train, his most intimate belonging, most exclusively his own.

She trembled afresh as this thought came home to her. Despite his assurances, marriage seemed to her a terrible thing. It was like parting, not only with the old life, but with herself.

She dressed mechanically, scarcely thinking of her appearance, roused only at length from her pre-occupation by the tread of hoofs under her window. She leaned forth quickly and discerned Scott on horseback, - a trim, upright figure, very confident in the saddle - and with him Billy still mounted on Rupert and evidently in the highest spirits.

The latter spied her at once and accosted her in his cracked, cheerful voice. "Hi, Dinah! Come down! We're going to tea at the Court. Scott will walk with you, and I'm going to ride his gee."

He rolled off Rupert with the words. Scott looked up at her, faintly smiling as he lifted his hat. "I hope that plan will suit you," he said. "The fact is the padre has been detained and can't get here before tea-time. So we thought - Eustace thought - you wouldn't mind coming up to the Court to tea instead of waiting to see him here."

It crossed her mind to wonder why Eustace had not come himself to fetch her, but she was conscious of a deep, unreasoning thankfulness that he had not. Then, before she could reply, she heard her father's voice in the porch, inviting Scott to enter.

Scott accepted the invitation, and Dinah turned back into the room to prepare for the walk.

Her hands were trembling so much that they could scarcely serve her. She was in a state of violent and uncontrollable agitation, longing one moment to be gone, and the next desiring desperately to remain where she was. The thought of facing the crowd at the Court filled her with a positive tumult of apprehension, but breathlessly she kept telling herself that Scott would be there - Scott would be there. His sheltering presence would be her protection.

And then, still trembling, still unnerved, she descended to meet him.

He was with her father in the drawing-room. The place was littered with wedding-presents.

As she entered, he came towards her, and in a moment his quiet hand closed upon hers. Her father went out in search of her mother and they were alone.

"What a collection of beautiful things you have here!" he said.

She looked at him, met his steady eyes, and suddenly some force of speech broke loose within her; she uttered words wild and passionate, such as she had never till that moment dreamed of uttering.

"Oh, don't talk of them! Don't think of them! They suffocate me!"

She saw his face change, but she could not have analysed the expression it took. He was silent for a moment, and in that moment his fingers tightened hard and close upon her hand.

Then, "I have brought you a small offering on my own account," he said in his courteous, rather tired voice. "May I present it? Or would you rather I waited a little?"

She felt the tears welling up, swiftly, swiftly, and clasped her throat to stay them. "Of course I would like it," she murmured almost inarticulately. "That - that is different."

He took a small, white packet from his pocket and put it into the hand he had been holding, without a word.

Dumbly, with quivering fingers, she opened it. There was something of tragedy in the silence, something of despair.

The paper fluttered to the ground, leaving a leather case in her grasp. She glanced up at him.

"Won't you look inside?" he said gently.

She did so, in her eyes those burning tears she could not check. And there, gleaming on its bed of white velvet, she saw a wonderful jewel - a great star-shaped sapphire, deep as the heart of a fathomless pool, edged with diamonds that flashed like the sun upon the ripples of its shores. She gazed and gazed in silence. It was the loveliest thing she had ever seen.

Scott was watching her, his eyes very still, unchangeably steadfast. "The sapphire for friendship," he said.

She started as one awaking from a dream. In the passage outside the half-open door she heard the sound of her mother's voice approaching. With a swift movement she closed the case and hid it in her dress.

"I can't show it to anyone yet," she said hurriedly.

Her tone appealed. He answered her immediately. "It is for you and no one else."

His voice held nought but kindness, comprehension, comfort.

He turned from her the next moment to meet her mother, and she heard him speaking in his easy, leisured tones, gaining time for her, making her path easy, as had ever been his custom.

And again unbidden, unavoidable, there came to her the vision of Greatheart - Greatheart the valiant - her knight of the golden armour, going before her, strong to defend, - invincible, unafraid, sure by means of that sureness which is given only to those who draw upon a Higher Power than their own, given only to the serving-men of God.

CHAPTER XVI

THE OPEN DOOR

Billy had already departed upon Scott's mount era he and Dinah set forth to walk to the Court. It was threatening to rain, and the ground beneath their feet was sodden and heavy.

"It is rather a shame to ask you to walk," said Scott, as they turned up the muddy road. "They would have sent a car for you if I had thought."

"I would much rather walk," said Dinah. Her face was very pale. She looked years older than she had looked at Willowmount. After a moment she added, "We shall pass the church. Perhaps you would like to see it. They were going to decorate it this morning."

"I should," said Scott.

He limped beside her, and she curbed her pace to his though the fever of unrest that surged within her urged her forward. They went up the lane that led to the church in almost unbroken silence.

At the churchyard gate she paused. "I hope there is no one here," she said uneasily.

"We need not go in unless you wish," he answered.

But when they reached the porch, they found that the church was empty, and so they entered.

A heavy scent of lilies pervaded the place. There was a wonderful white arch of flowers at the top of the aisle, and the chancel was decked with them. The space above the altar was a mass of white, perfumed splendour. They had been sent down from the Court that morning.

Slowly Scott passed up the nave with the bride-elect by his side, straight to the chancel-steps, and there he paused. His pale face with its light eyes was absolutely composed and calm. He looked straight up to the dim richness of the stained-glass window above him as though he saw beyond the flowers.

For many seconds Dinah stood beside him, awed, waiting as it were for the coming of a revelation. Whatever it might be she knew already that she would not leave that holy place in the state of hopeless turmoil in which she had entered. Something was coming to her, some new thing, that might serve as an anchor in her distress even though it might not bring her ultimate deliverance.

Or stay! Was it a new thing? Was it not rather the unveiling of something which had always been? Her heart quickened and became audible in the stillness. She clasped her hands tightly together. And in that moment Scott turned his head and looked at her.

No word did he speak; only that straight, calm look - as of a man clean of soul and fearless of evil. It told her nothing, that look, it opened to her no secret chamber; neither did it probe her own quivering heart. It was the kindly, reassuring look of a friend ready to stand by, ready to lend a sure hand if such were needed.

But by that look Dinah's revelation burst upon her. In that moment she saw her own soul as never before had she seen it; and all the little things, the shallow things, the earthly things, faded quite away. With a deep, deep breath she opened her eyes upon the Vision of Love....

"Shall we go?" murmured Scott.

She looked at him vaguely for a second, feeling stunned and blinded by the radiance of that revelation. A black veil seemed to be descending upon her; she put out a groping hand.

He took it, and his hold was sustaining. He led her in silence down the long, shadowy building to the porch.

He would have led her further, but a sudden, heavy shower was falling, and he had to pause. She sank down trembling upon the stone seat.

"Scott! Oh, Scott!" she said. "Help me!"

He made a slight, involuntary movement that passed unexplained. "I am here to help you, my dear," he said, his voice very quiet and even. "You mustn't be scared, you know. You'll get through it all right."

She wrung her hands together in her extremity. "It isn't that," she told him. "I - I suppose I've got to go through it - as you say so. But - but - you'll think me very wicked, yet I must tell you - I've made - a dreadful mistake. I'm marrying for money, for position, to get away from home, - anything but love. I don't love him. I know now that I never shall - never can! And I'd give anything - anything - anything to escape!"

It was spoken. All the long-pent misgivings that had culminated in awful certainty the night before had so wrought in her that now - now that the revelation had come - she could no longer keep silence. But of that revelation she would sooner have died than speak.

Scott heard that wrung confession, standing before her with a stillness that gave him a look of sternness. He spoke as she ended, possibly because he realized that she would not be able to endure the briefest silence at that moment, possibly because he dreamed of filling up the gap ere it widened to an irreparable breach.

"But, Dinah," he said, "don't you know he loves you?"

She flung her hands wide in a gesture of the most utter despair. "That's just the very worst part of it," she said. "That's just why there is no getting away."

"You don't want his love?" Scott questioned, his voice very low.

She shook her head in instant negation. "Oh no, no, no!"

He bent slightly towards her, looking into her face of quivering agitation. "Dinah, are you sure it isn't all this pomp and circumstance that is frightening you? Are you sure you have no love at all in your heart for him?"

She did not shrink from his look. Though she thought his eyes were stern, she met them with the courage of desperation. "I am quite - quite - sure," she told him brokenly. "I never loved him. I was dazzled, that's all. But now - but now - the glamour is all gone. I would give anything - oh, anything in the world - if only he would marry Rose de Vigne instead!"

Her voice failed and with it her strength. She covered her face and wept hopelessly, tragically.

Scott stood motionless by her side. His brows were drawn as the brows of a man in pain, but the eyes below them had the brightness of unwavering resolution. There was something rocklike about his pose.

The pattering of the rain mingled with the sound of Dinah's anguished sobbing; there seemed to be no other sound in all the world.

He moved at last, and into his eyes there came a very human look, dispelling all hardness. He bent to her again, his hand upon her shoulder. "My child," he said gently, "don't be so distressed! It isn't too late - even now."

He felt her respond to his touch, but she could not lift her head. "I can never face him," she sobbed hopelessly. "I shall never, never dare!"

"You must face him," Scott said quietly but very firmly. "You owe it to him. Do you consider that you would be acting fairly by him if you married him solely for the reasons you have just given to me?"

She shrank at his words, trembling all over like a frightened child. But his hand was still upon her, restraining panic.

"He will be so angry - so furious," she faltered.

"I will help you," Scott said steadily.

"Ah!" she caught at the promise with an eagerness that was piteous. "You won't leave me? You won't let me be alone with him? He can make me do anything - anything - when I am alone with him. Oh, he is terrible enough - even when he is not angry. He told me once that - that - if I were to slip out of his reach, he would follow - and kill me!"

The brightness returned to Scott's eyes; they shone with an almost steely gleam. "You needn't be afraid of that," he said quietly. "Now tell me, Dinah, for I want to know; how long have you known that you didn't want to marry him?"

But Dinah shrank at the question, as though he had probed a wound. "Oh, I can't tell you that! As long as I have realized that I was bound to him - I have been afraid! And now - now that it has come so close -" She broke off. "Oh, but I can't draw back now," she said hopelessly. "Think - only think - what it will mean!"

Scott was silent for a few seconds, then: "If it would be easier for you to go on," he said slowly, "perhaps - in the end - it may be better for you; because he honestly loves you, and I think his love may make a difference - in the end. Possibly you are nearer to loving him even now than you imagine. If it is the dread of hurting him - not angering him - that holds you back, then I do not think you would be doing wrong to marry him. If you are just scared by the thought of to-morrow and possibly the day after -"

"Oh, but it isn't that! It isn't that!" Dinah cried the words out passionately like a prisoner who sees the door of his cell closing finally upon him. "It's because I'm not his! I don't belong to him! I don't want to belong to him! The very thought makes me feel - almost - sick!"

"Then there is someone else," Scott said, with grave conviction.

"Ah!" It was not so much a word as the sharp intake of breath that follows the last and keenest thrust of the probe that has reached the object of its search. Dinah suddenly became rigid and yet vibrant as stretched wire. Her silence was the silence of the victim who dreads so unspeakably the suffering to come as to be scarcely aware of present anguish.

But Scott was merciful. He withdrew the probe and very pitifully he closed the wound that he had opened. "No, no!" he said. "That has nothing to do with me - or with Eustace either. But it makes your case absolutely plain. Come with me now - before you feel any worse about it - and ask him to give you your release!"

"Oh, Scott!" She looked up at him at last, and though there was a measure of relief in her eyes, her face was deathly. "Oh, Scott, - dare I do that?"

"I shall be there," he said.

"Yes, - yes, you will be there! You won't leave me? Promise!" She clasped his arm in entreaty.

He looked into her eyes, and there was a great kindness in his own - the kindness of Greatheart arming himself to defend his pilgrims. "Yes, I promise that," he said, adding, "unless I leave you at your own desire."

"You will never do that," Dinah said and smiled with quivering lips. "You are good to me. Oh, you are good! But - but -"

"But what?" he questioned gently.

"He may refuse to set me free," she said desperately. "What then?"

"My dear, no one is married by force now-a-days," he said.

Her face changed as a sudden memory swept across her. "And my mother! My mother!" she said.

"Don't you think we had better deal with one difficulty at a time?" suggested Scott.

His hand sought hers, he drew her to her feet.

And, as one having no choice, she submitted and went with him.

It was still raining, but the heaviest of the shower was over. A gleam of sunshine lit the distance as they went, and a faint, faint ray of hope dawned in Dinah's heart at the sight. Though her deliverance was yet to be achieved, though she dreaded unspeakably that which lay before her, at least the door was open, could she but reach it to pass through. She breathed a purer air already. And beside her stood Greatheart the valiant, covering her with his shield of gold.

CHAPTER XVII

THE LION IN THE PATH

A large and merry party of guests were congregated in the great hall at Perrythorpe Court, having tea. One of them - a young soldier-cousin of the Studleys - was singing a sentimental ditty at a piano to which no one was listening; and the hubbub was considerable.

Dinah, admitted into the outer hall that was curtained off from the gay crowd, shrank nearer to Scott as the cheery tumult reached her.

"Need we - must we - go in that way?" she whispered.

There was a door on the right of the porch. Scott turned towards it.

"I suppose we can go in there?" he said to the man who had admitted them.

"The gun-room, sir? Yes, if you wish, sir. Shall I bring tea?"

"No," Scott said quietly. "Find Sir Eustace Studley if you can, and ask him to join us there! Come along, Dinah!"

His hand touched her arm. She entered the little room as one seeking refuge. It led into a conservatory, and thence to the garden. The apartment itself was given up entirely to weapons or instruments of sport. Guns, fishing-rods, hunting-stocks, golf-clubs, tennis-rackets, were stored in various racks and stands. A smell of stale cigar-smoke pervaded it. Colonel de Vigne was wont to retire hither at night in preference to the less cosy and intimate smoking-room.

But there was no one here now, and Scott laid hat and riding-whip upon the table and drew forward a chair for his companion.

She looked at him and tried to thank him, but she was voiceless. Her pale lips moved without sound.

Scott's eyes were very kindly. "Don't be so frightened, child!" he said; and then, a sudden thought striking him, "Look here! You go and wait in the conservatory and let me speak to him first! Yes, that will be the best way. Come!"

His hand touched her again. She turned as one compelled. But as he opened the glass door, she found her voice.

"Oh, I ought not to - to let you face him alone. I must be brave. I must."

"Yes, you must," Scott answered. "But I will see him alone first. It will make it easier for everyone."

Yet for a moment she halted still. "You really mean it? You wish it?"

"Yes, I wish it," he said. "Wait in here till I call you!"

She took him at his word. There was no other course. He closed the door upon her and turned back alone.

He sat down in the chair that he had placed for her and became motionless as a figure carved in bronze. His pale face and trim, colourless beard were in shadow, his eyes were lowered. There was scarcely an inanimate object in the room as insignificant and unimposing as he, and yet in his stillness, in his utter unobtrusiveness, there lay a strength such as the strongest knight who ever rode in armour might have envied.

There came a careless step without, a hand upon the door. It opened, and Sir Eustace, handsome, self-assured, slightly haughty, strode into the room.

"Hullo, Stumpy! What do you want? I can't stop. I am booked to play billiards with Miss de Vigne. A test match to demonstrate the steadiness of my nerves!"

Scott stood up. "I have a bigger test for you than that, old chap," he said. "Shut the door if you don't mind!"

Sir Eustace sent him a swift, edged glance. "I can't stop," he said again. "What is it? Some mare's nest about Isabel?"

"No, nothing whatever to do with Isabel. Shut the door, man! I must be alone with you for a few minutes." Scott spoke with unwonted vehemence. The careless notes of the piano, the merry tumult of chattering voices, seemed to affect him oddly, almost to exasperate him.

Sir Eustace turned and swung the door shut; then with less than his customary arrogance he came to Scott. "What's the matter?" he said. "Out with it! Don't break the news if you can help it!"

His eyes belied the banter of his words. They shone as the eyes of a fighter meeting odds. There was something leonine about him at the moment, something of the primitive animal roused from its lair and scenting danger.

He looked into Scott's pale face with the dawning of a threatening expression upon his own.

And Scott met the threat full and square and unflinching. "I've come to tell you," he said, "about the hardest thing one man can tell another. Dinah wishes to be released from her engagement."

His words were brief but very distinct. He stiffened as he uttered them, almost as if he expected a blow.

But Sir Eustace stood silent and still, with only the growing menace in his eyes to show that he had heard.

Several seconds dragged away ere he made either sound or movement. Then, with a sudden, fierce gesture, he gripped Scott by the shoulder. "And you have the damnable impertinence to come and tell me!" he said.

There was violence barely restrained in voice and action. He held Scott as if he would fling him against the wall.

But Scott remained absolutely passive, enduring the savage grip with no sign of resentment. Only into his steady eyes there came that gleam as of steel that leaps to steel.

"I have told you," he said, "because I have no choice. She wishes to be set free, and - she fears you too much to tell you so herself."

Sir Eustace broke in upon him with a furious laugh that was in some fashion more insulting than a blow on the mouth. "And she has deputed you to do so on her behalf! Highly suitable! Or did you volunteer for the job, most fearless knight?"

"I offered to help her - certainly." Scott's voice was as free from agitation as his pose. "I would help any woman under such circumstances. It's no easy thing for her to break off her engagement at this stage. And she is such a child. She needs help."

"She shall have it," said Eustace grimly. "But - since you are here - I will deal with you first. Do you think I am going to endure any interference in this matter from you? Think it over calmly. Do you?"

His hold upon Scott had become an open threat. His eyes were a red blaze of anger. In that moment the animal in him was predominant, overwhelming. He was furious with the fury of the wounded beast that is beyond all control.

Scott realized the fact, and grasped his own self-control with a firmer hand. "It's no good my telling you that I hate my job," he said. "You'll hardly believe me if I do. But I've got to stick to it, beastly as it is. I can't stand by and see her married against her will. For that is what it amounts to. She would give anything she has to be free. She told me so. I'm infernally sorry. Perhaps you won't believe that either. But I've got to see this thing through now."

"Have you?" said Eustace, and suddenly his words came clipped and harsh from between set teeth. "And you think I'm going to endure it - stand aside tamely - while you turn an attack of stage-fright into a just cause and impediment to prevent my marriage! I should have thought you would have known me better by this time. But if you don't, you shall learn. Now listen! I am in dead earnest. If you don't drop this foolery, give me your word of honour here and now to leave this matter in my hands alone, - I'll thrash you to a pulp!"

He spoke with terrible intention. His whole being pulsated behind the words. And Scott's slight frame stiffened to rigidity in answer.

"You may grind me to powder!" he flung back, and in his voice there sounded a curiously vibrant quality as of finely-tempered steel that will bend but never break. "But you can't - and you shan't - force that child into marrying you against her will! That I swear - by God in Heaven!"

There was amazing force in the utterance, he also had thrown off the shackles. But his strength had about it nothing of the brute. Stripped to the soul, he stood up a man.

And against his will Eustace recognized the fact, realized the Invincible manifest in the clay, and in spite of himself was influenced thereby. The savage in him drew back abashed, aware of mastery.

Abruptly he released him and turned away. "You're a fool to tempt me," he said. "And a still greater fool to take her seriously. As I tell you, it's nothing but stage-fright. She had a touch of it yesterday. I'll come round presently and make it all right."

"You can only make it right by setting her free," Scott made answer. "There is no other course. Do you suppose I should have come to you in this way if there had been?"

Sir Eustace was moving to the door by which he had entered. He flung a backward look that was intensely evil over his shoulder at the puny figure of the man behind him.

"I can imagine you playing any damned trick under the sun to serve your own interests," he said, his lip curling in in an intolerable sneer. "But the deepest strategy fails occasionally. You haven't been quite subtle enough this time."

He was at the door as he uttered the last biting sentence, but so also was Scott. With a movement of incredible swiftness and impetuosity he flung himself forward. Their hands met upon the handle, and his remained in possession, for in sheer astonishment Eustace drew back.

They faced one another in the evening light, Scott pale to the lips, in his eyes an electric blaze that made them almost unbearably bright, Eustace, heavy-browed, lowering, the red glare of savagery gleaming like a smouldering flame, ready to leap forth in devastating fury to meet the fierce white heat that confronted him.

An awful silence hung between them - a silence of unutterable emotions, more poignant with passion than any strife or clash of weapons. And through it like a mocking under-current there ran the distant tinkle of the piano, the echoes of careless laughter beyond the closed door.

Then at last - it seemed with difficulty - Scott spoke, his voice very low, oddly jerky. "What do you mean by that? Tell me what you mean!"

Sir Eustace made an abrupt gesture, - the gesture of the swordsman on guard. He met the attack instantly and unwaveringly, but his look was wary. He did not seek to throw the lesser man from his path. As it were instinctively, though possibly for the first time in his life, he treated him as an equal.

"You know what I mean!" he made fierce rejoinder. "Even you can hardly pretend ignorance on that point."

"Even I!" Scott uttered a short, hard laugh that seemed to escape him against his will. "All the same, I will have an explanation," he said. "I prefer a straight charge, notwith-standing my damned subtlety. You will either explain or withdraw."

"As you like," Sir Eustace yielded the point, and again he acted instinctively, not realizing that he had no choice. "I mean that from the very beginning of things you have been influencing her against me, trying to win her from me. You never intended me to propose to her in the first place. You never imagined that I would do such a thing. You only thought of driving me off the ground and clearing it for yourself. I saw your game long ago. When you lost one trick, you tried for another. I knew - I knew all along. But the game is up now, and you've lost." A very bitter smile curved his mouth with the words. "There is your explanation," he said. "I hope you are satisfied."

"But I am not satisfied!" Quick as lightning came the *riposte*. Scott stood upright against the closed door. His eyes, unflickering, dazzlingly bright, were fixed upon his brother's face. "I am not satisfied," he repeated, and his words were as sternly direct as his look; he spoke as one compelled by some inner, driving force, "because what you have just said to me - this foul thing you believe of me - is utterly and absolutely without foundation. I have never tried - or dreamed of trying - to win her from you. I speak as before God. In this matter I have never been other than loyal either to you or to my own honour. If any other man insulted me in this fashion," his face worked a little, but he controlled it sharply, "I wouldn't have stooped to answer him. But you - I suppose I must allow you the - privilege of brotherhood. And so I ask you to believe - at least to make an effort to believe - that you have made a mistake."

His voice was absolutely quiet as he ended. The dignity of his utterance had in it even a touch of the sublime, and the elder man was aware of it, felt the force of it, was humbled by it. He stood a moment or two as one irresolute, halting at a difficult choice. Then, with an abrupt lift of the head as though his pride made fierce resistance, he gave ground.

"If I have wronged you, I apologize," he said with brevity.

Scott smiled faintly, wryly. "If -" he said.

"Very well, I withdraw the 'if.'" Sir Eustace spoke impatiently, not as one desiring reconciliation. "You laid yourself open to it by accepting the position of ambassador. I don't know how you could seriously imagine that I would treat with you in that capacity. If Dinah has anything to say to me, she must say it herself."

"She will do so," Scott spoke with steady assurance. "But before you see her, I think I ought to tell you that her reason for wishing to be set free is not stage-fright or any childish nonsense of that kind; but simply the plain fact that her heart is not in the compact. She has found out that she doesn't love you enough."

"She told you so?" demanded Sir Eustace.

Scott bent his head, for the first time averting his eyes from his brother's face. "Yes."

"And she wished you to tell me?" There was a metallic ring in Sir Eustace's voice; the red glare was gone from his eyes, they were cold and hard as a winter sky.

"Yes," Scott said again, still not looking at him.

"And why?" The words fell brief and imperious, compelling in their incisiveness.

Scott's eyes returned to his, almost in protest. "I told her you ought to know," he said.

"Then she would not have told me otherwise?"

"Possibly not."

There fell another silence. Sir Eustace looked hard and straight into the pale eyes, as though he would pierce to the soul behind. But though Scott met the look unwavering, his soul was beyond all scrutiny. There was something about him that baffled all search, something colossal that barred the way. For the second time Sir Eustace realized himself to be at a disadvantage; haughtily he passed the matter by.

"In that case there is nothing further to be said. You have fulfilled your somewhat rash undertaking, and that you have come out of the business with a whole skin is a bigger piece of luck than you deserved. If Dinah wishes this matter to go any further, she must come to me herself."

"Otherwise you will take no action?" Scott's voice had its old somewhat weary intonation. The animation seemed to have died out of him.

"Exactly." Sir Eustace answered him with equal deliberation. "So far as you are concerned the incident is now closed."

Ethel M. Dell

Scott took his hand from the door and moved slowly away. "I have put the whole case before you," he said. "I think you clearly understand that if you are going to try and use force, I am bound - as a friend - to take her part against you. She relies upon me for that, and - I shall not disappoint her. You see," a hint of compassion sounded in his voice, "she has always been afraid of you; and she knows that I am not."

Sir Eustace smiled cynically. "Oh, you have always been ready to rush in!" he said. "Doubtless your weakness is your strength."

Scott met the gibe with tightened lips. He made no attempt to reply to it. "The only thing left," he said quietly, "is for you to see her and hear what she has to say. She is waiting in the conservatory."

"She is waiting?" Eustace wheeled swiftly.

Scott was already half-way across the room. He strode forward, and intercepted him.

"You can go," he said curtly. "You have done your part. This business is mine, not yours."

Scott stood still. "I have promised to see her through," he said. "I must keep my promise."

Sir Eustace looked for a single instant as if he would strike him down; and then abruptly, inexplicably he gave way.

"Very well," he said. "Fetch her in!"

CHAPTER XVIII

THE TRUTH

At Scott's quiet summons Dinah entered. What she had passed through during those minutes of waiting was written in her face. She looked deathly.

Sir Eustace did not move to meet her. He stood by the table, very upright, very stern, uncompromisingly silent.

Dinah gave him one quivering glance, and turned appealingly to Scott.

"Don't be nervous!" he said gently. "There is no need. I have told him your wish."

She was terrified, but the ordeal had to be faced. She summoned all her strength, and went forward.

"Oh, Eustace," she said piteously, "I am so dreadfully sorry."

He looked down at her, his face like a marble mask. "So," he said, "you want to throw me over!"

She clasped her hands very tightly before her. "Oh, I know it's hateful of me," she said.

He made a slight, disdainful gesture. "Did you make up your mind or did Scott make it up for you?"

"No, no!" she cried in distress. "It was not his doing. I - I just told him, that was all."

"And you now desire him for a witness," suggested Sir Eustace cynically.

Dinah looked again towards Scott. He stood against the mantelpiece, as grimly upright as his brother and again oddly she was struck by the similarity between them. She could not have said wherein it lay, but she had never seen it more marked.

He spoke very quietly in answer to her look. "I have promised to stay for as long as you want me, but if you wish to be alone with Eustace for a few minutes, I will wait in the conservatory."

"Yes, let him do that!" Imperiously Eustace accepted the suggestion. "We shall not keep him long."

Dinah stood hesitating. Scott was looking at her very steadily and reassuringly. His eyes seemed to be telling her that she had nothing to fear. But he would not move without her word, and in the end reluctantly she gave in.

"Very well," she said, in a low voice. "If - if you will wait!"

"I will," Scott said.

He limped across the room to the open door, passed through, closed it softly behind him. And Dinah was left to face her monster alone.

She did not look at Sir Eustace in the first dreadful moments that followed Scott's exit. She was horribly afraid. There was to her something inexpressibly ruthless in his very silence. She longed yet dreaded to hear him speak.

He did not do so for many seconds, and she thought by his

utter stillness that he must be listening to the wild throbbing of her heart.

Then at last, just as the tension of waiting was becoming unbearable and she was on the verge of piteous entreaty, he seated himself on the edge of the table and spoke.

"Well," he said, "we have got to get at the root of this trouble somehow. You don't propose to throw me over without telling me why, I suppose?"

His voice was perfectly calm. She even fancied that he was faintly smiling as he uttered the words, but she could not look at him to see. She found it difficult enough to speak in answer.

"I know I am treating you very badly," she said, wringing her clasped hands in her agitation. "You - of course you can make me marry you. I've promised myself to you. You have the right. But if you will only - only let me go, I am sure it will be much better for you too. Because - because - I've found out - I've found out - that I don't love you."

It was the greatest effort she had ever made in her life. She wondered afterwards how she had ever brought herself to accomplish it. It was so hard - so hideously hard - to face him, this man who loved her so overwhelmingly, and tell him that he had failed to win her love in return. And at the eleventh hour - to treat him thus! If he had taken her by the throat and wrung her neck, she would have considered him justified and herself but righteously punished.

But he did nothing of a violent nature. He only sat there looking at her, and though she could not bring herself to meet his look she knew that it held no anger.

He did not speak, and she went on with a species of desperate pleading, because silence was so intolerable. "It wouldn't be right of me to - to marry you and not tell you, would it? It wouldn't be fair. It would be like marrying you under false

Ethel M. Dell

pretences. I only wish - oh, I do wish - that I had known sooner, when you first asked me. I might have known. I ought to have known! But - but - somehow -" she began to falter badly and finally concluded in a piteous whisper - "I didn't."

"How did you find out?" he said. His tone was still perfectly quiet; but he spoke judicially, as one who meant to have an answer.

But Dinah had no answer for him. It was the very question to which there could be no reply. Her fingers interlaced and strained against each other. She stood mute.

"I think you can tell me that," Eustace said.

She made a small but vehement gesture of negation. "I can't!" she said. "It's - it's - private."

"You mean you won't?" he questioned.

She nodded silently, too distressed for speech.

He got to his feet with finality. "That ends the case then," he said. "The appeal is dismissed. You can give me no adequate reason for releasing you. Therefore, I keep you to your engagement."

Dinah uttered a gasp. She had not expected this. For the first time she met his look fully, met the blue, dominant eyes, the faint, supercilious smile. And dismay struck through and through her as she realized that he had made her captive again with scarcely a struggle.

"Oh, but you can't - you can't!" she said.

He raised his brows. "We shall see," he said. "Mean-time -" He paused, looking at her, and suddenly the old hot glitter flashed forth, dazzling her, hypnotizing her; he uttered a low laugh and took her in his arms. "Daphne, you will-o'-the-wisp, you witch, how dare you?"

She made no outcry or resistance, realizing in a single stunning second the mastery that would not be denied; only ere his lips reached her, she sank down in his hold, hiding her face and praying him brokenly, imploringly, to let her go.

"Oh, please - oh, please - if you love me - do be kind - do be generous! I can't go on - indeed - indeed! Oh, Eustace, - Eustace - do forgive me - and let me go!"

"I will not!" he said. "I will not!"

She heard the rising passion in his voice, and her heart died within her; she sank lower, till but for his upholding arms she would have been kneeling at his feet. And then quite suddenly her strength went from her; she hung powerless, almost fainting in his grasp.

She scarcely knew what happened next, save that the fierceness went out of his hold like the passing of an evil dream. He lifted and held her while the darkness surged around.... And then presently she heard his voice, very low, amazingly tender, speaking into her ear. "Dinah! Dinah! What has come to you? Don't you know that I love you? Didn't I tell you so only last night?"

She leaned against him palpitating, unstrung, piteously distressed. "That's what makes it - so dreadful," she whispered. "I wish I were dead! Oh, I do wish I were dead!"

"Nonsense!" he said. "Nonsense!" He put his hand upon her head, pressing it against his breast. "Little sweetheart, what has happened to you? Tell me what is the matter!"

That was the hardest to face of all, that he should subdue himself, restrain his passion to pour out to her that which was infinitely greater than passion; she made a little sound that seemed to come straight from her heart.

"Oh, I can't tell you!" she sobbed into his shoulder. "I can't think how I ever made such a terrible mistake. But if only - oh, if only - you could marry Rose instead! It would be so very much better for everybody."

"Marry Rose!" he said. "What on earth made you think of that at this stage?"

"I always thought you would - in Switzerland," she explained rather incoherently. "I - never really thought - I could cut her out."

"Is that what you did it for?" An odd note sounded in Sir Eustace's voice, as though some irony of circumstance had forced his sense of humour.

"Just at first," whispered Dinah. "Oh, don't be angry! Please don't be angry! You - you weren't in earnest either just at first."

He considered the matter in silence for a few moments. Then half-quizzically, "I don't see that that is any reason for throwing me over now," he said. "If you don't love me to-day, you will to-morrow."

She shook her head.

"Quite sure?" he said.

"Quite," she answered faintly.

His hand was still upon her head, and it remained there. He held her closely pressed to him.

For a space again he was silent, his dark face bent over her, his lips actually touching her hair. Of what was passing in his mind she had no notion, and she dared not lift her head to look. She dreaded each moment a return of that tornado-like passion that had so often appalled her. But it did not come.

His arms held her indeed, but without violence, and in his stillness there was no tension to denote its presence.

He spoke at length, almost whispering. "Dinah, who is the lucky fellow? Tell me!"

She started away from him. She almost cried out in her dismay. But he stopped her. He took her face between his hands with an insistence that would not be denied. He looked closely, searchingly, into her eyes.

"Is it Scott?" he said.

She did not answer him. She stood as one paralysed, and up over face and neck and all her trembling body, enwrapping her like a flame, there rose a scorching, agonizing blush.

He held her there before him and watched it, and she saw that his eyes were piercingly bright, with the brightness of burnished steel. She could not turn her own away from them, though her whole soul shrank from that stark scrutiny. In anguish of mind she faced him, helpless, unutterably ashamed, while that burning blush throbbed fiercely through every vein and gradually died away.

He let her go at last very slowly. "I - see," he said.

She put her hands up over her face with a childish, piteous gesture. She felt as if he had ruthlessly torn from her the one secret treasure that she cherished. She was free - she knew she was free. But at what a cost!

"So," Eustace said, "that's it, is it? We've got at the truth at last!"

She quivered at the words. Her whole being seemed to be shrivelled as though it had passed through the fire. He had wrenched her secret from her, and she had nothing more to hide.

Sir Eustace walked to the end of the room and back. He halted close to her, but he did not touch her. He spoke, briefly and sternly.

"How long has this been going on?"

She looked up at him, her face pathetically pinched and small. "It hasn't been going on. I - only realized it to-day. He doesn't know. He never must know!" A sudden sharp note of anxiety sounded in her voice. "He never must know!" she reiterated with emphasis.

"He hasn't made love to you then?" Sir Eustace spoke in the same curt tone; his mouth was merciless.

She started as if stung. "Oh no! Oh no! Of course he hasn't! He - he doesn't care for me - like that. Why should he?"

Eustace's grim lips twitched a little. "Why indeed? Well, it's lucky for him he hasn't. If he had, I'd have half killed him for it!"

There was concentrated savagery in his tone. His eyes shone with a fire that made her shrink. And then very suddenly he put his hand upon her shoulder.

"Do you mean to tell me that you want to throw me over solely because you imagine you care for a man who doesn't care for you?" he asked.

She looked up at him piteously, "Oh, please don't ask me any more!" she said.

"But I want to know," he said stubbornly. "Is that your only reason?"

With difficulty she answered him. "No."

"Then what more?" he demanded.

It was inevitable. She made a desperate effort to be brave. "I couldn't be happy with you. I am afraid of you. And - and - you are not kind to - to Isabel."

"Who says I am not kind to Isabel?" His hand pressed upon her ominously; his look was implacably stern.

But the effort to be brave had given her strength. She stiffened in his hold. "I know it," she said. "I have seen it. She is always miserable when you are there."

He frowned upon her heavily. "You don't understand. Isabel is very hysterical. She needs a firm hand."

"You are more than firm," Dinah said. "You are - cruel."

Never in her wildest moments had she imagined herself making such an indictment. She marvelled at herself even as it left her lips. But something seemed to have entered into her, taking away her fear. Not till long afterwards did she realize that it was her new-found womanhood that had come upon her all unawares during that poignant interview.

She faced him without a tremor as she uttered the words, and he received them in a silence so absolute that she went on with scarcely a pause. "Not only to Isabel, but to everyone; to Scott, to that poor poacher, to me. You don't believe it, because it is your nature. But it is true all the same. And I think cruelty is a most dreadful thing. It's a vice that not all the virtues put together could counter-balance."

"When have I been cruel to you?" he said.

His tone was quiet, his face mask-like; but she thought that fury raged behind his calm. And still she knew no fear, felt no faintest dread of consequence.

"All your love-making has been cruel," she said. "Only once - no, twice now - have you been the least bit kind to me. It's no good talking. You'd never understand. I've lain awake often in the night with the dread of you. But" - her voice shook slightly - "I didn't know what I wanted, so I kept on. Now that I do know - though I shall never have it - it's made a difference, and I can't go on. You don't want me any more now I've told you, so it won't hurt you so very badly to let me go."

"You are wrong," he said, and suddenly she knew that out of his silence or her speech had developed something that was strange and new. His voice was quick and low, utterly devoid of its customary arrogance. "I want you more than ever! Dinah - Dinah, I may have been a brute to you. You're right. I often am a brute. But marry me - only marry me - and I swear to you that I will be kind!"

His calm was gone. He leaned towards her urgently, his dark face aglow with a light that was not passion. She had deemed him furious, and behold, she had him at her feet! Her ogre was gone for ever. He had crumbled at a touch. She saw before her a man, a man who loved her, a man whom she might eventually have come to love but for -

She caught her breath in a sharp sob, and put forth a hand in pleading. "Eustace, don't! Please don't! I can't bear it. You - you must set me free!"

"You are free as air," he said.

"Am I? Then don't - don't ask me to bind myself again! For I can't - I can't. I want to go away. I want to be quiet." She broke down suddenly. The strain was past, the battle over. She had vanquished him, how she scarcely knew; but her own brief strength was tottering now. "Let me go home!" she begged. "Tell Scott I've gone! Tell everyone there won't be a wedding after all! Say I'm dreadfully sorry! It's my fault - all my fault! I ought to have known!" Her tears blinded her, silenced her. She turned towards the door.

"Won't you say good-bye to me?" Eustace said.

Her voice was low and very steady. The glow was gone. He was calm again, absolutely calm. With the failure of that one urgent appeal, he seemed to have withdrawn his forces, accepting defeat.

She turned back gropingly. "Good-bye - good-bye -" she whispered, "and - thank you!"

He put his arm around her, and bending kissed her forehead. "Don't cry, dear!" he said.

His manner was perfectly kind, supremely gentle. She hardly knew him thus. Again her heart smote her in overwhelming self-reproach. "Oh, Eustace, forgive me for hurting you so - forgive me - for all I've said!"

"For telling me the truth?" he said. "No, I don't forgive you for that."

She broke down utterly and sobbed aloud. "I wish - I wish I hadn't! How could I do it? I hate myself!"

"No - no," he said. "It's all right. You've done nothing wrong. Run home, child! Don't cry! Don't cry!"

His hand touched her hair under the soft cap, touched and lingered. But he did not hold her to him.

"Run home!" he said again.

"And - and - you won't - won't - tell - Scott?" she whispered through her tears.

"But I don't think even I am such a bounder as that!" he said gently. "Do you?"

She lifted her face impulsively. She kissed him with quivering lips. "No - no. I didn't mean it. Good-bye Oh, good-bye!"

He kissed her in return. "Good-bye!" he said.

And so they parted.

CHAPTER XIX

THE FURNACE

The bridal dress with its filmy veil still lay in its white box - a fairy garment that had survived the catastrophe. Dinah sat and looked at it dully. The light of her single candle shimmered upon the soft folds. How beautiful it was!

She had been sitting there for hours, after a terrible scene with her mother downstairs, and from acute distress she had passed into a state of torpid misery that enveloped her like a black cloud. She felt almost too exhausted, too numbed, to think. Her thoughts wandered drearily back and forth. She was sure she had been very greatly to blame, yet she could not fix upon any definite juncture at which she had begun to go wrong. Her engagement had been such a whirlwind of Fate. She had been carried off her feet from the very beginning. And the deliverance from the home bondage had seemed so fair a prospect. Now she was plunged, back again into that bondage, and she was firmly convinced that no chance of freedom would ever be offered to her again. Yet she knew that she had done right to draw back. Regret it though she might again and again in the bitter days to come, she knew - and she would always know - that at the eleventh hour she had done right.

She had been true to the greatest impulse that had ever stirred her soul. It had been at a frightful cost. She had sacrificed everything - everything - to a vision that she might never realize. She had cast away all the glitter and the wealth for this far greater thing which yet could never be more to her than a golden dream. She had even cast away love, and her heart still bled at the memory. But she had been true - she had been true.

Not yet was the sacrifice ended. She knew that a cruel ordeal yet awaited her. There was the morrow to be faced, the morrow with its renewal of disgrace and punishment. Her mother was furious with her, so furious that for the first time in her life her father had intervened on her behalf and temporarily restrained the flow of wrath. Perhaps he had seen her utter weariness, for he had advised her, not unkindly, to go to bed. She had gone to her room, thankful to escape, but neither tea nor supper had followed her thither. Billy had come to bid her good night long ago, but, though he had not said so, he also, it seemed, was secretly disgusted with her, and he had not lingered. It would be the same with everyone, she thought to herself wearily. No one would ever realize how terribly hard it had all been. No one would dream of extending any pity to her. And of course she had done wrong. She knew it, was quite ready to admit it. But the wrong had lain in accepting that overweening lover of hers, not in giving him up. Also, she ought to have found out long ago. She wondered how it was she hadn't. It had never been a happy engagement.

Again her eyes wandered to the exquisite folds of that dress which she was never to wear. How she had loved the thought of it and all the lovely things that Isabel had procured for her! What would become of them all, she wondered? All the presents downstairs would have to go back. Yes, and Eustace's ring! She had forgotten that. She slipped it off her finger with a little dry sob, and put it aside. And the necklace of pearls that she had always thought so much too good for her, but which would have looked so beautiful on the wedding-dress; that must be returned. Very strangely that thought pierced the dull ache of her heart with a mere poignant pain. And following it came another, stabbing her like a knife. The sapphire for friendship - his sapphire - that would have to go too. There would be nothing left when it was all over.

And she would never see any of them any more. She would drop out of their lives and be forgotten. Even Isabel would not want her now that she had behaved so badly. She had made Sir Eustace the talk of the County. So long as they remembered her they would never forgive her for that.

Sir Eustace might forgive. He had been extraordinarily generous. A lump rose in her throat as she thought of him. But the de Vignes, all those wedding guests who were to have honoured the occasion, they would all look upon her with contumely for evermore. No wonder her mother was enraged against her! No wonder! No wonder! She would never have another chance of holding up her head in such society again.

A great sigh escaped her. What was the good of sitting there thinking? She had undressed long ago, and she was cold from head to foot. Yet somehow she had forgotten or been too miserable to go to bed. She supposed she had been waiting for the soothing tears that did not come. Or had she meant to pray? She could not remember, and in any case prayer seemed out of the question. Her life had been filled with delight for a few delirious weeks, but it had all drained away. She did not want it back again. She scarcely knew what she wanted, save the great Impossible for which she lacked the heart to pray. And no doubt God was angry with her too, or she could not feel like this! So what was the good of attempting it?

Wearily she turned to put out her candle. But ere her hand reached it, she paused in swift apprehension.

The next instant sharply she started round to see the door open, and her mother entered the room.

Gaunt, forbidding, full of purpose, she walked in, and set her candle down beside the one that Dinah had been about to extinguish.

"Get up!" she said to the startled girl. "Don't sit there gaping at me! I've come here to give you a lesson, and it will be a pretty severe one I can tell you if you attempt to disobey me."

"What do you want me to do?" breathed Dinah.

She stood up at the harsh behest, but she was trembling so much that her knees would scarcely support her. Her heart was throbbing violently, and each throb seemed as if it would choke her. She had seen that inflexibly grim look often before upon her mother's face, and she knew from bitter experience that it portended merciless treatment.

Mrs. Bathurst did not reply immediately. She went to a little table in a corner which Dinah used for writing purposes, and opened a blotter that lay upon it. From this she took a sheet of note-paper and laid it in readiness, found Dinah's pen, opened the ink-pot. Then, over her shoulder, she flung a curt command: "Come here!"

Dinah went, every nerve in her body tingling, her face and hands cold as ice.

Mrs. Bathurst glanced at her with a contemptuous smile. "Sit down, you little fool!" she said. "Now, you take that pen and write at my dictation!"

Dinah shrank at the rough words. She felt like a child about to receive corporal punishment. The vindictive force of the woman seemed to beat her down. Writhe and strain as she might, she was bound to suffer both the pain and the indignity to the uttermost limit; for she lacked the strength to break free.

She did not sit down however. She remained standing by the little table.

"Mother," she said through her white lips, "what do you want me to do?"

She could scarcely keep her teeth from chattering, and Mrs. Bathurst noted the fact with another grim smile.

"What am I going to make you do would be more to the purpose, my girl, wouldn't it?" she said. "Sit down there, and you'll find out!"

Dinah leaned upon the little table to steady herself. "Tell me what it is I am to do!" she said.

"Ah! That's better." A note of bitter humour sounded in Mrs. Bathurst's voice. "Sit down!"

She thrust out a bony hand, and gripped her by the shoulder, forcing her downwards.

Dinah dropped into the chair, and sat motionless.

"Take your pen!" Mrs. Bathurst commanded.

She hesitated; and instantly, with a violent movement, her mother snatched it up and held it in front of her.

"Take it!"

Dinah took it with fingers so numb that they were almost powerless.

"Now," said Mrs. Bathurst, "I will tell you what you are going to do. You are going to write to Sir Eustace at my dictation, and tell him that you are very sorry, you have made a mistake, and beg him to forget it and marry you to-morrow as arranged."

"Mother! No!" Dinah started as if at a blow; the pen dropped from her fingers. "Oh no! I can't indeed - indeed!"

"You will!" said Mrs. Bathurst.

Her hand gripped the slender shoulder with cruel force. She bent, bringing her harsh features close to her daughter's blanched face.

"Just you remember one thing!" she said, her voice low and menacing. "You've never succeeded in defying me yet, and you won't do it now. I'll conquer you - I'll break you - if it takes me all night to do it!"

Dinah recoiled before the unshackled fury that suddenly blazed in the gipsy eyes that looked into hers. Sheer horror sprang into her own.

"Oh, but I can't - I can't!" she reiterated in an agony. "I don't love him. He knows it. I ought to have found out before, but I didn't. Mother - Mother -" piteously she began to plead - "you - you can't want to make me marry a man I don't love? You - you would never - surely - have done such a thing yourself!"

Mrs. Bathurst made a sharp gesture as if something had pierced her. She shook the shoulder she grasped. "Love!" she said. "Oh, don't talk to me of love! Do you imagine - have you ever imagined - that I married that fox-hunting booby - for love?"

A great and terrible bitterness that was like the hunger of a famished animal looked out of her eyes. Dinah gazed at her aghast. What new and horrible revelation was this? She felt suddenly sick and giddy.

Her mother shook her again roughly, savagely. "None of that!" she said. "Don't think I'll put up with it, my fine lady, for I won't! What has love to do with such a chance as this? Tell me that, you little fool! Do you suppose that either you or I have ever been in a position to marry - for love?"

Her face was darkly passionate. Dinah felt as if she were in the clutches of a tigress. "What - what do you mean?" she faltered through her quivering lips.

"What do I mean?" Mrs. Bathurst broke into a sudden brutal laugh. "Ha! What do I mean?" she said. "I'll tell you, shall I? Yes, I'll tell you! I'll show you the shame that I've covered all these years. I mean that I married because of you - for no other reason. I married because I'd been betrayed - and left. Now do you understand why it isn't for you to pick and choose - you who have been the plague-spot of my life, the thorn in my side ever since you first stirred there - a perpetual reminder of what I would have given my very soul to forget? Do you understand, I say? Do you understand? Or must I put it plainer still? You - the child of my shame - to dare to set yourself up against me!"

She ended upon what was almost a note of loathing, and Dinah shuddered from head to foot. It was to her as if she had been rolled in pitch. She felt overwhelmed with the cruel degradation of it, the unspeakable shame.

Mrs. Bathurst watched her anguished distress with a species of bitter satisfaction. "That'll take the fight out of you, my girl," she said. "Or if it doesn't, I've another sort of remedy yet to try. Now, you start on that letter, do you hear? It'll be a bit shaky, but none the worse for that. Write and tell him you've changed your mind! Beg him humble-like to take you back!"

But Dinah only bowed her head upon her hands and sat crushed.

Mrs. Bathurst gave her a few seconds to recover her balance. Then again mercilessly she shook her by the shoulder.

"Come, Dinah! I'm not going to be defied. Are you going to write that letter at once? Or must I take stronger measures?"

And then a species of wild courage entered into Dinah. She turned at last at bay. "I will not write it! I would sooner die! If - if this thing is true, it would be far easier to die! I couldn't marry any man now who had any pride of birth."

She was terribly white, but she faced her tormentor unflinching, her eyes like stars. And it came to Mrs. Bathurst with unpleasant force that she had taken a false step which it was impossible to retrace. It was then that the evil spirit that had been goading her entered in and took full possession.

She gripped Dinah's shoulder till she winced with pain. "Mother, you - you are hurting me!"

"Yes, and I will hurt you," she made answer. "I'll hurt you as I've never hurt you yet if you dare to disobey me! I'll crush you to the earth before I will endure that from you. Now! For the last time! Will you write that letter? Think well before you refuse again!"

She towered over Dinah with awful determination, wrought up to a pitch of fury by her resistance that almost bordered upon insanity.

Dinah's boldness waned swiftly before the iron force that countered it. But her resolution remained unshaken, a resolution from which no power on earth could move her.

"I can't do it - possibly," she said.

"You mean you won't?" said Mrs. Bathurst.

Dinah nodded, and gripped the table hard to endure what should follow.

"You - mean - you won't?" Mrs. Bathurst said again very slowly.

"I will not." The white lips spoke the words, and closed upon them. Dinah sat rigid with apprehension.

Mrs. Bathurst took her hand from her shoulder and turned from her. The candle that had been burning all the evening was low in its socket. She lifted it out and went to the fireplace. There were some shavings in the grate. She pushed the lighted candle end in among them; then, as the fire roared up the chimney, she turned.

An open trunk was close to her with the dainty pale green dress that Dinah had worn the previous evening lying on the top. She took it up, and bundled the soft folds together. Then violently she flung it on to the flames.

Dinah gave a cry of dismay, and started to her feet. "Mother! What are you doing? Mother! Are you mad?"

Mrs. Bathurst looked at her with eyes of blazing vindictiveness. "If you are not going to be married, you won't need a trousseau," she said grimly. "These things are quite unfit for a girl in your station. For Lady Studley they would of course have been suitable, but not for such as you."

She turned back to the open trunk with the words, and began to sweep together every article of clothing it contained. Dinah watched her in horror-stricken silence. She remembered with odd irrelevance how once in her childhood for some petty offence her mother had burnt a favourite doll, and then had whipped her soundly for crying over her loss.

She did not cry now. Her tears seemed frozen. She did not feel as if she could ever cry again. The cold that enwrapped her was beginning to reach her heart. She thought she was getting past all feeling.

So in mute despair she watched the sacrifice of all that Isabel's loving care had provided. So much thought had been spent upon the delicate finery. They had discussed and settled each dainty garment together. She had revelled in the thought of all the good things which she was to wear - she who had never worn anything that was beautiful before. And now - and now - they shrivelled in the roaring flame and dropped into grey ash in the fender.

It was over at last. Only the wedding-dress remained. But as Mrs. Bathurst laid merciless hands upon this also, Dinah uttered a bitter cry.

"Oh, not that! Not that!"

Her mother paused. "Will you wear it to-morrow if Sir Eustace will have you?" she demanded.

"No! Oh no!" Dinah tottered back against her bed and covered her eyes.

She could not watch the destruction of that fairy thing. But it went so quickly, so quickly. When she looked up again, it had crumbled away like the rest, and the shimmering veil with it. Nothing, nothing was left of all the splendour that had been hers.

She sank down on the foot of the bed. Surely her mother would be satisfied now! Surely her lust for vengeance could devise no further punishment!

She was nearing the end of her strength, and she was beginning to know it. The room swam before her dizzy sight. Her mother's figure loomed gigantic, scarcely human.

She saw her poke down the last of the cinders and turn to the door. There was a pungent smell of smoke in the room. She wondered if she would ever be able to cross that swaying, seething floor to open the window. She closed her eyes and listened with straining ears for the closing of the door.

It came, and following it, a sharp click as of the turning of a key. She looked up at the sound, and saw her mother come back to her. She was carrying something in one hand, something that dangled and east a snake-like shadow.

She came to the cowering girl and caught her by the arm. "Now get up!" she ordered brutally. "And take the rest of your punishment!"

Truly Dinah drank the cup of bitterness to the dregs that night. Mentally she had suffered till she had almost ceased to feel. But physically her powers of endurance had not been so sorely tried. But her nerves were strung to a pitch when even a sudden movement made her tingle, and upon this highly-tempered sensitiveness the punishment now inflicted upon her was acute agony. It broke her even more completely than it had broken her in childhood. Before many seconds had passed the last shred of her self-control was gone.

Guy Bathurst, lying comfortably in bed, was aroused from his first slumber by a succession of sharp sounds like the lashing of a loosened creeper against the window, but each sound was followed by an anguished cry that sank and rose again like the wailing of a hurt child.

He turned his head and listened. "By Jove! That's too bad of Lydia," he said. "I suppose she won't be satisfied till she's had her turn, but I shall have to interfere if it goes on."

It did not go on for long; quite suddenly the cries ceased. The other sounds continued for a few seconds more, then ceased also, and he turned upon his pillow with a sigh of relief.

A minute later he was roused again by the somewhat abrupt entrance of his wife. She did not speak to him, but stood by the door and rummaged in the pockets of his shooting-coat that hung there.

Bathurst endured in silence for a few moments; then, "Oh, what on earth are you looking for?" he said with sleepy irritation. "I wish you'd go."

"I want your brandy flask," she said, and her words came clipped and sharp. "Where is it?"

"On the dressing-table," he said. "What have you been doing to the child?"

"I've given her as much as she can stand," his wife retorted grimly. "But you leave her to me! I'll manage her."

She departed with a haste that seemed to denote a certain anxiety notwithstanding her words.

She left the door ajar, and the man turned again on his pillow and listened uneasily. He was afraid Lydia had gone too far.

For a space he heard nothing. Then came the splashing of water, and again that piteous, gasping cry. He caught the sound of his wife's voice, but what she said he could not hear. Then there were movements, and Dinah spoke in broken supplication that went into hysterical sobbing. Finally he heard his wife come out of the room and close the door behind her.

She came back again with the brandy flask. "She's had a lesson," she observed, "that I rather fancy she'll never forget as long as she lives."

"Then I hope you're satisfied," said Bathurst, and turned upon his side.

Yes, Dinah had had a lesson. She had passed through a sevenfold furnace that had melted the frozen fountain of her tears till it seemed that their flow would never be stayed again. She wept for hours, wept till she was sick and blind with weeping, and still she wept on. And bitter shame and humiliation watched beside her all through that dreadful night, giving her no rest.

For she had gone through this fiery torture, this cruel chastisement of mind and body, all for what? For love of a man who felt nought but kindness for her, - for the dear memory of a golden vision that would never be hers again.

CHAPTER XX

THE COMING OF GREATHEART

It was soon after nine on the following morning that Scott presented himself on horseback at the gate of Dinah's home. It had been his intention to tie up his animal and enter, but he was met in the entrance by Billy coming out on a bicycle, and the boy at once frustrated his intention.

"Good morning, sir! Pleased to see you, but it's no good your coming in. The pater's still in bed, and the mater's doing the house-work."

"And Dinah?" said Scott. The question leapt from him almost involuntarily. He had not meant to display any eagerness, and he sought to cover it by his next words which were uttered with his usual careful deliberation. "It's Dinah I have come to see. I have a message for her from my sister."

Billy's freckled face crumpled into troubled lines. "Dinah has cleared out," he said briefly. "I'm just off to the station to try and get news of her."

"What?" Scott said, startled.

The boy looked at him, his green eyes shrewdly confiding. "There's been the devil of a row," he said. "The mater is furious with her. She gave her a fearful licking last night to judge by the sounds. Dinah was squealing like a rat. Of course

Ethel M. Dell

girls always do squeal when they're hurt, but I fancy the mater must have hit a bit harder than usual. And she's burnt the whole of the trousseau too. Dinah was so mighty proud of all her fine things. She'd feel that, you know, pretty badly."

"Damnation!" Scott said, and for the second time he spoke without his own volition. He looked at Billy with that intense hot light in his eyes that had in it the whiteness of molten metal. "Do you mean that?" he said. "Do you actually mean that your mother flogged her - flogged Dinah?"

Billy nodded. "It's just her way," he explained half-apologetically. "The mater is like that. She's rough and ready. She's always done it to Dinah, had a sort of down on her for some reason. I guessed she meant business last night when I saw the dog-whip had gone out of the hall. I wished afterwards I'd thought to hide it, for it's rather a beastly implement. But the mater's a difficult woman to baulk. And when she's in that mood, it's almost better to let her have her own way. She's sure to get it sooner or later, and a thing of that sort doesn't improve with keeping."

So spoke Billy with the philosophy of middle-aged youth, while the man beside him sat with clenched hands and faced the hateful vision of Dinah, the fairy-footed and gay of heart, writhing under that horrible and humiliating punishment.

He spoke at length, and some electricity within him made the animal under him fidget and prance, for he stirred neither hand nor foot. "And you tell me Dinah has run away?"

"Yes, cleared out," said Billy tersely. "It was an idiotic thing to do, for the mater is downright savage this morning, and she'll only give her another hiding for her pains. She stayed away all day once before, years ago when she was a little kid, and, my eye, didn't she catch it when she came back! She never did it again - till now."

"And you are going to the station to look for her?" Scott's

voice was dead level. He calmed the restive horse with a firm hand.

"Yes; just to find out if she's gone by train. I don't believe she has, you know. She's nowhere to go to. I expect she's hiding up in the woods somewhere. I shall scour the country afterwards; for the longer she stays away the worse it'll be for her. I'm sure of that," said Billy uneasily. "When the mater lays hands on her again, she'll simply flay her."

"She will not do anything of the sort," said Scott, and turned his horse's head with resolution. "Come along and find her first! I will deal with your mother afterwards."

Billy mounted his bicycle and accompanied him. Though he did not see how Scott was to prevent any further vengeance on his mother's part, it was a considerable relief to feel that he had enlisted a champion on his sister's behalf. For he was genuinely troubled about her, although the cruel discipline to which she had been subjected all her life had so accustomed him to seeing her in trouble that it affected him less than if it had been a matter of less frequent occurrence.

Scott's reception of his information had somewhat awed him. Like Dinah, he had long ceased to look upon this man as insignificant. He rode beside him in respectful silence.

The country lane they followed crossed the railway by a bridge ere it ran into the station road. There was a steep embankment on each side of the line surmounted by woods, and as they reached the bridge Billy dismounted to gaze searchingly into the trees.

"She might be anywhere" he said. "This is a favourite place of hers because the wind-flowers grow here. Somehow I've got a sort of feeling -" He stopped short. "Why, there she is!" he exclaimed.

Scott looked sharply in the same direction. Had he been alone,

Ethel M. Dell

he would not have perceived her, for she was crouched low against a thicket of brambles and stunted trees midway down the embankment. She was clad in an old brown mackintosh that so toned with her surroundings as to render her almost invisible. Her chin was resting on her knees, and her face was turned from them. She seemed to be gazing up the line.

As they watched her, a signal near the bridge went down with a thud, and it seemed to Scott that the little huddled figure started and stiffened like a frightened doe. But she did not change her position, and she continued to gaze up the long stretch of line as though waiting for something.

"What on earth is she doing?" whispered Billy. "There are no wind-flowers there."

Scott slipped quietly to the ground. "You wait here!" he said. "Hold my animal, will you?"

He left the bridge, retracing his steps, and climbed a railing that fenced the wood. In a moment he disappeared among the trees, and Billy was left to watch and listen in unaccountable suspense.

The morning was dull, and a desolate wind moaned among the bare tree-tops. He shivered a little. There was something uncanny in the atmosphere, something that was evil. He kept his eyes upon Dinah, but she was a considerable distance away, and he could not see that she stirred so much as a finger. He wondered how long it would take Scott to reach her, and began to wish ardently that he had been allowed to go instead. The man was lame and he was sure that he could have covered the distance in half the time.

And then while he waited and watched, suddenly there came a distant drumming that told of an approaching train.

"The Northern express!" he said aloud.

Many a time had he stood on the bridge to see it flash and thunder below him. The sound of its approach had always filled him with a kind of ecstasy before, but now - to-day - it sent another feeling through him, - a sudden, wild dart of unutterable dread.

"What rot!" he told himself, with an angry shake. "Oh, what rot!"

But the dread remained coiled like a snake about his heart.

The animal he held became restless, and he backed it off the bridge, but he could not bring himself to go out of sight of that small, tragic figure in the old mackintosh that sat so still, so still, there upon the grassy slope. He watched it with a terrible fascination. Would Scott never make his appearance?

A white tuft of smoke showed against the grey of the sky. The throbbing of the engine grew louder, grew insistent. A couple of seconds more and it was within sight, still far away but rapidly drawing near. Where on earth was Scott? Did he realize the danger? Ought he to shout? But something seemed to grip his throat, holding him silent. He was powerless to do anything but watch.

Nearer came the train and nearer. Billy's eyes were starting out of his head. He had never been so scared in all his life before. There was something fateful in the pose of that waiting figure.

The rush of the oncoming express dinned in his ears. It was close now, and suddenly - suddenly as a darting bird - Dinah was on her feet. Billy found his voice in a hoarse, croaking cry, but almost ere it left his lips he saw Scott leap into view and run down the bank.

By what force of will he made his presence known Billy never afterwards could conjecture. No sound could have been audible above the clamour of the train. Yet by some means - some electric battery of the mind - he made the girl below aware of him. On the very verge of the precipice she stopped, stood poised for a moment, then turned herself back and saw him....

The train thundered by, shaking the ground beneath their feet, and rushed under the bridge. The whole embankment was blotted out in white smoke, and Billy reeled back against the horse he held.

"By Jove!" he whispered shakily. "By - Jove! What a ghastly fright!"

He wiped his forehead with a trembling hand, and led the animal away from the bridge. Somehow he was feeling very sick - too sick to look any longer, albeit the danger was past.

The smoke cleared from the embankment, and two figures were left facing one another on the grassy slope. Neither of them spoke a word. It was as if they were waiting for some sign. Scott was panting, but Dinah did not seem to be breathing at all. She stood there tense and silent, terribly white, her eyes burning like stars.

The last sound of the train died away in the distance, and then, such was their utter stillness, from the thorn-bush close to them a thrush suddenly thrilled into song. The soft notes fell balmlike into that awful silence and turned it into sweetest music.

Scott moved at last, and at once the bird ceased. It was as if an angel had flown across the heaven with a silver flute of purest melody and passed again into the unknown.

He came to Dinah. "My dear," he said, and his voice was slightly shaky, "you shouldn't be here."

She stood before him, pillar-like, her two hands clenched against her sides. Her lips were quite livid. They moved soundlessly for several seconds before she spoke. "I - was waiting - for the express."

Her voice was flat and emotionless. It sounded almost as if she were talking in her sleep. And strangely it was that that shocked Scott even more than her appearance. Dinah's voice had always held countless inflections, little notes gay or sad like the trill of a robin. This was the voice of a woman in whom the very last spark of hope was quenched.

It pierced him with an intolerable pain. "Dinah - Dinah!" he said. "For God's sake, child, you don't mean - that!"

Her white, pinched face twisted in a dreadful smile. "Why not?" she said. "There was no other way." And then a sudden quiver as of returning life went through her. "Why did you stop me?" she said. "If you hadn't, it would have been - all over by now."

He put out a quick hand. "Don't say it, - in heaven's name! You are not yourself. Come - come into the wood, and we will talk!"

She did not take his hand. "Can't we talk here?" she said.

He composed himself with an effort. "No, certainly not. Come into the wood!"

He spoke with quiet insistence. She gave him an inscrutable look.

"You think you are going to help me, - Mr. Greatheart," she said, "but I am past help. Nothing you can do will make any difference to me now."

"Come with me nevertheless!" he said.

He laid a gentle hand upon her shoulder, and she winced with a sharpness that tore his heart. But in a moment she turned beside him and began the ascent, slowly, labouringly, as if every step gave her pain. He moved beside her, supporting her elbow when she faltered, steadily helping her on.

They entered the wood, and the desolate sighing of the wind encompassed them. Dinah looked at her companion with the first sign of feeling she had shown.

"I must sit down," she said.

"There is a fallen tree over there," he said, and guided her towards it.

She leaned upon him, very near to collapse. He spread his coat upon the tree and helped her down.

"Now how long is it since you had anything to eat?" he said.

She shook her head slightly. "I don't remember. But it doesn't matter. I'm not hungry."

He took one of her icy hands and began to rub it. "Poor child!" he said. "You ought to be given some hot bread and milk and tucked up in bed with hot bottles."

Her face began to work. "That," she said, "is the last thing that will happen to me."

"Haven't you been to bed at all?" he questioned.

Her throat was moving spasmodically; she bowed her head to hide her face from him. "Yes," she said in a whisper. "My mother - my mother put me there." And then as if the words burst from her against her will, "She thrashed me first with a dog-whip; but dogs have got hair to protect them, and I - had nothing. She only stopped because - I fainted. She hasn't finished with me now. When I go back - when I go back -" She broke off. "But I'm not going," she said, and her voice was flat and hard again. "Even you can't make me do that. There'll be another express this afternoon."

Scott knelt down beside her, and took her bowed head on to his shoulder. "Listen to me, Dinah!" he said. "I am going to help you, and you mustn't try to prevent me. If you had only allowed me, I would have gone home again with you yesterday, and this might have been avoided. My dear, don't draw yourself away from me! Don't you know I am a friend you can trust?"

The pitiful tenderness of his voice reached her, overwhelming her first instinctive effort to draw back. She leaned against him with painful, long-drawn sobs.

He held her closely to him with all a woman's understanding. "Oh, don't cry any more, child!" he said. "You're worn out with crying."

"I feel - so bad - so bad!" sobbed Dinah.

"Yes, yes. I know. Of course you do. But it's over, it's over. No one shall hurt you any more."

"You don't - understand," breathed Dinah. "It never will be over - while I live. I'm hurt inside - inside."

"I know," he said again. "But it will get better presently. Isabel and I are going to take you away from it all."

"Oh no!" she said quickly. "No - no - no!" She lifted her head from his shoulder and turned her poor, stained face upwards. "I couldn't do that!" she said. "I couldn't! I couldn't!"

"Wait!" he said gently. "Let me do what I can to help you now - before we talk of that! Will you sit here quietly for a little, while I go and get you some milk from that farm down the road?"

"I don't want it," she said.

"But I want you to have it," he made grave reply. "You will

Ethel M. Dell

stay here? Promise me!"

"Very well," she assented miserably.

He got up. "I shan't be gone long. Sit quite still till I come back!"

He touched her dark head comfortingly and turned away.

When he had gone a little distance he looked back, and saw that she was crouched upon the ground again and crying with bitter, straining sobs that convulsed her as though they would rend her from head to foot. With tightened lips he hastened on his way.

She had suffered a cruel punishment it was evident, and she was utterly worn out in body and spirit. But was it only the ordeal of yesterday and the physical penalty that she had been made to pay that had broken her thus?

He could not tell, but his heart bled for her misery and desolation.

"Who is the other fellow?" he asked himself. "I wonder if Billy knows."

He found Billy awaiting him in the road, anxious and somewhat reproachful. "You've been such a deuce of a time," he said. "Is she all right?"

"She is very upset," he made answer. "And she is faint too for want of food."

"That's not surprising," commented Billy. "She can't have had anything since lunch yesterday. What shall I do? Run home and get something? The mater can't want her to starve."

"No." Scott's voice rang on a hard note. "She probably doesn't. But you needn't go home for it. Run back to that farm we passed just now, and see if you can get some hot milk! Be quick like a good chap! Here's the money! I'll wait here."

Billy seized his bicycle and departed on his errand.

Scott began to walk his horse up and down, for inactivity was unbearable. Every moment he spent away from poor, broken Dinah was torturing. Those dreadful, hopeless tears of hers filled him with foreboding. He yearned to return.

Billy's absence lasted for nearly a quarter of an hour, and he was beginning to get desperate over the delay when at last the boy returned carrying a can of milk and a mug.

"I had rather a bother to get it," he explained. "People are so mighty difficult to stir, and I didn't want to tell 'em too much. I've promised to take these things back again. I say, can't I come along with you now?"

"I'd rather you didn't," Scott said. "I can manage best alone. Besides, I'm going to ask you to do something more."

"Anything!" said Billy readily.

"Thanks. Well, will you ride this animal into Great Mallowes, hire a closed car, and send it to the bridge here to pick me up? Then take him back to the Court, and if anyone asks any questions, say I've met a friend and I'm coming back on foot, but I may not be in to luncheon. Yes, that'll do, I think. I'll see about returning these things. Much obliged, Billy. Good-bye!"

Billy looked somewhat disappointed at this dismissal, but the prospect of a ride was dear to his boyish heart, and in a moment he nodded cheerily. "All right, I'll do that. I'll hide my bicycle in the wood and fetch it afterwards. But where are you going to take her to?"

Scott smiled also faintly and enigmatically. "Leave that to me, my good fellow! I shan't run away with her."

"But I shall see her again some time?" urged Billy, as he dumped his long-suffering machine over the railing and propped it out of sight behind the hedge.

"No doubt you will." Scott's tone was kindly and reassuring. "But I think I can help her better just now than you can, so I'll be getting back to her. Good-bye, boy! And thanks again!"

"So long!" said Billy, vaulting back and thrusting his foot into the stirrup. "You might let me hear how you get on."

"I will," promised Scott.

CHAPTER XXI

THE VALLEY OF HUMILIATION

When Scott reached the fallen tree again, Dinah's fit of weeping was over. She was lying exhausted and barely conscious against his coat.

She opened her eyes as he knelt down beside her. "You are - good," she whispered faintly.

He poured out some milk and held it to her. "Try to drink some!" he said gently.

She put out a trembling hand.

"No; let me!" he said.

She submitted in silence, and he lifted the glass to her lips and held it very steadily while slowly she drank.

Her eyes were swollen and burning with the shedding of many scalding tears. Now and then a sharp sob rose in her throat so that she could not swallow.

"Take your time!" he said. "Don't hurry it!"

But ere she finished, the tears were running down her face again. He set down the glass, and with his own handkerchief he wiped them away. Then he sat upon the low tree-trunk, and drew her to lean against him.

"When you're feeling better, we'll have a talk," he said.

She hid her face with a piteous gesture against his knee. "I don't see - the good of talking," she said, in muffled accents. "It can't make things - any better."

"I'm not so sure of that," he said. "Anyhow we can't leave things as they are. You will admit that."

Dinah was silent.

He went on with the utmost gentleness. "I want to get you away from here. Isabel is going down to Heath-on-Sea and she wants you to come too. It's a tiny place. We have a cottage there with the most wonderful garden for flowers you ever saw. It isn't more than thirty yards square, and there is a cliff path down to the beach. Isabel loves the place. The yacht is there too, and we go for cruises on calm days. I am hoping Isabel may pick up a little there, and she is always more herself when you are with her. You won't disappoint her, will you?"

A great-shiver went through Dinah. "I can't come," she said, almost under her breath. "It just - isn't possible."

"What is there to prevent?" he asked.

She moved a little, and lifted her head from its resting-place. "Ever so many things," she said.

"You are thinking of Eustace?" he questioned. "He has gone already - gone to town. He will probably go abroad; but in any case he will not get in your way."

"I wasn't thinking of him," Dinah said.

"Then of what?" he questioned. "Your mother? I will see her, and make that all right."

She started and lifted her face. "Oh no! Oh no! You must never dream of doing that!" she declared, with sudden fevered urgency. "I couldn't bear you to see her. You mustn't think of it, indeed - indeed! Why I would even - even sooner go back myself."

"Then I must write to her," he said, gently ceding the point. "It is not essential that I should see her. Possibly even, a letter would be preferable."

Dinah's face had flushed fiery red. She did not meet his eyes. "I don't see why you should have anything to do with her," she said. "You would never get her to consent."

"Then I propose that we act first," said Scott. "Isabel is leaving to-day. You can join her at Great Mallowes and go on together. I shall follow in a couple of days. There are several matters to be attended to first. But Isabel and Biddy will take care of you. Come, my dear, you won't dislike that so very badly!"

"Dislike it!" Dinah caught back another sob. "I should love it above all things if it were possible. But it isn't - it isn't."

"Why not?" he questioned. "Surely your father would not raise any objection?"

She shook her head. "No - no! He doesn't care what happens to me. I used to think he did; but he doesn't - he doesn't."

"Then what is the difficulty?" asked Scott.

She was silent, and he saw the hot colour spreading over her neck as she turned her face away.

"Won't you tell me?" he urged gently. "Is there some particular reason why you want to stay?"

"Oh no! I'm not going to stay." Quickly she made answer. "I

am never going back. I couldn't after - after -" She broke off in quivering distress.

"I think your mother will be sorry presently," he said. "People with violent tempers generally repent very deeply afterwards."

Dinah turned upon him suddenly and hotly. "She will never repent!" she declared. "She hates me. She has always hated me. And I hate her - hate her - hate her!"

The concentrated passion of her made her vibrate from head to foot. Her eyes glittered like emeralds. She was possessed by such a fury of hatred as made her scarcely recognizable.

Scott looked at her steadily for a moment or two. Then: "But it does you more harm than good to say so," he said. "And it doesn't answer my question, does it? Dinah, if you don't feel that you can do this thing for your own sake, won't you do it for Isabel's? She is needing you badly just now."

The vindictive look went out of Dinah's face. Her eyes softened, and he saw the hopeless tears well up again. "But I couldn't help her any more," she said.

"The very fact of having you to care for would help her," Scott said.

Dinah shook her head. She was sitting on the ground with her hands clasped round her knees. As the tears splashed down again, she turned her face away.

"It wouldn't help her, it wouldn't help anybody, to have me as I am now," she said. "I can't tell you - I can't explain. But - I am not fit to associate with anyone good."

Scott leaned towards her. "Dinah, my dear, you are torturing yourself," he said. "It's natural, I know. You have had no sleep, and you have cried yourself ill. But I am not going to give in to you. I am not going to take No for an answer. You have no plans for yourself, and I doubt if in your present state you are capable of forming any. Isabel wants you, and it would be cruel to disappoint her. So you and I will join her at Great Mallowes this afternoon. I will deal with your people in the matter, but I do not anticipate any great difficulty in that direction. Now that is settled, and you need not weary yourself with any further discussion. I am responsible, and I will bear my responsibility."

His tone was kind but it held unmistakable finality.

Dinah uttered a heavy sigh, and said no more. She lacked the strength for prolonged opposition.

He persuaded her to drink some more of the milk, and made a cushion of his coat for her against the tree.

"Perhaps you will get a little sleep," he said, as she suffered herself to relax somewhat. "Will it disturb you if I smoke?"

"No," she said.

He took out his case. "Shut your eyes!" he said practically.

But Dinah's eyes remained open, watching him. He began to smoke as if unaware of her scrutiny.

After several moments she spoke. "Scott!"

He turned to her. "Yes? What is it?"

The piteous, shamed colour rose up under his eyes. Again she turned her face away. "That - that sapphire pendant!" she murmured. "I brought it with me. Of course - I know - the presents will have to be returned. I didn't mean to - to run away with it. But - but - I loved it so. I couldn't have borne my mother to touch it. Shall I - shall I give it you now?"

"No, dear," he answered firmly. "Neither now nor at any time.

I gave it to you as a token of friendship, and I would like you to keep it always for that reason."

"Always?" questioned Dinah. "Even if - if I never marry at all?"

"Certainly," he said.

"Because I never shall marry now," she said, speaking with difficulty. "I - have quite given up that idea."

"I should like you to keep it in any case," Scott said.

"You are very good," she said earnestly. "I - I wonder you will have anything to do with me now that you know how - how wicked I am."

"I don't think you wicked," he said.

"Don't you?" She opened her heavy eyes a little. "You don't blame me for - for - " She broke off shuddering, and as she did so, there came again the rumble and roar of a distant train. "Then why did you stop me?" she whispered tensely.

Scott was silent for a moment or two. He was gazing straight before him. At length, "I stopped you," he said, "because I had to. It doesn't matter why. You would have done the same in my place. But I don't blame you, partly because it is not my business, and partly because I know quite well that you didn't realize what you were doing."

"I did realize," Dinah said. "If it weren't for you - because you are so good - nothing would have stopped me. Even now - even now -" again the hot tears came - "I've nothing to live for, and - and - God - doesn't - care." She turned her face into her arm and wept silently.

Scott made a sudden movement, and threw his cigarette away. Then swiftly he bent over her.

"Dinah," he said, "stop crying! You're making a big mistake."

His tone was arresting, imperative. She looked up at him almost in spite of herself. His eyes gazed straight into hers, and it seemed to her that there was something magnetic, something that was even unearthly, in their close regard.

"You are making a mistake," he repeated. "God always cares. He cared enough to send a friend to look after you. Do you want any stronger proof than that?"

"I - don't - know," Dinah said, awe-struck.

"Think about it!" Scott insisted. "Do you seriously imagine that it was just chance that brought me along at that particular moment? Do you think it was chance that made you draw back yesterday from giving yourself to a man you don't love? Was it chance that sent you to Switzerland in the first place? Don't you know in your heart that God has been guiding you all through?"

"I don't know," Dinah said again, but there was less of hopelessness in her voice. The shining certainty in Scott's eyes was warring with her doubt. "But then, why has He let me suffer so?"

"Why did He suffer so Himself?" Scott said. "Except that He might learn obedience? It's a bitter lesson to all of us, Dinah; but it's got to be learnt."

"You have learnt it!" she said, with a touch of her own impulsiveness.

He smiled a little - smiled and sighed. "I wonder. I've learnt anyhow to believe in the goodness of God, and to know that though we can't see Him in all things, it's not because He isn't there. Even those who know Him best can't realize Him always."

"But still you are sure He is there?" Dinah questioned.

"I am quite sure," he said, with a conviction so absolute that it placed further questioning beyond the bounds of possibility. "Life is full of problems which it is out of any man's power to solve. But to anyone who will take the trouble to see them the signs are unmistakable. There is not a single soul that is left unaccounted for in the reckoning of God. He cares for all."

There was no contradicting him; Dinah was too weary for discussion in any case. But he had successfully checked her tears at last; he had even in a measure managed to comfort her torn soul. She lay for a space pondering the matter.

"I am afraid I am one of those who don't take the trouble," she said at length. "But I shall try to now. Thank you for all your goodness to me, Mr. Greatheart." She smiled at him wanly. "I don't deserve it - not a quarter of it. But I'm grateful all the same. Please won't you have your smoke now, and forget me and my troubles?"

That smile cheered Scott more than any words. He recognized moreover that the delicate touch of reserve that characterized her speech was the first evidence of returning self-control that she had manifested.

He took out his cigarette-case again. "I hope you haven't found me over-presumptuous," he said.

Dinah reached up a trembling hand. "Presumptuous for helping me in the Valley of Humiliation?" she said.

He took the hand and held it firmly. "I am so used to it myself," he said, in a low voice. "I ought to know a little about it."

"Perhaps," said Dinah thoughtfully, "that is what makes you great."

He raised his shoulders slightly. "You have always seen me through a magnifying-glass," he said whimsically. "Some day the fates will reverse that glass and then you will be unutterably shocked."

Dinah smiled again and shook her head. "I know you," she said.

He lighted his cigarette, and then brought out a pocket-book. "I want to write a note to Isabel," he said. "You don't mind?"

"About me?" questioned Dinah.

"About the arrangements I am making. She is motoring to Great Mallowes in any case to catch the afternoon express."

"Oh!" said Dinah, and coloured vividly, painfully.

Scott did not see. "I can get someone at the farm to take the message," he said. "And when once you are with Isabel I shall feel easy about you."

"And - and - my - mother?" faltered Dinah.

"I shall write to her this afternoon while we are waiting for Isabel," said Scott quietly.

"What - shall you say?" whispered Dinah.

"Do you mind leaving that entirely to me?" he said.

"She will be - furious," she murmured. "She might - out of revenge come after us. What then?"

"She will certainly not do that," said Scott, "as she will not know your address. Besides, people do not remain furious, you know. They cool down, and then they are generally ashamed of themselves. Don't let us talk about your mother!"

"The de Vignes then," said Dinah, turning from the subject with relief. "Tell me what happened! Was the Colonel very angry?"

Scott's mouth twitched slightly. "Not in the least," he said.

"Not really!" Dinah looked incredulous for a moment; then: "Perhaps he thinks there is a fresh chance for Rose," she said.

"Perhaps he does," agreed Scott dryly. "In any case, he is more disposed to smile than frown, and as Eustace wasn't there to see it, it didn't greatly matter."

"Oh, poor Eustace!" she whispered. "It - was dreadful to hurt him so."

"I think he will get over it," Scott said.

"He was much - kinder - than - than I deserved," she murmured.

Scott's faint smile reappeared. "Perhaps he found it difficult to be anything else," he said.

She shook her head. "I wonder - how I came to make - such a dreadful mistake."

"It wasn't your fault," said Scott.

She looked at him quickly. "What makes you say that?"

He met her look gravely. "Because I know just how it happened," he said. "You were neither of you in earnest in the first place. I am afraid I had a hand in making Eustace propose to you. I was afraid - and so was Isabel - you would be hurt by his trifling."

"And you interfered?" breathed Dinah.

He nodded. "Yes, I told him it must be one thing or the other. I wanted you to be happy. But instead of helping you, I landed you in this mess."

Something in his tone touched her. She laid a small shy hand upon his knee. "It was - dear of you, Scott," she said very earnestly. "Thank you - ever so much - for what you did."

He put his hand on hers. "My dear, I would have given all I had to have undone it afterwards. It is very generous of you to take it like that. I have often wanted to kick myself since."

"Then you must never want to again," she said. "Do you know I'm so glad you've told me? It was so - fine of you - to do that for me. I'm sure you couldn't have wanted me for a sister-in-law even then."

"I wanted you to be happy," Scott reiterated.

She uttered a quick sigh. "Happiness isn't everything, is it?"

"Not everything, no," he said.

She grasped his hand hard. "I'm going to try to be good instead," she said. "Will you help me?"

He smiled at her somewhat sadly. "If you think my help worth having," he said.

"But of course it is," she made warm answer. "You are the strong man who helps everyone. You are - Greatheart."

He looked at her still smiling and slowly shook his head. "Now, if you don't mind," he said, "I will write my note to Isabel."

CHAPTER XXII

SPOKEN IN JEST

The afternoon was well advanced when Scott returned to Perrythorpe Court. No sounds of revelry greeted him as he entered. A blazing fire was burning in the hall, but no one was there to enjoy the warmth. The gay crowd that had clustered before the great hearth only yesterday had all dispersed. The place was empty.

"Can I get you anything, sir?" enquired the man who admitted him.

His voice was sepulchral. Scott smiled a little. "Yes, please. A whisky and soda. Where is everybody?"

"The Colonel and Miss Rose went out riding, sir, after the guests had all gone, and they have not yet returned. Her ladyship is resting in her room."

"Everyone gone but me?" questioned Scott, with a whimsical lift of the eyebrows.

The man bent his head decorously. "I believe so, sir. There was a general feeling that it would be more fitting as the marriage was not to take place as arranged. I understand, sir, that the family will shortly migrate to town."

"Really?" said Scott.

He bent over the fire, for the evening was chilly, and he was tired to the soul. The man coughed and withdrew. Again the silence fell.

A face he knew began to look up at Scott out of the leaping flames - a face that was laughing and provocative one moment, wistful and tear-stained the next.

He heaved a sigh as he followed the fleeting vision. "Will she ever be happy again?" he asked himself.

The last sight he had had of her had cut him to the heart. She had conquered her tears at last, but her smile was the saddest thing he had ever seen. It was as though her vanished childhood had suddenly looked forth at him and bidden him farewell. He felt that he would never see the child Dinah again.

The return of the servant with his drink brought him back to his immediate surroundings. He sat down in an easy-chair before the fire to mix it.

The man turned to go, but he had not reached the end of the hall when the front-door bell rang again. He went soft-footed to answer it.

Scott glanced over his shoulder as the door opened, and heard his own name.

"Is Mr. Studley here?" a man's voice asked.

"Yes, sir. Just here, sir," came the answer, and Scott rose with a weary gesture.

"Oh, here you are!" Airily Guy Bathurst advanced to meet him. "Don't let me interrupt your drink! I only want a few words with you."

"I'll fetch another glass, sir" murmured the discreet man-servant, and vanished.

Scott stood, stiff and uncompromising, by his chair. There was a hint of hostility in his bearing. "What can I do for you?" he asked.

Bathurst ignored his attitude with that ease of manner of which he was a past-master. "Well I thought perhaps you could give me news of Dinah" he said. "Billy tells me he left you with her this morning."

"I see" said Scott. He looked at the other man with level, unblinking eyes. "You are beginning to feel a little anxious about her?" he questioned.

"Well, I think it's about time she came home," said Bathurst. He took out a cigarette and lighted it. "Her mother is wondering what has become of her," he added, between the puffs.

"I posted a letter to Mrs. Bathurst about an hour ago," said Scott. "She will get it in the morning."

"Indeed!" Bathurst glanced at him. "And is her whereabouts to remain a mystery until then?"

"That letter will reassure you as to her safety," Scott returned quietly. "But it will not enlighten you as to her whereabouts. She is in good hands, and it is not her intention to return home - at least for the present. Under the circumstances you could scarcely compel her to do so."

"I never compel her to do anything," said Bathurst comfortably. "Her mother keeps her in order, I have nothing to do with it."

"Evidently not." A sudden sharp quiver of scorn ran through Scott's words. "Her mother may make her life a positive hell, but it's no business of yours!"

A flicker of temper shone for a second in Bathurst's eyes. The scorn had penetrated even his thick skin. "None whatever," he said deliberately. "Nor of yours either, so far as I can see."

"There you are wrong." Hotly Scott took him up. "It is the duty of every man to prevent cruelty. Dinah has been treated like a bond-slave all her life. What were you about to allow it?"

He flung the question fiercely. The man's careless repudiation of all responsibility aroused in him a perfect storm of indignation. He was probably more angry at that moment than he had ever been before.

Guy Bathurst stared at him for a second or two, his own resentment quenched in amazement. Finally he laughed.

"If you were married to my wife, you'd know," he said. "Personally I like a quiet life. Besides, discipline is good for youngsters. I think Lydia is disposed to carry it rather far, I admit. But after all, a woman can't do much damage to her own daughter. And anyhow it isn't a man's business to interfere."

He broke off as the servant reappeared, and seated himself in a chair on the other side of the fire. He drank some whisky and water in large, appreciative gulps, and resumed his cigarette.

"If Dinah had seriously wanted to get away from it, she should have married your brother," he said then. "It was her own doing entirely, this last affair. A girl shouldn't jilt her lover at the last moment if she isn't prepared to face the consequences. She knows her mother's temper by this time, I should imagine. She might have guessed what was in store for her." He looked across at Scott as one seeking sympathy. "You'll admit it was a tomfool thing to do," he said. "I don't wonder at her mother wanting to make her smart for it. I really don't. Dinah ought to have known her own mind."

"She knows it now," said Scott grimly.

"Yes. So it appears. By the way, have you any idea what induced her to throw your brother over in that way just at the last minute? It would be interesting to know."

"Did she give you no reason?" said Scott. He hated parleying with the man, but something impelled him thereto.

Guy Bathurst leaning back at his ease with his cigarette between his lips, uttered a careless laugh. "She seemed to think she wasn't in love with him. We couldn't get any more out of her than that. As a matter of fact her mother was too furious to attempt it. But there must have been some other reason. I wondered if you knew what it was."

"I shouldn't have thought it essential that there should have been any other reason," Scott said deliberately. "If there is - I am not in her confidence."

He was still on his feet as if he wished it to be clearly understood that he did not intend their conversation to develop into anything of the nature of friendly intercourse.

Bathurst continued to smoke, but a faint air of insolence was apparent in his attitude. He was not accustomed to being treated with contempt, and the desire awoke within him to find some means of disconcerting this undersized whipper-snapper who had almost succeeded in making him feel cheap.

"You haven't been making love to her on your own account by any chance, I suppose?" he enquired lazily.

Scott's eyes flashed upon him a swift and hawk-like regard, and the hauteur that so often characterized his brother suddenly descended upon him and clothed him as a mantle.

"I have not," he said.

"Quite sure?" persisted Bathurst, still amiably smiling. "It's my belief she's smitten with you, you know. I've thought so all along. Funny idea, isn't it? Never occurred to you of course?"

Scott made no reply, but his silence was more scathing than speech. It served to arouse all the rancour of which Bathurst's indolent nature was capable.

"No accounting for women's preference, is there?" he said. "You ought to feel vastly flattered, my good sir. It isn't many women would put you before that handsome brother of yours. How did you work it, eh? Come, you're caught! So you may as well own up."

Scott shrugged his shoulders abruptly, disdainfully, and turned from him. "If you choose to amuse yourself at your daughter's expense, I cannot prevent you," he said. "But there is not a grain of truth in your insinuation. I repudiate it absolutely."

"My dear fellow, that's a bit thick," laughed Bathurst; he had found the vulnerable spot, and he meant to make the most of it. "Do you actually expect me to believe that you won her away from your brother without knowing it? That's rather a tough proposition, too tough for my middle-aged digestion. You've been trifling with her young affections, but you are not man enough to own it."

"You are wrong, utterly wrong," Scott said. He restrained himself with difficulty; for still something was at work within him urging him to be temperate. "Dinah has never dreamed of falling in love with me. As you say, the bare idea is manifestly absurd."

"Then who is she in love with?" demanded Bathurst, with lazy insistence. "You're the only other man she knows, and there's certainly someone. No girl would throw up such a catch as your brother for the mere sentiment of the thing. It stands to reason there must be someone else. And there is no one but you. She doesn't know anyone else, I tell you. She has no opportunities. Her mother sees to that."

Scott was bending over the fire, his face to the flame. His indignation had died down. He was very still, as one deep in thought. Could it be the true word spoken in ill-timed jest which he had just heard? He wondered; he wondered.

A golden radiance was spreading forth to him from the heart of those leaping flames, like the coming of the dawnlight over the dark earth. He watched it spell-bound, utterly unmindful of the man behind him. If this thing were true! Ah, if this thing were true!

A sudden sound made him turn to see Colonel de Vigne and his daughter enter.

They came forward to greet him and Bathurst. Rose was smiling; her eyes were softly bright.

"How happy she looks!" was the thought that occurred to him, but it was only a passing thought. It vanished in a moment as he heard her accost Bathurst.

"How is our poor little Dinah by this time?"

"You had better ask this gentleman," airily responded Bathurst. "He has elected to make himself responsible for her welfare."

Rose's delicate brows went up, but very strangely Scott no longer felt in the least disconcerted. He replied to her unspoken query without difficulty.

"Dinah felt that she could not face the gossips," he said, "and as Isabel was badly wanting her, they have gone away together. Except for old Biddy, they will be quite alone, and it will do them both all the good in the world."

Rose's brow cleared. "What an excellent arrangement!" she murmured sympathetically. "And - your brother?"

Scott smiled. "Needless to say, he is not of the party. His plans are somewhat uncertain. He may go abroad for a time, but I doubt if he banishes himself for long when the London season is in full swing."

Rose's smile answered his. "I think he is very wise," she said. "When Easter is over, we shall probably follow his example. I hope we shall have the pleasure of meeting you when we are all in town."

"Ha! So do I," said the Colonel. "You must look me up at the Club - any time. I shall be delighted."

"You are very kind," Scott said. "But I go to town very rarely, and I never stay there. My brother is far more of a society man than I am."

"You will have to come out of your shell," smiled Rose.

"Quite so - quite so," agreed the Colonel. "It isn't fair to cheat society, you know. If we can't dance at your brother's wedding, you might give us the pleasure of dancing at yours."

Bathurst uttered a careless laugh. "I've just been accusing him of cutting his brother out," he said lightly. "But he denies all knowledge of the transaction."

"Oh, but what a shame!" interposed Rose quickly. "Mr. Studley, we won't listen to this gossip. Will you come up to my sitting-room, and show me that new game of Patience you were talking about yesterday? Bring your drink with you!"

He went with her almost in silence.

In her own room she turned upon him with a wonderful, illumined smile, and held out her hand.

"I won't have you badgered," she said. "But - it is true, is it not?"

Ethel M. Dell

He took her hand, looking straight into her beautiful eyes. There was more life in her face at that moment than he had ever seen before. She was as one suddenly awakened. "What is true, Miss de Vigne?" he questioned.

"That you care for her," she answered, "that she cares for you."

His look remained full upon her. "In a friendly sense, yes," he said.

"In no other sense?" she insisted. Her eyes were shining, as if her whole soul were suddenly alight with animation. "Tell me," she said, as he did not speak immediately, "have you ever cared for her merely as a friend?"

There was no evading the question, neither for some reason could he resent it. He hesitated for a second or two; then, "You have guessed right," he said quietly. "But she has never suspected it, and - she never will."

To his surprise Rose frowned. "But why not tell her?" she said. "Surely she has a right to know!"

He smiled and shook his head. "Pardon me! No one has the smallest right to know. Would you say that of yourself if you cared for someone who did not care for you?"

She blushed under his eyes suddenly and very vividly, and in a moment turned from him. "Ah, but that is different!" she said. "A woman is different! If she gives her heart where it is not wanted, that is her affair alone."

He did not pursue his advantage; he liked her for the blush.

"Isn't it rather an unprofitable discussion?" he said gently. "Suppose we get to our game of Patience!"

And Rose acquiesced in silence.

CHAPTER XXIII

THE KNIGHT IN DISGUISE

A long, curling wave ran up the shingle and broke in a snow-white sheet of foam just below Dinah's feet. She was perched on a higher ridge of shingle, bareheaded, full in the glare of the mid-June sunlight. Her brown hands were locked tightly around her knees. Her small, pointed face looked wistfully over the sea.

She had been sitting in that position for a long time, her green eyes unblinking but swimming in the heat and glare. The dark ringlets on her forehead danced in the soft breeze that came over the water. There was tension in her attitude, the tension of deep and concentrated thought.

Into the midst of her meditations, there came a slow, halting step. It fell on the shingle behind her, reaching her above the roar of the breakers, and instantly a flood of colour rushed up over her face and neck.

Sharply she turned. "Scott!"

She was on her feet in a second with hand outstretched in welcome.

"Oh, how you startled me! How good of you to come so soon! I - shouldn't have left the house if I had known."

Ethel M. Dell

"I came at once," he said simply. "But I have only just got here. I saw you sitting on the shore and came straight to you. What news?"

His quiet, deliberate voice was in striking contrast to her agitated utterance. The hand that held hers was absolutely steady.

She met his look with confidence. "Scott, she is going. You knew it - didn't you? - when you were here last Sunday? She knew it too. She didn't want you to go really. And so - directly I realized she was worse - I sent for you. But - they say - even now she may linger for a little. But you'll stay, won't you? You won't go again?"

His grave eyes looked into hers. "Of course I will stay," he said.

She drew a quick sigh of relief. "She scarcely slept last night. Her breathing was so bad. It was very hot, you know. The nurse or I were fanning her nearly all the time, till the morning breeze came at last. And then she got quieter. She is asleep now. They say she will sleep for hours. And so I slipped out just for a little, so as to be quite fresh again when she wakes."

"Don't you sleep at all?" Scott asked gently.

The colour was fading from her face; it returned at his question. "Oh yes, any time. It doesn't matter for me. I am so strong. And I can sleep - afterwards."

He looked down at the thin little hand he still held. "You mustn't wear yourself out, Dinah," he said.

Her lip quivered suddenly, "What does it matter?" she said. "I've nothing else to live for."

"I don't think we can any of us say that," he answered. "There is always something left."

She turned her face and looked over the sea. "I'm sure I don't know what," she said, with a catch in her voice. "If - Isabel - were going to live, if - if I could only have her always, I should be quite happy. I shouldn't want anything else. But without her - life without her - after these two months, -" her voice broke and ceased.

"I know," Scott said. "I should have felt the same myself not so long ago. I have let you slip into my place, you see; and it comes hard on you now. But don't forget our friendship, Dinah! Don't forget I'm here!"

She turned back, swallowing her tears with difficulty and gave him a quivering smile. "Oh, I know. You are so good. And it was dear of you to - to let me take your place with her. None but you would have done such a thing."

"My dear, it was far better for her, and she wished it," he interposed. "Besides, with Eustace away, I had plenty to do. You mustn't twist that into a virtue. It was the only course open to me. I knew that it would lift her out of misery to have you, and - naturally - I wished it too."

She nodded. "It was just like you. And I - I ought to have remembered that it couldn't last. It has been such a comfort to - to have my darling to love and care for. But oh, the blank when she is gone!"

Scott was silent.

"It's wrong to want to keep her, I know," Dinah went on wistfully. "She has got so wonderfully happy of late; and I know it is the thought of nearing the end of the journey that makes her so. And when I am with her, I feel happy too for her sake. But when I am away from her - it - it's all so dreary. I - feel so frightened and - alone."

"Don't be frightened!" Scott said gently. "You never are alone."

"Ah, but life is so difficult," she whispered.

"It would be," he answered, "if we had to face it all at once. But, thank God, that is not so. We can only see a little way ahead. We can only do a little at a time."

"Do you think that is a help?" she said. "I would give anything - sometimes - to look into the future."

"I think the burden would be greater than we could bear," Scott said.

"Oh, do you? I think it would be such a relief to know." Dinah uttered a sharp sigh. "It's no good talking," she said. "Only one thing is certain. I'm not going to break with Billy of course, but I'll never go back to Perrythorpe again, never as long as I live!"

There was a quiver of passion in her voice. She looked at Scott with what was almost a challenge in her eyes.

He did not answer it. His face wore a look of perplexity. But, "If I were in your place," he said quietly, "I think I should say the same."

"I am sure you would," she said warmly. "I only tolerated it so long because I didn't know what freedom was like. When I went to Switzerland, I found out; and when I came back, it just wasn't endurable any longer. But I wish I knew - I do wish I knew - what I were going to do."

The words were out before she could stop them, but the moment they were uttered she made a sharp gesture as though she would recall them.

"I'm silly to talk like this," she said. "Please forget it!"

He smiled a little. "Not silly, Dinah," he said, "but mistaken. Believe me, the future is already provided for."

Her brows contracted slightly. "Ah, you are good," she said. "You believe in God."

"So do you," he said, with quiet conviction.

Her lip quivered. "I believe He would help anyone like you, but - but He wouldn't bother Himself about me. There are too many others of the same sort."

Scott looked at her in genuine astonishment. "What a curious idea!" he said. "You don't really think that, do you?"

She nodded. "I can't help it. Life is such a maze of difficulties, and one has to face them all alone."

"You won't face yours alone," he said quickly.

She smiled rather piteously. "I've faced all the worst bits alone so far."

"I know," Scott said. "But you are through the worst now."

She shook her head doubtfully. "I'm afraid of life," she said.

He saw that she did not wish to pursue the subject and put it gently aside. "Shall we go in?" he said. "I should like to be at hand when Isabel wakes."

She turned beside him at once. Their talk went back to Isabel. They spoke of her tenderly, as one nearing the end of a long and wearisome journey, and as they approached the little white house on the heath above the sea, Dinah gave somewhat hesitating utterance to a thought that had been persistently in her mind of late.

"Do you," she said, speaking with evident effort, "think that - Eustace should be sent for?"

"Does she want him?" said Scott.

"I don't know. She never speaks of him. But then - that may be - for my sake." Dinah's voice was very low and not wholly free from distress. "And again - it may be on my account he is keeping away. She hasn't seen him for these two months - not since we left Perrythorpe."

"No," Scott said gravely. "I know."

Dinah was silent for a brief space; then she braced herself for another effort. "Scott, I - don't want to be - in anyone's way. If - if she would like to see him, and if he - doesn't want to come - because of me, I - must go, that's all."

She spoke with resolution, and pausing at the gate that led off the heath into the garden looked him straight in the face.

"I want you," she said rather breathlessly, "to find out if - that is so. And if it is - if it is -"

"My dear, you needn't be afraid," Scott said. "I am quite sure that Eustace wouldn't wish to drive you away. He might be doubtful as to whether you would care to meet him again so soon, but if you had no objection to his coming, he wouldn't deliberately stay away on his own account. You know - I don't think you've ever realized it - he loves Isabel."

"Then he must want to come," she said quickly. "Oh, Scott, do you know - I said a dreadful - a cruel - thing to him - that last day. If he really loves her, it must have hurt him - terribly."

"What did you say?" Scott asked.

"I said -" the quick tears sprang to her eyes - "I said that he was unkind to her, and that - that she was always miserable when he was there. Scott, what made me say it? It was hateful of me! It was hateful!"

"It was the truth," Scott said. He looked at her thoughtfully for a few seconds, then very kindly he patted her hand as it rested on the gate. "Don't be so distressed!" he said. "It probably did him good - even if it did hurt. But I think you are right. If Isabel has the smallest wish to see him, he must come. I will see what I can do."

Dinah gave him a difficult smile. "You always put things right," she said.

He lifted his shoulders with a whimsical expression. "The magnifying-glass again!" he said.

"No," she protested. "No. I see you as you are."

"Then you see a very ordinary citizen," he said.

But Dinah shook her head. "A knight in disguise," she said.

CHAPTER XXIV

THE MOUNTAIN SIDE

When Isabel opened her eyes after a slumber that had lasted for the greater part of the day, it was to find Scott seated beside her quietly watching her.

She reached a feeble hand to him with a smile of welcome. "Dear Stumpy, when did you come?"

"An hour or two ago," he said, and put the weak hand to his lips. "You have had a good sleep, dear?"

"Yes," she said. "Yes. It has done me good." She lay looking at him with a smile still in her eyes. "I hope little Dinah is resting," she said. "She was with me nearly all night. I didn't wish it, Stumpy, but the dear child wouldn't leave till I was more comfortable."

"She is resting for a little now," he said. "I am so sorry you had a bad time last night."

"Oh, don't be sorry for me!" she said softly. "My bad times are so nearly over now. It is a waste of time to talk about them. She sent for you, did she?"

He bent his head. "She knew I would wish to be sent for. She fancied you might be wanting me."

"I do want you," she said, and into her wasted face there came a look of unutterable tenderness. "Oh, Stumpy darling, need you leave me again?"

He was still holding her hand; his fingers closed upon it at her words.

"I think the last part may be - a little steep," she said wistfully. "I would like to feel that you are near at hand. You have helped me so often - so often. And then too - there is - my little Dinah. I want you to help her too."

"God knows I will do my best, dear," he said.

Her fingers returned his pressure. "She has been so much to me - so much to me," she whispered. "When I came here, I had no hope. But the care of her, the comforting of her, opened the dungeon-door for me. And now no Giant Despair will ever hold me captive again. But I am anxious about her, Stumpy. There is some trouble in the background of which she has never spoken - of which she can never bear to speak. Have you any idea what it is?"

He moved with an unwonted touch of restlessness. "I think she worries about the future," he said.

"That isn't all," Isabel said with conviction. "There is more than that. It hangs over her like a cloud. It weighs her down."

"She hasn't confided in me," he said.

"Ah! But perhaps she will," Isabel's eyes still dwelt upon him with a great tenderness. "Stumpy," she murmured under her breath, "forgive me for asking! I must ask! Stumpy, why don't you win her for yourself, dear? The way is open. I know - I know you can."

He moved again, moved with a gesture of protest. "You are mistaken, Isabel," he said. "The way is not open." He spoke wearily. He was looking straight before him. "If I were to attempt what you suggest," he said slowly, "I should deprive her of the only friend to whom she can turn with any confidence besides yourself. She trusts me now implicitly. She believes my friendship for her to be absolutely simple and disinterested. And I would rather die than fail her."

"Then you think she doesn't care?" Isabel said.

Scott turned his eyes upon her. "Personally, I came to that conclusion long ago," he said. "No woman could ever hang a serious romance around me, Isabel. I am not the right sort. If Dinah imagined for a moment that I were capable of making love in the ordinary way, our friendship would go to the bottom forthwith. No, my dear; put the thought out of your mind! The Stumpys of this world must be resigned to go unpaired. They must content themselves with the outer husk. It's that or nothing."

Isabel's smile was full of tenderness. "You talk as one who knows," she said. "But I wonder if you do."

"Oh yes," Scott said. "I've learned my lesson. I've been given an ordinary soul in an extraordinary body, and I've got to make the best of it. You can't ignore the body, you know, Isabel. It plays a mighty big part in this mortal life. The idea of any woman falling in love with me in my present human tenement is ridiculous, and I have put it out of my mind for good."

Isabel's eyes were shining. She clasped his hand closer. "I think you are quite wrong, Stumpy dear," she said. "If your soul matched your body, then there might be something in your argument. But it doesn't. And - if you don't mind my saying so - your soul is far the most extraordinary part of your personality. Little Dinah found out long ago that you were - greathearted."

Scott smiled a little. "Oh yes, I know she views me through a magnifying-glass and reveres me accordingly. Hence our friendship. But, my dear, that isn't being in love. I believe that somewhere there is a shadowy person whom she cherishes in the very inner secrecy of her heart. Who he is or what he is, I don't know. He is probably something very different from the dream-being she worships. We all are. But I feel that he is there. Probably I have never met the actual man. I have only seen his shadow and that by inadvertence. I once penetrated the secret chamber for one moment only, and then I was driven forth and the door securely locked. I am not good at trespassing, you know, for all my greatness. I have never been near the secret chamber since."

"Do you mean that she admitted to you that - she cared for someone?" Isabel asked.

Scott's pale eyes had a quizzical look. "I had the consideration to back out before she had time to do anything so unmaidenly," he said. "Possibly the shadowman may never materialize. In fact it seems more than possible. In which case the least said is soonest mended."

"That may be what is troubling her," Isabel said thoughtfully.

She lay still for a while, and Scott leaned back in his chair and watched the little pleasure-boats that skimmed the waters of the bay. The merry cries of bathers came up to the quiet room. The world was full to the brim of gaiety and sunshine on that hot June day.

"Stumpy," gently his sister's voice recalled him, "do you never mean to marry, dear? I wish you would. You will be so lonely."

He lifted his shoulders. "What can I say Isabel? If the right woman comes along and proposes, I will marry her with pleasure. I would never dare to propose on my own, - being what I am."

"Being a very perfect knight whom any woman might be

proud to marry," Isabel said. "That is only a pose of yours, Stumpy, and it doesn't become you. I wonder - how I wonder! - if you are right about Dinah."

"Yes, I am right," he said with conviction. "But Isabel, you will remember - it was spoken in confidence."

She gave a sharp sigh. "I shall remember dear," she said.

Again a brief silence fell between them; but Scott's eye no longer sought the sparkling water. They dwelt upon his sister's face. Pale as alabaster, clear-cut as though carven with a chisel, it rested upon the white pillow, and the stamp of a great peace lay upon the calm forehead and in the quiet of the deeply-sunken eyes. There were lines of suffering that yet lingered about the mouth, lines of weariness and of sorrow, but the old piteous look of craving had faded quite away. The bitter despair that had so haunted Dinah had passed into the stillness of a great patience. There was about her at that time the sacred hush that falls before the dawn.

After a little she became aware of his quiet regard, and turned her head with a smile. "Well, Stumpy? What is it?"

"I was just wondering what had happened to you," he made answer.

Her smile deepened. "I will tell you, dear," she said. "I have come within sight of the mountain-top at last."

"And you are satisfied?" he said, in a low voice.

Her eyes shone with a soft brightness that seemed to illumine her whole face. "Satisfied that my beloved is waiting for me and that I shall meet him in the dawning?" she said. "Oh yes, I have known that in my heart for a long time. It troubled me terribly when I lost his letters. They had been such a link, and for a while I was in outer darkness. And then - by degrees, after little Dinah came back to me - I began to find that after all there were other links. Helping her in her trouble helped me to bear my own. And I came to see that ministering to a need outside one's own is the surest means of finding comfort in sorrow for oneself. I have been very selfish Stumpy. I have been gradually waking to that fact for a long while. I used to immerse myself in those letters to try and get the feeling of his dear presence. Very, very often I didn't succeed. And I know now that it was because I was forcing myself to look back and not forward. I think material things are apt to make one do that. But when material things are taken quite away, then one is forced upon the spiritual. And that is what has happened to me. No one can take anything from me now because what I possess is laid up in store for me. I am moving forward towards it every day."

She ceased to speak, and again for the space of seconds the silence fell.

Scott broke it, speaking slowly, as if not wholly certain of the wisdom of speech. "I did not know," he said, "that you had lost those letters."

Her face contracted momentarily with the memory of a past pain. "Eustace destroyed them," she stated simply.

His brows drew sharply together. "Isabel! Do you mean that?"

She pressed his hand. "Yes, dear. I knew you would feel it badly so I didn't tell you before. He acted for the best. I see that quite clearly now. And - in a sense - the best has come of it."

Scott got to his feet with the gesture of a man who can barely restrain himself. "He did - that?" he said.

She reached up a soothing hand. "My dear, it doesn't matter now. Don't be angry with him. I know that he meant well."

Scott's eyes looked down into hers, intensely bright, burningly alive. "No wonder," he said, breathing deeply, "that you never want to see him again!"

"No, Stumpy; that is not so." Gently she made answer; her hand held his almost pleadingly. "For a long time I felt like that, it is true. But now it is all over. There is no bitterness left in my heart at all. We have grown away from each other, he and I. But we were very close friends once, and because of that I would give much - oh, very much - to be friends with him again. It was in a very great measure my selfishness that came between us, my pride too. I had influence with him, Stumpy, and I didn't try to use it. I simply threw him off because he disapproved of my husband. I might have won him, I feel that I could have won him if I had tried. But I wouldn't. And afterwards, when my mind was clouded, my influence was all gone. I wish I could get it back again. I feel as if I might. But he is keeping away now because of Dinah. And I am afraid too that he feels I do not want him - " her eyes were suddenly dim with tears. "That is not so, Stumpy. I do want him. Sometimes - in the night - I long for him. But, for little Dinah's sake -"

She paused, for Scott had suddenly turned and was pacing the room rapidly, unevenly, as if inaction had become unendurable.

She lay and watched him while the great tears gathered and ran down her wasted face.

He came back to her at length and saw them. He stood a moment looking downwards, then knelt beside her and very tenderly wiped them away.

"My dear," he said softly, "you mustn't ever cry again. It breaks my heart to see you. If you want Eustace, he shall come to you. Dinah was speaking to me about it only a short time ago. She will not stand in the way of his coming. In fact, I gathered that if you wish it, she wishes it also."

"That is so like little Dinah," whispered Isabel. "But, Stumpy, do you think we ought to let her face that?"

"I shall be here," he said.

"Oh, yes, dear. You will be here." She regarded him wistfully. "Stumpy, don't' - don't let yourself get bitter against Eustace!" she pleaded. "You have always been so splendid, so forbearing, till now."

Scott's lips were stern. "Some things are hard to forgive, Isabel," he said.

"But if I forgive - " she said.

His face changed; he bowed his head suddenly down upon her pillow. "Nothing will give you back to me - when you are gone," he whispered.

Her hand was on his head in a moment. "Oh, my dear, are you grieving because of that? And I have been such a burden to you!"

"A burden beloved," he said, speaking with difficulty. "And you were getting better. You were better. He - threw you back again. He brought you - to this."

Her fingers pressed his forehead. "Not entirely, Stumpy. Be generous, dear! It may have hastened matters a little - only a very little. And even so, what of it, if the journey has been shortened? Perhaps the way has been a little steeper, but it has brought me more quickly to my goal. Stumpy, Stumpy, if it weren't for leaving you, I would go as gladly - as gladly - as a happy bride - to her wedding."

She broke off, breathing fast.

He lifted his head swiftly, and saw the shadow of mortal pain gathering in her eyes. He commanded himself on the instant and rose. Self-contained and steady, he found and administered the remedy that was always kept at hand.

Then, as the spasm passed, he stooped and quietly kissed the white forehead. "Don't trouble about me, dear!" he said. "God knows I would not keep you from your rest."

And with that calmly he turned and left her.

But Biddy, whom he sought a few moments later to send her to her mistress, saw in him notwithstanding his composure, an intensity of suffering that struck dismay to her honest heart. "The Lord preserve us!" she said. "But Master Scott has the look of a man with a sword in his soul!" She wiped her own tears away with a trembling hand. "And what'll he do at all when Miss Isabel's gone," she said, "unless Miss Dinah does the comforting of him?"

CHAPTER XXV

THE TRUSTY FRIEND

The trains from the junction to Heath-on-Sea were few and invariably late. Scott had been pacing the platform for half an hour on the evening of the day that followed his own arrival ere a line of distant smoke told of the coming of the train he was awaiting.

His movements were slow and weary, but there was about him the strained look of a man who cannot rest. There was no gladness of welcome in his eyes as the train drew near. It was rather as if he braced himself for a coming ordeal.

He searched the carriages intently as they ran past him, and a flicker of recognition came into his face at the sight of a tall figure leaning from one of them. He lifted a hand in salutation, and limped along the platform to meet the newcomer.

Sir Eustace was out of the train before anyone else. He met his brother with the impetuosity of one who cannot stop for greeting.

"Ah, Stumpy! I'm not too late?"

There was strain upon his face also as he flung the question, and in an instant Scott's look had changed. He grasped the outflung hand.

Ethel M. Dell

"No, no, old fellow! It's all right. She is looking forward to seeing you."

Sir Eustace drew a sharp breath. His dark face relaxed a little. "I've had a hell of a time," he said.

"My dear chap, I'm sorry," impulsively Scott made answer. "I'd have met you at the junction, only it was difficult to get away for so long. Do you mind walking up? They'll see to fetching your traps along presently."

"Oh, all right. Yes, let us walk by all means!" Eustace expanded his chest, and breathed again, deeply. He put his hand on Scott's shoulder as they passed through the barrier. "What's the matter with you, my lad?" he said.

Scott glanced up at him - a swift, surprised glance. "With me? Nothing. I am - as usual."

Eustace's hawk-eyes scanned him closely. "I've never seen you look worse," he said.

Scott raised his shoulder slightly under his hand, and said nothing. The first involuntary kindliness of greeting passed wholly away, as if it had not been.

Eustace linked the hand in his arm as they walked. "Tell me about her!" he said.

"About Isabel?" Scott spoke with very obvious constraint. "There isn't much to tell. She is just - going. These breathless attacks come very frequently, and she is weaker after each one. The doctor says it would not be surprising if she went in her sleep, or in fact at any time."

"And she asked for me?" The question fell curtly; Eustace was looking straight ahead up the white, dusty road as he uttered it.

"Yes; she wanted you." Equally curtly came Scott's reply. He ignored the hand on his arm, limping forward at his own pace and leaving his brother to accommodate himself to it as best he could.

Sir Eustace sauntered beside him in silence for a space. They were approaching the heath-clad common that gave the place its name, when he spoke again.

"And Dinah?" he said then.

Again Scott glanced upwards, his pale eyes very resolute. "Yes, Dinah is still here. Her people seem quite indifferent as to what becomes of her, and Isabel wishes to keep her with her. I hope -" he hesitated momentarily - "I hope you will bear in mind the extreme difficulty of her situation."

Sir Eustace passed over the low words. "And what is going to happen to her - afterwards?" he said.

"Heaven knows!" Scott spoke as one compelled.

Sir Eustace continued to gaze straight before him. "Haven't you thought of any solution to the difficulty?" he asked.

"What do you mean?" Scott's voice rang suddenly stern.

A faint smile touched his brother's face; it was like the shadow of his old, supercilious sneer. "It occurred to me that you, being a chivalrous knight, might be moved to offer her your protection," he explained coolly. "You are quite at liberty to do so, so far as I am concerned. I give you my free consent."

Scott started, as if he had been stung. "Man, don't sneer at me!" he said in a voice that quivered. "I've a good many things against you, and I'm damned if I can stand any more!"

There was desperation in his words. Sir Eustace's brows went up, and his smile departed. But there came no answering anger in his eyes.

He was silent for several moments, pacing forward, his hand no longer linked in Scott's arm. Then at last very quietly he spoke. "You're right. You have a good many things against me. But this is not one of them. I was not sneering at you."

There was a note of most unwonted sincerity in his voice that gave conviction to his words. Scott turned and regarded him in open amazement.

The steel-blue eyes met his with an odd, half-shamed expression. "You mustn't bully me, you know, Stumpy!" he said. "Remember, I can't hit back."

Scott stood still. He had never in his life been more astounded. Even then, with the direct evidence before him, he could hardly believe that the old haughty dominance had given place to something different.

"Why - can't you - hit back?" he said, almost stammering in his uncertainty.

Sir Eustace smiled again with rueful irony. "Because I've nothing to hit with, my son. Because you can break through my defence every time. If I were to kick you from here to the sea, you'd still have the best of me. Haven't you realized that yet?"

"I hadn't - no!" Scott's eyes still regarded him with a puzzled, half-suspicious expression.

Sir Eustace turned from their scrutiny, and began to walk on. "You will presently," he said. "The man who masters himself is always the man to master the rest of the world in the end. I never thought I should live to envy you, my boy. But I do."

"Envy me! Why? Why on earth?" Embarrassment mingled with the curiosity in Scott's voice. His hostility had gone down utterly before the unaccustomed humility of his brother's attitude.

Sir Eustace glanced at him sideways. "I'll tell you another time," he said. "Now look here, Stumpy! You're in command, and I shan't interfere with you so long as you take reasonable care of yourself. But you must do that. It is the one thing I am going to insist upon. That's understood, is it?"

Scott smiled, his tired, gentle smile. "Oh, certainly, my dear chap. Don't you worry yourself about that! It isn't of the first importance in any case."

"It's got to be done," Sir Eustace insisted. "So keep it in mind!"

"I haven't been doing anything, you know," Scott protested mildly. "I only came down yesterday."

"That may be. But you haven't been sleeping for some time. You needn't trouble to deny it. I know the signs. What have you been doing at Willowmount?"

It was a welcome change of subject, and Scott was not slow to avail himself of it. They began to talk upon matters connected with the estate, and the personal element passed completely out of the conversation.

When they reached the white house on the cliff they almost seemed to have slipped into the old casual relations; but the younger brother was well aware that this was not so. The change that had so amazed him was apparent to him at every turn. The overbearing mastery to which he had been accustomed all his life had turned in some miraculous fashion into something that was oddly like deference. It was fully evident that Eustace meant to keep his word and leave him in command.

Dinah met them in the rose-twined portico. There was a deep

flush in her cheeks; her eyes were very bright, resolutely unafraid. She shook hands with Eustace, and he alone was aware of the tremor that ran through her whole being as she did so.

"Isabel is asleep," she said. "She often gets a sleep in the afternoon, and she is always the stronger for it when she wakes. Will you have some tea before you go to her?"

They had tea in the sunny verandah overlooking the sea. Sir Eustace was very quiet and grave, and it was Scott who gently conversed with the girl, smoothing away all difficulties. She was plainly determined to conquer her nervousness, and she succeeded to a great extent before the ordeal was over. But there was obvious relief in her eyes when Sir Eustace set down his cup and rose to go.

"I think I will go to her now," he said. "I shall not wake her."

He went, and a great stillness fell behind him. Scott dropped into silence, and they sat together, he smoking, she leaning back in her chair idle, with wistful eyes upon the silvery sea.

Up in Isabel's room overhead there was neither sound nor movement, but presently there fell a soft footfall upon the stairs and the nurse came quietly through and spoke to Dinah.

"Mrs. Everard is still asleep. Her brother is watching her and Biddy is within call. I thought I would take a little walk on the shore, as I shall not be wanted just at present."

"Oh, of course," Dinah said. "Don't hurry back!"

The nurse smiled and flitted away into the golden evening sunlight.

Dinah turned her head towards her silent companion. "I wonder," she said, "if I could learn to be a nurse."

He blew a cloud of smoke into the air. "Are you still worrying about the future?" he said.

"I don't know that I am exactly worrying," she made low reply. "But I shall have to decide about it very soon."

Scott was silent for a space while he finished his cigarette. Then at last slowly, haltingly, he spoke. "Dinah, - I have been thinking about the future too. If I touch upon anything that hurts you, you must stop me, and I will not say another word. But, child, it seems to me that we shall both be - rather lost - when Isabel is gone. I wonder - would it shock you very much - if I suggested to you - as a solution of the difficulty - that we should some day in the future enter into partnership together?"

He spoke with obvious effort; his hands were gripped upon the arms of his chair. The wicker creaked in the strain of his grasp, but he himself remained lying back with eyes half-closed in compulsory inaction.

Dinah also sat absolutely still. If his words amazed her, she gave no sign. Only the wistfulness about her mouth deepened as she made answer below her breath. "It - is just like you to suggest such a thing; but - it is quite impossible."

He opened his eyes and looked at her very steadily and kindly. "Quite?" he said.

She bent her head, swiftly lowering her own. "Yes - thank you a million times - quite."

"Even if I promise never to make love to you?" he said, his voice half-quizzical, half-tender.

She put out a trembling hand and laid it on his arm. "Oh, Scott, - it - isn't that!"

He took the hand and held it. "My dear, don't cry!" he urged gently. "I knew you wouldn't have me really. I only thought I

Ethel M. Dell

would just place myself completely at your disposal in case - some day - you might be willing to give me the chance to serve you in any capacity whatever. There! It is over. We are as we were - friends."

He smiled at her with the words, and after a moment stooped and lightly touched her fingers with his lips.

"Come!" he said gently. "I haven't frightened you anyway. Have I?"

"No," she whispered.

His hand clasped hers for a second or two longer, then quietly let it go. "Don't be distressed!" he said, "I will never do it again. I am now - and always - your trusty friend."

And with that he rose in his slow way, paused to light another cigarette, smiled again upon her, and softly went indoors.

CHAPTER XXVI

THE LAST SUMMONS

There is nought in life more solemn than the waiting hush that falls before the coming of that great Change which men call Death. And it is to the watchers rather than to the passing soul itself that the wonder seems to draw most close. To stand before the veil, to know that very soon it must be lifted for the loved one to pass beyond, to wait for the glimpse of that spirit-world from which only the frail wall of mortality divides even the least spiritual, to watch as it were for the Gate of Death to open and the great Revelation to flash for one blinding moment upon the dazzled eyes that may not grasp the meaning of what they see; this is to stand for a space within the very Sanctuary of God.

The awe of it and the wonder hung night and day over the little rose-covered house on the heath above the sea where Isabel was breathing forth the last of her broken earthly life. Dinah moved in that strange atmosphere as one in a dream. She spent most of her time with Scott in a silent companionship in which no worldly thoughts seemed to have any part. The things of earth, all worry, all distress, were in abeyance, had sunk to such infinitesimal proportions that she was scarcely aware of them at all. It was as though they had climbed the steep mountain with Isabel, and not till they turned again to descend could they be aware of those things which lay so far below.

Ethel M. Dell

Without Scott, both doubts and fears would have been her portion, but with him all terrors fell shadow-like away before her. She hardly realized all that his presence meant to her during those days of waiting, but she leaned upon him instinctively as upon a sure support. He never failed her.

Of Eustace she saw but little. From the very first it was evident that his place was nearer to Isabel than Scott's had ever been. He did not shoulder Scott aside, but somehow as a matter of course he occupied the position that the younger brother had sought to fill for the past seven years. It was natural, it was inevitable. Dinah could have resented this superseding at the outset had she not seen how gladly Scott gave place. Later she realized that the ground on which they stood was too holy for such considerations to have any weight with either brother. They were united in the one supreme effort to make the way smooth for the sister who meant so much to them both; and during all those days of waiting Dinah never heard a harsh or impatient word upon the elder's lips. All arrogance, all hardness, seemed to have fallen away from him as he trod with them that mountain-path. Even old Biddy realized the change and relented somewhat towards him though she never wholly brought herself to look upon him as an ally.

It was on a stormy evening at the beginning of July that Dinah was sitting alone in the little creeper-grown verandah watching the wonderful greens and purples of the sea when Eustace came soft-footed through the window behind her and sat down in a chair close by, which Scott had vacated a few minutes before.

Scott had just gone to the village post-office with some letters, but she had refused to accompany him, for it was the hour when she usually sat with Isabel. She glanced at Eustace swiftly as he sat down, half-expecting a message from the sick-room. But he said nothing, merely leaning back in the wicker-chair, and fixing his eyes upon the sombre splendour of endless waters upon which hers had been resting. There was a massive look about him, as of a strong man deliberately bent to some gigantic task. A little tremor went through her as furtively she watched him. His silence, unlike the silences of Scott, was disquieting. She could never feel wholly at ease in his presence.

He turned his head towards her after a few seconds of absolute stillness, and in a moment her eyes sank. She sat in palpitating silence, as one caught in some disgraceful act.

But still he did not speak, and the painful colour flooded her face under his mute scrutiny till in sheer distress she found herself forced to take the initiative.

"Is - Isabel expecting me?" she faltered. "Ought I to go?"

"No," he said quietly. "She is dozing. Old Biddy is with her."

It seemed as if the intolerable silence were about to fall again. She cast about desperately for a means of escape. "Biddy was up and down during the night. I think I will relieve her for a little while and let her rest."

She would have risen with the words, but unexpectedly he reached forth a detaining hand. "Do you mind waiting a minute?" he said. "I will not say - or do - anything to frighten you."

He spoke with a faint smile that somehow hurt her almost unbearably. She remained as she was, leaning forward in her chair. "I - am not afraid," she murmured almost inaudibly.

His hand seemed to plead for hers, and in a moment she laid her own within it. "That's right," he said. "Dinah, will you try and treat me as if I were a friend - just for a few minutes?"

The tone of his voice - like his smile - pierced her with a poignancy that sent the quick tears to her eyes. She forced them back with all her strength.

"I would like to - always," she whispered.

"Thank you," he said. "You are kinder than I deserve. I have done nothing to win your confidence, so it is all the more generous of you to bestow it. On the strength of your generosity I am going to ask you a question which only a friend could ask. Dinah, is there any understanding of any sort - apart from friendship - between you and Scott?"

She started slightly at the question, and in a moment firmly, with a certain authority, his hand closed upon hers.

"You needn't be afraid to speak on Scott's account," he said, with that rather grim humility that seemed so foreign to his proud nature that every sign of it stabbed her afresh. "I am not such a dog in the manger as that and he knows it."

"Oh no!" Dinah said, and her words came with a rush. "But - I told you before, didn't I? - he doesn't care for me like that. He never has - never will."

"I wonder why you say that," Eustace said.

"Because it's true!" With a species of feverish insistence she answered him. "How could I help knowing? Of course I know! Oh, please don't let us talk about it! It - it hurts me."

"I want you to bear with me," he said gently, "just for a few minutes. Dinah, what if you are making a mistake? Mistakes happen, you know. Scott is a shy sort of chap, and immensely reserved. Doesn't it occur to you that he may care for you and yet be afraid - just as you are afraid - to let you know?"

"No," Dinah said. "He doesn't. I know he doesn't!"

She spoke with her eyes upon the ground, her voice sunk very low. She felt as if she were being drawn down from the heights she desired to tread. She did not want to contemplate the problems that she knew very surely awaited her upon the lower level. She did not want to quit her sanctuary before the time.

Sir Eustace received her assurance in silence, but he kept her hand in his, and the power of his personality seemed to penetrate to the very centre of her being.

He spoke at last almost under his breath, still closely watching her downcast face. "Are you quite sure you still care for him - in that way?"

She made a quick, appealing gesture. "Oh, need I answer that? I feel so - ashamed."

"No, you needn't answer," he made steady reply. "But you've nothing to be ashamed about. Stumpy's an awful ass, you know, - always has been. He's been head over heels in love with you ever since he met you. No, you needn't let that shock you. He's such a bashful knight he'll never tell you so. You'll have to do that part of it." He smiled with faint irony. "But you may take my word for it, it is so. He has thought of nothing but you and your happiness from the very beginning of things. And - unlike someone else we know - he has had the decency always to put your happiness first."

He paused. Dinah's eyes had flashed up to his, green, eager, intensely alive, and behind those eyes her soul seemed to be straining like a thing in leash. "Oh, I knew he had cared for someone," she breathed, "But it couldn't - it couldn't have been me!"

"Yes," Sir Eustace said slowly. "You and none other. You wonder if it's true - how I know. He's an awful ass, as I said before, one of the few supreme fools who never think of themselves. I knew that he was caught all right ages back in Switzerland, and - being a low hound of mean instincts - I set to work to cut him out."

"Oh!" murmured Dinah. "That was just what I did with Rose de Vigne."

His mouth twisted a little. "It's a funny world, Dinah," he

said. "Our little game has cost us both something. I got too near the candle myself, and the scorch was pretty sharp while it lasted. Well, to get back to my story. Scott saw that I was beginning to give you indigestion, and - being as I mentioned before several sorts of a fool - he tackled me upon the subject and swore that if I didn't put an end to the game, he would put you on your guard against me, tell you in fact the precise species of rotter that I chanced to be. I was naturally annoyed by his interference. Anyone would have been. I gave him the kicking he deserved. That was low of me, wasn't it?" as she made a quick movement of shrinking. "You won't forgive me for that, or for what came after. The very next day - to spite the little beast - I proposed to you."

Dinah's eyes were fiercely bright. "I wish I'd known!" she said.

"I wish to heaven you had, my dear," Eustace spoke with a grim hint of humour. "It would have saved us both a good deal of unnecessary trouble and humiliation. However, Scott was too big a fool to tell you. There is a martyrlike sort of cussedness about him that is several degrees worse than any pride. So he let things be, still cheating himself into the belief that the arrangement was for your happiness, till, as you are aware, it turned out so manifestly otherwise that he found himself obliged once more to come to the rescue of his lady love. But his exasperating humility was such that he never suspected the real reason for your change of mind, and when I accused him of cutting me out, he was as scandalized as only a righteous man knows how to be. You can't do much with a fellow like that, you know, - a fool who won't believe the evidence of his own senses. Besides, it was not for me to enlighten him, particularly as you didn't want him to know the real state of things just then. So I left him alone. The next day - only the next day, mind you - the silent knight opened his heart; to whom, do you think? You'll be horribly furious when I tell you."

He looked into the hot eyes with an expression half-tender in his own.

"Tell me!" breathed Dinah.

"Really? Well, prepare for a nasty shock! To Rose de Vigne!"

"To Rose!" Indignation gave place to bewilderment in Dinah's eyes.

"Even so; to Rose. She guessed the truth, and he frankly admitted she was right, but gave her to understand that as he hadn't a chance in the world, you were never to know. I am telling you the truth, Dinah. You needn't look so incredulous. She naturally considered that he was not treating you very fairly and said so. But -" he raised his shoulders slightly - "you know Scott. Mules can't compete with him when he has made up his mind to a thing. He gracefully put an end to the discussion and doubtless he has buried the whole subject in a neat little corner of his heart where no one can ever tumble over it, and resigned himself to a lonely old age. Now, Dinah, I am going to give you the soundest piece of advice I have ever given anyone. If you are wise, you will dig it up before the moss grows, bring it into the air and call it back to life. It is the greatest desire of Isabel's heart to see you two happy together. She told me so only to-day. And I am beginning to think that I wish it too."

His look was wholly kind as he uttered the last words. He held her hand in the close grip of a friend.

"Don't let that insane humility of his be his ruin!" he urged. "He's a fool. I've always said so. But his foolishness is the sort that attacks only the great. Once let him know you care, and he'll be falling over himself to propose."

"Oh, don't!" Dinah begged, and her voice sounded chill and yet somehow piteous. "I couldn't - ever - marry him. I told him so - only the other day."

"What? He proposed, did he?" Sheer amazement sounded in Eustace's voice.

Dinah was not looking at him any longer. She sat rather huddled in her chair, as if a cold wind had caught her.

"Yes," she said in the same small, uneven voice. "He proposed. He didn't make love to me. In fact he - promised that he never would. But he thought - yes, that was it - he thought that presently I should be lonely, and he wanted me to know that he was willing to protect me."

"What a fool!" Eustace said. "And so you refused him! I don't wonder. I should have pitched something at him if I'd been you."

"Oh no! That wasn't why I refused. I had another reason." Dinah's head was bent low; he saw the hot colour she sought to hide. "I didn't know he cared," she whispered. "But even if - if I had known, I couldn't have said Yes. I never can say Yes now."

"Good heavens above!" he said. "Why not?"

"It's a reason I can't tell anyone," faltered Dinah.

"Nonsense!" he said, with a quick touch of his old imperious-ness. "You can tell me."

She shook her head. "No. Not you. Not anyone."

"That is absurd," he said, with brief decision. "What is the reason? Out with it - quick, like a good child! If you could marry me, you can marry him."

"But I couldn't have married you," she protested, "if I'd known."

"It's something that's cropped up lately, is it?" He bent towards her, watching her keenly. "It can't be so very terrible."

"It is," she told him in distress.

He was silent a moment; then very suddenly he moved, put his arm around her, drew her close. "What is it, my elf? Tell me!" he whispered.

She hid her face against him with a little sob. It was odd, but at that moment she felt no fear of the man. He, whose fiery caresses had once appalled her, had by some means unknown possessed himself of her confidence so that she could not keep him at a distance. She did not even wish to do so.

After a few seconds, quiveringly she began to speak. "I don't know how to tell you. It's an awful thing to tell. You know, I - I've never been happy at home. My mother never liked me, - was often cruel to me." She shuddered suddenly and violently. "I never knew why - till that awful night - the last time I saw her. And then - and then she told me." She drew a little closer to him like a frightened child.

He held her against his breast. She was trembling all over. "Well?" he said gently.

Desperately she forced herself to continue. "I don't belong to - to my father - at all; only - only - to her."

"What?" he said.

She buried her shamed face a little deeper. "That was why - she married," she whispered.

"Your mother herself told you that?" Sir Eustace's voice was very low, but there was in it a danger-note that made her quail.

Someone was coming along the garden-path, but neither of them heard. Dinah was crying with piteous, long-drawn sobs. The telling of that tragic secret had wrung her very soul.

"Oh, don't be angry! You won't be angry?" she pleaded brokenly.

His hand was on her head. "My child, I am not angry with you," he said. "You were not to blame. There, dear! There! Don't cry! Isabel will be distressed if she finds out. We mustn't let her know of this."

"Or Scott either!" She lifted her face appealingly. "Eustace, please - please - you won't tell Scott? I - I couldn't bear him to know."

He looked into her beseeching eyes, and his own softened. "It may be he will have to know some day," he said. "But - not yet."

The halting steps drew nearer, uneven, yet somehow purposeful.

Abruptly Eustace became aware of them. He looked up sharply. "You had better go, dear," he whispered to the girl in his arms. "Isabel may be wanting you at any time. We must think of her first now. Run in quickly and dry your eyes before anyone sees! Come along!"

He rose, supporting her, turned her towards the window, and gently but urgently pushed her within.

She went swiftly, enough as he released her, went with her hands over her face and not a backward glance. And Eustace wheeled back with a movement that was almost fierce and met his brother as he set foot upon the verandah.

Scott's face was pale as death, and there was that in his eyes that could not be ignored. Eustace answered it on the instant, briefly, with a restraint that obviously cost him an effort. "It's all right, Dinah is a bit upset this evening. But she will be all right directly if we leave her alone."

Scott did not so much as pause. "Let me pass!" he said.

His voice was perfectly quiet, but the command of it was such that Eustace, taken unawares, gave ground as it were instinctively. But the next moment impulsively he caught Scott's arm.

"I say, - Stumpy!" An odd embarrassment possessed him; he shook it off half-angrily. "You needn't go making mistakes - jumping to idiotic conclusions. I'm not cutting you out this time."

Scott looked at him. His light eyes held contempt. "Oh, I know that," he said, and there was in his slow voice a note of bitter humour that cut like a whip. "You are never in earnest. You were always the sort to make sport for yourself out of suffering, and then to toss the dregs of your amusement to those who are not - sportsmen."

Eustace was as white as he was himself. He held him in a grip of iron. "What the - devil do you mean?" he said, his voice husky with the strong effort he made to control it.

The younger brother was absolutely controlled, but his eyes shone like a dazzling white flame. "Ask yourself that question!" he said, and his words, though low, had a burning quality, almost as if some force apart from the man himself inspired them. "You know the answer as well as I do. You have studied the damnable game so long, offered so many victims upon the altar of your accursed sport. There is nothing to prevent your going on with it. You will go on no doubt till you tire of the chase. And then your turn will come. You will find yourself alone among the ruins, and you will pay the price. You may repent then - but repentance sometimes comes too late."

He was gone with the words, gone as if an inner force compelled, shaking off the hand that had detained him, and passing scatheless within.

He went up the stairs as calmly as if he had entered the house without interruption. Someone was sobbing piteously behind a closed door, but he did not turn in that direction. He moved straight to the door of Isabel's room, as if a voice had called him.

And on the threshold Biddy met him, her black eyes darkly mysterious, her wrinkled face drawn with awe rather than grief.

"Ah, Master Scott, and is it yourself?" she whispered. "I was coming to fetch ye - coming to tell ye. It's the call; she's had her last summons. Faith, and I almost heard it meself. She'll be gone by morning, the blessed lamb. There'll be no holding her after this."

Scott passed her by without a word. He went straight to his sister's bedside.

She was lying with her face turned up to the evening sky, but on the instant her eyes met his, and in them was that look of a great expectation which many term the Shadow of Death.

"Oh, Stumpy, is it you?" she said. Her breathing was quick and irregular, but it did not seem to hurt her. "I've had - such a wonderful - dream. Or could it have been - a vision?"

He bent and took her hand in his. His eyes were infinitely tender. All the passion had been wiped out of his face.

"It may have been a vision, dear," he said.

Her look brightened; she smiled. "He was here - in this room - with me," she said. "He was standing there - at the foot of the bed. And - and - I held out my arms to him. Oh, Stumpy, I almost thought - I was going with him then. But - I think he heard you coming, for he laughed and drew back. 'We shall meet in the morning,' he said. And while I was still looking, he was gone."

She began to pant. He stooped and raised her. She clung to him with all her waning strength. "Stumpy! Stumpy! You will help me - through the night?"

"My darling, yes," he said.

She clung to him still. "It won't be - good-bye," she urged softly. "You will be coming too - very soon."

"God grant it!" he said, under his breath.

Her look dwelt upon him. Again faintly she smiled. "Ah, Stumpy," she said, "but you are going to be very happy first, my dear, - my dear."

CHAPTER XXVII

THE MOUNTAIN-TOP

The night fell like a black veil, starless and still. Up in Isabel's room the watchers came and went, dividing the hours. Only the nurse and old Biddy remained always at their posts, the one seated near one of the wide-flung windows, the other crouched on an ottoman at the foot of the bed, her beady eyes perpetually fixed upon the white, motionless face upon the pillow.

Only by the irregular and sometimes difficult breathing did they know that Isabel still lived, for she gave no sign of consciousness, uttered no word, made no voluntary movement of any sort. Like those who watched about her, she seemed to be waiting, waiting for the amazing revelation of the Dawn.

They had propped her high with pillows; her pale hands lay outside the coverlet. Her eyes were closed. She did not seem to notice who came or went.

"She may slip away without waking," the nurse whispered once to Dinah who had crept to her side. "Or she may be conscious just at the last. There is no telling."

Dinah did not think that she was asleep, but yet during all her vigil the white lids had not stirred, no spark of vitality had touched the marble face. She was possessed by a great longing to speak to her, to call her out of that trance-like silence; but she did not dare. She was as one bound by a spell. The great stillness was too holy to break. All her own troubles were sunk in oblivion. She felt as if she moved in a shadow-world where no troubles could penetrate, where no voice was ever lifted above a whisper.

As she crept from the room, she met Eustace entering. He looked gaunt and haggard in the dim light. Nothing seemed natural on that night of waiting.

He paused a moment, touched her shoulder. "Go and rest, child!" he muttered. "I will call you if she wakes."

She sent him a faint smile and flitted by him into the passage. How could she rest on a night like this, with the vague whisperings of the spirit-world all about her? Besides, in another hour the darkness would be over - the Dawn would come! Not for all the world would she miss that wonderful coming of a new day - the day which Isabel was awaiting in that dumb passivity of unquestioning patience. They had come so far up the mountain-track together; she must be with her when the morning found them on the summit.

But it was Eustace's turn to watch, and she moved towards her own room, through the open windows of which the vague murmur and splash of the sleeping sea drifted like the accompaniment of far-off music - undreamed-of Alleluias.

The dim glow of a lamp lay across her path, like a barrier staying her feet. Almost involuntarily she paused before a half-open door. It was as though some unseen force compelled her. And, so pausing, there came to her a sound that gripped her like a hand upon her heart - it was the broken whispering of a man in an agony of prayer.

It was not by her own desire that she stood to listen. The anguish of that voice held her, so that she was powerless to move.

"O God! O God!" The words pierced her with their entreaty; it was a cry from the very depths. "The mistake was mine. Let me bear the consequences! But save her - O save her - from further suffering!" A momentary silence, and then, more desperately still: "O God - if Thou art anywhere - hear - and help! Let me bear whatever Thou wilt! But spare her - spare her! She has borne so much!"

A terrible sob choked the gasping utterance. There fell a silence so tense, so poignant with pain, that the girl upon the threshold trembled as one physically afraid. Yet she could not turn and flee. She felt as if it were laid upon her to stand and witness this awful struggle of a soul in torment. But that it should be Scott - the wise, the confident, the unafraid - passing alone through this place of desolation, sent the blood to her heart in a great wave of consternation. If Scott failed - if the sword of Greatheart were broken - it seemed to her that nothing could be left in all the world, as if even the coming Dawn must be buried in darkness.

Was it for Isabel he was praying thus? She supposed it must be, though she had felt all through this night of waiting that no prayer was needed. Isabel was so near the mountain-top that surely she was safe - nearer already to God than any of their prayers could bring her.

And yet Scott was wrestling here as one overwhelmed with evil. Wherefore? Wherefore? The steady faith of this good friend of hers had never to her knowledge flickered before. What had happened to shake him thus?

He was praying again, more coherently but in words so low that they were scarcely audible. She crept a little nearer, and now she could see him, kneeling at the table, his head sunk upon it, his arms flung wide with clenched fists that seemed impotently to beat the air.

"I'm praying all wrong," he whispered. "Forgive me, but I'm all in the dark to-night. Thou knowest, Lord, how awful the dark can be. I'm not asking for an answer. Only guide our feet! Deliver us from evil - deliver her - O God - deliver my Dinah - by that love which is of Thee and which nothing will ever alter! If I may not help her, give me strength - to stand aside!"

A great shiver went through him; he gripped his hands together suddenly and passionately.

"O my God," he groaned, "it's the hardest thing on earth - to stand and do nothing - when I love her so."

Something seemed to give way within him with the words. His shoulders shook convulsively. He buried his face in his arms.

And in that moment the power that had stayed Dinah upon the threshold suddenly urged her forward.

Almost before she realized it, she was there at his side, stooping over him, holding him - holding him fast in a clasp that was free from any hesitation or fear, a clasp in which all her pulsing womanhood rushed forth to him, exulting, glorying in its self-betrayal.

"My dear! Oh, my dear!" she said. "Are you praying for me?"

"Dinah!" he said.

Just her name, no more; but spoken in a tone that thrilled her through and through! He leaned against her for a few moments, almost as if he feared to move. Then, as one gathering strength, he uttered a great sigh and slowly got to his feet.

"You mustn't bother about me," he said, and the sudden rapture had all gone out of his voice; it had the flatness of utter weariness. "I shall be all right."

But Dinah's hands yet clung to his shoulders. Those moments of yielding had revealed to her more than any subsequent word or action could belie. Her eyes, shining with a great light, looked straight into his.

"Dear Scott! Dear Greatheart!" she said, and her voice trembled over the tender utterance of the name. "Are you in trouble? Can't I help?"

He took her face between his hands, looking straight back into the shining eyes. "You are the trouble, Dinah," he told her simply. "And I'd give all I have - I'd give my soul - to make life easier for you."

She leaned towards him, and suddenly those shining eyes were blurred with a glimmer of tears. "Life is dreadfully difficult," she said. "But you have never done anything but help me. And, oh, Scott, I - don't know if I ought to tell you - forgive me if it's wrong - but - but I feel I must -" her breath came so quickly that she could hardly utter the words - "I love you - I love you - better than anyone else in the world!"

"Dinah!" he said, as one incredulous.

"It's true!" she panted. "It's true! Eustace knows it - has known it almost as long as I have. It isn't the only thing I have to tell you, but it's the first - and biggest. And even though - even though - I shall never be anything more to you than I am now - I'm glad - I'm proud - for you to know. There's nothing else that counts in the same way. And though - though I refused you the other day - I wanted you - dreadfully, dreadfully. If - if I had only been good enough for you - But - but - I'm not!" She broke off, battling with herself.

He was still holding her face between his hands, and there was something of insistence, something that even bordered upon ruthlessness, in his hold. Though the tears were running down her face, he would not let her go.

"Will you tell me what you mean by that?" he said, his voice very low. "Or - must I ask Eustace?"

She started. There was that in his tone that made her wince inexplicably. "Oh no," she said, "no! I'll tell you myself - if - if you must know."

"I am afraid I must," he said, and for all their resolution, the words had a sound of deadly weariness. He let her go slowly as he uttered them. "Sit down!" he said gently. "And please don't tremble! There is nothing to make you afraid."

She dropped into the chair he indicated, and made a desperate effort to calm herself. He stood beside her with the absolute patience of one accustomed to long waiting.

After a few moments, she put up a quivering hand, seeking his. He took it instantly, and as his fingers closed firmly upon her own, she found courage.

"I didn't want you to know," she whispered. "But I - I see now - it's better that you should. There's no other way - of making you understand. It's just this - just this!" She swallowed hard, striving to control the piteous trembling of her voice. "I am - one of those people - that - that never ought to have been born. I don't belong - anywhere - except to - my mother who - who - who has no use for me, - hated me before ever I came into the world. You see, she - married because - because - another man - my real father - had played her false. Oh, do you wonder - do you wonder -" she bowed her forehead upon his hand with a rush of tears - "that - that when I knew - I - I felt as if - I couldn't - go on with life?"

Her weeping was piteous; it shook her from head to foot.

But - in the very midst of her distress - there came to her a wonder so great that it checked her tears at the height of their flow. For very suddenly it dawned upon her that Scott - Scott, her knight of the golden armour - was kneeling at her feet.

Half in wonder and half in awe, she lifted her head and looked at him. And in that moment he took her two hands and kissed them, tenderly, reverently, lingeringly.

"Was this what you and Eustace were talking about this afternoon?" he said.

She nodded. "I had to tell him - why - I couldn't marry you. He - he had been - so kind."

"But, my own Dinah," he said, and in his voice was a quiver half-quizzical yet strangely charged with emotion, "did you ever seriously imagine that I should allow a sordid little detail like that to come between us? Surely Eustace knew better than that!"

She heard him in amazement, scarcely believing that she heard. "Do you - can you mean - " she faltered, "that - it really - doesn't count?"

"I mean that it is less than nothing to me," he made answer, and in his eyes as they looked into hers was that glory of worship that she had once seen in a dream. "I mean, my darling, that since you want me as I want you, nothing - nothing in the world - can ever come between us any more. Oh, my dear, my dear, I wish you'd told me sooner."

"I knew I ought to," she murmured, still hardly believing. "And yet - somehow - I couldn't bear the thought of your knowing, - particularly as - as - till Eustace told me - I never dreamed you - cared. You are so - great. You ought to have someone so much - better than I. I'm not nearly good enough - not nearly."

He was drawing her to him, and she went with a little sob into his arms; but she turned her face away over his shoulder, avoiding his.

"I ought not - to have told you - I loved you," she said brokenly. "It wasn't right of me. Only - when I saw you so unhappy - I couldn't - somehow - keep it in any longer. Dear

Scott, don't you think - before - before we go any further - you had better - forget it and - give me up?"

"No, I don't think so." Scott spoke very softly, with the utmost tenderness, into her ear. "Don't you realize," he said, "that we belong to each other? Could there possibly be anyone else for either you or me?"

She did not answer him; only she clung a little closer. And, after a moment, as she felt the drawing of his hold, "Don't kiss me - yet!" she begged him tremulously. "Let us wait till - the morning!"

His arms relaxed, "It is very near the morning now," he said. "Shall we go and watch for it?"

They rose together. Dinah's eyes sought his for one shy, fleeting second, falling instantly as if half-dazzled, half-afraid. He took her hand and led her quietly from the room.

It was no longer dark in the passage outside. A pearly light was growing. The splash of the sea sounded very far below them, as the dim surging of a world unseen might rise to the watchers on the mountain-top.

They moved to an open window at the end of the passage. No sound came from Isabel's room close by, and after a few seconds Scott turned noiselessly aside and entered.

Dinah remained at the open window waiting with a throbbing heart in the great silence that wrapped the world. She was not afraid, but she longed for Scott to come back; she was conscious of an urgent need of him.

Several moments passed, and then softly he returned. "No change!" he whispered. "Eustace will call us - when it comes."

She slipped her hand back into his, without speaking. He made her sit upon the window-seat, and knelt himself upon it, his arm about her shoulders, his fingers clasping hers.

She could see his face but vaguely in the dimness, but many times during that holy hour before the dawn, though he spoke no word, she felt that he was praying or giving thanks.

Slowly the twilight turned into a velvet dusk. The great Change was drawing near. The silence lay like a thinning veil of mist upon the mountain-top. The clouds were parting in the East, all tinged with gold, like burnished gates flung back for the royal coming of the sun-god. The stillness that lay upon all the waiting earth was sacred as the hush of prayer.

Their faces were turned towards the spreading glow. It shone upon them as it shone upon all beside, widening, intensifying, till the whole earth lay wrapped in solemn splendour - and then at last, through the open gates, red, royal, triumphant, the sun-god came.

There came a moment in which all things were touched with the glory, all things were made new. And in that moment, sudden as a flash of light, a bird of pure white plumage appeared before their eyes, hovered an instant; then flew, mounting on wide, gleaming wings, straight into the dawn....

Even while they watched, it vanished through the gates of gold. And only the gracious sunshine of a new day remained....

A low voice spoke from the chamber of Death. They turned from the vision and saw Eustace standing in the doorway.

He was very white, but absolutely calm. There was a nobility about him at that moment that sent a queer little throb to Dinah's heart. He held out his hand, not to her, but to Scott. "She is gone," he said.

Scott went to him; she saw their hands meet. There was no agitation about either of them.

"In her sleep?" Scott said.

"Yes. We didn't even know - till it was over."

They turned into the room, still hand grasping hand.

And Dinah knelt up and stretched out her arms to the shining morning sky. Something within her was whispering that she and Scott had seen more of the passing of Isabel than any of those who had watched beside her bed. And in the quiet of that wonderful morning, she offered her quivering thanks to God.

CHAPTER XXVIII

CONSOLATION

Of the long hours that followed that wonderful dawning Dinah never had any very distinct recollection. Even Scott seemed to forget her for a while, and it was old Biddy who presently found her curled up on the window-seat with her head upon the sill asleep - Biddy with her eyes very bright and alert, albeit deeply rimmed with red.

She came to the childish, drooping figure, murmuring tender words. She put wiry arms about her and lifted her to her feet.

"There! Come to your own room and rest, my lamb!" she said. "Old Biddy'll take care of ye, aroon."

Dinah submitted with the vague docility of a brain but half-awakened. To be cared for and petted by Biddy was no new thing in her experience. She even felt as if the old crystal Alpine days had returned, as Biddy undressed her and presently tucked her into bed. Later, still in semi-consciousness, she drank the hot milk that the old woman brought her, and then sank into a deep, deep sleep.

She awakened from that sleep with a sense of well-being such as she had never known before, a feeling of complete security and rest. The house was very quiet, and through the curtained window there came to her the soft, slumberous splash of the waves.

She lay very still, listening to the soothing murmur, gradually focusing her mind again after its long oblivion. The memory of the previous night and of the coming of the dawn came back to her, and with it the thought of Isabel; but without grief and without regret. They had left her on the mountain-top, and she knew that all must be well.

A great peace seemed to have fallen like a veil upon the whole house. Surely no one could be mourning over that glad release! She saw again the flashing of those free wings in the dawn-light, and her heart thrilled afresh. She remembered too the close, strong clasp of Scott's h and as he had watched with her.

Where was Scott now? The wonder darted suddenly through her brain, and with it, swift as a flying cloud-shadow, came the want of him, the longing for the quiet voice, the quivering delight of his near presence. She half-raised herself, and then, caught by another thought, sank down again to hide her burning face in the pillow. It would be a little difficult to meet him again. On the old easy terms of friendship it could not be, and they had hardly begun to be lovers yet. He - had not even - kissed her!

Another thought came to her - of an even more disturbing nature. Save for old Biddy and the nurse, she was alone with the two brothers now. Would they - would they insist upon sending her home until - until Scott was ready to come and take her away? Oh, surely - surely Scott would never ask that of her!

Nevertheless the thought tormented her. She did not see any way out of the difficulty, and she was terribly afraid that Scott would be equally at a loss.

"I don't think I could bear it," she whispered to herself. "And yet - if he says so - if he says so - I suppose I must. I couldn't refuse - if he said so."

The soft opening of the door recalled her to the immediate

present. She saw old Biddy's face with its watchful, guardian look peep stealthily in upon her.

"Ah, mavourneen!" she whispered fondly, coming forward. "And is it awake ye are? I've peeped round at ye this five times, and ye were sleeping like a new-born babe. Lie still, darlint, while I fetch ye a cup o' tay then!"

She was gone with the words, but in a very little she was back again with her own especial brew. She set her tray down by Dinah's side, but Dinah did not even look at it. She raised herself instead, and threw warm arms around the old woman's neck. "Oh, Biddy," she said, "Biddy, darling, I can't think what ever I'd do without you!"

Biddy uttered a sharp sob, and gathered her close. But in a moment, half-angrily, "And what is it that I'd be crying for at all?" she said. "Isn't my dear Miss Isabel safer with the Almighty than ever she was with me? Isn't she gone to the blessed saints in Paradise? And would I have her back? No, no! I'm not that selfish, Miss Dinah. I'm an old woman moreover, and be the same token me own time can't be so far off now."

But Dinah clung faster to her. "Please, Biddy, please - don't talk like that! I want you," she said.

"Ah, bless the dear lamb!" said Biddy, and tenderly kissed the upturned, pleading face. "Miss Isabel said ye would now. But when ye've got Master Scott to take care of ye, it's not old Biddy that ye'll be wanting any longer."

"I shall," Dinah vowed. "I shall. I shall always want my Biddy."

"And may the Lord Almighty bless ye for the word!" said Biddy.

When Dinah was dressed, a great shyness fell upon her, born partly of the still mystery of the presence of Death that wrapped the little house. She stood by the window of her room, looking forth, irresolute, over the evening sea.

The blinds were drawn only in the room of Death, for Scott had so decreed, and the air blew in sweet and fresh from the rippling water.

After a few minutes, Biddy came softly up behind her. "And is it himself ye're looking for, mavourneen?" she murmured at Dinah's shoulder.

Dinah started a little and flushed. She wondered if Biddy knew all or only guessed. "I don't know - what to do," she said rather confusedly.

Biddy gave her a quick, wise look. "Will I tell ye a secret, Miss Dinah dear?" she whispered.

Dinah looked at her. The old woman's face was full of shrewd understanding. "Yes, tell me!" she said somewhat breathlessly.

Biddy's brown hand grasped her arm. "Master Scott went to town this morning," she said. "He'll be back any minute now. Sir Eustace is downstairs. He wants to see ye - to tell ye something - before Master Scott gets back."

"Oh, what - what?" gasped Dinah.

"There, now, there! Don't ye be afraid!" said Biddy, her beady eyes softening. "It's something ye'll like. Master Scott - he's not the gentleman to make ye do anything ye don't want to do. Don't ye trust him, Miss Dinah?"

"Of course - of course," Dinah said, with trembling lips.

"Then ye've nothing to be afraid of," said Biddy wisely. "Faith, it's only the marriage-licence he's been to fetch!"

"Oh - Biddy!" Dinah wheeled from the window, with both her

hands over her heart.

Biddy nodded with grave triumph. "It was Sir Eustace made him go. Master Scott - he didn't think it would be dacent, not at first. But, as Sir Eustace said, there's more ways than one of being ondacent, and after all it was the dearest wish of Miss Isabel's heart. 'Don't you be a conventional fool!' he said. And for once I agreed with him," said Biddy naively, "though I think he needn't have used bad language over it."

"Oh - Biddy!" Dinah said again, and then very oddly she began to smile, and the tension went out of her attitude. She kissed the wrinkled cheek, and turned. "I think perhaps I will go down and speak to Sir Eustace," she said.

She went quickly, aware that if she suffered herself to pause, that overpowering shyness would seize upon her again.

Guided by the scent of cigarette-smoke, she entered the dining-room. Sir Eustace was seated at a writing-table near the window. He looked up swiftly at her entrance.

"Awake at last!" he said, and would have risen with the words, but she reached him first and checked him.

"Eustace! Oh, Eustace!" she said. "I - I - Biddy has just told me -"

He frowned, as she stopped in confusion, steadying herself rather piteously against his shoulder. But in a moment, seeing her agitation, he put a kindly arm around her.

"Biddy is an old fool - always was. Don't take any notice of her! What a ferment you're in, child! What's the matter? There, sit down!"

He drew her down on to the arm of his chair, and she leaned against him, striving for self-control.

"You - you are so - so much too good," she murmured.

He smiled rather grimly. "No one ever accused me of that before! Was that the staggering piece of information that Biddy has imparted to you?"

"No," she said, a fleeting smile upon her awn face. "It was - it was - about Scott. It took my breath away, - that's all."

"That all?" said Eustace with a faintly wry lift of one eyebrow.

She slipped a shy arm around his neck. "Eustace, do you - do you think I - ought to let Scott marry me?"

"I'm quite sure you'll break his heart if you don't," responded Eustace.

"Oh, I couldn't do that!" she said quickly.

"No. I shouldn't if I were you. It isn't a very amusing game for anyone concerned." Sir Eustace took up his pen with his free hand. "He's rather a good chap, you know," he said, "beastly good sometimes. He'll take a little living up to. But you'll manage that, I daresay. When he told me how things stood between you, I saw directly that there was only one thing to be done, and I made him do it. The idea is to get you married before the nurse goes, and she is off to-morrow." He paused, looking at her critically, and again half-cynically, half-sadly, smiled. "You took that well," he said. "If it had been to me, you'd have jumped sky-high. You're a wise little creature, Dinah. You've chosen the best man, and you'll never be sorry. I congratulate you on your choice."

He turned his face fully to her, and she stooped swiftly and kissed him. "I'm - dreadfully sorry I - treated you so badly first," she whispered.

"You needn't be," he said. "It did me good. You showed me myself from a point of view that I had never taken before. You taught me to be human. I told Isabel so. She - poor girl -" he stopped a second, and she saw that momentarily he was moved; but he continued almost at once - "she was grateful to you too," he said. "You removed the outer crust at a single stroke - just in time to prevent atrophy. Of course," he glanced down at the letter under his hand, "it was a more or less painful process, but it may comfort you to know that it didn't go quite so deep with me as I thought it had at the time. There's no sense in crying over spilt milk anyhow. I never was that sort of ass. You may - or may not - be pleased to hear that I am already well on the way to consolation." He lifted his eyes suddenly with an expression in them that completely baffled her. It was almost as if he had detached himself for the moment from all participation in his own doings, contemplating them with a half-pathetic irony. "Shall I tell you what I was doing when you came in just now?" he said. "I was writing to the girl you nearly sacrificed your happiness to cut out."

"Rose de Vigne?" she said quickly.

He nodded. "Yes, Rose de Vigne" He paused for a second, just a second; then: "The girl I am going to marry," he said quietly.

"Oh, Eustace!" There was no mistaking the gladness in Dinah's tone. "I am pleased!" she said earnestly. "I know you will be happy together. You were simply made for each other."

He smiled, still in that strange, half-rueful fashion. "I am doing the best I can under the circumstances. It is kind of you to be pleased. But now once more to your affairs. They are more pressing than mine just now. It may interest you to know that Scott - although under Isabel's will he is made absolutely independent of me - is willing to live at the Dower House, if that arrangement meets with your approval."

"Of course - I shall love it," Dinah said.

"I am glad of that, for it will be a great help to me to have him there. You will be able to have Billy to stay with you in the holidays and roam about as you like. Scott is making all sorts of plans. I am going to settle the place on him as a wedding-present."

"Oh, Eustace! How kind! What a lovely gift!"

Sir Eustace smiled at her. "I am giving him more than that, Dinah. I am giving him his wife and - the wedding-ring." The irony was uppermost again, but it held no sting. "It will fit no other hand but yours, and it will serve to keep you in constant remembrance of your good luck. I can hear him coming up the path. Aren't you going to meet him?"

She sprang up like a startled fawn. "Oh, I can't - I can't meet him yet," she said desperately.

There was a curious glint in Eustace's eyes as he watched her, a flash of mockery that came and went.

"What?" he said. "Do you want me to help you to run away from him now?"

She looked at him quickly, and in a moment her hesitation was gone.

"Oh, no!" she said. "No!" and with a little breathless sound that might have been a tremor of laughter, she fled away from him out into the evening sunshine to meet her lover.

CHAPTER XXIX

THE SEVENTH HEAVEN

They were married in the early morning at the little old church that had nestled for centuries among its trees in the village on the cliff. The absolute simplicity of the service deprived it of all terrors for Dinah. Standing with Scott in the glow of sunlight that smote full upon them through the mellow east window, she could not feel afraid. The whole world was so bright, so full of joy.

"Do you think Isabel can see us now?" she whispered to him, as they rose together from kneeling before the altar.

He did not answer her in words, but his pale eyes were shining with that steadfast light of the spirit which she had come to know. She wished she could have knelt there by his side a little longer. They seemed to be so near to the Gates of Heaven.

But they were not alone, and they could not linger. Sir Eustace who had given her away, Biddy who had tenderly supported her, the nurse who carried the fragrant bouquet of honeysuckle - the bond of love - which she had herself gathered for the bride, all were waiting to draw them back to earth again; and with Scott's hand clasping hers she turned regretfully and left the holy place.

Later, when Sir Eustace kissed her with the careless observation that he always kissed a bride, she had a moment of burning shyness, and she would gladly have hidden her face. But Scott did not kiss her. He had not offered to do so since that wonderful moment when he had first held her against his heart. He had not attempted to make love to her, and she had not felt the need of it. Grave and practical, he had laid his plans before her, and with the supreme confidence that he had always inspired in her she had acquiesced to all.

At his desire she had refrained from entering Isabel's death-chamber. At his desire she was to leave that day for the Dower House that was to be their home. Biddy would accompany her thither. The place was ready for occupation, for by Isabel's wish the work had gone on, though both she and Scott had known that they would never share a home there. It almost seemed as if she had foreseen the fulfilment of her earnest wish. And here Dinah was to await her husband.

"I won't come to you till the funeral is over," he said to her. "I must be with Eustace. You won't be unhappy?"

No, she would not be unhappy. She had never been so near to Death before, but she was neither frightened nor dismayed. She stood in the shadow indeed, but she looked forth from it over a world of such sunshine as filled her heart with quivering gladness.

He did not want her to attend the funeral at Willowmount, would not, if he could help it, suffer her so much as to see the trappings of woe; and in this Dinah acquiesced also, comprehending fully the motive that underlay his wish. She knew that the earthly formalities, though they had to be faced, were to Scott something of the nature of a grim farce in which, while he could not escape it himself, he was determined that she should take no part. He was not mourning for Isabel. He would not pretend to mourn. Her death was to him but as the opening wide of a prison-door to one who had long lain captive, pining for liberty. He would follow the poor worn body to its grave rather with thanksgiving than with grief. And realizing so well that this was his inevitable feeling, even as in a

Ethel M. Dell

smaller degree it had become her own, Dinah agreed without demur to his wish to spare her all the jarring details, the travesty of mourning, that could not fail to strike a false chord in her soul.

It was well for her that she had Biddy to think of. The old woman was pathetically eager to serve her. She had in fact attached herself to Dinah in a fashion that went to her heart. It was Miss Isabel's wish that she should take care of her, she told her tremulously, and Dinah, knew that it had been equally her friend's wish that she should care for Biddy.

And Biddy was very good. Probably in accordance with Scott's desire, she made a great effort to throw off all gloom, and undoubtedly her own sense of loss and bereavement was greatly lessened by the consciousness of Dinah's need of her.

"Time enough to weep later," she told herself, as she lay down in the room adjoining Dinah's on that first night in the Dower House. "She'll not be wanting old Biddy when Master Scott comes to her."

The two days that followed were very fully occupied. There were curtains and pictures to hang, furniture to be arranged, and many things to be unpacked. Dinah went to the work with zest. She did not know when Scott would come. But it would be soon, she knew it would be soon; and she thrilled to the thought. Everything must be ready for him. She wanted him to feel that it was home from the moment he crossed the threshold.

So, with Biddy's help, she went about her preparations, enlisting the old nurse's sympathies till at last she succeeded in arousing her enthusiasm also. There was certainly no time to weep.

That second day after her arrival was the day of the funeral. It was a beautiful still day of summer, and in the afternoon Dinah and Biddy sat in the garden overlooking the winding river, and read the Burial Service together. It was Dinah's suggestion, somewhat shyly proffered, and - though she knew it not - from that time forward Biddy's heart was at her feet. Whatever tears there might be yet to shed had lost all bitterness from that hour.

"I'll never be lonely so long as there's you to love, Miss Dinah darlint," Biddy murmured, when the young arms closed about her neck for a moment ere they went back to their work. "Ye've warmed and comforted me all through."

It was late in the evening when dusk was falling that there came the sound of an uneven tread on the gravel path before the Dower House.

Dinah was the first to hear it. Dinah wearing one of Biddy's voluminous aprons and mounted on a pair of steps, arranging china on a high shelf that ran round the old square hall.

The front-door was open, and the birds were singing in the gloaming. She had been listening to them while she worked, when suddenly this new sound came. Her heart gave a wild leap and stood still. She had not expected him to-night.

She sat down on the top of the steps with a swift, indescribable rush of feeling that seemed to deprive her of all her strength. She could not have said for the moment if she were glad or dismayed at the sound of that quiet footfall. But she was quite powerless to go and meet him. A great wave of shyness engulfed her, possessing her, overwhelming her.

He entered. He came straight to her. She wondered afterwards what he must have thought of her, sitting there on her perch in burning embarrassment with no word or sign of welcome. But whatever he thought, he dealt with the situation with unerring instinct.

He mounted a couple of steps with hands stretched up to hers. "Why, my Dinah!" he said. "How busy you are! Let me help!"

Her heart throbbed on again, fast and hard. But still for a few seconds she could not speak. She stooped with a soft endearing sound and laid her face upon the hands that had clasped her own.

He suffered her for a moment or two in silence; she thought his hands trembled slightly. Then: "Let's get finished, little wife!" he said gently. "Isn't the day's work nearly over? Can't we take off our sandals - and rest?"

"I have just done," she said, finding her voice. "Biddy and I have got through such a lot. Oh, Scott," as the light fell upon his face, "how tired you look!"

"It has been rather a tiring day," he made answer. "I didn't think I could get over here to-night; but Eustace insisted."

"How good of him!" she said, with quick gratitude.

"Yes, he is good," Scott's voice was tender. "I couldn't sleep last night, and he came into my room, and we had a long talk. He is one of the best, Dinah; one of the best. I'm afraid you've made - rather a poor exchange."

Something in his tone banished the last of Dinah's shyness. She gave him her basket of china and prepared to descend. He stretched up a courteous hand to help her, but she would have none of it. "You are never to say that - or anything like it - again," she said severely. "If - if you weren't so dreadfully tired, I believe I'd be really angry. As it is -" she reached the ground and stood there before him, a small, purposeful figure clad in the great apron that wrapped about her like a garment.

"As it is -" he suggested meekly, setting the basket on a chair and turning back to face her.

Two quivering hands came out to him in the gloaming, and fastened resolutely on his coat. "Oh, Greatheart," whispered a tremulous voice, "I love you so much - so much - I want - to kiss you!"

"My darling," answered Greatheart softly, "you can't want it - more than I do."

His arms closed about her; he drew her to his breast.

*   *   *   *   *

"Arrah thin, what would I cry for at all?" said Biddy, as she lay down that night. "I've got herself and Master Scott to care for, and maybe - some day - the Almighty will remember old Biddy for good, and give another little one into her care."

*   *   *   *   *

"And you left them quite happy?" smiled Rose to her lover two days later. "It's a very suitable arrangement, isn't it? I always used to think that Dinah and your brother should make a match."

"Oh, quite suitable," agreed Eustace lazily, an odd blend of irony and satisfaction in his tone. "They will be happy enough. Stumpy, you know, is just the sort of chivalrous ass that a child like Dinah can appreciate. They'll probably live in the seventh heaven, and fancy that no one else has ever been within a million miles of it."

"Poor little Dinah!" murmured Rose. "She will never know what she has missed."

And, "Just as well perhaps," said Sir Eustace, with his faintly cynical smile.

Choose from Thousands of 1stWorldLibrary Classics By

A. M. Barnard
Ada Leverson
Adolphus William Ward
Aesop
Agatha Christie
Alexander Aaronsohn
Alexander Kielland
Alexandre Dumas
Alfred Gatty
Alfred Ollivant
Alice Duer Miller
Alice Turner Curtis
Alice Dunbar
Ambrose Bierce
Amelia E. Barr
Amory H. Bradford
Andrew Lang
Andrew McFarland Davis
Andy Adams
Anna Sewell
Annie Besant
Annie Hamilton Donnell
Annie Payson Call
Annonaymous
Anton Chekhov
Arnold Bennett
Arthur Conan Doyle
Arthur M. Winfield
Arthur Ransome
Atticus
B.H. Baden-Powell
B. M. Bower
Baroness Emmuska Orczy
Baroness Orczy
Basil King
Bayard Taylor
Ben Macomber
Bertha Muzzy Bower
Bjornstjerne Bjornson
Booth Tarkington
Boyd Cable
Bram Stoker
C. Collodi
C. E. Orr
C. M. Ingleby
Carolyn Wells
Catherine Parr Traill
Charles A. Eastman
Charles Dickens

Charles Dudley Warner
Charles Farrar Browne
Charles Ives
Charles Kingsley
Charles Klein
Charles Amory Beach
Charles Hanson Towne
Charles Lathrop Pack
Charles Whibley
Charles Willing Beale
Charlotte M. Braeme
Charlotte M. Yonge
Charlotte Perkins Stetson
Clair W. Hayes
Clarence Day Jr.
Clarence E. Mulford
Clemence Housman
Confucius
Cornelis DeWitt Wilcox
Cyril Burleigh
D. H. Lawrence
Daniel Defoe
David Garnett
Dinah Craik
Don Carlos Janes
Donald Keyhoe
Dorothy Kilner
Dougan Clark
Douglas Fairbanks
E. Nesbit
E.P.Roe
E. Phillips Oppenheim
Earl Barnes
Edgar Rice Burroughs
Edith Van Dyne
Edith Wharton
Edward J. O'Biren
Edward S. Ellis
Edwin L. Arnold
Eleanor Atkins
Eliot Gregory
Elizabeth Gaskell
Elizabeth McCracken
Elizabeth Von Arnim
Ellem Key
Emerson Hough
Emilie F. Carlen
Emily Dickinson
Enid Bagnold

Enilor Macartney Lane
Erasmus W. Jones
Ernie Howard Pie
Ethel Turner
Ethel Watts Mumford
Eugenie Foa
Eugene Wood
Eustace Hale Ball
Evelyn Everett-green
Everard Cotes
F. H. Cheley
F. J. Cross
Federick Austin Ogg
Ferdinand Ossendowski
Francis Bacon
Francis Darwin
Frances Hodgson Burnett
Frances Parkinson Keyes
Frank Gee Patchin
Frank Harris
Frank Jewett Mather
Frank L. Packard
Frank V. Webster
Frederic Stewart Isham
Frederick Trevor Hill
Frederick Winslow Taylor
Friedrich Kerst
Friedrich Nietzsche
Fyodor Dostoyevsky
G.A. Henty
G.K. Chesterton
Gabrielle E. Jackson
Garrett P. Serviss
Gaston Leroux
George A. Warren
George Ade
Geroge Bernard Shaw
George Durston
George Ebers
George Eliot
George Gissing
George MacDonald
George Meredith
George Orwell
George Sylvester Viereck
George Tucker
George W. Cable
George Wharton James
Gertrude Atherton

Grace E. King
Grace Gallatin
Grant Allen
Guillermo A. Sherwell
Gulielma Zollinger
Gustav Flaubert
H. A. Cody
H. B. Irving
H.C. Bailey
H. G. Wells
H. H. Munro
H. Irving Hancock
H. Rider Haggard
H. W. C. Davis
Hamilton Wright Mabie
Hans Christian Andersen
Harold Avery
Harold McGrath
Harriet Beecher Stowe
Harry Houidini
Helent Hunt Jackson
Helen Nicolay
Hendrik Conscience
Hendy David Thoreau
Henri Barbusse
Henrik Ibsen
Henry Adams
Henry Ford
Henry Frost
Henry James
Henry Jones Ford
Henry Seton Merriman
Henry W Longfellow
Herbert A. Giles
Herbert N. Casson
Herman Hesse
Homer
Honore De Balzac
Horace Walpole
Horatio Alger Jr.
Howard Pyle
Howard R. Garis
Hugh Lofting
Hugh Walpole
Humphry Ward
Ian Maclaren
Inez Haynes Gillmore
Irving Bacheller
Israel Abrahams
Ivan Turgenev
J.G.Austin

J. Henri Fabre
J. M. Barrie
J. Macdonald Oxley
J. S. Fletcher
J. S. Knowles
J. Storer Clouston
Jack London
Jacob Abbott
James Allen
James Andrews
James Baldwin
James DeMille
James Joyce
James Lane Allen
James Lane Allen
James Oliver Curwood
James Oppenheim
James Otis
James R. Driscoll
Jane Austen
Janet Aldridge
Jens Peter Jacobsen
Jerome K. Jerome
John Burroughs
John Cournos
John F. Kennedy
John Gay
John Glasworthy
John Habberton
John Joy Bell
John Kendrick Bangs
John Milton
John Philip Sousa
Jonas Lauritz Idemil Lie
Jonathan Swift
Joseph A. Altsheler
Joseph Carey
Joseph Conrad
Joseph E. Badger Jr
Joseph Hergesheimer
Joseph Jacobs
Jules Vernes
Julian Hawthrone
Julie A Lippmann
Justin Huntly McCarthy
Kakuzo Okakura
Kenneth Grahame
Kenneth McGaffey
Kate Langley Bosher
Kate Langley Bosher
Katherine Cecil Thurston

Katherine Stokes
L. A. Abbot
L. T. Meade
L. Frank Baum
Latta Griswold
Laura Lee Hope
Laurence Housman
Lawrence Beasley
Leo Tolstoy
Leonid Andreyev
Lewis Carroll
Lewis Sperry Chafer
Lilian Bell
Lloyd Osbourne
Louis Hughes
Louis Tracy
Louisa May Alcott
Lucy Fitch Perkins
Lucy Maud Montgomery
Lydia Miller Middleton
Lyndon Orr
M. Corvus
M. H. Adams
Margaret E. Sangster
Margaret Vandercook
Margret Penrose
Maria Edgeworth
Maria Thompson Daviess
Mariano Azuela
Marion Polk Angellotti
Mark Overton
Mark Twain
Mary Austin
Mary Catherine Crowley
Mary Cole
Mary Hastings Bradley
Mary Roberts Rinehart
Mary Rowlandson
M. Wollstonecraft Shelley
Maud Lindsay
Max Beerbohm
Myra Kelly
Nathaniel Hawthrone
Nicolo Machiavelli
O. F. Walton
Oscar Wilde
Owen Johnson
P.G. Wodehouse
Paul and Mabel Thorne
Paul G. Tomlinson
Paul Severing

Percy Brebner
Peter B. Kyne
Plato
R. Derby Holmes
R. L. Stevenson
R. S. Ball
Rabindranath Tagore
Rahul Alvares
Ralph Bonehill
Ralph Henry Barbour
Ralph Victor
Ralph Waldo Emmerson
Rene Descartes
Rex Beach
Rex E. Beach
Richard Harding Davis
Richard Jefferies
Richard Le Gallienne
Robert Barr
Robert Frost
Robert Gordon Anderson
Robert L. Drake
Robert Lansing
Robert Lynd
Robert Michael Ballantyne
Robert W. Chambers
Rosa Nouchette Carey
Rudyard Kipling
Samuel B. Allison

Samuel Hopkins Adams
Sarah Bernhardt
Sarah C. Hallowell
Selma Lagerlof
Sherwood Anderson
Sigmund Freud
Standish O'Grady
Stanley Weyman
Stella Benson
Stephen Crane
Stewart Edward White
Stijn Streuvels
Swami Abhedananda
Swami Parmananda
T. S. Ackland
T. S. Arthur
The Princess Der Ling
Thomas A. Janvier
Thomas A Kempis
Thomas Anderton
Thomas Bailey Aldrich
Thomas Bulfinch
Thomas De Quincey
Thomas H. Huxley
Thomas Hardy
Thomas More
Thornton W. Burgess
U. S. Grant
Valentine Williams

Various Authors
Vaughan Kester
Victor Appleton
Virginia Woolf
Walter Camp
Walter Scott
Washington Irving
Wilbur Lawton
Wilkie Collins
Willa Cather
Willard F. Baker
William Dean Howells
William le Queux
W. Makepeace Thackeray
William W. Walter
Winston Churchill
Yei Theodora Ozaki
Yogi Ramacharaka
Young E. Allison
Zane Grey

Lightning Source UK Ltd.
Milton Keynes UK
UKOW04n1903100515

251238UK00002B/3/P